A]

CW01498702

We have entered the sixth great extinction of this planet's history. The loss of habitat, conversion of landscapes and demise of vital ecosystems is unprecedented and relentless. Our false measures of economic prosperity that drive GDP growth fail to recognise human insubordination to the very systems that support life on earth. We are losing species faster than we can identify, yet our governance systems and global management institutions fail to effect meaningful change. The paradigm shift that we have spoken of for decades has to happen now. Systemic change of the global community is required – but who is going to effect it?

Ecochain transports us to a world where nature's spirit is alive and flourishing, served on tap and chilled for those lucky enough to taste it. We are carried in the slipstream of Bird, a young man with the knowledge of genius at his fingertips but the burden of a broken soul resting upon his shoulders. He is delivered into a world diametrically opposed to his and given a ringside seat to one of nature's finest predators in their quest for survival on the outlandish Sukula Plains in Africa. It is there that he realises the precarious nature of the ecochain and the threat that mankind poses, even to the kings of this terrain. Together with a team of dedicated researchers, he embarks on a journey that aims to deliver a message to the masters of our fate: that we are part of the fabric of our natural world and its survival is intricately woven into our own, not a simple diversion to be hung on our decorative walls.

An IUCN report published in March 2019 concluded that big game hunting in Africa lacks the capacity to fund its own activity and conservation, yet still the onslaught continues. And until the day that we stop wildlife exploitation for its hide, its horn and its teeth; until the day that we recognise the intrinsic value of our intact forests versus their commercial timber value; until the day that our corporations, our politicians and our financial institutions are held wholly accountable for their impacts on the ecochain – until that day, the sixth great extinction will continue unabated.

ECOCHAIN

DORIAN TILBURY

For Clarence and Clearwater

1

TAKE FLIGHT

Fall in Massachusetts. It inspires the mind with enigmatic visions of primeval forests raging and ablaze, drenched in a thousand shades of golden brown as nature's Chronos shifts from exuberant to dormant in the blinking of an eye.

Autumn in England, however, does not. And as October's grey dusk light draped itself across the contours of this sleepy English coastal village, a school bus hissed and squealed to an abrupt halt at the top of Shadycombe Road and scraped its battered doors apart. The obligatory rabble of screeching children alighted amidst a torrent of bickering taunts and frantic arm gestures, and then subdivided like the segments of a dismembered earthworm as they trickled and meandered their separate paths down the hill.

A young boy aged nine peeled away from the seething mass and continued on his way home alone. His grey flannel trousers were tired and worn, and the emblem on his blazer melted into a grimy haze of remnant school dinners and tuck-shop quarries, as yet unwashed from its awkward drape. His tie was pulled to one side, concealed beneath the frayed, white collar of his untucked shirt, and the striped school cap lay sideways across his head, releasing sporadic, curly locks of his unkempt hair.

He trundled along, all feet and knees, the classic paradigm of developing youth as bone, sinew and muscle compete for adolescent growth spurts in their quest for maturity, consistent only in their portrayal of ungainly disequilibrium. This untimely and lethargic gait, coupled with a pair of oversized second-hand shoes, compelled him to drag his heels across the concrete and occasionally knock his knees together, while a school bag thumped and bounced across his back. It gave him the demeanour of a clumsy circus freak with every bumbling step. But in an instant of fleeting grace, he suddenly swung the brown satchel from his shoulder and caught it effortlessly in his arms. He broke into a rapid trot and sidestepped his way down the pavement, skipping and accelerating as he went, tossing the bag in the air and catching it repeatedly as if it were passing through numerous pairs of imaginary hands.

"Bird catches the ball on his own twenty-two and sells the dummy, then turns on the pace and steps past two tackles," he shrieked in an exaggerated whisper.

"What a find this young man is, Bill... so much talent... so much flair... just what England needs right now..." The commentary continued as he tucked the satchel beneath his right arm and sped down the street, immersed in his rugby game – weaving and dodging, turning and tearing, stepping, sliding and ripping up the turf of this whimsical arena.

"Over the half-way... hands off a tackle... steps off his left... then his right... just the fullback to beat now... show of the ball... that blistering pace again – and he scores in the corner! What unbelievable skill from the young winger!" he yelped, racing across the street and placing his bag down on the opposite side.

A sneer crept across his lips as he threw the satchel back across his shoulder and held his arms aloft, twisting left and then right as if acknowledging the cheers from his imaginary crowd.

"Bird... Bird... Bird..." His name rang out from the stands like the incessant chant of some rhythmic revolution, and he stood in his stadium and revelled in it – absorbed and savoured the praise with the grace and virtue of a true, untainted athlete. Worthy, yet somehow unassuming.

Then spots of rain dabbed against the concrete walkway and the haze of England's all-too-familiar drizzle nestled along the brim of his cap and gently dampened the lapels of his blazer.

"Weather's a-comin' in, boy, best be getting on home now," he muttered to himself as he turned up the collars of his jacket, hunched his shoulders in and dug the heels of his shoes into the ground, as if intent on carving out a path in the pavement, or at least destroying his shoes whilst trying.

He walked along a row of nondescript tenement houses, all steeped in the familiar ambiguity of 1970s sameness, and turned into a pathway in the middle of the block. All that seemed to separate these invariable dwellings were the pale shades of exterior paint colour charts, now tired and worn from underfunded council-estate maintenance programmes that had about as much individuality as the post-war modernist mass-housing drive that had put them there in the first place. Row upon row of unoriginal functionality that crammed the masses into archetypal boxes emblazoned with the slogan 'Two up, two down and a roof over your head', as if to imply, 'You should be so lucky, mate!'

Aaahh, home sweet home, he thought to himself somewhat sarcastically as he glanced at the flowerbed of weeds and overgrown lawn sprawling away to the battered fence that divided their meagre segment of garden from that of the neighbours.

Look at this mess, he thought. What would my father say?

Bird (as he was affectionately known to his family and friends) had been fatherless for a little over three years now, but even when he had been around, his dad had never been much of a gardener. Staring at the ill-kept lawn suddenly sparked that last unsavoury memory of him, and the boy seemed to shudder at the thought. All those sombre, grey strangers that barked at him in their austere compassionate tones about how his father would not be coming home any time soon. How they had locked him up and thrown away the key, and Bird would be well advised to use the situation to his advantage – to see how not to live his life and to choose a different path. And he remembered his father's expression as they led him away in disgrace on that fateful day, how he had caught Bird's eye and smiled a wink at him across the courtroom, mouthing the word 'bollocks' as he went.

His father had always told him of the ills of society, a ghastly machine of conformity that crushed the spirits of the free and forced the intuitive into conventional stables of everyday monotony. He warned him of its power and oppression and the need to evade its consuming grasp. He advised him to steer well clear – to avoid the damn thing at all costs – to live under the radar and not to believe the hype – to make his own path – to follow the dreams in his heart, even when society scorned him. Yes, he constantly warned his son of this social nemesis and always referred to it as 'bollocks', seemingly unrepentant and somewhat self-righteous, even as it dragged him down to the gallows.

Yet, in spite of this blatant disregard for the system and the heinous crime for which his father had just been convicted, society still went through the motions of outreach support and enacted the compassionate façade of counselling for the innocent victim, who in this case happened to be Bird.

"At least he's young enough not to notice the gap in his life. He has time to forget the past and build a positive future," the social worker had explained to his mother on one of her court-ordered home visits. "The younger they are, the better chance they have," she had said, sympathetically. "It's up to you to make sure he has the opportunity to do something different and not follow the same path as his father – you know, make a useful contribution to society. It's very important at this stage – young boys are heavily influenced by their fathers and it is crucial that he does not see him as some kind of hero. Crime never really pays, you do understand that, don't you?"

And whilst she had smiled and nodded profusely, Bird's mother had her own set of issues in dealing with this crap hand of cards that life had obnoxiously thrown at her. Issues that she chose never to face, but rather to drown in a sea of hard liquor and remorse. Smoothing the ride for her innocent child as well had proven to be something of a juggling act that fast became difficult to perform.

"Hi, Mum, I'm back!" Bird called, pushing open the door and collecting the meagre offering of junk mail that lay on the doormat inside. He always liked to forcefully announce his arrival home, as his mother had something of a nervous disposition and in her state it was never a good idea to startle her. She was usually three sheets to the wind by half past four in the afternoon, and in a drunken stupor with her mind on other things, surprises were not well handled.

Bird never quite knew what kind of reception would be in store for him. Sometimes there was intoxicated hysteria, sometimes cold and quiet despair; occasionally there was euphoric nostalgia; but mostly he was met with a glazed stare and incoherent anguish. Today, though, all was silent.

In the lounge, a soft melody strummed from the record player in the corner and a song suddenly jumped into life. He peered around the door, half expecting to see her dancing, but the room was bare.

"Mum?" he called again towards the kitchen, but no one answered.

Maybe she's passed out upstairs…

He put down his bag and the sorry excuse for mail he'd retrieved and stomped his way up the faded stairwell and along the short landing to her room. Again, there was no sign, not even the usual sprawl of yesterday's laundry scattered across the bed. The house was pretty much vacant. He shrugged his shoulders nonchalantly and went back down to the kitchen to fetch himself a sandwich and a glass of milk – after all, England's blistering new talent had to keep his energy up.

There was no surprise in this scenario for Bird; he often came home to a house with no life, just a note on the kitchen table to say she was down the pub and would be back soon, that there was dinner in the fridge and tea in the pot, which he could fix for himself. So he wasn't surprised to see the paper underneath an overflowing ashtray on the kitchen table, and casually went about his business. He could still hear the record player in the lounge scratching out a vinyl tune, but he couldn't make out the song. He whistled along anyway as he laid out two slices of white bread and reached inside the stark fridge for butter, jam and the remnants of yesterday's milk.

Through the kitchen window, he could see the iridescent sheen of a blackbird sitting on the back fence preening itself in the fading light, while sparrows and white-eyes flicked through the hedgerow and a robin darted in and out of view. In the sky beyond, the ever-present seagulls twisted and soared, and a magpie, hidden from view, screeched out its raucous call.

That was why they called him Bird. His fascination with avian life and his uncanny ability to pick out their intricate nuances, varied calls and individual habits at such a young age had everyone convinced that one day he might just evolve wings of his own and drift away from humanity to live among them forever. And even he had secretly wished for the impossible, but always consoled himself with the fact that he'd have to be human to fulfil that dream of one day playing for England and scoring the winning try in the corner at Twickenham. That was the one and only thing mankind had over birds in his opinion – the ability to play rugby.

Bird's appreciation of the coastal avifauna of southern England had been nurtured and sculpted over his short years with the help of his mother's cousin, Alfred Weiss, who lived by himself in the woods at the end of a beaten path and was hailed as one of Britain's leading ornithologists. Bird spent most weekends with Alfred and absorbed his eccentric enthusiasm like a sponge, feeding off the barrage of scientific information that seemed to flow effortlessly from every breath he exhaled. And whilst the paternal skills of a quirky mad scientist will always leave a lot to be desired, Alfred was inadvertently bumbling his way into the vacant, fatherless chasm now available for rent inside the boy's soul.

Bird replaced the whistle with a distorted hum as he bit into his sandwich and sat himself down at the kitchen table to read his mother's note. He wondered where she would be this time – the King's Arms, the Queen Vic, the Ferryboat Inn? Which of these fine establishments would she have chosen to grace today? Whichever had the most accessible line of credit to exploit – that was his guess. He skimmed through the note, half anticipating the familiar flow of words without actually reading them; it was only when he got to the end that a bewildered frown crumpled the skin between his eyebrows, forcing him to put down the sandwich, swallow hard and start reading from the beginning again, this time scrutinising each and every word on the page.

My dearest Bird,

I hope that one day you may be able to forgive me. I know this is hard to understand but I can't go on anymore. I don't think this is good for either of us and you deserve a chance to spread your wings and soar like an eagle. I have to go away for a while to sort some things out and I can't say when I will be back. You know what to do and you know where to go. There is some money under the ashtray which is all I can spare right now. I am so sorry my boy but I think we both know that this is for the best. No matter what happens, you must know that I will always love you.

Mum.

He placed the note down on the table, unsure whether to laugh out loud or scream hysterically; then he snatched it up again and read the words one more time, just to be sure that it said what he thought it said. It did. He reached under the ashtray and pulled out a ten-pound note, unfolding and inspecting it as if there might be some clue hidden there, a trace of sanity to make sense of this bizarre situation. There wasn't.

"She's gone," he whispered to himself. "She's really gone."

He got up slowly from the table and wandered towards the lounge, his mind skipping through an embellished symphony of synaptic ballads in a desperate quest for answers among its young and limited archive. There were few there to be found, but the words "*You know what to do and you know where to go*" seemed to guide him through a mechanical stagger, focussing his attention on a telephone in the far corner of the room. He turned the volume down on the record player in an attempt to make space in his head, then fixed a glazed stare on the phone, realising that making the call would mean closure and his mother would not come bursting out of a closet screaming "Surprise!" with a bottle of wine in one hand, a cigarette in the other and a smile across her lips as she squashed his cheeks together and told him how much she loved him.

But no one was there. He was alone in the murky lounge, now silent and somewhat unfamiliar as he gazed at paltry artefacts scattered about the room that had once symbolised a family's unity. It was getting dark outside, and the stillness of the room began to disturb him. A voice in his head was telling him to put the lights on, but the switch was across on the other side and the phone was right there. He needed to make that call before it was too late – before desperate realisation of the magnitude of this event sent him diving for cover in the familiar refuge underneath his bed and held him there for the rest of the night, quaking and alone. An unfamiliar wave of anxiety suddenly rippled across his skin and hunched up in between his shoulders with an abrupt shiver, throwing him off balance for a second, but he gathered himself and drew a deep breath.

He picked up the receiver and started dialling a four-digit number that by now was as familiar as the lines on his own face. Each number clicked mechanically in the earpiece as the rotary-dial phone wound its way back to zero, and then there was a pause as the call routed itself through an analogue switchboard, connected and whistled with the familiar staccato ring tone.

"Hello?" came a voice on the other end.

"Hello, Alfred, it's me."

"Ah, hello Bird, everything all right?"

"I don't think so, not really all right this time, Alfred." He trembled. "This time I think she's gone, I really think she's gone."

On the other end of the phone, there was a pause as Alfred weighed this situation for a moment, thinking only of his own consequences. He didn't need to be a rocket scientist to have predicted that this day would come, and secretly he'd been both dreading and preparing for it for the last three years. He shook his head and sighed as a thousand thoughts crashed through his mind, then suddenly remembered the boy and how he must be feeling. Bird was in need of help, and now that he came to think of it, everything else was superfluous to that fact.

"OK, son." His elusive paternal instinct was now guiding him. "You just hang on there and I'll be over shortly, you hear? Everything's gonna be all right, Bird, you'll see. Everything's gonna be just fine, son. Don't you worry about anything, you hear?" But there was no sound at the other end of the line.

To Bird, Alfred's words barely registered. He gazed around the room, drifting in and out of the situation, still searching for a sign that would tell him that actually, it wasn't really happening – still staring into the dark corners to see if she was there, hoping to catch the glow of her cigarette.

"Bird?" Alfred called again, jolting him into the present.

"Yes…"

"Are you sure you're all right, Bird? Is anyone else there with you? Bird?" Alfred kept using his name, clearly trying to keep his attention.

"Yes, I'm sure I'm OK. No one else is here, I'm all alone. I'll just wait for you here… just like you said… I'll wait here… but, Alfred…"

"Yes, son?"

"Don't be long."

Alfred must have felt the pain in his voice, because he loosened up his tone.

"I'll be there in a flash, boy, before you can even say *jack diddly*. Now go and put the kettle on, 'cos I have a feeling I'll be needing a cup o' tea when I get there. I

shan't be long, Bird, do you hear me? I shan't be long."
And then the phone went dead in his hands.

"Jack diddly," Bird uttered in soliloquy as he placed
the receiver back in its cradle.

Outside, evening was rapidly drawing in. A street lamp
rained down a dull, yellow glow that partially illuminated
the dark room, streaming light through the window but
casting black shadows in its corners. Bird turned slowly
back to the record player and reached for the volume, now
desperate to drown out the silence of despair and postpone
the inevitable feeling of abandonment that lurked
somewhere in the depths of his soul. These next few
minutes waiting for Alfred would be long and painful and
he'd need something to take his mind off the circumstance.
In the absence of television, the record player was his only
available option, and he cranked the volume as high as it
could go.

The boy slowly sank down into the couch and buried
his head in his hands. The acoustic melody of bittersweet
guitar riffs wafted aimlessly around before the striking
harmony of a male-voice requiem broke away in a delicate
paradox of haunting prose.

But the darkness would not be his friend.

And the silence would remain inside him until the
bitter end.

2

A WALK IN THE PARK

"Bird… Bird… Bird…" There was a knocking on the door, faint but monotonous, and someone in the distance calling his name – though for a second there he swore he was back at Twickenham with a thousand screaming fans chanting it after a winning score in the corner.

"Burrd? Are ye awake, Burrd?" It was Maggie, the cleaner. Twickenham would have to wait for another day – or another dream.

"Yeah, Maggs… Morning."

"It's aarfternoon actually and Cracker's doown stairrs in t' pub. He told me you and he wurr s'posed to be goin' somewhere teday and you'rre late. D'you know what I said? I said, funny thaart, not like Burrd to be late. Thart's what I said to him, Burrd. I mean, it's not like I have to come up here every murnin' to wake you from yer slumber now is it? NOOOOOOHOA, not Burrd, I said, he's the most punctual person…"

"Yeah, right, Maggs, don't you have a toilet to clean or something?" he quipped, pulling the edges of the pillow around his ears.

Her face curled into a disapproving sneer and she paused momentarily, glaring steel blades into the closed door through which she'd been shouting at him whilst shuffling around in the corridor outside. This was an all-too-familiar routine for these two unlikely associates –

only today was Bird's day off and under normal circumstances she'd have let him sleep, but Cracker had asked her to wake him and she had politely obliged.

Maggie was an old widow, her husband having gone to that grave in the sea after a lifetime on the fishing boats. His foot got snagged in rigging as they were shooting away crab pots to the ocean floor one dark winter's morning. Eighteen pots lashed together on a line, flying in quick succession over the edge. Next thing they knew, there was old Tom flying with them, rope around the ankle – too quick – dragged down to the bottom of the English Channel, grave of rancid graves. Maggie had no kids and Tom had no pension. Destiny would have her work as a cleaner and a barmaid until she was no longer able to walk, talk or think, then maybe the kind people at the National Health Service would throw her into one of their fabulous institutions that smelt of bleach and overcooked peas. She probably deserved better.

"Thanks, Maggs, I'm on my way."

"So you blurrdy should be, this is noo time t' be sleepin'," she clucked in a strong West Country accent that drew out her a's and rattled her r's. She was a true Devonshire lass – prone to leaving out letters, syllables and sometimes even words through sheer idleness of speech, and oftentimes those that she chose to enunciate she did with little articulation. Bird had somehow managed to avoid the dreaded farm-boy drawl despite having spent most of his life in England's West Country. His accent was bland – neutral, English and bland.

He lived above the pub in which he worked – the Wound and Bandage, shortened by those who frequented it to 'the Wound', occasionally 'the Bandage', though more often than not, simply 'the boozer'. Cracker was perched at the bar negotiating the dregs of a bottle of Pilsner swindled off the barmaid after some friendly chat and emotional blackmail when Bird appeared at the door. Bird had grown up with Cracker and had given him the nickname years before as he was always cracking something, and it was generally something illegal. If there was ever anything untoward, unjust, morally inappropriate or just plain stupid to be done, Cracker cracked the nod – each and every time.

"All right, Cracks? You look like shit, mate."

"All right, Bird? You too, dude. Fancy a breakfast?"

"Yeah, man. Starved." They continued their enamoured conversation as they ambled out of the pub and down the main drag towards Arthur Black's cafe.

"So, what'd you get up to last night, Birdman?"

"Cards at DZ's, usual routine. You know how it is."

"Oh yeah, poker night was it? And just how are the cards falling for you at this time of year, Feather Boy? Still got the luck of the dogs or did you clean the boys up?"

"Fuck all, mate, I lost fifty sheets," replied a foot-scuffing Bird.

"Fifty quid! Are you nuts or wot?" yelped Cracker, incensed. "That's half an ounce of bud or a gram of chang or… or…" He paused in a moment's distorted contemplation and raised his screwed eyes to the heavens, stroking his stubbled chin. "Or a shit-load of acid, man." His eyes rested on Bird's, his hand still on the stubble. "You're not all there, are you, mate? You is lost somewhere in the clouds, man… high up in them clouds."

"Yeah, you're right Cracks, but what can I do? I just love to play. It's six hours of hellish entertainment where I actually stand a chance of winning." He paused momentarily, not too dissimilarly to his mate's previous action but lacking the chin gig. "Not much chance of winning with the drugs, man."

"Ah, you're talking like a rehab case, Bird." And with an accent that resonated like a drugged-up Keith Richards, Cracker continued his mock. "Yeah, man, like rehab did it for me, know wot I'm saayin'? Just, like, ironed out da creases, man. 'Cos no matter how you looks at it, its ve drugs man, vey just strip your soul and, like, realign your cosmic atoms, yeah, and completely like take over, yeah – but rehab roight, I mean that's the gig, yeah – the rebirth – the manifestation…"

"Cracker – shut the fuck up."

They walked into the café, greeting Arthur as they entered with Cracker still droning on behind Bird like a gibbering basket case, and took a table by the window overlooking the sea. A voice bellowed from the depths of the kitchen, out of sight but very audible. With the accent it could have been Maggie's clone, but it wasn't; it was Big Beth the waitress.

"Mornin' laads – usual today?"

"Murrnin' Berrth," mocked Cracker. "Aye, ay'll be 'aarvin the usual please, me daaarlin'!"

"Yeah, you'll be gettin' it up yer aaarse too if ye keeps mockin' me, bay!" snorted Beth, with an evil glint that suggested not only her ability to perform such an action but an extreme willingness to execute it as well.

"Before we eat, Mr. Bird, let's consume." With a wicked glint adorning his sunken blue eyes, Cracker produced from his pocket two small squares of blotting paper that had an emblem of dragons etched in red on the face.

"Red dragons, mate. Double dips. Mental trips, man. Neck 'em now so they start to take effect before we drown them in cholesterol."

They swallowed the acid simultaneously and felt the unmistakable taste of chemicals on their gums.

"Got two more if we need to double up in the day." Cracker winked at the bemused soul sitting opposite him, wincing as the blotter crept down his throat.

"What the fuck will we need to double up for if these are 'double dip, mental trip' red dragons in the first place?" Only Cracker would know – Bird didn't.

At that moment the door opened and two young ladies walked in. They were yachting types but here out of season. Henley's Hooray Henrys usually only gathered during the summer when they descended en masse, desperate to justify the existence of their forty-thousand-pound yachts that sniffed wind once a year but hosted super parties and did wonders for the balance sheets at tax time. They were easy pickings for the likes of Bird and Cracker, who took great pride in manipulating the wallets of such folk in order to subsidise their various and extensive drug habits. And whilst the wallets were comprehensive enough to handsomely reward these acts of subliminal intent, in a world without Fagin the habits just grew wider while Oliver Twist sank forever deeper.

It was only the die-hard yachty yuppies that usually came down this way outside of summer and they were all genuine sea dogs, too. But these two girls were precious little angels, beautiful from every angle. They carried a certain naivety about them, yet a distinct confidence and charm that private school and university had instilled. You could put money on them being successful young associates in the city – publishing or fashion, something arty, not law or finance or gangster shit.

They took the table next to Bird and Cracker, not even registering their presence, which was a sure sign they were from out of town – everyone here greeted each other. Cracker didn't even notice them, he was still drivelling on about some mindless crap that only sounds good when you're completely off your head, which he usually was anyway.

Bird, on the other hand, studied one of the angels' cleavages. He was busy undressing her in his mental theatre, peeling away her blouse and loosening a soft silk slip which would fall off her smooth shoulders as he ran his lips down her silken neck. She would be groaning with pleasure at the feel of his gentle touch, begging him not to stop and… ooh… ooh… Bird… ooh … yes… Bird…

"Breakfast, boyos. Enjoy, and don't forget my tip!" Bird hit reality with a thump as Big Beth thrust two plates of fried stuff swimming in baked beans in front of them before taking the order from the angels. He was still lost somewhere in angel one's cleavage and she was aware of it, repulsed by his obvious intentions to strip her of her underwear and then her dignity.

And she could sense it. "Filthy man!" she hissed through the edges of her twisted lips.

Bird didn't impress her much, but she thought Cracker could be a potential dish. Just needed a bit of work on the hair, a change of clothes and posture, perhaps a good scrub – oh, and some elocution lessons – then he could actually pass for acceptable. Well, marginally. Pity he was so obviously into drugs like the rest of these fouled-up creatures living in this town. No career, no future, no hope. A burden, that was all, just a burden on taxpayers' money – her money, her beautiful untainted money – her reason for being. Money, money, money, status, position, success.

"I'll have a crab sandwich on wholewheat with herbal tea, please."

"Oh, that sounds delish, make that two. Thanks awfully." They curled up their lips and snarled a foxy smile at each other as Miss Cleavage slid her elbows onto the table and rested her chest on her forearms.

Bird and Cracker tucked into their fry-ups. Bird was sure this girl was on for him really, she just didn't know it yet. It was his day off; maybe she'd be in the pub tonight for the pool match. She'd surely swoon over him after seeing what a demon he was on the table, wouldn't she? He resolved to himself that if she was there, he would play his heart out and she would see that he was different. She would understand that a Birdman only comes along once a millennium and if he happens to be staring at your chest, you damn well better seize the opportunity. Tonight would be the night.

With strengthened resolve and joyous heart he cut into his sausage, which was now coated in tomato sauce and bean juice and steaming with the latent heat released from its inner core. It was an action he had performed flawlessly thousands of times and today should have been no different. He didn't really know what happened. Didn't even know how it happened, or why, but it did – something happened – something bad. A little slip – too heavy on the knife, not firm enough with the fork, who knows…

…Don't know… just kinda happened, man…

But before he had time to realise it, an object was airborne.

The knife had slid sharply across his plate, catapulting a piece of sausage off the edge and giving it a life of its own – a target – a mission – AWOL and loving it. With the inclined edge of his plate accelerating its elevation, the meaty accord had launched itself skyward, whereupon slow motion of the visual receptors involuntarily ensued.

The missile glided its way through the air, catching all molecules of light as it went, illuminated like a flashing satellite – rotating, flickering, orbiting an unmistakable path guided by destiny. Bird watched helplessly as it gradually sailed towards the target as if equipped with a homing device. Miss Cleavage saw the thing just in time to register 'missile incoming' but not soon enough to dodge it.

With the greatest of ease and in the slowest of motions, it exploded against her chin and sent remnants of ketchup and bean juice splattering across her angelic face. It seemed to hang there for a second, suspended like a raindrop on a grass stem, before easing itself off and rolling gently down inside her shirt –exposed by the way she had been sitting – and into the cleavage that was the cause of all this attention in the first place. The acid had already started creeping up Bird's spine and any minute now would be exploding into his head sending him careering out of control.

Shit – what's that? It's the acid, isn't it – I can feel the acid – I can feel it already – it's mutant, man – any acid that hits within ten minutes has got to be mutant. Where's that sausage? It hit her chin – yes, her chin, the sausage –

oh dear. Why is this happening to me – why now? Wait. What's happening? Ah, bollocks!

There was a pause that seemed to last a lifetime as Miss Cleavage buried fourteen thousand visual daggers into Bird's heart – but then it happened. The calm of the café, the cool of the air, the beautiful silence of slow motion, shattered by a mind-crushing scream as the hot sausage embedded itself into her bra.

"AAAAAAAAAAAAAGGGGGGGGGGGGHHHH HHHHHHHH!"

She stood up, still screaming, and turned her gaze on Bird, her face speckled with bean juice.

"You bloody idiot!" She spat the words at him like a cat facing a new puppy brought into its house for the first time, and then stormed out to the bathroom.

"God, you're pathetic," spat her feline friend as she followed Miss Cleavage to the ladies' for support.

"Uhh, s-s-sorry," whimpered Bird to their backs as they left the room. "Sorry…"

Cracker fell off his chair and gripped at his sides in an attempt to contain his raucous laughter. Beth joined him from the kitchen before burying her shaking head into her open hands, and even Arthur forced out a grin. Bird actually cracked up himself for a second, but then it all started to dawn on him and suddenly he was not enjoying it that much, after all. He was now into a full-blown trip and the walls were starting to sway and contort around him. The acid was rushing up his spine and filling his head with something that felt like liquid – endorphins? He didn't know, the word was just swimming around his head with multicoloured fish.

Endorphins.

He kept forgetting the incident and rushing into tangent thoughts but was aware all the while that some bad shit was going down around him – he just couldn't remember what. It made him kind of anxious, like the plot was sailing away from him on a rabid sea with multicoloured fish.

Cracker picked himself up off the floor.

"God, you got style, man. You got style like no one I ever seen, Feather Boy. No wonder you ain't been laid in three years."

Fish… endorphins… colours… shit, did you see… what was that… man, that looks cool… what is it… just can't remember… something bad is going down, I'm sure… what is it… what's bad?

"Wow, three years, is it really that long?" His speech interjected his fluid thought.

Shit, the birds, the screaming birds, the rabid, hellfire girls, fish… endorphins… sausage… what was that? The birds, they'll be back any minute… they're my problem… one's gonna kick my ass… the birds… the sausage…

Is this the end… my beautiful friend… is this the end?

"Cracks, we gotta get outta here, man." Bird looked across at Cracker, his eyes alive with fear. "I gotta get on the cliffs – like, fast! Screaming chicks, dude – flying sausages… and I'm comin' up, man!"

Cracker straightened his gaze, aware of the acid now for the first time. "God yes. Screaming chicks and sausages. Let's get outta here."

They hurried down the rest of their food, paid Beth and shuffled out of the café just as Miss Cleavage was returning from the bathroom, restored.

"It means you're in love!" yelled Cracker as they disappeared up the street. He was laughing again, and Bird started to relax once in the fresh air and away from the neurotic, bean-coated woman. Cracker always had the last word – no matter what.

It means you're in love... Cupid's arrow... a sausage. This is mental acid, man.

The walk to the cliffs happened, but it wasn't registered or measured by any means known to man. So much had occurred – was still occurring. Their heads were exploding with images and lights, screaming with the barrage of incoherent thoughts. It was windy on the cliffs, with sporadic cloud cover throwing intermittent blankets over the sun, but they weren't really aware of feelings towards the weather – so much else was going on.

No time to consider the weather. Whether I'm hot or cold, wet or dry, black or white, human or dragon – yeah, dragon. Dragon's what fucked us up...

Bird gripped Cracker's arm and stared hard at his face.

"Dragon's what fucked us up, man, red dragon." His eyes were on fire and his face was contorting in and out of mutating shapes.

Cracker stared hard at Bird, as if unaware of who he was and why he was talking to him. He tried hard to focus, as if knowing that there was a connection somewhere, but gave up the mission and had to ask himself about his socks to be sure he was in control.

"Did I put odd socks on this morning? I saw them on the chair. What's that?" His head moved away, leaving a sparkling tracer behind it. He was following an imaginary flying object, brightly lit and conspicuous yet never really identified.

"That's it, man – the gig's blown. I haven't eaten all day." Bird released his grip on Cracker's arm and stared out to sea.

They were perched on the edge of a rock jutting out from a cliff where, two hundred feet below them, the waves crashed into its face with relentless ease. They had been sitting in silence for some time, just taking in the scene, and this was their first communication. Bird was unhappy about the exchange; it hadn't exactly gone according to plan.

What was the plan again? Shit, this is all too much – too much, man – this is mental acid.

He gazed out to sea and relaxed his face. His eyes seemed to roll in their sockets like pneumatic shutters and he suddenly found himself staring inside – into his own head. It was fairly bare, painted a brilliant white, and dome-shaped with an attic window on one side shining a beam of light into the centre of a wooden floor. Two people sat on either side of the beam, cross-legged and facing each other. They looked exactly the same – both perfect replicas of Bird himself, even down to the clothes they were wearing. They stared at each other for a while and then started talking.

"So, what do you think of the acid?" the first clone ventured.

"Red dragons, man – kicked my ass!" came an indignant reply.

"Yeah, mine too. Don't really know what I think of them 'cos they never gave me a second to think."

"You're not supposed to think, fool – this is LSD, we take it so we don't have to think. It thinks for us. It alters our perception – not just sensory."

"Yeah, I know, but I have to have an opinion about it or there's simply no point in doing it."

"What the fuck d'you need a point for?"

They seemed drone-like at first, two-dimensional spectres born of a dormant consciousness, but as they began to speak a reality was consuming them, manifesting his own humanity into the alien lair that had spun a myriad of illusions inside his head. The drone of reason continued his defence.

"Well, I just think we need some kind of mission with this trip, that's all – you know, like sensory enhancement or spiritual levitation – something cool and sixties-like. But I guess that's wasted on you, isn't it? For you it's just about getting high."

"Piss off! Don't get self-righteous with me, we do 'em 'cos we do 'em – end of fuckin' story."

So that probably makes him the drone of contempt?

"Fair enough, I shouldn't have expected much more I guess, what with you being Neolithic and all."

The drone of contempt ignored the remark and stared sulkily away. Mr. Reason, however, continued.

"Anyway, this stuff will take an age to wear off and we will be having many an inane conversation until it does, so I just thought I'd get an opinion from the outset, that's all. Hmm… maybe it'll never wear off, maybe we'll trip like this forever. Now there's an interesting concept; what do you think of that?"

The drone of reason was apparently trying his damnedest to keep some form of communication going, painfully aware that the prospect of riding six hours in hallucinogenic mayhem with a sulky companion does not bode well on the old paranoia front. It stimulated a response, at least.

"What do I think?" The drone of contempt emerged from spontaneous indifference. "I think we should never come down." Albeit just for a fight. "I think we should live in this state of mind forever and just live the trip for the rest of our lives. Remember Scotty?" He smirked cheekily. "Scotty was forever out of it. He was forever on the run – forever being chased – forever ducking – forever diving – but never really escaping… *the dragon!*"

There was a pause. Everything went quiet. They stared at each other a while and contemplated their mate, Scott. Even Bird, hovering around outside the drone dome, suspended his animation and spared a thought for his old friend. Scott had taken one tab too many and literally lived in a mental acid trip for a whole year, despite not actually consuming any LSD during the period. It was kind of scary, even to the drones, not to mention Bird.

"That's your answer to everything, isn't it?" The minute's silence for their bombed-out friend was suddenly broken. "Do it all, get a habit, be an addict. I remember Scotty, I remember him well and I don't want to be how he was, no way. Could anyone really want to be addicted to acid?"

"Yeah man, why the fuck not?"

"Why the fuck why?" came a short, sharp response. "Why excess on everything that is potentially damaging to us? You've wanted to get addicted to every substance we've ever tried – thank God we only flirted with heroin. You did this last time we tripped, too, and I still don't think it's physically possible to be addicted to LSD anyway, so when are you going to grow a brain cell that works?

'Addict' has a certain ring that kind of suits you – it suits you, but it doesn't suit me."

The drone of reason's voice was rising in pitch, having remained stoically calm throughout the exchange so far, and a waft of sarcasm drifted into his dialogue, resonating disdain for his companion.

He continued, "I don't actually want to be addicted, you know – I just want to be free, can you understand that? Why do we always have to have excess – why do we have to OD on everything life throws at us? I just wanna be normal, moderate, considerate, know what I'm saying? Do such words feature in your prehistoric vocabulary?"

"I want, I want – always thinking about yourself, aren't you?" the drone of contempt snorted. "Well, get it into your head, pal, there's three of us here, not just you – and sometimes the things that you want will have to take a back seat for the good of the community. You, yeah you…" The drone pointed at Bird who considered himself somewhat of a prowler, an intruder looking through a strange bedroom window. "You're in this too, you know?" he mocked, gesticulating towards Bird. "He sees us, man… he's part of the gig, don't forget that – we are three. It's not just a one-happy-man show in here, mate. We all have a say in what goes on and there's three of us – got it?" They were talking about Bird – he was talking about Bird, he was talking about himself.

Who are these guys?

"Since when did you become so concerned about the good of the community? I don't see you consulting anyone when the stimulants are flowing and you want to get wasted – you just go right ahead, and he always follows. You bully him just as much as you do me. You just shout and scream about what you want, and we all trudge along and do as we're told for fear of you losing the plot and going off on one again. Don't talk to me about community. Your rhetoric doesn't quite work the same with me as it does with him. I live in here with you, I know you and I tolerate you for the sake of peace and harmony. He doesn't." The drone of reason now pointed at Bird. "He's got no clue what you're really like, he doesn't know the half of it. He walks around half asleep, hoping life will all just go away, but me, I'm wide awake, man. The only one round here that is, too, and possibly the only chance we have of salvation in this hallucinogenic storm."

"You don't know shit, Mr. Righteous. You walk around with your thumb up your own arse and your nose up his. Always trying to be so reverent, so correct, so beneficial to society; well, bollocks to it, mate – the gig is blown. Life ain't worth the grief of getting attached to this society 'cos it'll rip our hearts out and split our souls, then ask for praise when the day is done. This is the gig, man – this is the only one left to play – it is here and it is now. Ride that wave into oblivion, 'cos you never know when it might be your last!" A victorious snarl had crumpled the edge of his lips, and both drones scowled with aggressive intent.

"Yeah yeah, quote your clichés, live in your fantasy world. When are you going to grow up and sniff that coffee, mate? Gonna hide all your life in imaginary sports arenas and home movies only shown in your mental theatre?"

They were still sitting cross-legged on the floor, but there was now much waving of the arms and voices were steadily rising in pitch. They had suddenly become very real to Bird.

Who are these guys?

"What are you talking about? This is *our* mental theatre, it's *our* mind – we all live here you know, we all share this thinking space."

"Oh, don't I know it. Don't I know that I have to share this sacred temple with the likes of you two? Think about what I've done with my share of this mind, think about what we've learnt, what we've seen, what we've proven. Think about the work we've done with birds, the studies that we made, the papers delivered to Oxford, the identifications, the academics of it all. We have a wealth of scientific knowledge flowing around in here, yet we do nothing with it – absolutely nothing. We could really make a difference in this life, we could research birds in the Amazon or whales in the Arctic or lions in Africa, but you steamroll around here, pumping drugs into his mouth as soon as he opens it because you cannot handle the past. Come to think of it, you can't handle the present or the future, either. When are you going to let it lie?"

Bird cocked his head to the side and raised his eyebrows; the drone had a point.

Lions in Africa?

"Piss off. I'm not letting anything lie," Mr. Contempt retorted. "Don't see you wanting to stop when the coke's flowing and there's an audience to spout your bird bollocks to. And since when could we research whales in the Arctic or lions in Africa?"

"I don't know, I just thought about it. The fact is that these drugs are killing us – we need to get away. What is the point if we can't even think?"

"God, you got no clue? We – aren't – supposed – to – think!"

Who the hell are these guys?

The argument was now cascading into catalytic obscurity and Bird could feel the tension rising inside his own head. These guys sure looked like him and they sure knew a lot about how he viewed life, but who on earth were they and why were they arguing so?

And then it began.

At first there was just a tingling in his feet that rumbled across his knees, but then it started to quake in his groin until his whole body suddenly felt the static gyration. An alien force had somehow manifested itself in the base of this rock, causing his stomach to flutter, his nerves to quiver and his skin to crawl as the whole universe began shaking around him. The feeling welled up from the pit of his soul and gained momentum as it rushed through his being, electrifying every morsel of potential energy as it summoned its resources.

Endorphins?

The pressure built up inside him like massive turbines propelling themselves towards optimum revolution, and the two characters began groping at the floor as this monstrous quaking intrusion released itself in a shattering flash. It had started in his stomach, rushed up his torso and burst through the wooden floor inside his head, sending exploding debris everywhere and igniting a thousand fireworks. Mayhem – World War III – that AWOL sausage again. *"KABOOM"* right inside his brain.

Through the explosive flashes of incendiary smoke clouds, a pillar was emerging up the centre of his head, rising like a rocket ship blasting away from its rigging. The tower inched its way forward, up the apex of his mind, until it ground to a gradual and somewhat mechanical halt just short of the inside of his crown.

As the air began to clear, Bird could make out an object perched on the pillar's summit. It was another replica of him, but this time aged six and butt-naked sitting crossed-legged on top of the Nelson's illusory Column now firmly rooted inside his head. The kid waited for calm as the roar subsided through a sea of dust. When it was clear enough to have an audience, he stood up on his pillar and looked straight at Bird. He held the stare for just a second then clicked his fingers, reciting as only a six-year-old can:

> *"He thinks he's right*
> *But you know that he's wrong;*
> *He writes the music*
> *And we all sing the song;*
> *But the truth you will find*
> *Down here deep in our soul:*
> *I am the rock*
> *And you have to let it roll..."*

He paused momentarily, the floor belonging solely to him. The two characters that had previously held it were now huddled in separate corners of Bird's head, shivering with fear. The boy delivered his epilogue with a wink and a grin.

"This is the gig, boys – the only one left to play – you've got to let it roll." And then he was gone.

Led Zeppelin's 'Stairway to Heaven' burst into life as Bird's eyes rolled out of his head and he was once again staring at the sea. It took a few seconds to comprehend the shattering event, even with the tune thumping in his brain, but eventually a trigger was squeezed and endorphins were released, inducing a bemused Bird to gently pat his now restored and intact head.

Endorphins?

He suddenly sprang to his feet, rubbed Cracker's head and then thrust his air guitar across his chest and began rocking out to the tune. He whined and screeched his unique rendition of the iconic guitar solo and pranced around the rock, completely oblivious to life, let alone the elderly couple walking their dog on a nearby footpath. Had he seen them he would have undoubtedly been consumed by paranoia and frozen to this granite outcrop for hours on end with no chance of salvation, but as it was, he was lost in the ultimate composition with just one question on his mind.

Is there really a stairway?

"It's one of those lunatics from the village, Harry. Let's walk on," muttered the disgruntled rambler.

Cracker was still rooted to the rock with his elbow resting on his knee. He didn't shift his gaze from the ocean – not once.

3

IT'S LADIES' NIGHT – OH WHAT A NIGHT

"YEEEEESSSSSSS PLEEEAASSSEE!"

It had been all one motion for Cracker. He shot the line of cocaine up his nose with a loud snort and a disposition that so deservedly earned him the name and rose up, grabbing Bird by the face and squashing his cheeks together, saying:

"Why in God's name do we keep doing it to ourselves, my little feathered friend?"

Bird had the look of a confused puppy about him. All he needed to do was cock his head to one side and raise an ear and the set would be complete. Thankfully he didn't. He was yet to do any coke and was still a bit shaky from the trip. He'd been pacing up and down in serious contemplation with his hands behind his back and his lips puckering until Cracker grabbed him and welcomed him back to humanity. It was all a bit much.

"Gotta get it together, Cracker – gotta play a pool match. I'm the team fucking captain and the guys will be looking to me for leadership, guidance, organisation…" He stared away for a second and then looked at Cracker with the fear of an imaginary god in his eyes. "And I'm still trippin', man."

"Do a line, it'll sort you out. Damn, I gotta smoke – like, hard." Cracker was rocking from the narcotic and in a completely different place from Bird, who was feeling vulnerable and alone, unsure whether the coke would actually sort him out or shove him over the edge of a precipice that would send him floating on a sea of LSD forevermore. But he followed Cracker's lead anyway… he always did.

The very sensation of hitting a substance up his nose gave him the feeling of shooting a lightning bolt into the brain. This was especially compounded when coming down from hectic double-dip mental trips and snorting badly-cut cocaine, which this definitely was. It burned a hole in Bird's nose as it screwed its way into his deluded mind.

"You know, Mr. Cracker, I believe you were right." And in an instant, one persona was buried as another one was born. "A line has definitely sorted me out. Let's have a go on your smoke, mate." He pulled hard on the cigarette and blew out a thin line of blue smoke as he licked non-existent granules from his fingertips and flicked aimlessly at his gleaming nostrils.

"I think the time has come for me to do a little territory markin', Mr. Cracker. This is my gig, after all, and I've got a match to win. We are fourteen games without loss and the Birdman here remains unbeaten all season." Suddenly matter-of-fact and chirpy, he tugged at his shirt collar and straightened imaginary lapels. "Folk startin' to talk about me, Cracks – gone and got meself a reputation I have. Demon on the table, that's I – demon on the motherfuckin' table. Apparently I am the dude to beat, the man with the plan, the cat with the crock, know wot I'm sayin'? Yep, guess my time is now. Fifteen years of fortune – Andy Warpo said that. Gonna fuck these boys up tonight – Royale wi' cheese style."

"That's fifteen minutes of fame and it was Andy Warhol who said it. And you can bet your bones he weren't talkin' about pool, neither, featherhead. 'Notha line, Birdyboy?" He was holding a rolled-up fiver.

Bird had been talking with some limp-rendition-of-a-London-gangster type voice, which, let's face it, wasn't that convincing at the best of times, and Cracker had just done a fine job of deflating his bloated ego in one swift action. But riding the crest of that frosted wave with life stretching out before him and the chemical pumping through his veins, well, nothing would really topple him.

"Go on, then."

The pub was busy and bustling, full of regulars all down to support their lads in the pool team and perhaps snag a free sandwich from the players' platter at half time. Everyone knew each other except for the visiting team and their assorted entourage of unappealing women and toothless mates, but the mood was buoyant enough. As usual, Ray Branner was late – Bird contemplated getting stressed about it for a moment but decided to get drunk instead. There was time, DZ was just getting going on his game and he was always first up. Bird played number six and Ray usually played fifth. He was a useful player, without a doubt the best on the team, but just so majorly unreliable.

Across town, Ray Branner sat in his one-room bedsit, slumped across a ragged armchair with a tourniquet twisted around his scant bicep. An empty syringe protruded from the vein in his arm and a broken smile crumpled his cracked lips. Moments earlier, he had been tussling with a voice inside his head about the pool match he was due to be playing in at the pub, but his favourite obsession had recorded a resounding victory and taken precedence over all extracurricular activities for the rest of the evening. A melancholic tune ambled out of his music box and drifted around the room as the poison seeped deeper inside his brain. Ray Branner was going nowhere.

The pool team comprised six players. A contest against neighbouring pubs entailed playing six games of singles and then three games of doubles to get the best of nine. There is never a draw in pool, so basically the first team to win five frames took the game. The Wound had some of the most talented players in the region but they all had various and associated stimulant habits, so Bird and two friends known as DZ and Iceberg seemed to be the only three that ever got it together to play each week. Ray was one of the best pool players that Bird had ever known, but his 'habit' seemed to take priority over everything else in his life, so it was no surprise when he was late or indeed never showed. As the match progressed, however, it began to sway the opposition's way, making the need for Ray even greater – which only added to Bird's potential pressure levels.

More alcohol is needed!

Four games down and the Bandage boys were losing three-one. Ray was nowhere to be seen and Bird was now officially stressed, not to mention a bit inebriated, and getting ever more desperate to find a replacement.

"I'll do it, Birdman, I'll play for Ray." Cracker was leaning on the table talking to Bird under its hanging light while he racked up the balls. Bird looked at him, unable to respond – he was mesmerised by the image of a dragon that faded in and out of focus across Cracker's face.

Cracker smiled and picked up the cue. His opponent spun a coin and slammed it down on the edge of the table.

"Heads, mate." And so it began.

This was bad. It was worse than bad. Cracker couldn't play to save his life and this frame was as vital as they come in any match, but something had Bird's tongue wrapped up tight and neither Heaven nor Earth could release it.

God help me, what have I done?

In spite of his deepening concern, the vehicle was in motion and had already started to roll. Cracker was just one of those people that you couldn't say no to. Bird stood back and watched as his fears of Cracker's shiteness at pool coalesced into a horrifying reality right there before his eyes. And to rub salt into the gaping wound of distorted morality, his opponent was shit-hot and on a roll. But by some freak of an erratic power known only as Lady Luck, he potted the black with three balls left on the table and forfeited his game. And Cracker wasn't shy about taking the credit, either. He threw his victorious fists into the air as the black trickled off the edge of the table and into obscurity.

"Double JD 'n' Coke, ta mate." He smiled as he shook his disgruntled opponent's hand. "Bad luck, eh…" wink wink. The guy wasn't amused; he thought Cracker was a complete and utter clown.

"JD 'n' Coke? Fuckin' twat," he murmured as he sauntered to the bar.

Three-two down and one to play in the singles games. It was time for the Birdman to assert his dominance and show the gathered crowds just exactly what this game was all about.

Ping… craaaackk.

Bird potted the white ball on his break and immediately forfeited two shots to his opponent, who wasted no time. He began slotting balls left, right and centre, swooping around the table like a whirlwind, always thinking a couple of shots ahead, potting well, getting good position and manipulating the table like he had a premeditated plan for each ball. He was fired up and looked like he might clean the slate with the first visit, but his last colour juggled in the jaw of the pocket and refused to drop, which threw Bird a much-needed lifeline. They played cat-and-mouse safety for a few shots but it just wasn't happening for Bird; his usual pool-table flair was in some other pub tonight and he was kind of floundering around without it.

Bastard dragon!

Then suddenly, without fear, countenance or warning, her face appeared in the crowd – just like that – Miss Cleavage. She was watching the game – watching his game – him – making an arse of himself – again. She surely was an angel. The prettiest angel he'd ever seen. He looked up at her and the AWOL sausage flashed into his mind for the first time since that morning. Cupid's arrow – fired straight from his plate and into her heart. Cupid's sausage in Uncle Arthur's café – yes, she would be his. Tonight.

He had fluked one ball in on his break and so had six left on the table. Everything went quiet as he breathed out a deep sigh and focussed all his attention on the white ball perched at the end of his sliding cue. For the first time in the frame he felt relaxed and natural. This was a game he had spent thousands of hours playing; it was an extension of his life. Like putting one foot in front of the other until the destination is attained. Like breathing the sweet, sweet air of a hardwood forest, safe in the knowledge that this is the heart of the world's lungs – the purest breath he could ever take. This was his arena and this was his game and if anyone should taste the sweetness of victory here, it should be him.

He took the shot and his ball gently rolled into its pocket. Game on. One by one he began potting the rest, slow and methodical, the white ball locked on like a predator, opening up the table as it went. Every shot was genetically coded into his mind – the roll of the ball, the nature of the cloth, the positioning, the strength, the angle – all there, he didn't have to even think about it. This was instinctive.

She was here, watching – there was purpose now, real purpose. He slowly chalked his cue. Six balls down and cueing for a long, straight black – top left corner – full in the face. Bang! And away she blows. He knew from the moment he struck it, she was going down straight as a die – not even touching the sides. He was up and walking before the black had even slammed home like there was never an element of doubt in his mind, and who knows, maybe there wasn't. A roar of appreciation went up from the home crowd as the black ball found its mark and disappeared from view.

"Pint of Guinness, thanks mate," he said, shaking the hand of his bemused and head-scratching opponent.

Miss Cleavage flashed an approving smile as she ducked and turned for the bar. She didn't make eye contact, but he was sure it was for him. Various people were congratulating him and slapping his back as a long, dark pint got thrust into his midrib.

"You 'un really play, me bay. You gaart talent – reeaaal talent, bay." His slightly inbred farmer-dude opponent smiled a toothless grin at him.

Bird turned for the bar with his arms aloft and called out loudly, "Do you see me? DO – YOU – SEE – ME? My name is Mr. Bird and this is my place! Long may we live, boys!" And with that, he wolfed down his pint.

"Yeah, long may we live!" echoed Dave the barman in a somewhat mocking tone.

"I see you're as accurate with a pool ball as you are with a sausage."

He spluttered into the drink and thick, black liquid shot out of the top of his glass. She was standing right next to him, leaning on the bar – Miss Cleavage herself. The cocaine was wearing off fast and the alcohol was beginning to disorientate him. He looked at her face with a calm smile, trying to buy some time. I mean, what do you say to a girl this attractive when your only point of contact had been scalding her breasts with your breakfast and you've got Guinness all over your face?

"It was Cupid's arrow – the sausage." The words came out before he had time to even think about it, and his mind suddenly started doing backflips. As soon as he said it, he remembered her face spitting at him in the café. "You bloody idiot," that's what she had said, "you bloody idiot."

What's she gonna say now?

He stood looking at her as a paranoiac sweat gathered on his spine. He was waiting for the reaction, checking his escape routes and mentally brushing up on his jujitsu defence moves in anticipation of Miss Cleavage's impending assault. But instead, she burst out laughing.

"Sorry, my mistake," she blurted. "In that case you're not such a great shot with the sausage after all – you hit my chin!" Her accent was crisp and fresh, classy but not fake, and still she laughed. Bird could taste the sweetness of victory rolling across his gums – she had bought the tacky line, and his confidence exuded.

"Quite the contrary." He smiled. "It touched your face and then your heart and tonight I have done the same – to remain there forever – like a vampire locked in the coffin of your love."

He gestured with the back of his hand as he spoke, softly stroking her cheek then retreating quickly enough to avoid too much familiarity. He approved of his form though; it was almost as if he was still in the game and would have this girl eating out of the palm of his hand any minute now. She smiled and delicately touched her bottom lip with her tongue.

"Forever, you say?" She moved her face close to Bird's, trying to be as seductive as she could, though she barely needed to try at all. His heart started to pound – she was definitely on for him – wasn't she?

As her face drew in, her top lip began to curl and she suddenly looked like a vixen defending her cubs from attack. Bird's heart leapt into his mouth.

"You burnt my cleavage with your sausage, you stupid twat. The only place you're going to remain forever is the septic tomb that you end up lying face down in after a good night out with the lads!"

She smiled a cold, heartless smile and rubbed her hand up the inside of his thigh as she walked out. Bird felt like his heart had just been ripped out of his chest – or his mouth, as that's the last place it was.

The Big Country ballad 'Broken Heart' snaked its way out of the jukebox and he shuddered at the irony as he stared towards the door. He had wandered numerous valleys that morning – let alone thirteen – and for a moment there he did think he was the one that she dreamed of. But not only was her bed made elsewhere, she'd kicked him out of it before he even saw it – kicked him for sure, right in the balls of his pride, and left him panting and deflated. The mirror of the ladies' toilet reflected her victorious sneer as she gave herself a flattering glance and adjusted her lips with thumb and forefinger before taking a cubicle.

"C'mon, Bird, it's time for doubles."

The pool was elementary now. Come to think of it, life was pretty elementary. The acid was preparing to leave with a contented smirk on its face. It was like a demon that had possessed his soul for a while and was now moving on to another gig, collecting its hat and coat, leaving him huddled, naked and shivering in the corner as it wiped its feet on the remainder of his sanity and bid him farewell. He could taste the chemical in his mouth and its paranoid fear was now setting in. Miss Cleavage's reaction had left him miles out of his crease, and he'd been badly stumped just as he was starting to get his eye in and looking like he would make a half-century.

Never was much of a cricketer.

The opposing pool team had regressed into a drunken stupor and lost all interest in the match, so it wasn't difficult for the Bandage boys to clean them up and win the game six-three. Alcohol seemed to flow freely, and the Wound was once again in full swing. Ram Jam's 'Black Betty' blared its way out of the jukebox, grinding out guitar riffs that battled against raised voices, harsh accents and clinking glasses, and only just prevailed.

Bird was leaning on the bar talking intermittently to Dave, who was working. It wasn't much of a chat, though.

Dave hadn't stopped all night, but he was trying to console Bird, being the only witness to the evening's earth-shattering event.

"Why are you looking so sad, Birdman?"

It was her, she was back to taunt him. "That is your name, isn't it? At least, that's what your fan club calls you." She was slurring her words and swaying from side to side. The pints of snakebite and black had rendered her manual dexterity skills temporarily unstable and she was now sailing one too many down the line.

"My name is Bird – man is my gender," he sneered sarcastically.

"Strange name, wouldn't you say?"

"Not really."

"Should be called Sausageman." She giggled.

"Ah yeah, you got it! Look, I'm really sorry, what can I say? I genuinely didn't fire the sausage on purpose. It just happened, now please, can't you just let it lie?"

"Ooooohh – tantrums," she mocked, then dropped her head and swayed from side to side like an innocent schoolgirl. "I'm sorry, I was only joking. Just wanted to see if it really was Cupid's arrow."

She suddenly relaxed and became human for the first time. Every encounter with her so far had been enigmatic and fantasy-filled, and it was strange to see her as just another girl.

"Maybe it wasn't, after all," she crowed.

Had he read this situation correctly? Did she just open the door again there, ever so slightly? Perhaps. Perhaps he could get back in if he acted quickly? Instinct took control.

"Yeah, but maybe it was," he whispered.

She smiled and stared deep into his eyes, saying nothing, happy just to share the moment with him, share space and not feel compelled to have a reason for doing so. His face was being drawn to hers like a magnet unable to reverse its polarity. She moved up to him and started to close her eyes. She was so close that he could almost taste her, and he was just about to, when…

"That's time at the bar now, folks. Start drinking up now, please!"

Dave was clanking the bell for all it was worth just five feet from where they stood and Miss Cleavage fell into Bird's arms, bursting out into staccato laughter. The moment was gone. He held her close and put his right hand on the back of her head, and it felt somehow alien – yet somehow so natural. Had it really been three years?

"We're going to a friend's house to have a smoke now, would you like to come?" He was searching for something. "Sorry, I don't even know your name."

"Burnt tits, pleased to meet you, Birdman!" She laughed a drunken laugh again and swayed forward, resting her hand on his chest to stabilise herself and perhaps offer a tantalisingly flirtatious touch. "No, really, Samantha. Samantha Cowley; call me Sam. This is Tiffany. TIFF, TIFF!" she yelled over her right shoulder, waving violently. "COME AND MEET THE BIRDMAN!" Then she returned her glazed stare to Bird and gently hiccupped. "Can Tiff come and smoke ganja, too?"

Amazing that alcohol is legal when this is what it reduces us to.

"Yeah, why not indeed?"

They found themselves back at DZ's sleek pad. It was an intimate, almost subdued affair but it was just what Bird needed – chilled. Talking Heads was playing in the background and he sat on the floor, packing his hash pipe and rolling joints while DZ tried to convince him to take another gram of the coke he'd just scored. He needed some extra cash for Ingrid's birthday, but Bird was skint and credit wasn't going to help either of them much.

Are we on that road to nowhere?

DZ had done well for himself over the years working seasons of fishing in the English Channel, but winter was a time when the hardcore fishermen caught boats that sailed to Scotland and ravaged the North Sea for its quarry of crustaceans, which never really interested DZ that much. Instead he subsidised his winter expenditure by dealing hash, weed and occasionally cocaine to the many takers on the sleepy shores of this English coastal town.

His nickname stood for 'drop zone' – a parachuting term for the circle of ground where one must aim to land after a jump. Rumour had it that DZ had missed the drop zone years ago and had been floating in drug-induced bliss ever since, never really committing to anything save having a good time, and never really catching the penultimate wave that would wash him up on the beach of society where so many before him had been dumped after a lifetime of youthful surf-riding. The classic paradigm of middle-aged casualties beached on the midlife crisis of under-achievement and family disappointment wasn't exactly DZ's scene. He tried to distance himself from those floundering fools who seemed desperately repentant of their misspent youth and endeavoured to make up for lost time by finally facing their responsibilities, all the while evading the reality that the only skill to be achieved in the break was coolness and calm and they seemed to have lost even that.

Where did it go, he wondered – the ability to really and truly not give a toss? It's so prevalent when we're young, and then suddenly we wake up to paranoiac cold sweats about the future, family values and our role in society – qualities that were so well and truly beneath us when all that mattered was the break, the board and how cool we were to be the dudes out there riding it.

DZ was substantially older than the gathered troops but he had kept the quality of cool, and whilst he may no longer be paddling out to where the breakers curled, he knew about the ride and understood the tales of the rip because he really did know what it was like to surf the back line of excitement.

"Do you have a real name, Mr. Bird? I take it that's a nickname." Sam was restored to her former angelic status since the smoke. She had calmed down and her accent was once again crisp and seductive.

"Real name?" DZ scoffed, interjecting before Bird could draw breath. "Real name? Bird? Ha! There's no name in the world that would be appropriate for this boy, isn't that right, mate?" DZ snorted, rubbing Bird's matted head.

"These are my friends, who needs enemies?" Bird smiled at Sam.

DZ huffed at him through his lips. "Listen mate, if you were like a normal human being, perhaps you'd have a name, but as you're caught somewhere between the avian order and God knows what kind of life form, there's no name been invented to describe the likes of you yet."

"See what I mean?"

"Hey, come on Birdy boy, I mean, let's be honest here, what would you be called? The-Lesser-Spotted-Long-Legged-Blue-Bellied-Powder-Snortin'-Reefer-Smokin'-Acid-Droppin'-Featherbrain? Just too much of a mouthful, man. What would that abbreviate to? The LSLLBBPSRSADF bird. Nope, just don't work. Hi, I'm DZ and this is me mate, LSLLBBPSRSADF? I don't think so!"

"Long may you live, dude," Iceberg calmly interjected as Bird passed him a smouldering bowl. DZ was off on one – it was too late to stop him now, he was away.

"This one's the dog's bollocks, sweetheart. Today's Tom Sawyer. There is no name to describe his likes. The human side of this man is one of Britain's leading ornithologists. The drug-takin', head-bangin', lateral thinkin', shit-kickin', long-livin' son of a feathered side, well that's pure avian, man. Mutant avian, granted, but avian all the same. In fact…" He paused and cocked his head to one side, gazing at the ceiling. "He *IS* a bird. He just defected to the other side to infiltrate our species and gather information for the real rulers of this planet, the real evolutionary race." DZ settled himself next to Sam and began on his speech, gesticulating profusely with his hands. It didn't bode well for Bird; he'd only just managed to salvage this deal with Miss C and now, on the home straight, it was his mates that proved to be a bigger handicap than his own stupid self. No justice.

"Since I've known this Birdman," DZ continued with a Cheshire cat's grin, "and it's been quite a while now, he has been on a quest to become… well… a bird. He knows all there is to know about our little feathered gods and loves them more than life itself. How does it go, mate?

Cormorants found swimming seventy feet under the North Sea, migrating storks interfering with long-distance jets at thirty thousand feet, the polar caps, the highest peaks, the forests and savannahs, the city streets and the tower blocks, in the middle of the oceans and at the heart of the desert dunes, in every piece of every sky that you ever see above you – they are found. Our avian mentors who turned scales into feathers and took to the sky for immortal freedom. The composers of life's sweet melody and the creators of the rainbow's spectrum. Alas, Mr. Bird, are we just mortal clones consumed by a world more powerful than we could ever imagine? Indeed we are, and none are more aware of this than Feather Boy here himself. This guy is the full nine, darlin' – ain't that right, Birdyboy?"

"The whole nine."

"What's that?"

"The whole nine," Sam continued. "It's the whole nine yards, not the full nine."

"Whatever!"

DZ had been subjected to Bird's rhetoric so many times now, he knew it off by heart. Bird was blushing and self-conscious. The feathered ones were his life, his love and his passion. Nothing else mattered save getting high, but that freed him, freed his soul from these earthly ties and allowed him to fly – to get up there with them and soar on the thermals, rush on the pressure fronts, ride the cyclones of oblivion that invisibly rotate around all our heads, beckoning us to find a board and just ride, baby, ride.

"That's right, man," he relented. "I just love birds, can't help myself. They're such perfect creatures in every sense of the word and there isn't much perfection left in this world, Samantha Cowley." He flashed a smile at her and put a light up to his pipe, inhaling a deep well of smoke before passing it to DZ with a sarcastic growl.

Miss Cleavage had been grappling with her desires all night. Ever since she saw him play pool she knew he was different. There was something about him – something untamed, mysterious, secretive. Yes, this was a man of secrets – secrets, hidden agendas and social roleplays. A man who throws his breakfast on you at lunchtime and calls it Cupid's arrow. A man who works rough bars and hustles pool tables. A man who sits here rolling joints and making cocaine deals, but somewhere else, he's respected and admired, an expert in his field, genius even – the dog's bollocks. She should despise him but there was something about him that strangely charmed her, awakened a primal urge that she never knew was there.

But now it started to dawn on her – the paradox – he was a total paradox. She still didn't know his name but it didn't matter, she was sold – this was to be hers, he was to be hers. Just for one night she would gamble with her soul and dance with the devil, bugger the consequences. She was going to catch this Bird tonight, in her parents' holiday cottage on her weekend away. The freedom of this spirit, freedom that she lacked in her own but desired so much, would be caged, because if she couldn't have it then why should he? Nothing was going to stop her – I mean, let's face it, she always got what she wanted. Daddy made sure of that. The desire began to pound through her heart and reverberate inside her throat. She couldn't take her eyes off him – not for a second.

Her parents weren't there, but Sam had her own set of keys to the holiday cottage and came and went at leisure. Tiff and Dave the barman staggered upstairs to Tiff's room and slammed the door behind them. Sam could hold it no longer – the pheromonal exchange kicking off in her vicinity was too much for her feminine hormones to cope with, and she was on to him like a panther hitting unsuspecting prey. She pounced, touching his lips with hers, darting her tongue in and out of his mouth seductively and running her hands over his chest.

God it feels good. Three years really is a long time, thought Bird through his euphoric nostalgia.

She tasted amazing and smelt even better – angel – would she really be his tonight? He closed his eyes and prepared to slip into the chasm of unexplored sex in an untamed land – that crushing feeling in his chest and stomach, still not really believing it's happening but knowing all the same that it is and…

…And oh my God, any minute now I'm going to explode with desire!

But instead he was consumed with an image – an image so real that he could touch it. He could feel it – smell it, live it, be consumed by it.

Burning… flames… fire… smoke…

He was on his knees, looking at a car that was burning furiously and billowing out huge clouds of smoke. Small explosions were going off inside it, as if incendiary devices were being systematically detonated throughout the vehicle, and a frantic girl was sitting in the driver's seat, trapped by her seatbelt. She hammered on the window with her fists then battled with the belt, all the while screaming his name.

"BIRD… BIRD… BIRD…"

He sat and watched, unable to move as she burned, dripped and melted right before his eyes. He lost her in the flames for a moment and strained his gaze into a hard stare... searching. Then she was back... hammering... screaming... begging. Begging him to do something... to help her... to free her... but he didn't move... he was rooted to the spot by a horrific paralysis. He lost her again... those piercing screams consumed and liberated with the flames forging them on... higher... brighter... hotter still. He stared and stared, but she was gone and all that was left was fire. Fire and billowing smoke.

Bird screamed out loud and threw Sam away from him. She had her top off and he could see the cleavage that had aroused him in the café. It looked kind of sordid.

"Bird – are you all right? Did I do something?"

Sam was confused, if not surprised and maybe a little embarrassed. He was rooted to the spot, staring at nothing but staring hard. Was it her? Did she do something? Didn't she do something? It had been three months since she'd split up with Gabriel and this was to be her bit of rough, a waltz with Lucifer, a walk on the wild side. Wasn't she good enough? She looked at Bird, aware for the first time of the expression in his eyes – they were on fire.

"Bird – speak to me please, you're scaring me. Are you all right?"

His eyes flashed across in a psychotic glance and fixed her fearful gaze. A terrifying chill shot down her back. Who is this man – *what* is he?

"No, Sam, I'm not. I'm very fuckin' not all right at this moment in time. I gotta go, man, I'm really sorry. You are perfect in every way, it's just that three years is a very long time. She might be gone, but I'm still burning. I'm sorry – really I am."

And then he was gone – disappeared into the night, leaving Miss Cleavage alone with her fears once again.

"I couldn't even make it with the barman – I didn't even catch his name. Gabriel, you bastard."

4

THE DAY OF RECKONING

The walk to Alfred's house was always filled with nostalgia and belonging. Bird had travelled the cliff road a thousand times and the woods behind had been his stomping ground as a child, the site of many hard-fought battles against intergalactic foes destined to destroy the world but for the brave intervention of three superheroes: Bird, Cracker and Iceberg.

From the road he could see the estuary snaking its path inland from the ocean, cutting through steep cliffs that slid down to meet it in undulating greens, oranges and reds. Massive boulders held testament to the centuries of pounding by the relentless sea, isolating them from the mainland which had banished them to a whittling existence in oceanic purgatory for a death they had eluded. The waves rolled in endlessly and crashed onto a sand bar in the middle of the channel, creating swirls and backflows that thrashed about in random and sustained motions like a sixties hippie chick high on acid and flailing about at a Jimi Hendrix gig. And behind it all, beyond the great rising shores and battered rocks, lay the deep expanse of ocean that stretched away to eternity – a rolling, breathing, living mass of formidable might.

No matter how many toxins we pump into her or how much sewage we pour down her throat or how many tons of nuclear waste we float on her surface, we will never stop the waves from rolling in, day after day, year after year, time after time. The moon will rise and it will set, taking its tidal partner in hand performing a slow and rhythmic embrace to the melodies of time.

We are not the rulers of this planet, nor keepers of forests or wardens of mountain ranges. No. We are a putrid intrusion on the tranquillity of evolution – a thorn in the foot of natural selection – a cancer in the beauty of creation. God made the world and then made Man to rule over all that reside upon it, but who made God? And if he made a creation so pure and self-sustaining, why did he put Man in control – an egocentric race of inadequate half-wits motivated only by fear and greed? The fear of what we cannot control fuels greed to cast its web of deceit upon all that can be consumed beneath its sordid shroud. And like the emaciated creature that lurks in the depths of our soul, we ravage all that falls into the net and cast aside the bones for the paltry animals that remain. Except those we so proudly proclaim as Man's best friend, for they may share in the spoils of war.

Dogs – never did care for them much.

He turned off the cliff road and up onto a path leading into the woods. It was one of those rare sunny autumn days and the sunlight cast crisp, dappled shadows around his feet. A squirrel shot out from a hole, saw Bird, froze and scampered off into another hole, all in the space of a second. Bird chuckled to himself. Squirrels were always in such a hurry. If they could talk, *"Shit, I'm late"* would be all they would say.

All around him, ancient willow, oak and beech trees draped heavily over his path and absorbed the majority of the light that was casting its way down to the shrubs below. He could make out the call of a jay in the middle distance doing a poor impression of a goshawk. A song thrush also burbled out its jumbled message of territorial definition somewhere above his head, and various warblers, tits and robins clucked, screeched and twittered all around him. The sun had brought out the forest's street performers to proclaim their existence and advertise their dominance in the cyclical hierarchy of territorial boundaries, and it seemed they were all now seizing the moment.

Nestled in a woodland clearing, deep in the heart of this English coastal forest, the white picket fence ran its random and unsustained course around Alfred Weiss' cottage. Sections of it were missing, blown down and trampled by the harsh October winds that had ravaged this coastline for years. A line of smoke twisted its way out of a chimney, advertising the comforting warmth of a living room fire at its feet. Bird pushed open the door and went inside. His visits were becoming less frequent now and he was aware of the solitude he was leaving behind.

"Hi Alfie, it's me," he called.

"I'm in the shed. Get yourself a tea and bring me one, too." The reply echoed from an inconspicuous outpost in the forested garden. Bird gazed through the back door towards an outside shed and noticed that England was once again dark and gloomy, the autumn sunshine having been swallowed by her clouds.

As he walked into the kitchen, a photograph caught his eye and he stopped and stared at it for a while, tracing the outline with his finger. It was a rugby team with their trophies and cups displayed on the ground before them. The title read: 'National County Champions. Under 19s Squad 1990.' With his index finger, he gently touched the image of a boy standing on the back row, second from the right. It was him, aged eighteen and erupting with the glow of proud mettle that crowned one of the greatest moments of his life, not to mention Alfred's; the old man had even forfeited a raptors field trip to watch the final match that had earned them the title. He hadn't been disappointed – it was a blinder of a game and they had won the tournament for the first time in thirty-nine years.

Bird had come from very different beginnings to most of the players in his team. They were all private-school boys from wealthy families who had grown up together and played for their respective schools for years. Bird was the only one from a state school where football had been the favoured sport, but a gym teacher had noticed his hand-eye co-ordination at a young age and pushed him towards the town, and ultimately county, rugby squads.

He was very far removed from the kids he joined there – in status and in breed – and it was a wonder he ever prevailed. Rugby had been a part of their lives forever, and so had class and etiquette; these boys were being groomed for tomorrow's aristocracy. There was no doubt of their mastery over the ideology and masculinity of the sport, but their one weakness lay in a fear of being tackled – of being put down hard on the deck. Bird soon identified this and exploited the flaw. He started to hit anything that moved and hit it hard. His upbringing with the likes of Cracker and Iceberg prepared him beautifully for this task, and going in like a freight train and putting these spoilt wankers on their backs gave him immense satisfaction. He was perfect for the job. I mean, why risk your precious gentry of tomorrow if there's a demented 'village boy' who's prepared to go in like a raging psychopath for you? No reason.

And that was it. Psychotic tendencies to put private-school boys on their backs with a thump had earned him the position of fullback for the county rugby squad. Once his mettle had been proved he was able to develop some semblance of camaraderie with the members of his team, which gelled over the years. After the final when they had won, there was Bird, sharing in the glory, one of tomorrow's elite cavaliers – just for a brief moment in time. It had felt wonderful. The victory was sweet and the moment would be savoured forever, but time ambles into perpetual change and our mortal souls amble along with it – our lives become the chronicles of history and this is where his chapter would end. The train had stopped and the athlete alighted.

Wonder where all that aggression went? I think I lost it somewhere beneath a mountain of drugs, alcohol and regret… yes… regret… that's the big one.

"Hi, Alfred. What you up to?" Now in the shed, he handed him his tea.

"Hello stranger, I was just thinking about you. A lady recovered this ringed sedge warbler in some netting on the rocks of her fish pond and thought I might be interested in the ring."

"And are you?"

There was a pause. Alfred was now lost somewhere in the bird and unable to sustain a conversation for any length of time.

"Mmm? Yes, well, uuummm… oh, absolutely dear boy; this ring is from Africa – South Central to be precise." Alfred's geographical mind thought in terms of bird distribution regions rather than specific countries. "And it was placed there in March, just as this little chap was bulking up for his flight back here. He'll be moving on again soon, so I'm replacing the ring with one of mine in the hope that they might recover the same bird and carry on the process. I'll send this ring off to them tomorrow but I've been warned about the post over there – can take months for stuff to get through. Anyway, what've you been up to lately, Bird? Have you been to see any of the waders down on the mudflats when the tide is out? All sorts of stuff about at the moment, I even saw a little ringed plover there yesterday – he's a bit off course, normally doesn't venture past Bournemouth but this chap obviously sneaked off without anyone noticing."

Bird smiled. Alfred was an information obsessive – the classic mad scientist. He was without doubt one of Britain's leading ornithologists and a paramount cog in her avian science machine, and he'd been moulding Bird over the years to follow in his footsteps. But lately plans had been going awry. Something was missing these days. A fire had gone out inside the lad, which he just couldn't rekindle.

And it's true to say that for Bird, the enthusiasm was dying. He'd learned as much as he probably ever wanted to about local birds, and getting into foreign avia was difficult without actually being there and seeing them for himself. He'd been through some books and documents where they were relevant to the migration hypothesis that he and Alfred had worked on some years before, but without watching these wondrous creatures exalt themselves in their natural state, the whole thing seemed to be losing its purpose. Those faraway lands had such diverse habitats that attracted hundreds of exotic species that he could well have got excited about, but there was simply no way of getting there, so what was the point? Having the migration hypothesis shot down in the way it was seemed only to corroborate these disillusions and enable society to hammer one final nail into the regressive social coffin that justified his resignation from ornithology.

"No, Alfie, haven't been to see much recently. I did go for a walk on the cliffs yesterday but I wasn't really in the frame of mind for birding. There was a beautiful flock of goldfinches though, must have been at least fifty."

"Mmmmm, fifty, hey? Not bad."

Oh God, tell me it was fifty, tell me it wasn't three and the acid intervening again. No, I saw them, I'm sure I saw them; it was one of my moments of clarity!

"How's the Wound?" Alfred candidly changed the subject.

"Oh, much the same, quietening down for winter now. It's been a good month for sales and we're kickin' ass on the pool. Mike's as happy as any landlord can be and he seems to be off my case now."

"He still talking about sending you on that cellar master's course? Might be a useful bit of paper for you at some stage."

"Yeah, there's talk, but you know how he is. Anyway, dunno if I really want to be a cellar master, not exactly prime on my list of careers – know what I mean?"

"Well, what is?" Bird shrugged up his shoulders and gazed away. "Can't go on ignoring it forever, Bird. It's fine when you're young but the years are starting to tick by now and the longer you leave it, the more you'll forget all you've learnt."

Alfred had momentarily lost concentration on the ringed warbler in his hand. It flapped about his face, which contorted into a strained expression before he caught the bird again and regained his composure. He placed it in a small hutch. He'd finish it later.

"How long's it been now, Bird? Two and a half? Three years?"

"Yeah, thereabouts." Alfred was up to something – Bird knew the old man well enough to know that the idle banter about the pub was not to further his local knowledge. Was it coming now?

"You're not happy, son; I see it in your eyes."

Bird sighed and rolled his head to one side. He didn't need a lecture on society, family values or careers – just didn't need it, not today, not with the chemical hangover he had.

"I won't lecture you, Bird," Alfred said, as if reading his thoughts. "You know that's not my style. Everything you have learnt from me has been your own making – I haven't forced anything on you, now have I?"

"No, Alfie, you haven't, so please don't start now."

"Look, son – you're all I have and I'm all you have. Your mother walked out on you all those years ago and you haven't heard from her since. You knew that all I had to offer was birds, and that's what I've passed on. You're the only hope we have of salvaging anything and we all know you can do the job. The papers you prepared in the migration hypothesis were brilliant, boy, everyone agreed, but take a look around you now. Surely you see the destruction? You see the demise, the loss of habitat and the diminishing numbers in species. We're heading for the sixth great extinction. Someone has to be there to stop it. Can you imagine a world without birds? Would you want to imagine that? The future lies with you, son, you and your misguided friends. If they don't understand what's happening, it's up to you to make them or we don't stand a chance."

"What do you think I am, Alf? Some kind of apostle? A disciple that will go out there and preach the good word to the heathen masses – 'Don't destroy the world!' 'Save our birds from extinction!'" A chemical mood swing was welling up inside him, but this was Alfred's place and such behaviour just didn't belong here.

Alfred stared deep into Bird's eyes. His smile was so calm and assuring, genuine – an ageing phenomenon trying to leave behind its prodigy. Of all the people in the world, he got Bird as his protégé. A disillusioned, mixed-up kid with the knowledge of a genius at his fingertips and the burden of a broken life resting on his shoulders. Alfred Weiss deserved more; there wasn't a bad bone in his body.

"Yes, Bird, that's exactly what I think you are," he said, maintaining the stare. "You have it, son, you can capture the hearts and minds of people, and God knows you have the knowledge. It has to become 'cool' to be concerned. Don't you see, a global awareness has to take place soon or everything will disappear right before our eyes."

"It already has, Alfred. If you ask me, we're beyond the point of no return. It's time to hang up the gloves and marvel at the last of it before everything is consumed beneath a mountain of human gluttony."

"I can understand the cynicism, Bird, really I can. I see the desperation too. But what I don't understand is the defeatism. D'you remember the rugby trials of 1990? Remember how marginal your place was back then? That kid from the posh school in the northern county rallying for your spot? It was the first time your place in the team had been threatened and being in the final meant everything to you. Let's face it, they were ready to drop you, but you never gave up and what's more, you got into that team. You trained hard, you fought, you struggled, you endured the bad times just to be a part of that squad – and you did it because it was important." He paused and gazed away momentarily before focussing his stare on Bird once more. "Where's that tenacity gone? Is this not important to you anymore? Are you ready to just throw it all away for a cheap thrill? Did that fighting spirit die in the accident, too?"

Bird dropped his head in despair. At first he'd held it together as best he could, but the last year had been hard – nothing had really improved since the crash. A cavity remained in his heart and all that seemed to fill it was the temporary release that mind-altering substances were offering. He knew he was slipping but he didn't have the strength or the will to fight it.

Someone losing the battle with himself was not exactly a prime mover to save the planet from global destruction – the sixth great extinction.

"I lost a lot in that crash, Alfie – lost nearly everything. Maybe it did take my spirit."

"A body without a spirit is the walking dead, Bird."

Alfred moved across the shed and reached up onto a shelf, removing an old card and blowing off its dust.

"Remember this?" He handed the card to Bird, who opened it and saw his own handwriting. The inscription read:

We all have spirits that can fly,
But not all of them reach their destination.
Never give up the quest, Alfred.

From Bird.

"This must be eight years old, maybe more. Did I write this? Should have been a lyric." Bird stared hard at the card and felt a twinge in his stomach.

"You gave it to me at a time when my work was being heavily criticised. I don't think you knew the significance of the words – I don't even think you were aware of what was happening at the time – but this card and these words gave me a new strength, a new purpose, new eyes with which to focus on the mission. You didn't lose everything in the accident, Bird, just the vision, and all you need to have vision is to open your eyes. That's the real question here, son. You've been closing your eyes, hoping for it to go away, for so long now – are you ready to actually open them and make it go away?"

Bird's head was still hung. The day of reckoning had to come sometime, he just didn't want it to be today.

"Let's go in the house, I have something to show you."

The room was poorly lit and musty, in need of a good clean and the woman's touch that had eluded Alfred and his house for so many years. He'd been married before but the obsession with birds had presided over all nuptial emotions, forcing his wife on to greener pastures and more devoted men, as elusive now as Alfred's misguided passion. Bird slumped into an armchair in one corner of the lounge, tossing newspapers and media debris to one side.

Typed papers were stacked in uneasy piles on every available surface. Some had spilled over onto the furniture and then the floor, forcing back enemy lines and now threatening to take the whole room. Framed pictures were dotted around the murky walls in random, crooked lines. Some were enlarged photographs of birds in various habitats; others were old paintings of country scenes passed down through generations. And by the cabinet near the kitchen, Bird's team photo and an assortment of action shots taken by Alfred during the final.

Alfred was shuffling through some documents at his desk, which resembled an exploded bank vault with paper and the associated trash of a genius scattered all over it. As he pried a piece of paper from the wreckage, he slowly eased himself into a rickety padded office chair and leaned back.

"Ah, here it is." Triumphantly he held up the tattered document, which he squinted at through librarian spectacles perched precariously on the edge of his nose. He began to orate like a preacher delivering Sunday morning's service, clearing his throat and pushing out his chest.

"There is a research station somewhere in Central Africa. It's been around for some time studying a variety of environmental attributes in the area. They have a lion project going on, an antelope study, various plant and grass analyses and a bird project."

A bewildered look was creeping onto Bird's face.

What's he telling me about research stations stuck out in the middle of the African jungle for? This is too weird. Didn't I hallucinate something about lions in Africa just yesterday? Déjà vu, man.

Alfred cleared his throat once again as he prepared for oratory deliverance. "Now, it says here that they've hit a bit of a snag with personnel and are looking for volunteer assistants to help out for a couple of months until they get themselves organised. It'd be the real thing, Bird, real field work in an uncontrolled environment," he said, peering over the document, down his nose and through his spectacles perched at the end of it.

"It's a vast flood plain that spends about eight months a year underwater. As it floods and recedes, hundreds of different habitats are created and exposed and some three hundred species exploit it at the various stages, but no two years are ever the same. The waders are there in huge numbers, sometimes thousands of birds in a single flock. An analyst documented three thousand six hundred birds from forty-eight species feeding in one waterhole as it began to recede after the rains. It says here…" he lazily nudged the spectacles up his nose as he held the paper towards the light, "…that flocks of a thousand white-faced ducks are not uncommon, four to five hundred openbill storks, two to three hundred yellow-billed storks…" His glasses crept further down his nose with every movement from his lips. "Four to five hundred white pelicans… teals, ducks, geese, plovers, rails, stilts, stints, herons, egrets, darters, cormorants, ibises, kingfishers and skimmers – and those are just some of the aquatic birds. There's raptors, too, and vultures, cranes, passerines, owls, sandgrouse, doves, and much much more! Plus they have longclaws, Bird – pink-throated longclaws, in the wild." Alfred smiled triumphantly at him, dropping the paper slightly to gain a clear line of sight over it and his glasses, now resting in their familiar place on the end of his nose once again.

Bird had to admit, it did sound wonderful. He remembered the stuffed longclaw that he'd seen once in a university display cabinet and marvelled at the bedraggled specimen it had become. He'd always wondered how it would look alive and well in its natural habitat. The specimen's keeper had played them a recording of its territorial call, sung whilst perched on a tussock of grass on the open plains, displaying the striking bib of pink on its throat. The call was crisp and clear, fluting and melodic, and cut through every audible sound both on the tape and in the room in which they were standing.

Longclaws belong to the pipit family, the epitome of drab brown birds with marginal plumage variation between the numerous species. In the Amazon, there are reputed to be more than three hundred species of pipit, but quite what differentiated them was always something of a mystery to Bird. Africa has a dozen or so and he'd found it hard enough to get enthusiastic about them, never mind three hundred.

Pink-throated longclaws, however, are the Cinderellas of the family. Ostensibly, they're drab brown birds too, until they turn around and expose their throats, bearing a bib of brilliant pink bordered by a thick, black band. It truly was a bird to convert any non-believer to the marvels and mysteries of bird-watching, and it had always been a dream of Bird's to see one in the wild. But it was just a dream, like fantasising about what car he'd buy if he ever won the lottery. Never had he contemplated the reality, and anyway he knew the dream would be better – it always was. This was all a bit sudden and a bit quick, and he was having trouble absorbing the scene. Denial would be the only defence.

"Well, the first thing that comes to mind for me, Alfie, is what all these thousands of fowl are feeding on. Majority has got to be insects – biting, stinging, disease-ridden, mutant jungle insects, and anyone who ventures there to see the birds runs the gauntlet of despair with these little bastards that will undoubtedly be attracted to the fair, lily-white skin that covers the likes of me. I don't think

I'm ready for jungle fevers and jungle critters just yet, thanks. Besides, you said they have a lion project there? That means living in the general vicinity of lions, and everyone knows lions eat anything that moves. Come on man, you know what I'm like, it'd be just my luck to walk into a marauding band of stinking cats and get served up as a feline feast. No thanks, Alf, I don't think I'm ready to go Kentucky-fried in Africa just yet."

Alfred took off his specs and dropped his hands down by his sides. He seemed physically deflated, and his body language tugged at the emotional strings attached to Bird's heart.

"So, what will you do, Bird? Drop acid and go cliff walking for the rest of your life hallucinating goldfinch flocks? Two years ago you'd have jumped at this. I mean, it's not like you'll spend the rest of your life there, just a few months to help them out and get a bit of invaluable experience."

The dormant thespian in Alfred leapt into life once again and jumped about, flailing his arms in the air.

"Get out there, Bird, go and sample some other life for a while. Clear your head, boy, let go of the past, find that spark again and do something to stop the rot instead of sitting here and letting it consume you too – come on, dude! I'm the closest thing to family that you've got so I'm exercising a bit of parental guidance and strongly recommending that you take this opportunity. Besides, I have to get this ring back to them somehow and you can take it – same research station, I'm sure. Bloody post."

Alfred didn't like getting personal with Bird and he hadn't done it for a good while now, but he could see that some proverbial ass needed kicking here, else his prodigy would be lost and this boy that he had grown to love like his own would drown in a sea of despair. He had no parents and as his only legal guardian, Alfred Weiss really was morally obliged to convince him. Besides, he really couldn't trust the postal service with this ring.

"Think about it, Bird, and let me know in the next couple of days. I don't see this vacancy lasting forever, so be decisive – and as you used to say yourself, get a life, man! Fancy some more tea?"

5

RAY OF LIGHT

Bird was awoken by the resonant clink of glasses and the relentless chattering of people. The morning's activity rang out with a seagull's cry and a diesel engine's groan as boats shunted up and down the estuary with sluggish intent. He went over to the window and looked out on another sunny morning, enticing punters into the Wound's beer garden that overlooked the water. The *Mary Jane* was steaming out for another week at sea, and he could see the guys piling and stacking gear and generally shuffling about in fisher-boy style on her decks. The crew were all Bandage regulars, and although they made a pretty packet taming the rabid seas and dredging up her crustaceans, Bird didn't envy their lifestyle – not a bit.

Africa now consumed his every thought, and as he gazed out to sea, beyond the mouth of the estuary, he wondered what sort of view he might have from the research camp. It wouldn't be the English Channel, that's for sure, but it might still be the sea. Yes – a sea of grass with white-tufted tussocks waving gently in the wind. A sea of waves that flowed through Africa's savannah with every breath from Mother Earth. A sea of life in tranquillity where the cancer of modern society had not yet grown. Yes, still the sea, a green sea whose fishing boats would be a million wildebeest bobbing on the eternal carpet of life.

Long, wiry African men with bones through their noses would perform freaky trance dances around massive bonfires. They would frantically wave shield and spear whilst chanting hallucinogenic-induced rhyme and punching out a tribal beat in honour of the Birdman's gracious arrival. The skies would be alive with birds, and Africa would be calling out her symphony of cycles within life – within cycles within life. And he would be there, he would be in it – Bird, the barman from the Wound and Bandage. His eyes began to sparkle at the excitement of his thoughts.

Alfred's offer had ignited a flurry of synaptic transmissions across his clouded mind, and a multitude of questions rose up from the ashes. Could he really find happiness so far from home? Would he have anything tangible to offer the research institute? Would it have anything to offer him? How hot would it be? What would the Africans be like? How would they receive him? Did they eat people? How would he survive without Cracker and the lads in a barren and landlocked desert?

It would be tough – no denying that. This nautical paradise had been his home for as long as he could remember, and the whole place reeked of familiarity. But something was still amiss. The real purpose driving his thoughts was still somewhat elusive. A monumental decision to make a move like this should be based on burning ambition or zealous aspiration like a childhood fantasy or barbiturate reverie, not just some whim to escape potential drug addiction and repressive boredom. Paranoiac interjection on decision-making suddenly intervened.

Hang on, I haven't decided anything yet. I can't be justifying the move until I decide to make it. Or am I just weighing up the odds? Weighing up the heavy shit, more like!

Officially of course, he was still in the thinking phase – no final decision had yet been reached – but he had to admit, it did excite him. A mystic thrill rippled through his head as his hand moved semiconsciously into his shorts and scratched his backside, just as it did every morning of his life. He was still smiling at the thought of warriors welcoming the white man from across the great skies into their homes. In spite of the dread his presence symbolised in the ancient tales of their elders, they would undoubtedly honour him on arrival and bow at his feet – just as they'd done for Livingstone. Maybe they'd even present virgin teenage girls as a gift, smooth chocolate-brown skin and firm, pouting breasts. What would he do with them? Then, in mid-perverted thought, he rubbed his nose and ran his fingers through his hair, freezing momentarily at the sudden realisation that this was the same hand that moments ago was rummaging around inside his shorts. He frowned and shrugged.

Grabbing his smoking wares off the table, he pressed play on a beat-box and stumbled back into bed. Music piled out of the speakers and tumbled uncontrollably around the room, agitating cosmic atoms and disturbing the rancid tranquillity of a well-slept pit.

He skinned up a joint and lay back on his pillows as he lit it. The hash hit him hard, threatening to send him back to sleep at any moment before kicking in and elevating him to the precipice that he had spent so many years precariously balanced on. A beam of sunlight cast its ray through the window, catching his eye and illuminating a photograph next to his bed. Song lyrics filtered into the room as the morning sun lit up the image. He lay back on his pillows, gazing at the picture as he chuffed on his reefer.

> *Ray of light illuminates the man I used to be,*
> *Reverential apparition, or just a distant*
> *memory?*

The photograph was of Bird and Alfred dressed in their Sunday best and standing proudly in front of the science faculty at Oxford University. They had just delivered a research paper detailing Alfred's controversial theories on avian migratory navigation, and the triumphant look on their faces was captured as a wondrous moment in time. The triumph was short lived as the theory was scoffed at and thrown out less than a month later, but the moment was caught on film and represented a pinnacle in Bird's life that he had been falling from ever since.

The music stirred an unfamiliar sensation in the pit of his stomach like a cold steel blade tearing at his insides, and a chilling sweat crept over his body, rippling through his skin and breaking out on its surface. A fearful panic began to envelop him and he started to shiver uncontrollably. He pawed at his chest and felt a clammy residue. His lungs were being crushed by an imaginary vine growing tighter and tighter in super-quick time, and confusion rampaged through his senses.

Fuck me, what is going on? Should I be panicking? Can't fuckin' breathe. Yes, panic – panic for all you're worth, man! Just calm down now, be cool, it's in my mind – all in my mind – I can allow it to be there, and I can not allow it – I choose not – I choose not!

He gasped for breath as he squeezed his hair, as if trying to pull the skin away from his mouth in a frantic bid to open an orifice – any orifice – to suck in the air. Holding his pose, he focussed every ounce of concentration on instinctive survival skills. It seemed that Death was aiming to roll for the last of his earthly remains until, finally, the sensation eased and air began to fill his parched mouth, leaving Death to grimace a smile and pack away his dice for another day.

He slugged on a glass of water that sat next to his bed and finally felt relief. The glass seemed to ooze in his hands and he noticed the grime that was collecting on its surface. When he held it up to the light, white flecks drifted through the unclear, greasy water. He frowned benignly.

What the hell am I drinking? How long have I been filling my body with this shit?

He held up the spliff in his other hand and asked the same question.

"Years."

And it had been. Years and years of substance abuse, from tobacco to temazepam, heroin to speed, alcohol to Big Macs. So long burying his head in a drug-induced haze because the rot in this world had become so prevalent that its stench was unavoidable.

The way he saw it – like his father before him – was that everyone had a choice with this society: they could join or they could abstain, be part of it or be banished. Buy into the media-driven crap about careers and mortgages, bank balances and life insurance, or drop into the numerous forms of societal exile – none of which held any real allure for him.

But it hadn't always been this way. Bird had once dined at the banquet of spiritual fulfilment on the project with Alfred, and every minute had felt bloody marvellous. He knew what it meant to have a mission that inspired him to achieve its entirety because he was wholly committed to the cause; he knew what it meant to have a dream. Real purpose, real reasons to leap out of bed every morning and embrace the beauty of life. But that was gone now – she was gone now, and along with her went that dream. He had lost his childhood sweetheart in one crushing moment three years before and life had long since lost its purpose. The drug-induced haze was a tightrope he tried to walk while searching for alternatives and a rather convenient excuse not to face the future just yet. It was a springboard that could bounce in either direction – the trick was knowing which way to go before the haze itself consumed him. Having friends like Cracker sure helped in situations like this.

Bird and Cracker had spent many an hour contemplating the alternatives to this dreaded society. They'd even delved into mythical worlds, places where they could hide from its hounds of hell – from the institutions and regulations, the regimes and conditions – even from life itself. And on a fine winter's morning while briskly walking along the cliffs, they came up with a solution that would end their dilemma once and for all and answer every question that had ever been asked.

It had begun as one of the many profound conversations that they often found themselves engaged in and ended in the key that would unlock the meaning of life forever. Because beneath their brazen exteriors and apparent disregard for humanity as a whole, there was kindness and compassion inside these psycho hippies, even sensitivity and awareness, intrigue and sometimes extreme intellect.

"Yeah like, you take Hitler for example," Bird had expounded. "Here's a dude that starts a regime to ethnically cleanse the world, annihilating half its population and leaving a temporary ecological breakdown in its wake 'cos he wants to build this massive evil empire that separates people by their class and creed. He wants a New World Order of conditioning and societal cloning, where all must conform to the ethnic scriptures of a vicarious dictator breathing hellfire and damnation to those who dare oppose the machine."

"Yeah?" came Cracker's informed reply.

"Well, everyone was up in arms about the horror of it all, weren't they? They're all like shocked and dismayed at his nerve, yeah?"

"Yeah," proffered Cracker again.

"Well, hang on a minute, didn't we once colonise a few minor countries of our own at one time? And didn't we trash the odd ancient tradition in the name of some other dictatorial regime? Yes, I'm sure we did. Well, we did it for God and of course for Queen and country. But our regime was acceptable, some even considered it good – after all, these were heathen natives who needed to be educated in our Western ways because we had 'God' and they had 'gods'. The poor misguided souls worshipped absurd things like trees, birds, animals, clouds, air and rain, which is all cute and cuddly, dudes, but it don't give you redemption at the end of the day. Know what I'm saying?"

"No."

"Well, what makes empirical or religious colonisation any different from the gig Hitler was on?"

"We were doing it, that's what."

"Exactly my point, mate!" Bird resounded triumphantly. "And who are we to stand in judgement of what's right and what's wrong? Old Churchill gives it all… *'We'll fight them in the fields and in the streets – we'll fight them on the hills and the landing grounds – we will never surrender'* bollocks, and then sends his own colonies into battle to fight for him – to keep England's green and pleasants green and pleasant. The King's African Rifles – bloody marvellous regiment. So what's the difference here, man – what's right and what's wrong?"

"We were right and Hitler was wrong – end of fuckin' story, mate." It was a cold winter's morning and Cracker was battling a hangover from the night before, so he sure as shit wasn't in the mood to enter into the realms of Bird's profound resolution, no matter what.

"OK, put it another way." Bird was not about to give up. "What if you take into account the fact that when…"

"Bird mate, just shut the fuck up and accept the fact, man, it's all a load of bollocks. Nothing more and nothing less, just a complete load of bollocks."

Cracker's interruption had the desired effect and silenced Bird's march for prophetic prosperity, but it also placed the key into a lock that would ultimately open the door to an untold bounty that housed all their answers.

The 'bollocks theory' was conceived at that very moment and ended up evolving into the parameters of the New World Order that was born of the decay that encapsulated Bird's broken soul and Cracker's despondency to life in general. And its prime objective? Well, to put it simply – bollocks. Bollocks to it – bollocks to it all – it's all a load of bollocks. Live life according to your own morals, your own rules and your own code of conduct that has absolutely nothing to do with society, because it's all a load of bollocks anyway.

No one could explain to them why the British Empire was acceptable when Hitler's quest was not, in spite of the blinding similarities between the two regimes – oppression, destruction of local custom, theft of land and wealth. No one could say why the Muslim belief was more plausible than the Hindu one, why Catholics and Protestants should hate each other so, why they all fought endless wars over whose God was right and whose was wrong, so bollocks to them, bollocks to the lot of them. If they all thought their way was right, then why shouldn't Bird and Cracker invent their own code that could be just as right?

Bird reasoned that on a fundamental level, society tried to accommodate mankind's cultural diversity, but the dynamics of what we as people have evolved into don't exactly fit into neat and tidy boxes. So they export this Western democratic system to the far corners of the globe and attempt to institutionalise the planet in order to shape these random strands into symmetrical packages of DNA that may be manipulated and managed – and it almost works. Most people do just trudge along in the system and toe the line of societal cloning, believing that what they are told is the absolute truth. Unlike Bird and Cracker, they believe the hype that's fed to them by their politicians, their preachers, in their newspapers and on their TV sets. They believe it and they accept it.

They accept the myth that reality talent shows really do showcase undiscovered talent rather than make a select few individuals morosely wealthy. They accept that Iraq housed weapons of mass destruction and is now better off for the 'Allied' invasion. They accept that climate change may or may not be real, depending on whose point of view they choose to follow. They accept that combustion engines are still the best way to power our manic machinery in spite of the fact that we can land space probes on Mars. They accept it and they believe it. The engines in our cars remain pretty much unchanged for over a century and choke the atmosphere a little more with each waking minute, but there's stuff driving around Mars analysing the soil, and that kind of raised a couple of questions for the boys.

"Yeah, like, ask your grandma how many space missions she witnessed as a child and she'll tell you none, but ask her if some dude in the area had a car and she might say one," Cracker had proffered once back off the cliffs and in his warm room with a cup of tea and a spliff, now prepared to indulge Bird's ranting at last.

"Yeah man, that car remains virtually unchanged, but now that granny's old and wrinkly, we've walked on the moon and sent probes onto Mars," agreed Bird. "Should that tell us something about technological advancement?"

"Only if we're listening, my little feathered friend."

"Or not, as the case may be – not listening to the trashy media or the lying politicians. I mean, they're the ones who never highlighted this gaping moral hole between knowing so little about the limitations on our own environment yet trying to know so much about a rock several hundred light years away. If they don't say it, we don't accept it, but the FTSE index dropped by sixteen points in the night and the Dow Jones remained stable while the London stock exchange saw a dramatic increase after the Spice Girls played a sell-out gig in Tokyo. It's such a load of bollocks, man, but everyone seems to accept it. They accept it because it's on their TVs and in their newspapers," Bird continued in a dramatically mocking tone. All Cracker could do was shake his head and smile as he flicked the ash from his reefer.

"I fuckin' hate the mainstream media, man. They create news that thirty years ago never mattered to us because it wasn't such big business. It's all about money, mate, a self-righteous machine that formulates our opinions and shapes our minds about shit we will never understand, but it will captivate our attention just enough to keep us hanging through the commercial break. So is it the story that's important or the marketing that punctuates it?"

"All right, all right, I think I got your point." Cracker was now desperate to stop this fool before he got all emotional and distressed.

"Just like you said, Cracks, it's all a load of bollocks," was Bird's parting remark as he sat back down.

The life of a societal clone didn't much appeal to Bird. What society deemed to be right and wrong was totally different from his perception. He didn't need a licence to drive a car, he just needed to know how. He didn't need to be of a certain age to drink, he just needed to look it. He didn't need a qualification to do a job, he just needed the ability. He didn't need to go to school if it challenged his general sense of well-being, and it usually did, so he usually didn't. He didn't need to observe the law because it wasn't his to observe. He didn't need education about drugs, he just needed money to buy them – and so it went on.

But money presented a slight problem to Bird within this anarchic paradigm of 'bollocks', because straight survival kind of depended on it. To buy something from a shop, he needed some form of finance. Occasionally he was able to barter, but of course the shopkeeper always preferred cash. There were instances when he would accept Bird's meagre offering of a sock, which would be placed on the shelf as an exchange for the item just lifted, but he was usually unaware of it. The drug dealer only took cash and you didn't offer him anything else.

But straight theft also presented a problem to Bird as he was a firm believer in the words and music of Bob Marley, who expounded the virtue that what you put out is what you get back. So he was always careful to absolve his conscience by initiating some form of exchange for acts that may be construed as theft when they came back to him in later life. He lost a lot of socks and caused grave discomfort to his feet demonstrating this sacrifice, but it helped to ease the spiritual burden and hopefully avoid any altercations with Mr. Marley in the afterlife.

It comes as no surprise to learn, then, that this kind of philosophy is liable to get one into certain establishments that perhaps one doesn't want to be in – like prison. Bird's father was inside and had been since he was six. He knew all about this prison place and didn't fancy it too much as it would entail spending time with his Dad. So to follow his ideal, he needed to know how society worked, to have been a part of it at some time getting to know loopholes, dodging points and camouflage that would hide him when the bloodhounds were on his trail. That was the only drawback. Society had ways of enforcing its regime, and staying out of the clutching claws was paramount to his survival when walking this tightrope. Escaping the system, its institutions and its media conditioning was essential when living life according to 'bollocks'.

Bird and Cracker were the instigators of the 'bollocks theory' and the makers of its rhetoric – it was their life's philosophy and they lived by it. Their rules, their parameters, their way of life for the last five years. But something had happened to Bird in this experience with the glass – what alcoholics might call a moment of clarity. It wasn't that he had been reborn or seen the light, or even recognised any error in his ways – not at all. I mean, he was still tugging on the last of his spliff whilst contemplating the lightning-bolt emotion that had just shot through his body when the ray of sunlight illuminated the photograph. And no matter what happened, he would continue to live by the rhetoric that he and Cracker had manifested on that crisp and cold 'bollocks theory' morning. But a higher purpose seemed to have been awakened within him and enlightenment had consumed him, forcing the question over and over again:

Reverential apparition or just a distant memory?

All those years of scrabbling through the undergrowth, under dripping forest canopies, along thistle-filled hedgerows and on windswept cliffs. Those thousands of hours spent observing and marvelling at the specimens that had become the basis of their paper delivered to Oxford. The theories they had assembled on physical migratory preparations – the bodily changes that migrating birds encounter when preparing to fly. All they had learned of these creatures' amazing ability to cross the oceans of the world. Was it just a memory or did it actually mean something to him?

Yes… yes it did… and it still does…

Alfred's prime mover with science had always been to try to rationalise the existence of man as undisputed ruler of this planet, because he was old school. Study other organisms to draw parallels with our world to benefit society and show how much further evolved we are. It had been drummed into him for over sixty years that humans were evolutionarily superior to every race on the planet, because they possess a higher level of consciousness and spatial awareness that allows them lateral thought patterns to communicate and co-operate their intentions in a clear and concise way.

But Bird had never been able to swallow that pill, especially once the special interests got involved and money was able to skew results into favourable conclusions to maximise profits. He knew we were not the highest evolved species on the planet – he had been watching birds with Alfred from the age of three, and for as long as memory possessed him, he had been consumed by their overwhelming beauty, colour and song, and their unparalleled ability to take to the sky and soar on the thermals of our world. This, he thought, separated birds from every single species on the planet – especially one so easily swayed by financial gains.

His theories on all this had once been so sound, and living was once so easy, but that old-school mentality that he fought as a zealous and inspired teenager had sucked the life out of him and left him drained and deflated. The grip of society was so strong that even the kids he had grown up with, the infantry in their anarchic militia, had been consumed by it.

Get a job, get a career, get a bank account, a home, a mortgage, a debt to the speeding wheels of industry that tempt us with the freedom of our own life but really fasten the chains around our ankles that enslave us in a system that was once our nemesis – bollocks!

Bird's life had been a melting pot of misfortune and mishaps. He had the mind of a genius but risked being trapped within the boundaries of financially-manipulated intuitive prisons, which he fought hard to avoid. Had his true spirit been allowed to fly, he would surely have circled with the rest of them in that mythical cyclone of scientific discovery, allowing him the freedom to upturn rocks of urban legends and push the envelope of understanding. As it was, the system had beaten him and left little purpose for him to continue with it. When the element of discovery is removed from science and a programme of maintenance on old findings takes effect to satisfy special interests, the likes of Bird become very disinterested. Call it snobbery, call it arrogance, call it French-fried potatoes with mayonnaise – he saw no point in reanalysing a specimen for the four-hundredth time to find that actually it should be separated into three further dimensions than previously separated into because someone paying the bills needs it justified. Bollocks!

And so that was it – out with the science of it all, remain with the appreciation, and nothing else matters because we all know in our heart of hearts at the end of the day that it's all a load of bollocks. Nothing more, nothing less. Everything is about perceptive interpretation, which is individual, erratic and changeable with enough cash, and therefore bollocks. Simple.

In the wake of several emotional disasters, the appreciation of birds was all that had kept him alive. He saw these creatures as refined individuals with intricate dialects, social structures, class systems, territories and governments. They were able to sustain worlds within our world that with human interpretation could appear frighteningly familiar. Did we learn from them? Do they pull the puppet strings after all? Maybe. But for Bird, they represented more than just a scientific exhibit – they stood for freedom itself.

They say that Africa was the birthplace of mankind as *Homo sapiens* – the place where *Homo erectus* laid down and gave way to his greater-evolved cousin to carry the evolutionary torch forward and press its boundaries on towards the stars. Maybe Africa would hold the answers for him, too. Maybe there he could cross that divide and dip a wing into the undiscovered side for just a brief moment in time. Maybe there he could rekindle the fire that society was sucking out of him and re-form a militia to topple this existence once and for all. Yes, just maybe. Maybe Africa.

6

TRAVEL PLANS

For a man whose life had revolved around reinventing himself into a bird for the purpose of spiritual flight, one would think that the physical action of boarding an aircraft for a journey would be a natural one, but this was not the case. Bird had never actually flown anywhere. He'd never been on a plane, nor a helicopter, nor bungee jumped off a three-hundred-foot bridge for that matter. He'd never physically left the ground for longer than a few seconds, and the very prospect of flying to Africa filled him with dread. Flight, he thought, should be an unaided surf ride across a rip in the deep blue sky reserved for those creatures physically adapted to it, not some prehistoric heap of scrap metal with four bloody great turbines strapped to its wings.

Everything about planes he found ugly and unnatural. Great big fuck-off metal tubes that blast themselves into orbit with a thousand miniature explosions in their armpits. People crammed like sage and onion stuffing in the intestines of these beasts with nothing but a paltry offering of synthetic sustenance during their harrowing ordeal. Delays and diversions – queues and quarrels – chalk lines and checkpoints – X-rays and sock shufflings. Everyone he knew that had ever flown anywhere had a nightmare tale to tell about the inadequacies of airlines, the endless mind-numbing waits, the shocking food and service on board, and all at the price of a small fortune. Getting to Africa would not be easy.

Travel plans – airports – flying. How the hell do I do that? Where's Cracker? He'll know.

"Well, thank heavens for that. I'll make arrangements. More tea?" That was all Alfred had to say on the matter before proceeding to make Bird a presentation. "You'll be needing a good pair out there, son," he said, offering a wrapped package to Bird. "Rough terrain, great distances – you'll be needing a pair and they'll need to be good. Look after them, lad. Been around a while."

"Thank you, Alfie." Bird unwrapped the parcel and removed a pair of 1968 Zeiss binoculars and a reference book in a leather-bound case with a notepad and pen tucked neatly into the front pocket. *Roberts' Birds of Southern Africa* was emblazoned on the book's title page, above a scribble from Alfred wishing Bird luck. The binos really were state of the art.

"I thought I was going to South Central Africa, Alf, what's with the Roberts? Isn't this book for Southern African birds only?" he muttered while thumbing through the pages.

"Hmmm? Yes… problem with that region… blast, must fix this kettle." Alfred's head appeared momentarily from the kitchen; he was now making tea and burning himself on the dodgy kettle for the umpteenth time that day.

"Bugger all reference material for the area…" His face disappeared, consumed by the kitchen, his voice now echoing around its door. "Part of the job you'll be doing – referencing habitats, food resources, migration routes, breeding grounds, that sort of thing. Very similar to what we've done in the past, only this will be virgin territory."

He was still fumbling with the sketchy mains connection on his kettle, cursing under his breath in between bouts of mission debriefing. "You'll be working out what's there, what isn't, what should be there, what could be there…" He gazed momentarily at the kitchen ceiling and stroked imaginary whiskers on his chin, having temporarily relieved his hands of kettle duties. "What could be there…" he echoed quietly to himself. "Yes, bloody hell, never thought of it like that – what *could* be there."

He suddenly ceased all activities simultaneously – chin stroking, dodgy kettle, ceiling gazing, the lot – and stared across in Bird's general direction without actually looking at him. Cats sometimes do that; they stare at a wall or the leg of a chair or the back of a sofa for hours on end. Alfred reminded him of a cat. He never really looked *at* him, just kind of looked his way.

"Have you any idea what could be there?" he wheezed in staccato excitement.

"Not really, have you?" Bird replied almost nonchalantly.

Alfred's eyeballs shot back into their sockets and bounced into position to refocus on Bird once again. "None, boy – not a bloody one – and do you know how exciting that is?" He rubbed his hands with glee and disappeared into the bowels of his kitchen to grapple with the burny kettle once more – Agincourt would be his!

That's why Bird loved Alfred. That's the dude he was – an amazing and unparalleled enthusiasm for birds. No one could be in his presence for any length of time and not feel inspired. Whacky professor or not, this cat had character. He had passion, drive, motivation, desire and emotion – qualities that become harder to find in oneself as time rolls on. They become diluted particles in the bloodstream of life that finally dissolve in a heart filled with regressive desire.

"You'll be needing a farewell, Birdman," was all Cracker had to say. "How about a night out at the Wound followed by a trip for us all to the airport, to make sure you get on that plane? I quite fancy a train ride up to London for the day."

"Where does it come from, Cracks?" answered a bemused Bird. "You seem to open your mouth and all this gob shite just falls out, all over the place, polluting the air."

"Shall we smoke a bong?" Cracker proffered with a look of genuine offence on his face.

Cracker's parents had taken him abroad many times in his life and he'd had the good fortune of flying from a very young age. His parents did this in spite of his numerous drug habits and associated criminal lifestyle, which rated them as fairly cool by Bird's standards – and indeed they were. Quite what they'd done to deserve a son like Cracker was beyond everyone.

He'd been a heroin addict for a while, Cracker had, constantly moving around the country and pulling various 'bad' scams to support his habit. One of his favourite tales to regale anyone that would listen was about a time when he walked into a haberdashery shop one fine London morning and promptly picked up a six-foot roll of material. Thrusting it onto his shoulder, he proceeded to walk out of the establishment, as cool as can be.

Cool, that is, until he hit the pavement, where he did a Linford Christie and legged it. But the geezer in the shop decided that Cracker was worth a run and promptly gave chase. Cracker had been on the gear for some time and wasn't exactly in the finest physical form, but he gave it as large as he could on the old athletic front anyway. Eight seconds into his marathon, the adrenaline wore off and he couldn't be bothered to run anymore, so he stopped on the pavement and grabbed a skanky works[*] from his pocket – needle and all – and held it up as a dagger while panting like a jackrabbit as he turned to his assailant and yelled:

"I'm a fuckin' smakky wiv AIDS – how much do you earn? Is it really worth it? Eh?"

Taking into account the physical state of Cracker after his sprint – face all gaunt and thin, flushed from the energy expenditure, eyes bloodshot and bulging like a goldfish, sweat and skank dripping profusely from every orifice and the general demeanour of something your neighbour's dog puked up, all the while panting and wheezing like a ninety-year-old wino, with the look of the devil in his eyes and a hypodermic syringe in his fist – the shop geezer soon decided Cracker wasn't worth the run after all and let him walk. It wasn't his shop anyway. And the conclusion of the story? Well, Cracker picked up the roll of material and walked off, as cool as can be.

"Don't you worry about a thing, little Birdyboy, Uncle Cracks is gonna be right there beside you to put your feathered ass on that plane – nice an' easy."

"If you think for one moment you're coming to the airport, Cracker, you have a sorely mistaken think pattern. I'm sure we ascertained that some years ago, anyway."

"And if you think for one moment, *MR. BIRD,* that I'm gonna let you be in any state to put yourself on a bar stool, let alone a plane, on your last night here before

---

[*] A hypodermic syringe lacking in medical hygiene

97

flying off to Africa, then you indeed have a similar predicament with *your* thought patterns. Bong?"

He held up a rancid plastic drink bottle stained brown from excessive smoke passage, with a smoking hash bowl poking out of one side. Bird held his thumb over a shotgun hole and sucked through what was the semblance of the top while Cracker stoked the bowl with a pen-sized blowtorch. The bubbled smoke was cool but heavy, and it sank to the pit of his lungs. As he sat back, he exhaled a mushroom cloud of smoke towards the ceiling with a loud snort and was momentarily winded.

"Fuuhhhkinn aaeerropl…pl…lanes…s…s…s…" he wheezed, forcing the smoke from the depths of his soul.

"Fuckin' aeroplanes," echoed Cracker as he packed another bong. "You will have to have a party." Bubble, bubble, bubble!

"I'll need to pack as well. What sort of kit am I gonna need, being in the jungle for two months?" Bird's throat revived and he regained breath.

"Chhh…hoh…hocolate   maa…aa…aan. Ta…ha…hake   as   much   cho…ho…hocolate as…hhas…hhas you can." Cracker paused and sucked in some more air. His face was beaming red with the pressure of trying to keep the bong smoke down.

"One th…hi…hing's for sshh…sshhh…sure, no cor…hherr…ner shh…hhop where you're going… where ya gho…ho…hoing again?" WWHHHOOOOOSSSHH, he released the pent-up bong smoke.

"Good question, mate – good fucking question. Where am I going and why am I going there?"

"You're leaving when? I can't believe you Bird, just can't believe you, you're so bloody unreliable. How the hell am

I gonna get someone to replace you at such short notice? Don't you ever think about anyone besides yourself?" was all Mike the landlord had to say.

"Take it easy, Mike. It's coming into winter – there's never any punters around in winter, you just need a couple of casuals. There's loads of folk about and it's only a couple of months – don't have a heart attack, man."

"Yeah, how about me, Mike? I'll do a stint for ya," Cracker smirked.

"Cracker? I don't even trust you as a punter in my bar, do you really think I'd be stupid enough to put you behind it? And don't call me 'man', hippie boy!"

"I didn't."

"Not you, dickhead – him," he said, motioning towards a grinning Bird.

"Ah, go easy Mike, Cracks is a good lad – sound as. You can trust him. He's right as rain now he's off the gear." Cracker simulated a punch into Bird's ribs.

"The only rain he's right as, Bird, is acid rain, and as you might have noticed, there's more of it about these days – the rain and the acid. So don't think for one moment that Cracker's going behind the bar. I can't throw him and I don't trust him." Cracker looked across at Bird, confused and eyebrows raised.

"Enough already," Mike continued. "Get your shit together and I'll organise some cash for you. I suppose tonight will have to be your last shift..." He paused momentarily and looked knowingly at Bird and Cracker. "You'll be needing a going-away party too, no doubt? Notify the troops and I'll let the cops know on my way out of town. You're such a dick, Bird." And then he spun away, still muttering to himself as he walked.

"Does that mean I'll get my job back when I come home?" Bird yelled after Mike's disappearing figure.

"NO! Now piss off and pack. You dick." And then he was gone.

"Landlords – who needs 'em?" Bird said, shaking his head.

"Better notify the troops, Bird. You heard the man – your leaving party starts now."

"No, Cracks, I gotta work and I gotta pack and so far all we've established I'll need is skins, rolling tobacco, underpants and chocolate, and I don't know why but I have a sneaking suspicion that that won't be enough. Will I need a passport?"

"Let's go up to your room and have a look at your kit. I've got us some snortable chang and once we've had a line everything will become clear, my little friend – clear as a budgie's bell."

Cracker was looking at Bird in that way again, that way he'd looked at him since they were three. It got him into trouble then and it was getting him into trouble now, almost thirty years later. But Bird and Cracker had an understanding that went way beyond friendship. They'd been through so much together, endured such feats, surfed so many rips and experienced a multitude of emotions – contrived, chemical or natural – with the other right by their side. They had formulated each other's characters, evolving in similar habitats yet still juggling with the propensities of independent identities that allowed them to veer off on tangents quite opposed to one another. Joined by the umbilical cord of life, they reversed the societal division of humanity's zygote to bond the diverse genes of strangers and formulate the cohesion of two individuals who ran bumper-to-bumper in the traffic jam of life. Packing and cocaine it would be.

7

THIS INDECISION'S BUGGING ME

"Yeah, like I say, we're *really, really sorry*," Cracker wheezed in a desperately patronising tone, emphasising the words just a little more than he needed to. "He's had an accident and kind of passed out but I promise you, it's just a mild psychiatric condition and once he's actually airborne he'll be just fine." He leaned in close with a glance across each shoulder and lowered his voice, as if sharing some tragic secret. "Look, I know this is hard to believe but flying is a really huge issue in his life – like, massive – and this is the kind of reaction he has to any situation that causes him severe stress. It's like being in denial. He thinks that if he passes out and doesn't register getting on the plane, then he was forced into it and now just has to endure it – kind of like his cross to bear – know what I mean?" He leant back, smiling benignly and exposing the tar stains on his teeth, which probably didn't help matters, then uttered such a condescending epitaph that all and sundry shuddered a double-take and seriously questioned the logic of using Cracker as an ambassador in such a circumstance: "He'll be right as rain when he wakes up. I promise you, sweetheart, everything will be just fine." And then he winked.

Sympathetic nods went round the four or so heads that were standing around Bird surreptitiously supporting him, as he was currently unable to stand or hold his head upright for any length of time. For some reason best known to no one in particular, Cracker had been designated as speaker, and although they all acknowledged his ridiculous effort, in their heart of hearts they knew that this ship was slowly sinking.

"Sir. Your friend looks very drunk to me – absolutely smashed in fact – and I don't think you should try to tell me otherwise," retorted the uniformed girl somewhat authoritatively. "He is a danger to himself and this flight, and we have every right to refuse him entry to the aircraft if we deem him unsafe. What if he wakes up to be an axe murderer or a hijacker – or he has some kind of psychotic fit because he realises that he is now on a plane? What then?"

This was the fourth time the check-in desk girl at Heathrow Airport had had to explain this to Cracker, and she was now tired of the story and fast becoming tired of him. One look at the state of Bird had convinced her that she was dealing with a bunch of complete muppets here, and so far Cracker hadn't done much to repudiate that fact. He had been persistent, though. The anxiety of Bird not making this flight and losing his only shot at this stupendous opportunity because they had trashed him with shooters at his leaving party was now starting to weigh heavily on Cracker's mind. He'd made Bird drink more alcohol on the train up to London as well, whilst everyone else had had coffee and plastic burgers, and now, with the fun behind them and the cold light of a brand-new day settling like frost along the ledges of paranoid despair inside his head, Cracker was starting to wish he'd just put Bird on the train in Plymouth and pointed him in the direction of London with a fond farewell.

Bird, on the other hand, was blissfully unaware. The last thing he could actually recall was being in the Wound and Bandage the night before, doing Polish spirit shots on top of a number of pills, a few lines of coke and many pipes of skunk thrown in for good measure. It had been shooters night at the Wound and a bottle of Polish spirit – 80% proof – was the designated drink of choice, courtesy of a cross-Channel fishing boat that had smuggled it in from France the week before. They had mixed it with Blue Label vodka to water it down a bit and take the edge off it, then racked it up behind the bar for all to enjoy on the understanding that each shot was to be taken with Bird, as he was the one going away and this was his party.

At first it had been really fun. Bird was surrounded by loads of his mates all lining up to share a farewell drink with him, jostling for a sliver of his precious pie and extolling the great virtues of his impending trip to Africa and the noble cause for which he was departing. Coming up on four pills and hitting the shots one after another just added to the allure, and Bird was loving it – telling everyone how much they meant to him, how much he'd miss them, how he had always felt so 'right on' with them and how he had come to think of them as family.

The chemicals had kept him in the moment and allowed him enough control to hit the shots with a joke and a smile, rushing sporadically off each line of coke then gently surfing the waves of welling ecstasy that filled him with loving emotions, and wrapping the whole enchilada in a man-sized ego of Polish spirit to indulge the appetites of this madding crowd. The Wound and Bandage was rocking at full steam and all the usual suspects had been drawn out of their lairs to celebrate. Bird was reviving old acquaintances and strengthening new ones as this merry band of misfits all convened for the momentous occasion.

And that was really the last time he was able to walk, talk or even think for himself: in the middle of it all at the Wound, revelling in his fifteen minutes of fame and loving every second of it. He vaguely remembered someone standing up at the jukebox, yelling, "Hey Birdyboy, this one's for you, mate!" and the next thing he knew, The Clash was blaring out of every corner and a multitude of people suddenly appeared at his feet, all flailing their arms around and screeching along with the song... *Should I stay or should I go?*

It was great!

But then the Polish spirit kicked in, and everything just got plain messy. Quite what happened for the rest of the night was something of a mystery. They always ended up at DZ's house after a night out at the pub, so it was safe to assume that the usual protocol had been followed, but Bird had no clue as to what had actually transpired. Memory eluded him at this stage, but snippets of the evening laced themselves into the fabric of his distorted thoughts, and every so often he leapt to life and squealed some incoherent gibberish, then receded sheepishly back into his shell.

"...If I go there will be trouble... but if I stay it will be double..." he scowled in one such instance, making the check-in desk girl shake her head slowly in complete disbelief as he withdrew once again, his outburst contained.

"Excuse me, Ma'am, if you'd allow me just one second of your time?" Iceberg stepped forward, simulating the action of taking cap in hand despite the fact that he wasn't wearing one and his bright red hair had been sawn to a fresh grade-one crewcut of stubble across his gleaming scalp. The other three shuffled their grip on Bird and steadied him as Iceberg walked towards the desk. "I have here a copy of the application letter made on Mr. Bird's behalf to the research station that he is on his way out to in Africa," he continued. Surprised that she was even listening, he humbled himself further. "If you would be so kind as to take five minutes to read his brief resumé before brutally condemning my learned friend here to the pitiful realms of axe murderer, we would appreciate it greatly. Would you do that?" he asked with genuine heartfelt sincerity. "I know it's a lot to ask but this really is his one and only chance to get out there and show the world what he knows about avian dynamics. You see, he's been working on a bird migration hypothesis for Oxford University and he now has to go into the field to test it. If what he believes is correct, it will change our whole understanding about bird migrations and possibly alter the way that people fly, too. Look, let's be honest..." he continued with a knowing smile, "these are not normal circumstances and Mr. Bird here is not the most normal of cats you'll ever meet – believe me, we all fully appreciate that but please, he has to fly, he has to get where he's going for the sake of science. Surely there must be something you can do for him?"

He fluttered a heart-stopping glance at her and then took a step back, sliding the letter onto the counter as he went.

The check-in girl looked daggers at Iceberg. She was the classic Essex Girl and she could smell it on these boys – her pheromone detectors identified them as the rude-boy low-lifers they were, and she didn't like them, not one bit

– rude boys. There was an awkward pause as she gazed in disbelief at the sorry rabble of imbeciles in front of her, shuffling from side to side in an unconvincing attempt to conceal Bird's true Polish spirit colours, yet somehow failing miserably. They all stared back at her with expectant eyes the size of saucers.

"I'll read it," she said, picking up the letter. "Now go and stand over there and wait for me. I'll have to talk to my supervisor."

What the hell did I go and do that for? she asked herself as she disappeared behind the baggage carousel.

"Nice one Icy, let's hope she comes right else we're in major shit, man. I'm beginning to think this feathered clown might not make the flight after all. I doubt he'd ever forgive us, either."

"No, Cracker, *you're* in major shit and it's you he'd never forgive. What is it with you two, anyway? You're always on such a trip to screw each other up it's a wonder you're actually mates at all. Can't you fools let your egos lie for just one moment? Always gotta prove that one can get more twatted than the other. You looked like you were on a mission to nail him last night and if you were, then I can safely say that you won, hands down."

"I know, ain't it great?" Cracker smiled his 'what the fuck' smile that nobody could really disagree with and proceeded to explain.

"Same rules as always, Iceman – he knows 'em and he plays the game better than most of us. It's what he'd do and it's what he expects. Only reason I've won today is 'cos this one is such a big gig – possibly the biggest ever. Going to Africa has become so important to him that he couldn't let all them pretty feathers fly. He's normally the one doing the wasting, man – you know how hardcore he is – but he's been surfin' against the rip all night and that's the bottom line. We all know where the break is, mate, and don't think for one moment that he doesn't know how to ride – this is the world heavyweight champion at getting fucked up. It's just that tonight's was such a major gig and he couldn't get the importance of it out of his head to let rip and take me on. It was always gonna be mine. Know wot I mean?" Cracker sniggered.

"You're still facing the music if the bands are marching, mate. Make no mistake, if he doesn't catch this plane, I'm offering you as a sacrifice for the slaughter. And you can pay for my train ticket, too – if he wasn't so wasted we could have said goodbye to him in Plymouth."

"She's back, lads. Go and sort it, Iceman," came a hurried interruption.

Iceberg did not acquire his name through any magnificent behavioural trait of coolness or calm. No. He got his name simply because his head was the shape of a lettuce – an Iceberg lettuce. He walked purposefully to the counter and resumed negotiations with the check-in girl.

"It's completely against regulations," the girl whispered, flashing paranoid glances around the hall, "but if your friend is who this letter says he is then I feel I have to let him fly." She raised her voice for the benefit of them all and continued as she eyed each and every one of them. "I want you all to know that I am not happy about this though, I could lose my job here. I don't even know why I'm doing it, but something is telling me that your friend has to get to where he is going, and I appreciate that." They all nodded enthusiastically. "Strangely enough, I even believe that the work he is doing is vitally important – but let me tell you, if this backfires I'm the one who will pay and I don't like that part of it, not one bit." She held their stare for a moment then leant over her keyboard and began punching his details into the computer. "But tell me this," she asked Iceberg without looking up. "If he is this hot-shot ornithologist, why's he so drunk?"

"Ah man, it's not his fault, he just gets like that sometimes and, well, it's true, he's never been on a plane before and he's shit-scar… I mean, petrified. It was the only way he knew how to deal with it. Doesn't touch a drop normally, that's probably why he got so wasted. Thank you for your help – I promise you, it won't backfire, and he is not a hijacker, he's just a bit of a mixed-up kid – it's a sign of genius, you know?"

She didn't believe a word of it – and with this bunch of psychos as his mates, who could blame her? He didn't exactly look like Mr. Goody Two Shoes.

"Well, I've organised a wheelchair for him and two stewards to put him on the flight. I've pulled a couple of strings here, so he just better be who you say he is or God help me, I'll hunt you down and make you pay for my lost pension." She glared at them all once again, then focussed her stare on Cracker. "And I can guarantee it won't be a teddy bear's picnic I'll take you to, neither!"

She still didn't know why she was doing it – maybe Iceberg was part of the reason. Maybe underneath that rough and brazen exterior, there was care and compassion inside these people. It gave her a kind of hope for humanity.

Iceberg didn't really give a shit what her reasons were – he was just relieved to get the guy out of here. He raised his eyes to heaven before resting them on hers, and clasped his hands together dramatically.

"God bless you, Ma'am. God bless you. One day you shall be rewarded for this noble deed, I promise you that. None of us will ever forget you." Then he suddenly realised that this girl actually wanted nothing more than to be forgotten by these half-wits, so he pulled back before he undid all his good work. He was still gesticulating profuse gratitude as he backed away, but it was more relief than actual gratitude that he felt.

The last they saw of their lifelong companion was two stewards in asylum-type uniforms carting him off in a wheelchair towards the departure lounge. It looked kind of sad, really. Society's answer to the enormity of our environmental crisis slumped across a wheelchair, being shipped off by men in white coats to faraway lands. The five of them stood speechless on a gleaming airport floor, still somewhat bemused by the chain of events they had just witnessed, and marvelled at the image of Bird as he faded from view. They knew where he was going and they knew why he was going there, but knowing him the way they did, something just didn't quite add up. Who was this guy?

This the prophet going out into the wilderness for sixty days and sixty nights that he may find his soul and a true spiritual purpose?

This the 'Agent Green' specially selected to build an environmental militia to cripple the toxic giants of our world and change the course of history?

This the envoy, summoned for the purpose of enlightenment that he may deliver a message to the distorted race in the mutant lands who hold little understanding of the priceless jewel on which they stand?

This the heathen from the Western world that shall be converted to guide this poetic prophecy and save our floundering earth?

This the prodigy?

"God help us, man. God fucking help us." The four solemn heads that surrounded Cracker nodded in agreement as they stared at the disappearing image of the wheelchair.

The raven had left the tower. Bird was gone – into Africa.

8

BEGIN THE BEGINNING

Darkness.

There is a darkness that envelops us in the womb. Liquid darkness. It is all around – consuming yet supporting. Our eyes are open but there is nothing to see. It's comforting and it is safe. There is no knowledge of what surrounds the darkness because it is all we know. The tyranny of our awaiting world features nowhere in the womb. There is no preparation for the transition we are about to make, but the gap between darkness and light is suddenly breached, opening the floodgates of life and washing us up on the floor of humanity like a floundering fish.

Birth and rebirth. Begin the beginning.

What was that? Ow, my head – feels like I've split it open with an axe. Where am I? What's that smell, what's that noise? Why is it so dark? Wait, what was that? Man, it's loud. I recognise it but I haven't heard it before. Robin, got to be a robin of sorts? Ah man, my head is splitting, I need a drink. Where am I?

He was in a bed with starched sheets and woven hospital blankets, inside a small room with brick walls. He'd been sweating and could smell a sharp, pungent odour emanating from inside the linen, but it was different to the skank smell of his unwashed bed at the Wound –

this was kind of a raw skank, like it had been clean for ever and virginally soiled. It smelt strange.

A dim light was being cast through an opening in the wall in front of him. He could see no glass, but it was a window of sorts. A few crickets whistled and faint rustling noises could be heard at a distance, though all sounds were seemingly engulfed within a crushing silence so profound it was almost deafening. But just as light splits the eternal confines of darkness, so this silence was ripped by a high-pitched shriek that resonated through the air in a tumbling crescendo of piping notes.

What the…? Can only be a robin?

The call seemed to spark an orchestra of birds into life, and within seconds the whole place was alive with twittering, fluting, whistling, screeching and howling calls that sent Bird into a frenzied panic. He didn't know any of them – he was not at home. Not only was he not at home, he was not in England.

Holy Mary Mother of God, I must be in Africa!

Images began flashing into his mind. He was on his knees in a cubicle throwing up, but a soothing woman's voice was in the background. There was turbulence. Was it a plane?

Fuckin' aeroplanes!

He was in a vehicle stinking of fish, lying on rough hessian sacks. It was hot and dusty; trees were flashing past; other people were there, foreign people. Things were flying around the confined space – brown things, fly-type things – they were biting – they hurt. His hand moved onto his legs and began scratching – this is in real time. Big welts and scabs had formed on them.

What the hell?

He ran his fingers over the wounds – they were indeed insect bites, and they now itched like hell. Then, suddenly, a voice echoed within his confusion. The accent was foreign and distorted but the voice was calm and distant – or so it seemed.

"Good morning, saa."

Who is that?

The voice came again. Bird lay still and tried to listen to the reaction of whoever it was being woken up – it would help gauge his surroundings, give him some vital information as to where on Planet Earth he was. Might not even be Earth – alien abduction? His only real recollection of time was going through travel plans with Alfred, but there were still a couple of days left before flying, weren't there? Then he remembered the Wound. Polish spirit shooters – he could still taste them in his mouth.

"Good morning, saa."

Shit, man, why isn't someone answering this dude? Is he on a telephone? Bad line? Is anyone picking up?

There was a faint tapping on a door really close to where he was – his door perhaps?

"Good morning, saa."

Paranoia crept over his skin like a morning mist creeping across the moors back home. The voice was talking to him.

"Um, g… g… good morning. Are you talking to me?"

"Yes, saa. Good morning, Bwana Berd."

"Yes, good morning."

What the hell is 'bwana'?

"I have here some tea."

"Oh great, how civilised. Hang on, I'll open the door." His voice croaked from too many cigarettes at the

Wound. "Where the hell is it?" he whispered, clearing his throat, still consumed with the paranoia as he tried to get out of bed. Then suddenly a fearful howl erupted from his lungs as an alien lair engulfed him.

"Evfing OK, saa?"

"BASTARD... aaagggghhh get off... get this shit off me... what is it... aaaggghhh!"

"Saa?"

Bird hadn't realised he'd been sleeping under a mosquito net, and he was now rolling around the cold concrete floor, struggling with this mutant shroud that had crashed down from a beam above his head and enwrapped him like a web.

"Are you OK, saa?"

"Yes, fine, sorry. Sorry, just hit something with my toe trying to get this shit off me."

Bastard net – is this some kind of sick joke? How did I even get into this thing? Oh bollocks, did I even put myself to bed? Where am I? What's going on? Please tell me, someone?

He was now hopping around the dim room holding up a stubbed toe, dressed in underpants and a sweaty T-shirt, looking for some clothes. This in itself was futile because he couldn't even find the door, and all he kept bumping into was the bastard net.

"May I enter, saa?"

"Yes, hold on, hold on, just looking for the... oowww... for the... ahhssh... the door. Yes, one second."

He had manoeuvred himself to the wall with a window-like opening and was fumbling along it searching for a door – it had to be there somewhere. He stole a quick glance through the window and saw trees, only trees, thick green trees, right there, right outside – nothing but trees.

The jungle, man, I'm in the jungle.

He felt the wooden frame and ran his hands over the door, searching for the handle.

"Right, just coming, sorry, sorry. Now, where's the blasted handle? God, I sound like Alfred already." But this was Alfred's world, after all. It wouldn't be long before he started talking that familiar language again.

The door handle wasn't coming easy. He was poking around in the corner like a blind man in a pharaoh's tomb, but he just couldn't find it. Then suddenly, he heard a metallic device click and the opposite side of the door opened without his intervention, illuminating his lily-white, skinny frame wearing a pair of oversized, baggy underpants and a skanky shirt with welts all over his legs. A short African man stood in front of him dressed in a brilliant white uniform and bearing a tray across his outstretched arms.

"Your tea, saa?"

Bird said nothing. He had never been served tea before and certainly not by such a distinguished gentleman. The man was short and stocky, muscular and toned. His skin was smooth and chocolate black, a pungent antithesis to the clothes he wore, but they fitted him like a glove. His sleeves were short, revealing the immaculately toned biceps on his upper arms with prominent veins traversing down their midsection. His hair was short, jet black and in tight curls, shaved bald at the sides. He was impeccably neat and tidy. His clothes rested perfectly on his athletic frame and military creases ran centrally down the sleeves and legs. Everything about this guy was symmetrical, including the teeth in his smile, which lit up his clean-shaven, perfectly rounded face. He was beautiful.

"Th…th…thank you. Is this for me?"

By contrast, the African stared at a skinny white man with long, straggly, dark hair that was matted and grimy. His face was unshaven, and sweat and dribble marks were visible around his lips. The holey creased T-shirt hung loosely over his ribbed chest and was wet with perspiration, turning it a shade of grimy yellow in the dim morning light. Two long, skinny arms waved about self-consciously at his sides, their only compliment being a pair of similarly-built legs with hairy, knobbly knees that dangled awkwardly out of the bottom of some baggy underpants – all covered with beaming red bite welts.

"Good morning, Bwana Berd. My name is Isaac. I have some tea for you."

His English was broken and the accent strained as if his mouth just wasn't programmed to speak this language, but the articulation effort was flawless, and whilst his pronunciation left something to be desired, his execution left Bird feeling very much in awe of his enterprise.

Behind Isaac, Africa's dawn chorus was unfolding in the thick trees. The sun was crawling up to its horizon with every ticking second, and any minute now a molten Armageddon would explode in the east as Earth's illuminating star crept beyond the deep blue sky.

"The baffloom is just here. The Madam say you must see camp and relax this morning. She com' back later to speak wif you. Is OK?"

"Yes fine, thank you. Um, sorry, Isaac, who is the Madam?"

"Madam Sarah. This her camp. You werk for her, yes? You come to see rions, yes? Many rions here, Bwana Berd – soooo many rions, I think you rike this prace, yes?"

"Haa, yeah, I like it already."

117

What the hell is a rion and why is he calling me 'bwana'?

"Jacob also is out. Him rooking the rions now but maybe him come back for runch. You see him when he come. Him happy to see you for help wif rions." Isaac smiled again and it filled Bird with a warm glow that made him forget how rough he was feeling.

And rough was indeed the word. Yes, the Wound, Manic's party, loads of drugs… shooters, bastard shooters. It was coming back to him now. Cracker and the lads had fucked him up royally before putting him on the plane. He didn't remember flying or being met at an airport, but he must have; he was here, in the jungle, in the middle of nowhere, having an inane conversation with a dude that made little sense and seemed to mix up his Rs and his Ls. Still, he'd brought Bird some tea, which was kind, and had tried to make him welcome, even if he did call him 'bwana' and talk about rions.

What the hell is a rion? Never heard of a bird called rion, maybe it's a special of the area. And what is 'bwana'? Wonder if he's cussin' me?

Then he sniggered at his own ridiculous thought.

After wincing down a gulp of strong, sweet tea, Bird hobbled his way to the small bathroom next to his room. The building stretched away from him, with many green doors along it like horse stables, and what had looked like a glassless window from his bed was indeed a window without glass, but it was covered with mosquito gauze. The roof of the building was supported with heavy beams and thatched with thick grass, its rooms fairly basic with little attention paid to any aesthetic detail. There were definitely no frills or spills in the bathroom either – just a toilet, a shower and a sink, and the floor was again cold concrete. A broken mirror hung lopsidedly on a wall and revealed the state of his appearance.

Great. Must have made a healthy first impression on this lot – comatose, covered in puke and looking like Iceberg's dog. Nice one, lads, really helped me out there. Who needs enemies when you have mates like Cracker? God, I hope I haven't blown the gig already – Alfred would never forgive me. All depends on what this Sarah is like. I hope I haven't met her yet – I would remember that, wouldn't I?

Poking at the reflection of his substance-abused face in the dilapidated mirror, he continued his thought pattern.

I wonder if she's a pothead? She might be some intense Dian Fossey-type creature out here studying furry animals that look like us, or a freaky entomologist looking at termites, or maybe a botanist with mutant homegrown… hey man, this is the jungle, anything's possible.

He paused for a moment to stare out of the open bathroom door towards the thick bank of trees that seemed to surround him, and to marvel at the cacophony of bird sounds. The dawn chorus was now steamrolling into a crescendo of audial chaos that threatened to erupt into an avian holocaust at any moment – which is, after all, its subliminal purpose, or anti-purpose: the avoidance of conflict through display. As far as their song could be heard was the territory they proclaimed to defend; should others challenge it, a battle would be imminent – do or die. Bird knew the theory all too well, but he was used to knowing all the players within the symphony as well. Out here, nothing was familiar.

And as this intricate maze of recitals unfolded around him, it struck Bird that in Africa, the territorial boundaries seemed so fiercely contested by so many different parties that it was a wonder any of the creatures knew where they were to defend – but somehow they did. Chaotic as it may have sounded to a hungover, welt-ridden, knobbly-kneed Englishman, these fluting, whistling males knew exactly what they were doing and took it very seriously indeed. This was as much a part of life as finding food or dressing themselves up in elaborate breeding plumages to attract a mate. This was the first step to securing the partner who would fulfil their evolutionary objective, perpetuate their progressive existence, gird the loins of their genetic procrastination – it's all about getting laid.

Securing a place of their own that was safe and aesthetically pleasing to their female partner demonstrated an independence and reliability, not just to their mate but to the competition as well. They couldn't rely solely on their pretty tail feathers to bring her to their door, even if they did complement them with a funky breeding dance. She needed a wholesome environment to raise her offspring and the males had to provide it.

This place was definitely Africa – it was smack bang in the middle of the jungle, no doubt about it. These guys didn't mess around. There was immense competition out here and only the strong would survive; there was no place for the weak or faint-hearted. Do or die, you eat what you kill. They had to think with their wits and be cool enough to dodge the badass motherfucker next door who might want to steal their hard-earned mate or, worse still, eat her. Very real considerations in Africa's radical pastures.

And then, for the first time within the limitless boundaries of such considerations, Bird felt suddenly very alone. The birdcalls were not familiar to him, nor were the trees. Everything about this place felt so removed from what he'd been used to. He'd been served tea by a real

African man who could barely speak English and awoken to an alien net that engulfed him in its deadly grasp during a struggle to get out of bed. He was surrounded by unfamiliarity in sight, sound and smell, and it was now thirty degrees in the shade – just around dawn.

But it was the insignificance of his presence that really got him. The conflict going on in these trees was monumental. Great powers were rising and falling, societies were creating and destroying themselves, an intense struggle for life was awakening around him, and it stirred a consciousness inside. If this is how tough it is for the birds, what was in store for him? What awaited the lonely boy hiding behind a green door in a faraway land that he had no comprehension of?

There were untold perils here; there were beasts that could kill him in the blinking of an eye. There were carnivores that could eat him, hippopotami that could trample him, elephants that could blast him, crocodiles that could munch him; and then there were lions – yes, Alfred had said there were lions here. He knew all too well that lions ate people, and they were here – lots of them, lots of slobbering, man-eating lions. A sudden realisation sent a chill creeping over him.

Rions? No, can't be. He can't be talking about lions. I'm here for birds – as a volunteer. Not lions – surely not. No, can't be!

The thought of lions gave Bird an uneasy sensation. The realisation that he was alone kept rebounding through his head and punching him softly in the guts, which didn't help this gentle paranoiac induction. The fact was, no one really knew him here and no one really cared – it's survival of the fittest and this was someone else's environment. If the shit went down, someone else would know exactly what to do, where to go and how quickly they would need to get there. That someone else was simply not Bird.

They'd leave me for dust – and rions. NO! I mean lions. Well, they'd leave me for the lions, too. Oh no!

The hard-hitting reality of where Bird was suddenly culminated in his stomach. Sweat gathered in his armpits and then crept onto his chest. His oesophagus tightened, and he lunged violently towards the toilet bowl, heaving bile from the pit of his being. Pains shot through his body and his muscles constricted to force out the filth that was now dribbling over his limp bottom lip and into the bowl he was clutching for dear life. What was it and where did it come from?

Cracker, shit like this always comes from Cracker… bastard!

After an age of head-splitting heaving, he dragged himself away from the toilet bowl and stripped off his clothes. The shower was powerful and hot and he stood under it with his mouth open, trying to cleanse every inch he could.

Enough of this shit, now. It's time for a new beginning. No more drugs, no more alcohol, no more Cracker and no more Wound and Bandage. Just birds, lots and lots of birds. And Africa – this is Africa, man. Let the beginning begin.

9

SYMMETRY IN CHAOS

Bird scratched his head, standing in the doorway of his newly acquired room, looking in and pondering his own stupidity. It couldn't have been that blatant, could it? There must have been a brain in there at some stage, mustn't there? He glanced back along the row of doors to make sure he was at the right one.

Have I been moved to another room? Doesn't look like anyone's slept here. That's my kit, though, and those are my boots. They can't have cleaned up already – surely not?

Everything was spotless. His bed was made, his boots and pack were neatly arranged at its foot, the mosquito net was once again hanging from a hook in the ceiling and his bird book and binoculars were in the middle of a small desk. Symmetrical. This had to be Isaac's work – like the man himself, it was all so damn symmetrical.

He took a deep breath and went inside to get changed and sort himself out before the Madam got back. Madam Sarah – his new boss. What was she going to be like? Alfred had never told him he would be working for a lady and Bird was unsure how he felt about it. He had never had a female boss before and his social skills with the species left something to be desired. He just prayed for good governance over his decaying memory and bird knowledge so as to make a positive impression and hopefully gain favour from the onset. God knows how much shit he was already in if she had been there to greet him when he got off the vehicle the night before. Maybe the gig was already blown – time would tell.

He unpacked his kit, threw some clean clothes on his back and strolled out of the door to get acquainted with this new environment. It was hot, of that he was sure, hot and bright with no clouds to blot out the deep blue sky that stretched to infinity above him and made his eyes wrinkle up into a squint. The ground underfoot was hard, brown and dusty. Sporadic patches of grass burst out of the soil in a desperate bid to defy the diminishing water table and infiltrate the ground above their roots, but the deep and compact dirt was definitely in control. Huge trees stood tall in defiance of the parched earth, and small buildings seemed to gather beneath their limbs to maximise the shade they cast and protect their clay walls and thatched rooves from the intense heat. The air was still alive with its avian orchestra of unfamiliar calls, and he could hear the gentle hum of a diesel engine somewhere in the distance.

There were African men in green overalls and boots scurrying around the site carting firewood, opening water pumps, sweeping dust and generally keeping busy in this sun-dappled island. They all stopped to look at him as he came into their line of sight, saying nothing and making no gestures of welcome, just stopping momentarily and staring before continuing with their tasks. He felt very self-conscious. In England, it was rude to stare, and not many people did it. But Africa would have a different rulebook, a different modus operandi, a different way of being that he would have to get used to for these two months. Their stares were not malicious nor threatening, they were more inquisitive about who the new white man was and how long he was going to be here.

Isaac appeared out of one of the buildings and emptied some rubbish into an outside dustbin. He caught Bird's eye and gestured to him.

"Bwana Berd, Bwana Berd, com' into the kitchen and I make you som' blekfast." At last, a familiar and friendly face. Bird liked Isaac. He didn't understand him, but he liked him.

The kitchen was a small and poky circular building made of clay bricks with a high, conical, thatched roof and was devoid of any substantial windows. A large table took up most of the central floor space, with various utensils scattered around its surface. A chest freezer was off to one side, purring away contentedly. It never occurred to Bird that they were a million miles from any electric grid and he didn't even give the freezer a second thought. Instead, he marvelled at square shelves that dangled awkwardly against the round walls inside the kitchen and soon realised that this was Isaac's domain – even within the physical limitations of a square peg in a round hole, his symmetry shone through and the tools of his trade were neatly arranged along them. Foodstuffs were simmering in frying pans on gas hobs, and a pleasing aroma began to fill the air.

"Blekfast leddy in some few minets. You want som' tea fest?"

"Yes, thank you Isaac, tea would be good."

"Yes, Bwana – how men' shooga?"

"Oh, no sugar thanks, just milk."

"You don' want shooga wif tea? Not even one?"

"Not even one, thank you."

"Fank you, saa."

"Isaac, why do you call me 'bwana' – what does it mean?"

"Him mean 'saa'. It is respect that African make for *muzungu*. You are my boss."

"I thought Sarah was the boss?"

"Madam Sarah the big boss. You the littol boss, yes – *mwanyike nani*? You muzungu, so you the boss."

"Ha ha, yes. I don't quite think so somehow."

"Saa?"

"Nothing, never mind. What is 'muzungu'?"

"Muzungu mean 'white man' in our langwedge – you white man, me *muntu*. Muntu alweys werk for muzungu."

"And what is 'muntu'?"

"Oh Bwana, you never been in Africa before, no? You not know about we African peoples? We peoples called muntu. Muntu mean 'man' in African langwedge – black man."

Wow, this dude is really strung out on the old black/white thing.

Isaac had brewed fresh tea leaves with hot water and milk inside a mottled teapot. He selected a mug from the shelf with contemplated precision, then poured the tea through a wire strainer and presented the mug to Bird. "Your tea, saa."

"Thank you, Isaac. Did you put sugar?"

Isaac's face lit up with his electric smile again. "Bwana say no shooga, me no put shooga. Sum they like shooga very much bot muzungu, him no want shooga for tea. Why? Only muntu like shooga in tea. Even Madam Sarah, she not like shooga in tea. Me no undastand, shooga good with tea. Savongo, him take shooga but only half.

Imagine, half shooga in tea. No, no, no, no!" Isaac moved back to his sizzling pans, chuckling to himself.

White people were indeed very strange to him. He'd met quite a few in his time and received countless hours of training on how to prepare their meals, but it sure didn't help his understanding of the race or their eating habits. They kept their food in tins and plastic packages and when you opened them, the food was often a strange colour. Then they would eat many different things from a variety of bizarre containers all at the same time, on the same plate and coated in sauce or gravy. He had also encountered some that only ate vegetables, didn't touch the meat at all, and this he found to be most unnatural. To Isaac and his tribe, meat was like gold, a highly marketable commodity that could be traded for a variety of life's necessities. His people risked life and limb to get hold of meat because it was wholesome and nourishing, and without it their food was both bland and non-nutritious. Quite why someone would refuse to eat it out of choice was a very strange phenomenon and contributed nicely to the weirdness of white in Isaac's world.

Then there was the rationalisation for the white folk to be out here in the first place. They came to look at the animals and write stuff down, but why? To Isaac, animals fell into two categories: there were those you could eat and there were those that could eat you. You stay away from the ones that can eat you and try to catch as many of the others as possible so you, your numerous wives and assorted children can have food and be merry. To sit for hours on end in the scorching African sun, watching lions sleep or antelope graze or elephants bathe or termites forage or baboons groom, seemed a completely bizarre concept.

Take lions, for example. They had attacked and eaten his people since the dawn of time. His tribe lived around what was now a huge national park, having been relocated to its man-made borders in the 1930s in an effort to maintain the natural wildlife resource inside. But they had lived in this area, with these animals, since before time began. They all knew of the ferocity and indiscriminate killing ability of lions, and they were therefore creatures to be feared and avoided at all times. Why someone would actively track them down to watch them sleep was just plain madness to him. He did his job, though, and toed the line he was given. It was not for him to reason why, just for him to do or die.

"Isaac, who is Savongo? You mentioned his name earlier."

Isaac momentarily stopped what he was doing and stared into a vacant chasm. He looked like he was about to speak but fell silent again. Bird was perplexed by the reaction – maybe there were things out here that a white man was not supposed to know. He knew African people were sensitive about culture and tradition, and he wondered if Savongo might be some sort of god that he should not be asking questions about. He felt awkward – like a bumbling fool that had just knocked his pint over in the pub.

"Savongo no more a person." The confounding silence was finally broken. "Him a spirit. Him watch ova animals, trees and berds. Him god for all creatures of this world, but him stay with us peoples and protect us when we are going into the boosh. Him watch us to make sure no rions come. Him very much respect by my peoples – we love Savongo much, too, because him protect us. But him only take half shooga in tea – imagine?"

Bird smiled to himself. This guy was amazing. He was a real African man from a real African tribe. He had ancient customs and mysterious gods that protected him from all the dangers in his home environment. He probably left offerings for Savongo under some sacred shrine to give thanks for his guardianship when looking danger right between the eyes. Could it be that these offerings to this great god would be cups of tea with half a sugar? Yep, these folks were as weird to Bird as white folks were to Isaac.

Maybe, he reasoned, Savongo was a great hunter from centuries ago who got himself into the religious chronicles of these people by doing some hugely heroic deed and, therefore, he will always stay with them. Protector from evil.

"Will I ever meet Savongo?" he pried.

"Ha ha ha. No, Bwana Berd. No, no, no! Savongo, him gone. Him no longa a peoples, him now a god. I told you that."

"Yes, you did, and I hope Savongo is able to look after me while I'm here too because I have a feeling that all is not so fine and dandy in this place."

"Saa?"

A huge fry-up breakfast was presented to Bird and he sat at the table destroying the plate in front of him. He was hungry. It seemed an age since he last ate, and all the drugs and alcohol had sapped every ounce of energy from him. The food was good and his appetite seemed endless.

Isaac continued pottering around the kitchen, singing out a sweet harmony in his tribal tongue while he cleared away pots and pans and returned his kitchen to its familiar state of symmetry. As he worked, a voice addressed him from outside, and he responded instantly. Bird stopped a while and tried to listen to the language. He'd heard Africans talk on the TV before and it had always sounded rash and harsh, employing many strange clicking sounds. By contrast, this exchange seemed gentle and mellow, flowing like a mountain dew waterfall tumbling graciously over rock and crevice. It was somehow touching. There was nothing familiar about it in any way, shape or form but it was subtle and tender – like Isaac himself, his language seemed kind and endearing.

A lump welled up in Bird's throat and emotions shot through his body like laser beams. People had actually come to this continent and hunted these people down – hunted them, trapped them and wrapped them in chains. They had linked them all together and shipped them off to distant shores, that they may be sold as slaves. White men did this, his ancestors did this, and look at the way these people were. Everything about them was gentle, peaceful and harmonious, and yet they were hunted down like dogs and strung up from trees.

And now, since the Colonies had fallen away and slavery was dead and buried, their own politicians had embarked on another form of enslavement – oppressive dictatorships – leaving the people no better off than they were before. It wasn't right. Bird had given the topic some thought before his arrival and wondered how his conscience might react, but no matter how he looked at it, these people seemed to have been dealt a rougher hand than most. He consoled himself with the fact that he couldn't be held responsible for these atrocities and it wasn't his fault that they had ever occurred, but the fact that he even considered such things meant he would be viewing life in a far more profound way in Africa, and he needed to be open to that.

This place seemed like the cutting edge of reality. It beckoned him to be more in tune with the issues in his soul; it demanded that he be considerate of the cultural divide and accept that Africans did what they did for their own reasons. It would be do or die out here and he had to respect that – he couldn't go around preaching the 'bollocks theory' like some kind of prophet. Africa could eat him up and spit him out and no one would even blink an eye. He would have to operate under a new schedule, with new priorities, and the important issues of his English life would not be relevant out here. Thank God Cracker wasn't around – they wouldn't last five minutes in this environment together.

"Thank you very much, Isaac, that was a wonderful meal." Bird held his scraped-clean plate and tea mug in his hands. "Where can I wash the plate?"

"No problem, saa, I will clean for you."

"Are you sure? You don't have to do everything for me you know, I can wash a plate."

"Oh no, saa, muzungu no wash plate. Is muntu who wash plate, no problem, saa."

"Whatever you say, man. This is your place, dude, I do as you say. To me, Isaac, you're the Bwana."

"Ha ha ha! No, no, no, no, saa. Ha ha ha!"

Isaac clearly found this remark hilarious, and Bird was glad to have made him laugh.

Isaac was still chuckling as he took the plate and mug from Bird's hands. It wasn't about slavery or subservience to Isaac; it was just about position and job description. Within his tribe, there was a very definite social structure and hierarchy. They were born into the domain in which they lived and if that happened to be lower than the guy next door, then so be it – that would be their position. They didn't question it, they didn't argue and they didn't fuck with it. They answered to those above them, who in turn answered to those above them. The highest point of answering rested with the tribal chief and to go higher meant entering into the realms of gods, like Savongo. The very nature of Bird's white skin labelled him a visiting scientist and set him above the likes of Isaac in their community hierarchy. Amongst other things, it determined that he wasn't allowed to wash his own dishes or clean his own room – it was just not his job.

"I'm going to take a walk around the camp, Isaac, is that all right?" Bird asked him.

"No problem, saa. You may follow the road to the edge of ma trees but don't walk onto ma prains, OK?"

"What are ma prains?"

"The grass prains, Bwana. Follow the road and you can see. Beeg, beeg ma prains. So, so beeg and so many animals."

"OK man, whatever you say, Bwana."

Isaac once again burst into uncontrollable laughter as his hands splashed water from the sink. He liked this Bird dude; he wasn't like any other white boy he'd met before – he called Isaac Bwana – imagine.

Bird stepped out into the dappled brightness once again and crumpled his face into a squint. He could feel energy flowing back into his body from the food and it felt good. He was going to be healthy again, he was going to use his brain as he had once before and he was going to put all his training with Alfred to good purpose. He would sort out their bird project for them in whatever capacity they required and get their wheels turning on the rusty old tracks again.

The men in green overalls now greeted him as he walked past them, all calling him 'Bwana' or 'saa', and he acknowledged them with a deep smile and slight gesture of the hand. He found the dusty track leading out of camp, which he assumed was the road Isaac had referred to, and trudged slowly along, his head rotating like a radar. The track wound its way into obscurity, adorned on all sides by magnificent trees, each ablaze with a myriad of colours from bright yellows through oranges and reds, gently coalescing into a thousand shades of green. The trunks were tall, sometimes thin, sometimes thick, themselves awash with colours from brown to red to grey and even yellow.

The forest floor was again sparse and looked as if it had been burnt at some stage. Various shrubs, plants and flowers sprouted up, their stems thick with silvery hairs and their buds sticky and colourful. They all looked so radical – nothing looked quaint and pretty like in an English country garden. There were no roses or daffodils or buttercups or dandelions. He didn't know the names of these plants, but if they had any they would be called Panzers, Messerschmitts or AK-47s.

Then something caught his eye. It was a striking mauve purple in colour, a small plant with a long stem and three or four sweet-pea-like flowers sprouting from the top. He smelled it – the scent was strong and perfumed, the flowers dainty and cute and beautifully coloured – deep and sensual. The petals were soft and inviting, almost good enough to eat, but it just seemed so out of place here. Several bumbling bee-type creatures were probing the depths of its stamens, sucking out the sweet nectar and collecting its genes to carry to the next willing pistil to induce its pollination. Poetry in motion.

He stood in the forest and took several deep breaths. The air was sweet – he was at the heart of our world's lungs, sucking the pure life that emanates from these organic beings, and it felt bloody marvellous. He stared at the trees and thought about their precious function – the exchange of gas from these simple organisms that induces life on Planet Earth as it creates an atmosphere for everything to breathe. The blue glow that envelops the world as seen from outer space all comes from these humble beginnings. The evaporation of water that is returned to the soil as rain is only made possible by these static creatures who, like a permeable filter, transform the shit that we exhale into the life's blood that induces our existence.

Ah yes, trees are gods. They are life-givers in so many ways.

Everything that he took so blindly for granted back home seemed so critical and significant out here. No man had planted this forest; no architect had planned it; no town council controlled or monitored it; no worker bazzers in yellow reflector jackets manicured it and took endless tea breaks in it; no Town Mayor had cut a fancy pink ribbon strung across it to declare it open and legal. Mother Earth was in control here – she called the shots, she named the plays, she manifested the existence and she determined the persistence.

It was as if Nature had vacated England, or she'd been evicted and put into temporary accommodation while she waited for her name to appear on top of a welfare housing list. She was nowhere to be found, save in small pockets on the cliffs and in the forests on the way to

Alfred's house, though even there, man had zoned a small sanctuary for her, like she'd been granted temporary severance due to extenuating circumstances. But out here in this forest, her spirit was everywhere. It was in the soil, the AK-47 plants, the buzzing, bumbling bees, the beautiful chaotic trees and the birds that fluttered in their crowns.

Then suddenly, from out of nowhere and through this divine contemplation of prophetic purgatory, a series of shattering cries sent a monstrous surge of adrenaline through his pounding heart and he hit the deck like the Viet Cong under napalm, covering his head with his arms and burying his face in the dirt. He gingerly peered through his arm guard as a small cluster of missiles shot through the trees, screeching and hollering their way above him.

They were fast – *very* fast – weaving and rolling an intricate path through the maze of this towering forest. He lifted his dusty head from the earth and tried to catch a fleeting glimpse of the birds as they disappeared into the woodwork.

What in God's name is going on here? They were birds, weren't they? They're why I'm here, aren't they? So what am I doing eating dirt? This place is all too much – too much, man – it's got me fired up and wired up and I ain't even done any drugs. Parrots, gotta be parrots, screeching and flying like that – can only be parrots, man.

And indeed, parrots they were. Catching the tail end of the squadron as it disappeared into the trees, he picked himself up, brushed himself down and frantically flicked through the pages of his book.

Could be brown-necked or Meyers. There was a distinct flash of green and the unmistakable parrot-like call as they shot through my airspace.

He jotted down some notes and realised that he had been so consumed by the alien nature of this whole place and its radical plant-life that the bird list had been kind of neglected. He should have been noting birds all morning instead of messing about with Isaac, talking about ancient gods and half sugars in cups of tea. He would need to get focussed on his mission, particularly if Sarah had met him off the vehicle the night before. He'd have a lot of ground to make up with her. Each time he thought about it, cold shivers rippled down his spine.

His encounters with Miss Cleavage before he left home were not good omens for his first ever time working for a woman. He was obviously emitting some kind of desirable pheromone that her acute maternal detectors managed to pick up on. And if that was indeed the case, it would be a negative balance on his account out here, because the sort of lady who lives on her own in a place like this is probably fiercely independent and tragically in touch with those pheromone detectors. Sarah the research 'Madam' would not be interested in any of Bird's sob stories about how emotionally neglected he'd been and how he might need some mollycoddling to get him acquainted with all this ornithological stuff again because he'd been excessing on drugs, alcohol and regret for the last eight years. Sarah was busy trying to get her struggling research institute on the map and she would be needing some fairly hearty support from the likes of Bird. The bottom line was that he was going to have to get his act together before she got back, and diving for cover from a small flock of Meyers parrots was not exactly the grandest way of opening that brand-new high-interest super saver's pheromonal account.

Gotta get my eye in again – gotta get it together.

With his dignity restored, he set about finding birds in the forest to start his list. It wasn't difficult. Everywhere he looked something fluttered, dived, soared, climbed, receded, pecked, scraped, popped, preened, displayed, chilled and drilled. There were sunbirds and woodpeckers, bulbuls and orioles, chats and rollers, weavers and white-eyes, buntings and canaries, twinspots and firefinches, waxbills and starlings, swallows and helmetshrikes and… and… and before he knew it, he had over thirty species on his list and… well, he had kind of… well, you know… kind of… also lost the track.

In a forest in Africa on his first day on the job that was to redeem his sinking soul, he had arrived half-dead from an excessive drug and alcohol binge, he had trapped himself in the mosquito net that hung above his bed, he had thrown up wretched bile all over his newly-acquired bathroom, he had learned of a god that takes half a sugar in his tea, he had dived for cover from a marauding band of Meyers parrots, he had got covered in dirt and grime from a short walk in the woods, and to add to it all he had now got lost in the radical African jungle, where any number of demons were about to consume his pathetic self and leave his bones to the slobbering hyenas.

Great – this is just bloody marvellous.

It wasn't funny and he wasn't amused. There were lions out here, there was everything out here and everything knew its way around – and he didn't. He was a sitting duck and he didn't even need to quack. But surprisingly, it wasn't fear that he felt, more disappointment. He couldn't quite explain it. His calculating brain was screaming to find a landmark that he could orientate to, but a feeling in his chest was telling him which way home was, and funnily enough, the instinctive chest feeling was riding higher than the mind's panic, leaving him decidedly calm.

Without even thinking, he looked to his right and saw that there was a large area of light emanating from the trees. Isaac had told him that if he followed the track, he would come to "ma prains" – the large, grassy plains. There would be no trees on the plains so they would be much lighter than the forest. Yes, they would be much lighter because there would be no shade. If he got to the tree line, he could orientate himself, hang a right, follow the trees and hopefully meet the track.

At the forest edge, the trees stopped in a long, horizontal line – they just stopped altogether. Thousands upon thousands of advancing trees halted in their tracks, in this spot that gave way to the endless plains reaching into eternity and beyond. A deep golden shade of wispy grass ebbed and flowed in the gentle breeze with its white-tipped tussocks waving in random and sustained motions, just like the sea's waves that used to roll up the estuary in front of the Wound. The grassy sea that he had dreamed of that morning in his bedroom was now here, right at his feet, and he was a part of it.

The resounding thud of exasperated discovery pounded his gut and rendered all faculties temporarily mesmerised. He squinted in disbelief and gently scratched his scalp, his mouth open and agape. Waves of emotion welled up inside him as his eyes tried to absorb the big-picture scene, but it was just too much to take in all at once – there was simply too much to see. Endless horizons on the oceans back home, or even rolling fields stretching across undulating cliffs, were big-picture gigs too, but nothing was like this. It was almost as if he could see the curve of the earth somewhere out there in the grass. It had to curve, for it was so vast that surely this could never end.

But it was not only an endless golden meadow that halted his pattern of logical thought. For there, stretching out in front of him, dotted all over this outlandish prairie, in the middle, far and eternal distance, were thousands upon thousands of animals – animals in numbers he never knew possible. They weren't wildebeest like he'd seen on television, but they were animals – spread out as far as life could exist and even beyond, to places where the heart would never beat. Animals grazing peaceably on the carpet that had been in his Tintin dreams when he contemplated whether Africa was right for him. How could he ever have thought that this would not be right for anyone? This was paradise.

The animals were medium-sized antelope, golden brown in colour, some with majestic, sweeping horns, others with their heads bare. Their brilliant white bellies contrasted deeply with their golden backs, and the black tips to their tails flicked an endless, rippling pattern across the distant heat haze, warning of the mid-day swelter sailing on its horizon.

The vastness had consumed him at first, but his eyes now drifted across the scene and tried to absorb things in slightly more detail. The plain was broken up by small pockets of vegetation – essentially islands in this quantum grass lake. They were erratic and irregular, sprouting out in clusters of sometimes ten or twelve grouped together, and other times the odd one here and the odd one there. The trees on these islands were a mixture of palms and various deciduous species such as large figs or African sausage trees or huge, straight-stemmed leadwoods with their characteristic silvery bark and limited foliage. Huge fronds swept off the palms in a bizarre contrast to the scene, as if they belonged on the ocean. Some palms were short and bushy; others had very tall, thin trunks and exploding crowns thirty metres off the ground – a haven for birds. The island refuges would also suit browsing antelope escaping the midday sun, perhaps a sleepy jackal lair or extensive mongoose tunnel network, and maybe also predators snoozing away lazy days while they waited for a more suitable temperature in which to become active. Whatever lurked within them, these islands stretched into the invisibility of the grassland's heat haze at the back of the plains and all the way forward to where he now stood.

He looked carefully at the fauna that was around him and started to see that there was not just one kind of antelope here. Scattered around a pair of close-set islands was a small herd, maybe fourteen in all, of much larger antelope. They looked like horses in stature and all had long horns, slightly curving towards their backs. They were large with a chestnut-brown tinge in their coat and a pair of hugely oversized ears that flopped out either side of their 'Mardi Gras' painted faces – black masks with spooky, white eyeholes that looked like they had been scored out by a young child learning how to operate a pair of scissors for the first time. They were truly majestic creatures.

In the far distance, out on the grasslands, he could see family groups of zebra milling in and out of small wildebeest herds, their traditional counterparts, in groups of fifteen to twenty. In time he would come to know their mutual symbiotic dependence with the grass that they ate but for now, like the freezer, it was all just another mystery.

A small family of warthogs with about six youngsters trotted out from an island and busily shuffled themselves across an open area towards a neighbouring island. The hoglets were very small, about a quarter the size of their parents, but they all ran in a perfectly synchronised straight line with their tails in the air. They looked absurd and Bird couldn't help but chuckle.

There were also family groups of very small, dainty little antelope scattered around the tree line and into the local islands that were off to one side of him. They again had white bellies and golden backs, but their stature was dwarfed by the mighty horse-like creatures and their horns were short and straight, in contrast to the sweeping horns of the creatures in their thousands.

The abundance and variety of life in front of him made him weak at the knees. In all the bird work he'd done with Alfred, they'd conducted a fair amount of habitat analysis, looking at how the migrating birds used their habitats to support themselves whilst in them and how these changed with the rolling seasons to force them away and find greener pastures in which to breed. Similarly, they had looked at the habitats that birds travelled to and tried to assess what made one place favourable over another in order to justify thousands of miles of migrating flight. This had really been Alfred's baby and Bird didn't have much to do with it, save that he had assisted with data collection, which made him reasonably familiar with some of Africa's hugely diverse flora. He didn't need to be a rocket scientist to see that there was a superabundance of lush food here and a fair amount of diversity with the plains, the islands and this forest behind him. This place could host the whole spectrum of life on earth – all that appeared to be missing was water and he was sure that, as a massive floodplain that floods and recedes each year, there had to be water on it somewhere.

He smiled at his flow of thoughts and felt more confident that he would begin thinking in the scientific way that Alfred had taught him during the research era. It wouldn't take long to get back into it all and there was plenty to see and do, so a new life might prove to be more exciting than boring and hopefully take his mind off the fact that there would be no drugs out here – a very real consideration when trying to change the habits of a lifetime.

He could have stood there all day but figured he would be in it for most of the time he was here, so he could get properly acquainted then. The task of finding his path and meandering back to camp still loomed over him like a cloud as he scuffed along the treeline in a homeward direction. He was feeling his way along the edge to where he thought the road might be, and soon enough he stumbled on a track that bisected the trees and wound its way back into the woods. He stood at the junction with a deep sense of pride that he'd survived his first endurance test in Africa and safely got himself home – well, at least onto a yellow-brick road that would take him back to his wizard and safe-keeper, Isaac.

Turning back to take in a last image of the majestic scene, he noticed that a bird was twittering and fluttering above him, seemingly very agitated at something. It settled momentarily, and he put the glasses up to his eyes and took a long and involved look. It was drab, dull and brown.

Seeing that it had his attention, the creature began hopping madly again and jabbering constantly. It took off from its perch, displaying two brilliant white windows down either side of the tail. It circled him several times and then flew up to another perch, where it seemed to beckon him some more. The creature's behaviour was unfamiliar and intriguing – as if it was asking Bird to follow. He did. As he approached its perch, it flew off again with dipping flight and a chattering din before reaching another perch in another tree and settling again, still constantly calling. He followed it for some way, repeating this manoeuvre, but then remembered his most recent encounter with navigational failure and halted his quest while the going was good and the track still visible. He was learning. Out here, there were many distractions that could take one's eye off the ball when traversing dangerous pastures. He needed to keep his wits about him at all times.

"Not this time, dude. Just got lost in this here jungle and I don't fancy doing it again. Maybe next time?" The bird twittered more irately as he turned to leave, raising its pitch and quickening the tempo. "Relax, man, it can't be today – sorry for that, but hey, I'm in the neighbourhood, I'll be around for a while, look me up in a couple of days and we'll make a date – I promise. But for now, I gotta go. Laters." Twitter twitter!

Raymond, a general worker from the camp – one of the green overalls and boots brigade – stood perplexed as he watched the crazy white boy standing and staring into the tree, having a fairly reasonable conversation with a bird that seemed to twitter back to him. Raymond was not unfamiliar with the greater honeyguide and had followed it to honey on several occasions, but he was sure that this bird could not talk, and even if it could, he was sure it would not speak English. His local tongue would have been a much better option for the bird as there was an abundance of people who spoke it, enabling the creature to converse with many rather than few, as were the English speakers. He concluded that the white man must have special powers to be able to communicate with the bird; after all, this man had come a very long way to be out here and his name in his own native tongue was Bird, so maybe this was his gift – bird talker?

The men at camp had discussed this newcomer at length the night before and concluded that he was most unlike all the other scientists they had ever met, in particular the lion specialists. When he was met at the airport, he was in a wheelchair and covered in vomit and the attendants had informed his driver that he was sick from alcohol poisoning. He was spluttering incoherent gibberish as they threw him on the back of a Land Rover loaded with rations for the camp and seemed to respond better to being treated like a sack of the aforementioned supplies than a patient. He was immediately given the nickname 'Bwana Noni', meaning 'boss Bird', but in light of recent events Raymond concluded that the name should be changed to 'Isamba Noni' – 'the talking bird' or, as it stood in his language, 'The Bird Talker'. Yes, this was much more appropriate. He would tell the others tonight and they would agree to change the white man's name in light of these recent events. 'Isamba Noni'.

As for now, he had been instructed by Isaac to go and find the white boy for fear that he was lost in the woods. His mission had been accomplished; he now just had to get the mysterious alien back to camp and ensure his safe and swift return.

10

SARAH

The rest of the day subsided through bouts of wandering around the camp and meeting the rest of its staff. Their team was eleven strong, headed up by a man named Jacob whom Bird was yet to meet, though so much reference had already been made to him that by now he seemed strangely familiar. He was the longest-serving member of the institute, which earned him the title of staff foreman, and as a result of his extensive and intricate local knowledge, the reins of the ailing lion project had been placed in his hands some years previously. Sarah was English with a PhD in Molecular Genetics and although she had spent the best part of four years in Africa, she was still grappling with some of the traditions and customs, so Jacob had become her crucial link between Western practicality and African idiosyncrasy. She obviously ruled with an iron fist and was referred to with a reverence that indicated respect laced with a small dose of fear. The more he found out about Sarah, the more fearful Bird became of not lasting two months in this establishment.

Everything about this camp was different from any place he had ever spent time in before. The buildings were unsymmetrical, hashed together and mostly made out of coarse clay bricks, with roofs that were oblong or conical and thatched with thick grass. The ground in between was again baked, bare and dusty from being trampled by too many feet over too many years. Whilst the rainy season lasted for at least a quarter of the year and always yielded plenty of water, so much vegetation had been stripped away from the topsoil that the rain just ran off its surface without even dribbling on the dormant root system below. As long as people were here walking these paths, the grass didn't stand a chance. Outside of the trampled zones, however, life paradoxically blossomed from every inch of soil.

Huge trees dictated the flow of construction and restricted development to isolated areas, resulting in the apparent random and planless feel. Mother Earth called the play out here and the camp worked according to her plan or none at all. She did not adhere to manmade workflow charts, yet in the face of this seemingly anarchic disorder they had got the place to run in a very efficient and quick-step style. Africa has a tidy knack for creating order through chaos, inasmuch as things are done in a roundabout and seemingly illogical way but eventually objectives are achieved. The parameters governing an operation in an area such as this were so wide and so varied that much was left to chance and many a gamble was taken on a whim, with a prayer that they might pay off. They often did.

The buildings fulfilled a variety of functions and made up the activity zones in the camp. There was the staff accommodation block – the stable-like house that Bird had woken up in. Then there was the kitchen where he had had breakfast and learned of the god who took half a sugar in his tea. Another was a motor vehicle workshop with rough shelving around the edges and the entrails of an assortment of machinery lying in, around and above every protruding surface. A number of skeletal machines lay twisted, Mad

Max style, around the perimeter of this workshop, and an old Series II Land Rover stood in its yard, mouth wide open and two self-fashioned Land Rover dentists resting on its gums. They were getting to work with huge spanners, removing decaying teeth and installing fillings and crowns that it might once again gnash at the hard, African terrain that had rendered it like this in the first place.

He met all the men but was unable to remember any of their names, even moments later. They were all very pleasant and smiled profusely at him, but their English was poor. All communication at the camp went through Isaac, Jacob, or Raymond who knew just enough to get by but not quite enough to warrant philosophical, religious or political debate. Isaac would proudly present Bird to the men and declare his name, title and brief resumé in English, which he would then translate as they had not one clue what had just been said. However, it was considered rude to speak only in their native tongue when a foreigner was present as they could insult him without his knowledge, therefore both languages were employed. Africans in general are very conscious of this and tend to speak loudly in public places because to be discreet means they may be talking ill of someone, which could be construed as insulting, so it's best to be heard by all.

The title bestowed upon him during such introductions was 'Rion Man', which Bird did not argue with as he was sure there had been some terrible misunderstanding with his job description. He was now painfully aware that 'rions' were in fact lions and the nature of him being a 'Rion Man' would entail actually doing something with these slobbery beasts – though quite what, he was not sure. Whatever it was, he was not the man for the job; this had all been a dreadful mix-up that he would sort out with Sarah when he met her. Isaac meant well – he was just the chef, after all; it wasn't his job to allocate research scientists to their functions and Bird couldn't really blame the chap for it.

Isaac had fed him well all day, and by late afternoon Bird was feeling somewhat feline in his own special way – gorged, replete and ready for a nap. He wallowed in a deckchair that had teleported itself from some tacky seaside resort and was busy absorbing the scene of trees and more trees whilst acquainting himself with the commencement of dusk when, far in the distance, he heard the hum of a machine – a motor car.

It struck him for the first time that day – the peaceful serenity of a place with only the sound of the turning Earth to disturb its silence. As dusk drew in, the momentum of bird calls had picked up from its midday slump, when it was just too hot to sing, into an orchestral roar of last-minute territorial definition. Crickets and beetles chirped and whirred with quivering precision. A breeze tapped out its tune on the trunks of trees and whispered a cymbals chime through their trembling leaves as miniature life forms scuttled through the leaf litter, picking and rummaging minuscule beats to the crescendo of sound in this 'Big Picture Symphony'. The noise of the engine was an audible cancer that grew like a putrid sore on the face of their untainted melody and echoed mankind's obstinate incompatibility to this world.

It drew nearer and nearer.

Ripples of anticipation started up his spine as he rose to his feet and prepared for an initial encounter with Sarah, his stomach turning itself over and over until a knot formed. It felt like he had been waiting all day for a schoolmaster to reprimand him for some mindless offence, and he wanted to get it over with and get back to the adventures of the playground as quickly as possible. He walked to where the road entered camp and stood waiting for the car to pull up. Some of the guys had shuffled into the spot, this for them part of their daily routine – to meet the vehicle and offer assistance to Sarah – and they stood quietly laughing and joking to themselves.

The peaceful sedateness of the beautifully tranquil scene from moments before was then suddenly blasted with the advent of a festering mechanical mule, spat from the bowels of this forest and screeching to a dusty halt that forced the assembled crowd to close their eyes and hold their breath. Sarah had arrived.

People jumped off the vehicle, barking in their local tongue, while the awaiting entourage hustled around the car picking up boxes, cases and research scientist gear. The unmistakable voice of an English lady boomed out, giving orders and firing questions through the settling dust, and feet scurried in all directions in obedience. From within the cloud, a figure emerged and presented itself to Bird with a warm smile and an outstretched hand as her voice cut through the air.

"Mr. Bird? Hi, how are you doing, my name's Sarah… Sarah Whitfield. Sorry I'm so late but I've had quite a day and just couldn't get back till now. Hope Isaac looked after you and gave you a tour of the camp. Are you settled in? Is everything OK?"

She shook his hand and avoided extended eye contact with him as she fired out her questions. Her accent was sharp. She was obviously well educated and incredibly motivated, confident in herself yet seemingly more than a little apprehensive about her new colleague. He perceived her as a fired-up fast bowler on a hat trick, looking to take out his middle-stump first ball.

Never was much of a cricketer.

"Yes, thank you, all's well," Bird stammered and stumbled, somewhat nervously. "Isaac has been w…wonderful."

"Good. Let's go inside and have some tea." Used to scientists who were not the greatest of socialites, it was clear Sarah was expecting no airs or graces from this man.

"Come on, follow me. ISAAC – ISAAC," she yelled, "I'm home. Please bring tea to the office for me and Mr. Bird." And then she spun, marching away emphatically.

Bird scuttled along behind her like a dictator's frightened advisor and thanked all his imaginary gods that she obviously hadn't met him the night before. Her screen door screeched and thumped as they went inside, catching Bird's heel and bouncing awkwardly before it slammed shut. He spun around and frowned, then skipped gingerly inside to avoid further assault.

The room was poorly lit, again with small windows covered in mosquito gauze and an open pair of screen doors leading to a wooden deck. A large desk took up one wall, not too dissimilar to Alfred's, just more orderly and adorned with reference books – some open, others waiting – and a laptop computer. A pair of reading glasses and an old tea mug were set to one side, and on the wall above, a massive map hung in a poorly made wooden frame. The map indicated a floodplain surrounded by forests with finger-like streams sprawling through it. String lines were pulled over magnets designating lion home ranges, and yellow post-it notes and old photographs of lions were scattered across the scene referencing names, numbers, lineages and inter related data. Bird scanned it for information but nothing really made sense.

"That is the Sukula Plains. You'll get to know them well enough," Sarah offered. "Come in, make yourself comfortable. Let's go out on the porch and watch the last of the sunset."

With that, she began to twist like a whirlwind in a confined space. Her large-brimmed hat was tossed from her head, releasing a full crown of dusty brown hair that she ruffed up before tying it back into a ponytail. Her jacket followed and landed perfectly on the arm of a decaying chair as she jettisoned it from her shoulders. The once-khaki collared shirt and shorts were dirty and hung loosely around her frame as she perched herself on a rickety office chair and attacked the laces on her boots.

"Sorry about this, but I've got to get these boots off." She smiled at Bird, glancing momentarily at him before returning her attention to the footwear. Her deep blue eyes pierced through the grime on her face, and Bird caught himself looking at her.

He had not expected this. It was not on the expected list, nor was it planned or even remotely contemplated in any way. She was not supposed to be beautiful, she was supposed to be a dragon. Was she beautiful? She was dirty and dusty and perhaps not looking her best, but her skin was tight around her limbs and tanned a deep brown without stain or blemish. Her legs were long and perfectly formed, and her arms were muscular and toned. The features on her face were prominent and proportioned, but nothing had prepared him for her eyes. The contrast between their indigo blue and her chestnut face was astounding. It set them deep into her head and gave her a penetrating stare, as if she looked at him directly from her brain. She'd only flashed a glance at him, but he was temporarily mesmerised until that gut-wrenching sensation that had burned him with Miss Cleavage stirred once again and brought him back to the present. He looked away and motioned to the porch.

"W…w…will we sit out here?" He signalled meekly towards the chairs.

"Yes. That's the porch – go ahead, take a seat. The view's not great unless you like trees but it's the best we've got at the moment. Ah Isaac, thank you. Everything OK – no problems?"

"No probrem Madam, evfing OK."

"Good. Put the tea outside on the porch, please. We'll eat at seven – usual time, thank you Isaac."

"Fank you, Madam."

Isaac backed away and out of the room. His demeanour was different now, somehow more subservient. Rather than the jovial, chuckling clown that Bird had eaten breakfast with, he was serious and timid, minding his Ps and Qs and stepping gracefully around the whirlwind that was by now running out of steam and calming itself down. He was gone as silently as he had arrived.

"Thank God for that. Tea and a moment to put my feet up. What a day this has been. How d'you take it?"

"Hmm?"

"Tea, how do you take it?"

"Oh, s…s…sorry, ahh… m…milk no sugar, please."

"Milk is compulsory out here. It's already in the pot. Some colonial relic I feel. No sugar? I see you are a fellow Pom."

"I beg yer pardun?"

"Pom? Englishman? It's what we get called out here – well, by the colonials who call themselves Africans, anyway. Some of them are a bit strung out on their roots and heritage now that the empire has fallen and they have to answer to black politicians. Not part of their fine constitution, you see, and forty-something years after independence, some of them still believe that the colonies are not dead."

"Oh, right. What people? Um… I mean, who are these people? I haven't seen any white people all day and I know I'm a bit slow, but it seems to me that we are some way from civilisation here. Who calls you Pom?"

Sarah looked at him, a frown crossing her face. "Well, they're not here, Mr. Bird." She spoke slightly slower, as if patronising his idiocy. "They're mostly in town. There are a few who live in the vicinity at safari camps and the likes." She paused in mid-pour of the mottled teapot. "But they're just as insufferable as the rest. No, I'm talking generally about the few narrow-minded old-school colonials and long-serving expats left in this country. I'm sure you've encountered them before."

Bird could sense that she was starting to sniff out his charade. He had to pretend to be a serious scientist who knew his stuff, he couldn't let on that he'd been doing sod all for the last three years or else she'd have him on the first Land Rover out of here, and he was determined to do his time.

"Oh yeah, them. Ha ha. Yeah, bloody colonials, ha ha, who needs 'em, hey? Fuck the lot of them, errmm… ha ha… yeah…"

I said fuck. I did, didn't I? I said fuck. I don't believe it, I said fuck. You're not in the pub now, boy, liven up and get with the programme – no swearing.

153

Sarah smiled. This guy was weird, but he definitely had the look of genius about him. So, he says the odd swear word, what the hell? She often swore. She did wonder, though, about his seeming confusion at the mention of colonials. She had heard that this guy was a bit 'out there' in the normality stakes, but he couldn't have been in the bush so long that he had forgotten who the white people were?

More importantly, though, she had been told he was one of the best, and by God, did the project ever need the best to save it and the institute from extinction. She decided she liked him – she wasn't on his wavelength, but she liked him.

He was a bit green though, and she wondered where and how this young, lily-white, straggly-haired English boy got all his experience from. He must have been in Africa before – he couldn't have studied lions at London Zoo or Windsor Safari Park. Maybe he was just a complete social lunatic. It's a well-known phenomenon with people who live around animals for extended periods of time that they lose touch with society and essentially with our reality as well, sometimes only thinking in the first person and absolute present.

She decided to probe a bit more. "So, tell me of your experience, Mr. Bird. You come highly recommended."

"Oh, ah, um yes… yes, ha ha, that'll be Alfred… likes to blow trumpets that aren't meant to be blown. I'm just a volunteer and I'm sure I won't be able to do too much for you, but I have plenty of field experience and my observations are normally fairly watertight. I've been… ahem… uh… kind of diverging for the last couple of years, but you never really lose your eye and identification is always fairly easy. I hope I can be of some use to you – I'm certainly full of enthusiasm." He beamed a foolish grin.

Sarah leaned back in her chair and cupped her tea in both hands. A warm smile had adorned her face and she felt an easy glow tingle into her body. He was modest. He fumbled a lot. He was uneasy in her company – these were all the signs she needed. He was the man she had been hoping for, the man who could take up the reins of their floundering lion study and put it on the map to secure extra finance. He was the genius that she had been promised who would bumble and fumble his way around but come up with the groundbreaking work that they had been on the verge of here for the last eight years. He was the man that she would present to the donors as her ace in the hole when the grant cheque was ready for signing. He would sway public opinion and enable her to see out the dream, putting her on the map of scientific discovery and proving to all those back home that she was not a failure. But above all, he was the key to saving this beautiful place that she had now fallen so deeply in love with. Mr. Bird – the answer to her prayers – her man!

An unfamiliar glow warmed inside Bird as those deep blue eyes creased into the contours of her face. "Modesty is good, Mr. Bird." She smiled.

"You can call me Bird, if you like. May I call you Sarah?"

A gentle frowned crumpled across her forehead. "Why, of course. What's your real name?"

"My name is Bird. I only get called Mr. Bird if I'm being nicked… or in the shit." Sensing his undoing and fumbling profusely with his hands, he hastily tried to cover his tracks. "Ha, yes… ha ha… of course it's… um… well… um, it's usually for removing a specimen that I'm not supposed to touch for further faecal analysis and the likes. They sometimes get very edgy about scientific interference on scat, but there's so often a vital clue hiding in what they would call 'turd' but what I would see as an intricate web of information regarding diet, and even foraging ranges when a prey analysis is conducted from the surrounding area. Much to be gained from turd, Sarah – much."

What the hell am I saying? God, I hope she's buying this.

"Right, yes, I see what you mean. Have you ever been picked up by the police in Africa for stealing, um… 'turd'?"

"In Africa? Well, no, I've only just got here, haven't had time to make a nuisance of myself yet. Huh huh!" A nervous chuckle followed his ridiculous statement.

Sarah looked at him intently. Bird saw the bemusement written across her face and desperately changed the subject, hoping to shift the spotlight off himself.

"Anyway, enough of that. Can you fill me in a little bit about this place?"

"Yes, sorry, yes of course. I don't suppose you were given that much information on us. I know it was short notice and I believe you were pulled off another project to come here…"

Another project? Are you mad? I was pulled out of the Wound and Bandage to come here. Only project I was working on was drugs, man – taking too many mind-altering, mood-enhancing drugs and trying to analyse their effects – oh, and maybe Miss Cleavage. God, it seems so far away now.

"Sorry about that, but David had to pull some strings for me, it's a desperate situation. I'll begin at the beginning."

Sarah cleared her throat, swigged at her tea and relaxed back into the chair as she began to recount the familiar tale. The cavalry had at last arrived. The defining moment of real support that she had dreamt of for so long was now here and the enormity of this crisis would no longer be hers to weather alone. Help had arrived. Her man was here – this was her man.

11

UNDOING THE DONE

"The Sukula Research Institute has been going for just over eight years now. I've been here for four and I've been running it virtually single-handed for the last eighteen months. This region is politically stable, which is a godsend in Africa, but economically, it's screwed." Sarah shuffled in her seat and tossed back her head, spewing tea from the edge of her cup, and stopped momentarily to regain her balance and stop the liquid from scalding her bare legs. "Anyway," she continued, "our main donors are starting to get restless because we are not really breaking new scientific ground and the institute seems to be in direct conflict with the local communities. Most research grants in Africa are given on the basis that studies will benefit the communities directly and mankind indirectly, and the donors can feel that they are appeasing their consciences by saving people with needy causes whilst furthering the development of man."

"So why are you in conflict with the communities?"

"Well, I don't know how far you went out of camp today, but you can see that we are sitting on a fairly substantial wildlife resource here. There's lots of animals out there."

Bird nodded. "Judging by what I saw today, yes, there is a shit-load of animals here."

"Well, the people of this region are traditionally hunter-gatherers and have been since before time began. With the economy being the way it is, there has been no investment in the area since the sixties, and therefore there is no infrastructure on which to base any sort of wildlife industry. The people live below Western-set poverty levels, but they aren't actually starving thanks to well-stocked rivers and good rainfall for crops. It's just that they have no means of generating income to get extra food and much-sought-after accessories. As a result, they have reverted back to their ancestral ways of hunting, only now the rules have changed – they've been labelled poachers. You see, the area was zoned a national park in the fifties and the tribes living within its boundaries were relocated into their wet-season homelands for permanent habitation."

Bird's eyebrows were wrinkling in a kind of bemusement and she could see that she was starting to lose him already. She didn't know whether it was her poor explanation or his stupidity that caused his confusion but hoped it was neither. Surely he'd encountered this kind of relocation in his previous work in Africa? She continued regardless.

"Back then, the way these people lived was that they had two sets of villages – one within what is now the National Park and one without. The villages outside the park were not prone to so much flooding and made it easier for transport and crop growing. Equally, though, they did not host as much wildlife nor have as good fishing spots. The villages inside the park were teeming with wildlife, but when it rained, they were not ideal places to live purely because of the floodplain syndrome that I'm sure you know of?" Bird nodded.

"Anyway," Sarah continued, "the deal was that these tribes would live permanently in their summer villages outside the park but would be given special concessions for hunting and fishing. The park would then be turned over to tourism, which would generate cash, and they would receive their share in lieu of the land they had sacrificed. It also meant wildlife would give a tangible benefit and therefore be of some value to them. Of course, fifty-odd years later, the concessions are virtually hunted out because there has been no control and the money that was promised to these people in the first place has been squandered."

"Was there ever any development for tourism?"

"Initially, yes. Camps were built and roads were made, but the socialist government of the seventies deemed those Western influences on this country to be negative and they closed them all down. The whole point of trying to put an intrinsic value on the wildlife to stop local people killing it all was then diminished. They didn't know what to believe anymore, especially as government officials themselves used to come here and hunt – and seemingly quite legitimately – but when the locals tried it, they were arrested for poaching. The cash reward for losing their land has never been forthcoming and they've now been done out of the deal. Of course, trophy hunting has been the only money-making scheme that's actually survived here, which again is legal and just confuses the whole situation further. Meat is a major source of nourishment for these people, but they're not allowed to hunt anything and it's a million miles to the closest butcher. The colonials taught them all they ever needed to know about mass annihilation and the hunter up the road brings fat Americans here to shoot whatever he can find, but the local guys get arrested if they so much as dare try to hunt a single antelope for the pot. If it's OK for us to do it, why shouldn't it be OK for them? They were never after trophies – that seemed to be just our wasteful indulgence – but food is precious and desperately needed."

"What do you mean?"

He is stupid, she thought. It's not just me, he is actually stupid, isn't he? Thick as a plank. But what the hell, I'm on a roll.

"OK. The park is the park and there's no hunting of any kind permitted there. The hunting concessions are large areas surrounding the park where controlled trophy and meat hunting is permitted. Now people, mainly Americans and Germans, pay a healthy fee to come here and shoot wildlife."

"What do they shoot?" Bird huffed in a most disconcerted way.

Sarah sighed loudly. She was right, this guy was pretty damn slow for a lion expert, but maybe that was just his way. Maybe he had never encountered hunting before. It was all right, it was just that he was strange – she knew that. She'd play his game and give him all the info he needed; after all, he was going to help her salvage the sinking dream – he was her man.

Bird had experienced a range of emotions while Sarah spoke, and the chemical hangover was certainly not helping. At first he'd followed her reasonably well. It was the sort of stuff that the BBC did documentaries about – ancient tribes being translocated in the name of conservation and all. It was always the subject of TV documentaries though, never real life and certainly never his real life; yet now, here he was, out in the thick of it, on the front line like some sort of Eco-Warrior saving the floundering Earth from extinction.

As Sarah continued to speak, the hairs on the back of his neck started to stand up. He was going to do something with his life at long last – he was going to be instrumental in change that would save birds, animals and people from extinction in Africa. It felt amazing.

Then Sarah had started talking about trophy hunting, and she'd lost him. It was all getting a bit too technical, and it raised the question of his authenticity. Trophy hunting? Trophy hunting what? And why? And who does it? And what for? And where's the trophy?

"What do they shoot?" he asked in consternation.

"Everything, Mr. Bird – they shoot absolutely everything. All the antelope, warthog, hippo, buffalo, crocodile, lion, leopard, even elephant in some areas and rhino where it's allowed."

"WHAT?" Bird was incensed. "They shoot rhinos and elephants? What the hell for?"

"Trophies, Mr. Bird. Trophies. They shoot them, cut off the heads, cure the skins and decorate their houses with them. Surely you know about trophy hunting?"

"No, man – you gotta be kidding me? People don't do that anymore. It's the new millennium, for God's sake. Everyone knows we're sitting on a potential environmental meltdown, people don't kill like that anymore... do they?"

Sarah leaned in close and stared deep into Bird's soul. Her eyes were the colour and depth of the ocean and her voice became soft and full, as if she were about to tell a child some horrific ghost story. She exaggerated every syllable, every expression, every emotion, hissing a cymbal's deathly chime from the tip of her darting tongue.

A demon lurked in her eyes, but she was closer to Bird now than she had ever been, and he was suddenly consumed with erratic waves of lustful temptation pulsating through his chest. Her stare was beautiful and he lost himself in it.

"Do you know how they hunt lions, Mr. Bird?" He shook his head slowly to indicate he did not, with his eyes still fixed on hers. "They shoot a hippo and they cut it in half…"

She started with her tale, oblivious to the glaring fact that this so-called highly decorated lion expert knew nothing of lion hunting. If she hadn't been so caught up in the beautiful innocence written across his face and her natural maternal instincts to tell him of the evil ways they killed her lions, she would have surely sussed there and then that actually, this was not her man at all.

"…then they drag the carcass behind a vehicle through the lion's territory and get a good, strong scent going." Her words were now slow and deliberate. "They drag it to a spot and chain it in a tree, just high enough so the lion can't get to it. Then they sit in a purpose-built hide about fifty metres away, downwind and concealed from the view of investigating lions. They sit in this hide with high-powered, scoped-up rifles and wait for the animal to come and start sniffing out the bait. If he's big enough, they shoot him. If not, they wait until another comes along. Sometimes they shoot both, just in case the 'other one' doesn't appear."

Bird stared intently at her. He had never before heard of such a thing, and certainly not from the Angel of Death herself. He did ponder what kind of sick punters would actually come here and do this kind of stuff, though – I mean, where was the high? Where was the kick?

"Anyway, where the hell have you been all this time?" Sarah sat back in her chair, consumed by her own charade – the Jackanory moment gone. "Never mind. The end result is that we are losing study animals left, right and centre to the hunters, who are baiting them out of our area and sometimes even shooting them within it. The hunters are making plenty of cash from the business, which is fully legal and legitimate I might add, and are paying a healthy subsidy to the local communities. We are a non-profit organisation, so contribute very little in terms of hard cash to the villagers, and on top of all that, we are trying to curb the meat poaching because the prey animals that you saw today are an all-important balance in this equation. Our attempt to control the lion hunting will mean less of it and therefore less cash to the communities as well. Consequently, we are compromising them and they are not happy about it, and when they aren't happy, the donors aren't happy. So I need to get the whole thing rolling again, and there is nothing that generates attention like lions because everyone reveres them. I want to use the fact that we have a unique population of lions here as the reason to keep the institute alive, and that's why I need a lion expert to prove it and finally push this rock off its cliff."

"Well, what is it that you do here? Why don't you prove the lion theory yourself?" Bird was confused. Why didn't *she* do this study and save everyone the time and him the potential danger?

"I have a Masters in Biodiversity Conservation and a PhD in Molecular Genetics. I'm using isotope variants to measure ecosystem functionality and the relationships between the vegetation, the flood, the fire and the antelope, and as they constitute the majority of prey for our lions, I need to complement my work by understanding the relationship between them and the predators – make a whole enchilada, if that makes any sense?" It didn't but he nodded anyway. "But to put weight on the argument," she continued, oblivious, "it has to be done by someone who has experience and is known by the scientific community for work done with lions in the past. Someone like you, who has published papers on lion behaviour."

Bird coughed and spluttered to himself. She was not getting his ignorance and it was now painfully clear to him that he was not out here to look at fluffy tweety birdies. Sarah went on.

"But we have trophy hunters in this area and their livelihood kind of depends on the lions. The last thing they want is a group of bleeding hearts like us running around, trying to stop all the killing. We know that if we don't stop them, or at least attempt to control them, our unique lions will be dead and if that happens, we may as well pack up and go home. One more for man to notch up on his belt of decimated species." She took a well-earned sip of her tea and cleared her throat to continue the onslaught. Letting out a long sigh, she went on.

"Anyway, the hunters have chased away the last two lion specialists and are doing some considerable damage in town when it comes to us getting study permits for new ones. See what I'm up against? The last scientist left three months ago and he wasn't exactly great. The work he did while he was here could have been done by Jacob, so we are really about a year behind and the donors are starting to get restless. They will only buy my excuses and sob stories for so long. I need something concrete to show them – I need a reason to conduct a study that they will finance, or we stand to lose everything. That's why you're here."

Bird stood up, his pale complexion gleaming in the dim moonlight. It hit him like a freight train – all at once. He was quite literally shitting himself at the thought of lion specialists being chased out of this place by rabid hunters and didn't fancy this cock-up at all. It was time to come clean.

Nervously, he touched his chin with his right hand and gazed off into the distance as his left hand slipped deep into his pocket and pushed up his shoulder, giving his body an awkward stance. His voice was soft and shaky as he spoke and for a moment he thought he sounded like Frank Spencer, but hoped to God that he didn't.

"Sarah, I don't know what you've been told about me but I am no lion specialist – I'm not an anything specialist. I think some serious mistake has been made here. I have never even been to Africa before," he murmured, glancing momentarily across at Sarah to gauge her reaction but finding none there to gauge. "The only headway I have ever made in life has been with birds. I know a little bit about English birds, but I don't claim to be an expert. I have come here as a volunteer for two months to help out with ringing migrating birds and maybe some habitat analysis. Ten minutes ago I never even knew that people hunted lions in the wild, now you are asking me to go onto the front line and take these people on. I've been working bars, snorting cocaine and dropping acid for the last two years. I'm no SAS Bad Barry and I'm no lion man either, I'm just a small-town English barman who likes birds – I'm sorry, but I don't think I'm your man. I think there's been a monumental fuck-up here, actually."

He looked at her with compassion as he sat back down and that knot tightened itself in his gut again. At first, he had wanted to hide everything and just play along so he could keep the job, but no one had told him of hunters. Hunters killed things – they killed living things with high-powered rifles from seedy ambushes in hidden dens. They blasted unsuspecting animals for reasons that no one has accurately been able to explain to the world yet, but nevertheless, they do. Hunters are men who kill for pleasure. You take these punters on, you think seriously about the consequences. In fact, you only think about the consequences as you ask yourself, 'Am I really the best qualified dude needed for this heavy-duty shit or could it be that there is someone more, how shall we say, suitable for the task?'

I mean, let's face some home truths here. Bird was a hippie, he was a new-age-reefer-smoking-funkadelic-psycho-hippie, and these boys would have him for breakfast.

Sarah was bemused. She smiled at Bird.

"Mr. Bird, you simply must be mistaken. Your CV said you had worked in Tanzania with the Serengeti Research Institute and in Botswana with the Kalahari lion study. Were you lying on your CV?"

"I don't have a CV, Sarah – I've never written one in my life."

"I'll show you, Mr. Bird, I've got your CV here – I was looking at it last night."

She got up, shaking her head and smiling as she disappeared into her office. She'd heard that this guy had taken some time away from field work, and David had told her over the radio that he was a bit of an odd character, but there couldn't have been a mix-up like this – not at this stage of the game – not when she was so desperate. Maybe he was just a bit nervous of the hunters, maybe she had been a little too heavy on the story and he was trying to back out by claiming there'd been a logistical error. She'd talk him round. I mean, there was the CV in her hand. It said all the things she'd told him it had said. He must just be the modest type. She'd talk him round, he'd see – he was her man, after all.

"Maybe this will jog your memory, Mr. Bird." She tossed the resumé onto his lap and slumped herself back into her chair, still smiling whilst wrapping her legs over one arm. Aware of her body language, she made sure to face him in a relaxed and open manner. If she was to sway him, she had to appear to be as welcoming as she could. It was him, she knew it was him. Yet there was something about him that was dark and mysterious. He wasn't giving her the full story, but she would get it and he would be him – and together they would solve her problem. This was him – he was here – this was her man!

Bird read through the paper and felt his heart sink with each sentence. This was not him, it simply wasn't. This was some dude who'd done a lot of work with lions. It said that he had delivered a paper to Oxford on his findings from three years of research. Well, he did do that in an indirect way, but that was with birds. It was also with Alfred.

He didn't know who the geezer on this sheet was, but it certainly wasn't him – well, part of it wasn't, but part of it most definitely was. His vital stats were all there and correct and the name on the top of the sheet read 'Mr. Bird' – but why all the other junk? This was Alfred, it had to be

Alfred – I mean, it wasn't Bird, so it had to be Alfie. Alfred must have lied to get him employed. But he'd given Bird a copy of the same resumé – the one that Iceberg had pulled at the airport to get him on the flight. That was all about birds, though, and what's more, it was mostly true – he'd read it, it was all true. This was a heap of shit – a minging, reeking, festering turd stewing in his hands – and it was now starting to smell pretty bad. It was Alfred. The most honest man you could ever meet. Bastard.

"It was Alfred – this has to be Alfred's work," he murmured softly.

"Sorry, what was that?" Sarah asked in a mildly sarcastic tone. "Remember who you are now?"

"Sarah, this simply isn't me. I'm really, really sorry, man, but this shit just isn't mine. Alfred must have written this to get me the job. I don't know what to say."

"Alfred? Alfred Weiss the ornithologist, is that who you mean?"

"Do you know him?"

"I did my PhD at Oxford. I don't know him but I've heard of him and I know there was a recommendation from him somewhere along the line to hire you."

"Hire? You're not going to pay me, are you?"

"Well, we were. But not if you're not who you say you are. Or at least who that says you are. How do you know Alfred Weiss?"

"He's my mother's cousin. Look Sarah, I'm not this, I'm just not, I'm not anything. I'm really sorry. Please don't pay me – oh God, I feel terrible."

Sarah stared off into the distance. She'd been scoobied – bowled middle stump on the last ball of the over when it was all starting to look like a healthy knock. This was supposed to be her man, her batting partner to see out the innings and clinch the game. For a while, she had even thought that he was – for a while there she had been taken in by his charade. The line he threw caught her fair and square, and she had wriggled on the hook for just a moment. The anger began welling up inside her. How had this happened? How could she have relied so heavily on this and been let down so desperately? How had she let herself get sucked into it, and when would she get a break from all this grief? Thoughts shot through her mind like anti-aircraft fire splitting the night sky in Jerusalem.

He isn't my man – he's not even close. He's a filthy little junkie boy. He's a filthy, dirty, drug-pushing shit who lied on his resumé to get the job. He doesn't know anything about anything and he's come here pretending to be Craig fucking Packer – to have a jolly old time in the bush. Well, not on my watch, boy – you don't come and play these games around me at a time like this, you just don't do that. Bastard men – can never be trusted – not one bloody inch. Look at him – the little shit...

She flashed a stare of Satan's own fire across at Bird's hanging head, but his eyes were fixed to the floor and he didn't notice.

You can tell at a glance – I mean to say, he's just a fucking barman.

The words ran around her head, getting louder and louder as the pressure built up inside her like a kettle ready to sing a symphony of brewed tea to the world. Tension pulsated in her veins, and they swelled and bulged at the side of her face. Her eyes opened wide and her lips began to quiver – she just couldn't hold it any longer. More tea, vicar?

"YOU'RE JUST A FUCKING BARMAN?" Sarah screamed, shattering the silence and charging across the room towards him with her fists tightly clenched. She looked like the psycho chick out of Tomb Raider but less endowed, and Bird yelped out loud as a dog does when his tail is crunched. He cringed – she was holding all the power and there was absolutely nothing he could do about it. His body physically recoiled and instinctively he threw his arms around his head as she hovered above him like some mythical demon.

"Yes, I'm just a barman, I'm sorry," he whimpered from under his pathetic guard.

The lid could be contained no more. His words were a formidable catalyst to Vesuvius Sarah, and as she began to erupt the immediate world felt the wrath of her core as it shook itself free and unleashed its entrails all over him – ash and molten slander.

"WHAT THE HELL DO YOU THINK THIS IS?" She started stuttering and stammering with the force of the quake. "I…I…IS THIS SOME K…K…KIND OF SICK F…F…FUCKING JOKE?" Spots of phlegm flew from her raging mouth, catching the dusty light behind her and flashing like anti-aircraft fire in that Jerusalem night sky again. "DO I LOOK LIKE I NEED PRACTICAL JOKES IN MY LIFE? DO I LOOK LIKE A COMPLETE AND UTTER FOOL? DO I? WELL, DO I?"

"No, no you don't. I'm very sorry," he whimpered, lifting up one knee to try to hide some more of his pitiful self from this hounding beast, but the barrage continued. She was still towering over him and threatened to break his quaking form at any moment.

"'Sorry'? What the hell is 'sorry' going to do for me? Is it going to get me the funding I need? Is it going to put us back on the map? Is it going to save our fucking lions and their fucking habitat from complete fucking ANNIHILATION? Well? Is it?" She paused and stared at him, as if letting her questions melt into his skull to make sure they had full effect.

This was an all too familiar cycle for Sarah. It was the power she always held over men, the power that Daddy had always held over her to make her achieve those greater accolades that put prizes on her wall and medals in his soul. But Daddy wasn't here now, there was just this fool cowering below her like a dog, ready to beg for forgiveness at her command. Oh yes, she ought to make this piece of slime beg. He ought to beg for all those wrongdoings from the hunters, but it would be an insult to her power. Instead, she continued in a calmer tone laced with psychotic overtones.

"Do you really think that sorry will save all the animals that you saw today?" She paused and drew breath. "Is sorry going to make the hunters throw away their livelihoods for the sake of saving a few poxy lions? What do you think is going on here, Mr. Bird? Do you think we're all just having some kind of picnic? Do you think we're all out to lunch?" She paused again – the 'out to lunch' bit was good and she congratulated herself. "It's dying, you know." Her tone became soft, melancholic. "It's dying right before our eyes. In two years it could all be gone. Does that mean anything to you?"

She sensed him starting to relax, thinking that now she'd calmed down he might be able to level with her. What he didn't know was that she was just trying to coerce him gently out of his shell to watch that pathetic face wince in fear again as she hit it with another West Bank barrage.

Without warning, she raised her voice to a scream once again and was rewarded as he thrust his head into his chest and brought up his broken guard.

"Sorry won't cut it, mate – you're going to have to do better than fucking sorry – do you hear me? Now, get out; get out of my sight. Tomorrow I will find a vehicle to send you away – out of here and away from me. You worthless piece of shit – go and play your sick jokes somewhere else – go on, get out!" She pointed towards the door.

"B…b…b…but Sarah, I can stay and help for a while, can't…"

She flashed a glare across at him and he took the cue, ceasing all activities simultaneously as he got up and strode purposefully for the door.

Bird scuttled off to his room, fearing for his life. He'd blown it. The worst of his fears had been realised and he'd blown the gig. The chance was gone – the bitch was bad. She was a bad, bad Tomb Raiding bitch.

God, I came so close. Alfred, you fool, why weren't you honest? You're always bloody honest. I'm on my way tomorrow. What a dickhead. What a total dickhead. I can't believe I actually blew it so bad – and so soon into the gig, too. Did Miss Cleavage call me a worthless piece of shit? No, she called me a stupid twat – amounts to the same, I guess.

The feeling inside him was hollow and sickening as he sat on the edge of his bed, rocking gently backwards and forwards, staring at the blank walls around him. He had no drugs to soothe away this dilemma and he was left to contemplate it with a smokeless head and a worrying lump that consumed an Adam's apple of fear inside his throat.

He deliberated long and hard in his room about what she had said. He remembered the animals he had seen that day and clumsily groped for the feeling of discovery that had enveloped him so beautifully on the plains. He thought of the wonderful people he'd met, like Isaac and Raymond, and how badly he wanted to be with them, to learn from them. He would think hard of a way to help Sarah. He would strengthen his resolve to do something useful with his life and be on the front line of Africa's conservation. He would formulate a plan to become the lion specialist that she needed to save her institute, and she would accept his proposals because she would know deep down that he could make everything better for her – for those beautiful eyes and that fearful wrath. He would convince her to let him stay and she would ultimately be glad of his help, and one day he would look into those eyes and not feel the gut-wrench of Miss Cleavage and all the others since his accident.

And then reality hit him, and desperation once again cloaked itself around his mildly oscillating form.

Later, Isaac brought him dinner in his room and told him not to worry. He insisted emphatically:

"Madam Sarah, she jost like shouting, shouting too much. This happen for all ma guys. You, Bwana Berd, you no difflent. You now ma guy – same like us. She can be calm in morning – you see."

He would have liked to believe Isaac, but the sombre Pink Floyd ballad would roll around his head all night and consume any positivity inside him, further highlighting the rancid mess he was now in. He would pray that Isaac was right. He would pray for a brighter day tomorrow. He would pray that he would be able to sleep tonight and not lie awake worrying about the fucked-up gig. He stared at the blank walls and traced the outline of bricks with his eyes. He swore he heard his mother's voice and jerked his head sideways to listen.

"Hush now baby… baby don't you cry…"

But the room was bare. Pink Floyd would traverse the contours of distorted transgression inside his mind and sleep would evade him – all night long.

12

I RISE ABOVE

Excessive anxiety ran like a rampant chemical through Bird's blood. It altered his understanding of events by inducing random exchanges through a synaptic window to reality – kind of similar to what those red dragons had done to him a few days before. LSD interfered with his natural filter of information, a mechanism that literally sifted through the mass of data sent to his brain by sight, sound, smell, touch and sensory receptors. His filter determined the material in order of priority and processed it accordingly, allowing his logical mind to make an interpretation in the way it saw fit. LSD simply scrambled that filter – dropped his guard, inducing mass flooding of information that the brain could not prioritise or explicate. Hence, random images poured into his senses and created visions that he would normally have filtered out – the much-loved hallucinations.

Alcohol and various other stimulants retarded the transfer of neural messages by a split second, thereby deceiving his mind with information that did not exist. The delay across its synaptic gap would be sufficient to instigate a moment in limbo, which the brain filled with arbitrary data either sent by the subconscious, or distorted in the conscious mind. That's why he often got feelings of immortality when he was drunk. Ecstasy messed with his natural levels of serotonin, a chemical that induced feelings of general well-being and excellentness, but that's not really relevant right now.

Whilst on the subject of chemicals passing through the body and their negative residual effect, a similar effect could arise from having too few. A syndrome may occur where the body is being starved of stimulants that perhaps it had become quite used to over a period of time. Suddenly, for whatever reason, such influences are no longer traversing into its nerve centre, which in itself has the potential to increase substrate chemical anxiety levels and cause the patient – or victim, as is sometimes the case – a distortion of reality.

Such was the case for Bird. He had been lying awake all night, worrying and wondering – firstly about how he had blown the gig, but secondly about the fact that he was actually starting to feel something for this place – and for the Tomb Raider at its helm. Some twisted part of him seemed determined to find a way of staying, though he didn't really know why. If it wasn't enough that he had just had to deal with the whole Sarah episode, he was having to deal with it in a totally alien environment – one that was most definitely governed by the psycho druid herself – in the middle of the fucking jungle in Africa. To top all that, he hadn't had a spliff in a couple of days and he was coming down from excess bingeing on cocaine and ecstasy whilst trying to nurse that Polish spirit hangover. It wasn't really working. His perception of reality was kind of blown before he even fell off the plane, and now here he was, trying to reason the enormity of an environmental collapse in Africa while attempting moral sympathy for Lara bloody Croft. It was all too much.

It should therefore come as no surprise that, having finally fallen asleep at about four a.m., he woke up screaming and in a cold sweat forty-five minutes later when the robin from the morning before (which he had identified to be Heuglin's) began its dawn recital to the world. His senses were more acute on this second morning and he managed to take enough evasive action so as not to destroy his mosquito net. It was hard, but he contained himself. Sleep was now off all available menus and he was once again lying in his antimalarial cocoon deliberating his position.

Bollocks to it – bollocks to the lot of it. I mean really, what's she gonna do? We're in the jungle here, man – I may not be Mr. Lionman but I am something and what's more, I'm here. She needs me, she knows I can be of use to her. I just have to help her realise it – convince the girl. I'll get up early – well, just now in fact. I'll have a shower and meet her as she gets up. I'll be forceful and confident, I'll make her listen to what I have to say. I'll make her understand that the mistake was not my doing, and I will pledge to do whatever it takes to stay here and get this show on the road. First light is on its way; I'll be up for it and I'll be looking my best. I'll show her that I am efficient and I can do whatever it is she needs me to do. I'll impress her on my first morning at work. This is my resolve. I feel a bit better now – fuckin' anxiety.

It was like he had blinked – that was all – just blinked. A simple lubrication of the retinas by rapidly running the eyelids over them. Just one quick blink. Doesn't take too long – less than a second, in fact – to blink, that is. Just to take one little blink.

All the same, it was now almost seven a.m. and Sarah had been up since six trying to get through to her office in town on the radio. Isaac had sneaked a cup of tea to Bird and woken him up again, only this time, his manual dexterity control was not so great and he once again found himself on the floor grappling with his destroyed mosquito net.

Oh no, I overslept, I can't believe it... bollocks!

He raced to the bathroom and washed himself up as best he could. It was still his resolve to talk her round and convince her to let him stay, only now he was going to have to do it with another healthy dose of that chemical anxiety flowing through his veins. Look, it wasn't impossible, not at all; it would have just been easier if he wasn't so damn anxious – and if he hadn't fallen asleep again.

This is life, man. Life ain't easy, sometimes you gotta fight for the shit you believe in and sometimes that shit is hard. But if you truly believe, man, you can break through those barriers, you can come out the other side with your resolve intact, and your short-term goals that make up the big-money prizes can be achieved.

"Believe in yourself. Believe in me – right now. Please?"

He was talking to himself whilst looking in a small mirror that hung in his bedroom, trying to tidy his hair and look somewhat presentable. It was a futile effort, bearing in mind his general unkempt appearance, but at least he tried. Grabbing his notebook and pen and straightening his clothes one final time he marched out of the door and over to Sarah's house, where he could hear her having a distorted conversation on an HF radio. The words kept flashing through his mind: *Strengthen your resolve to stay. You want to be a part of this place and its conservation. Make her understand. Be strong and forceful, don't let her trample you again, tell her of your plan...*

"Mr. Bird, it seems today is not our lucky day." The screen door on her house squeaked as it knocked against her foot. "You aren't getting away from me as quickly as we both might have hoped."

She had seen him approaching and gone to cut him off before he made it to her house. She didn't want to hear another word from him; he had hurt her and she didn't want to give him an opportunity to rub any salt into the wound. She had to strike first and explain the situation so there could be no misunderstanding.

"It seems the pontoon that you crossed on two days ago has miraculously sunk into the river and my supply vehicle is trapped on the other side. I don't have a vehicle to get you to the pontoon from this side as all are in use, so you will be staying here for a while until I can sort this mess out." There was not a single ounce of sympathy or remorse as she spoke. "You are no longer welcome to stay in the accommodation that you are in. You are not a scientist, nor are you of any use to me, so you will be given a hut in the staff compound. You will collect a ration of food from the store and live with the staff until I am able to send you away. Jacob will need a lackey so you will accompany him with his lion monitoring daily. Do you understand?" The question was rhetorical. There was no pause for reply and she didn't even look at him as she fired the next instruction hard and fast before turning back into the house, the screen door squeaking once again as it thumped closed. "I don't want to see you and I don't want to hear you. Make sure I don't."

And then she was gone.

Bird had said nothing. His mouth was frozen shut, his strengthened resolve cracked, crumbling and trickling out of his feet as dust. She had done it all for him anyway. He was staying – he hadn't even had to speak. One thing did kind of confuse him about the whole ordeal, though – where was he moving to? It had never occurred to him that the men in green overalls and Isaac might not have the same living and eating facilities as him. He had never even stopped to think that they just might not all be living in large rooms like his, with beds and mosquito nets and en-suite bathrooms with hot running water. Not once. But now that he had, he wanted to know where the hell they lived?

"Bwana Berd?" Isaac's voice came from behind him. "The Madam say you pack your things and I prepare the house for you in compound wif ma guys. When your things is packed I show you, it's OK?"

Bird turned to stare at Isaac, still a bit flummoxed by everything. "But what and where is the compound?"

"Is close Bwana, is not so far, you see."

"And what the hell is a pontoon?" His thoughts were random and disjointed, as if he'd been smacked on the nose and was now totally disorientated.

"Pontoon is big boat for taking vehicle across river. It attached to a wire and there are guys who pull it across, but sometimes it sinking because pontoon is vely old. You must go to packing now your things, Bwana, then I show you compound. I take lations from the store for your food. I get all for you. Go now."

Isaac turned and hurried away, frantic in this unusual task that Sarah had set for him – taking a white man to live in the compound with them – imagine! He had looked at Bird forlornly while he spoke and emanated a kind of sympathy that made Bird feel like he'd just been sentenced to prison. Where the hell was he going to live?

"Mr. Bird?" The voice of a well-spoken and distinguished African had him rotating on his heels once again. "My name is Jacob. I am the one working with lions. My men have informed me of what has happened. I am sorry for how the Madam is, but these are difficult times for her. Tomorrow you will come out with me, but for now I think you must try to settle in to your new hut and let Isaac help you. I will speak with the Madam to see if she will give you a mattress and a net for mosquitoes, otherwise you can die of malaria. I will see you this evening." He turned to walk away, seemingly uninterested in a response.

"It's good to meet you, sir – I have heard much about you." Bird held out his hand to Jacob, who stopped and spun around, staring deep into his eyes. This unknown white man had called him sir – why? He shook his hand without saying a word, never once shifting his gaze from Bird's.

Jacob's prominent cheekbones were set high in his face, which seemed only to extenuate the squaring of his jaw and give him a rigid, somewhat impetuous stare. Like Isaac, he was toned and muscular, though slightly taller and seemingly a bit older, the edges of his tightly-curled hair tinged a lighter shade of grey. His air was confident and self-assured, educated and informed, if not a little intense. He turned and disappeared towards Sarah's house, leaving Bird to once again ponder his sentence. His new abode didn't even have a mattress, let alone a bed.

He wrestled the rucksack onto his back and walked out of his small room for the last time. At least he wouldn't be getting snagged in the netting again, that would definitely be an advantage to this whole situation. He was still kind of in shock after all the events that had happened. Everything was now going so fast and changing so rapidly that it was a good thing he was all messed up from the drugs and alcohol; if these things happened to one in a rational mind-state, one might try to understand them with rational arguments. As it was, he was so tripped out from withdrawal in its various forms that these bizarre events added something of a light relief to what was really happening inside his head.

Now that's fucked up.

He found Isaac by a small storeroom behind the kitchen, busy piling some kit into a wheelbarrow. Bird didn't take much notice of what was in it and maybe that was a blessing.

"OK, saa, is finish. You leddy? Let's go." He picked up the wheelbarrow arms and began pushing in the direction of the workshop. The wheel squeaked rhythmically and Bird trudged along in time behind it. They walked out past the skeletal wrecks of the workshop, greeting yawning mechanics who were busy opening things up and getting on with their day. The well-worn path wound its way into the trees and meandered out to pastures as yet undiscovered by Bird.

The forest here was much the same as that he had walked through to get to the plains the day before. AK-47 plants and huge trees littered the pathway and beyond. Birds darted around their canopies and the constant buzz of crickets, nectar-feeding insects and bugs rang out in the air, as permanent as the sunshine. The wheelbarrow's squeak echoed recurrently and Bird could feel the weight of his pack straining at his shoulders. It had been a while since he'd tested his fitness levels and this was now proving to be hard work. He hoped it wouldn't be too much farther, but if he had taken a moment to lift his head from the footpath he was walking on, he would have seen the clearing up ahead and the first of the small, thatched mud huts that were now creeping into view. As it was, he didn't notice anything until he had walked right next to the first of many huts sprawling out across this hidden refuge.

"Whooaa shit, cool hut man but it's a bit small isn't it?" he exclaimed as he caught sight of the abode and stopped.

The hut was small and round with the customary thatched, conical roof. Its walls were made of mud and had visible hand marks all over their smoothed surface. The bottom of the roof was low, maybe only chest high, and the circumference of the hut would have been no more than a small garden shed in England or a large child's Wendy house. Brazen animal shapes had been etched onto the exterior with fading paint, together with traditional African patterns that looked almost infantile at first glance. But within a second of studying them, Bird was filled with a profound sense of awe as he realised that these might well be the drawings of an ancient culture passed down through a thousand generations. They looked like drawings he had seen in the National Geographic magazines that made up so much of Alfred's home furnishings in the cottage. It wasn't that the artists were not talented or hadn't taken the time to add a touch of class to their work, it was just that they continued an age-old tradition in the way it had begun – with civilisation itself. Seeing it here for himself, it seemed that time had just stood still for millennia.

There was a neat wall, no more than a few inches high, protruding from either side of a slender doorway and continuing around the foot of the structure, almost like a fence. Between this wall and the hut were simple plants, none of them flowering but all lush and green and very deliberately placed. The door itself was made of rough timbers lashed together with a fibrous binding and tied shut to a pole. The materials were all natural and untreated, representing a purity that resonated through these people, a suggestion that their beautiful innocence was yet to be tarnished by the relentless onslaught of our conceited electronic generation. And maybe it never would. Maybe even if it had, they'd have chosen to let it pass by without encroaching on their lives. Could such a thing be possible?

Bird contemplated the simplicity to himself, and he once again felt a twinge in his gut that filled him with both awe and fascination for the people he was now to live with. The naïve sincerity of an ancient race could be just the tonic he was searching for, to energise his soul and create the ambition that would lift him out of this despair and into an embellished future. He tingled with excitement and let his mind run through the maze of conjecture surrounding his heart. Anything was possible now.

His gaze eventually drifted away from the hut to the rest of its surroundings, where a small, traditional African village lay sprawling through the timber of the immediate forest. There were at least a dozen of these clusters varying in size and randomly scattered through the trees. Some were rectangular or square, some round. Each one seemed to be in a cluster of three or four buildings, as in front of the huts were smaller thatch-and-pole structures with no walls but a similar conical roof. Inside each of these open fabrications, large logs were positioned in a star-like configuration that trickled blue woodsmoke and indiscriminate licks of flame from their confluence. These were cooking huts – effectively kitchens – and some had one in front of their home, others two, but each one housed a fire. Then, behind the sleeping huts, were smaller, grass-walled rooms with no roofs – these were the bathrooms.

African ladies were moving through the complex, dressed in traditional fabrics that wrapped around their chests and flowed down past their knees. Each one carried a baby on her back and some had cargo on their heads – buckets of water, logs of firewood, packages wrapped in musty cloth. Their soft, harmonious voices rang out on the breeze as they hummed tribal songs to themselves and each other.

Young children darted in and out of view, wearing old rags loosely wrapped around their bony frames. The callous skin on their bare feet was cracked and pale, and shrieking cries indicated the climax of obscure objectives in their simple games. The ground in the village was bare dust, but all around its perimeter, small vegetable patches sprouted lush green leaves and multi-coloured fruits.

"This wey, saa." Isaac beckoned and Bird walked behind him – into the village.

There is a classic scene in old Western movies when the man with no name walks into a saloon, spurs clinking, boots clunking – and everything stops as the whole loudness of the place dissipates and all eyes focus on the stranger. Well, Bird's reception in the village wasn't quite like that, but bearing in mind the chemical anxiety racing through him and its associated imbalances, not to mention the fact that everyone in the village did freeze momentarily when they saw him, that's exactly how he felt. It only lasted a second, though, because as soon as the kids registered a white man's presence, they let out a bloodcurdling scream that sliced through the air and cut it like a cheese-wire. This then induced the women to do the same, and the next thing he knew, folk were scattering every-which way, howling like banshees and shedding their loads in order to get away from this demon in their midst. Bird was ready to dive for cover himself, but he soon came to realise that the commotion was all about him – he was the demon.

"What the hell's going on, Isaac? Haven't these people seen a white man before? Was it something I said? Is it the way I look?"

Searching eyes peered from within and behind the structures, and whispers penetrated their walls. Isaac shouted out in his local language and gestured towards the prying eyes, seemingly annoyed with their reaction, and continued cussing as he walked on with his squeaking barrow. His sentences were full of clucks and tschuks, expressing his displeasure at their response to Bird.

"Vely solly, saa. You know, these people, the wives and children, them no see white peoples so much so them aflaid. Is bad, I tell them is bad. You are ma guest – they shood 'ave lespect. Solly for that, saa."

"Don't worry, Isaac, I just can't believe they could be so openly scared of me."

"Them jost women and children. Them not know nuffing. They jost prepare food and house for the man. Them not know. You, saa, you live in house next to me. My wife prepare food for you and we share ma cooking hut – is OK?"

"Yeah, man, whatever you say."

"This your house and this ma kitchen." Isaac and his squeaky barrow halted simultaneously.

Bird stopped and slowly removed the pack from his back. It slid to the ground next to him and then toppled onto the floor. He paid it no heed. He was staring at his new accommodation and now kind of understood just how pissed Tomb Raider must have been to move him here.

The doorway was slim and no more than five feet high. The hut was round, about the same size as the first one he'd seen, but it was in need of some maintenance, with the mud peeling off its walls and exposing a frame of sticks and twigs onto which it had once been plastered. Two triangular slits were carved into the walls on either side of the doorway as windows, and a decaying piece of cardboard leant against one side, presumably the remnants of a door. Relics of some form of artwork showered the exterior where it remained intact, but they were scattered and faint. The roof was windblown and uneven with bare patches and holes, and the whole thing resembled a dishevelled goat shed to Bird.

"This is my house?"

Isaac nodded at him forlornly, his gaze dropped towards the floor. "We help to fix for you, saa. Me and ma guys, tonight when all finish ma werk. You see, we make nice house for you, saa, no plobrem. Solly, saa."

Isaac was ashamed. He'd never had to treat a white man like this before and he didn't think it was right, especially not for this muzungu. He was so nice, so friendly, so respectful, so interested in their culture and their place. He was a good man and this was how they rewarded him.

Isaac had encountered several white folk in his time, and most had been arrogant fools that he had cooked and cleaned for and they paid him little or no respect. They all had staff block accommodation with showers and brick walls and proper beds. They were all scientists who hadn't offended The Madam, yet they were so undeserving of the treatment they received. Now here was a humble man who showed gratitude and kindness, respect for his fellow man, and his reward was being thrown into a dilapidated hut. There was no justice in this situation for Isaac and he felt sick from it. He'd never had to show a white man to a hut like this before and it felt wrong.

Isaac's voice washed over Bird as he stared at the hut. He tried hard to focus on what Isaac was saying.

"Jacob, him fight for a bed for you so you no sleep on floor. Him talk wiv Madam and make plan for you. I put your food inside."

Up to this point, Bird was unaware that what Isaac had been pushing in the wheelbarrow was his ration of food, but now that he looked at it, he could see items and containers that resembled the stuff. There was a plump, green cabbage on top, a small bottle of cooking oil, a two-kilo packet of sugar, a bar of soap covered in pukey pink plastic, some coarse salt wrapped in newspaper, a bundle of ground nuts wrapped in a banana leaf and a small, plastic bowl containing whole-bodied, small brown fish. They looked like whitebait but were obviously sun-dried, and the smell reminded him of his rank journey on the Land Rover, hungover and comatose. These must have been the contents of the minging sacks he'd been lying on. There was another container, an old coffee tin, that was full of uncooked beans, and then the odd tomato rolling around on top of a large, white sack that took up the whole bottom of the wheelbarrow. The sack contained 25 kilograms of crushed maize. It resembled flour.

"What is that, Isaac?"

"Is *nshima*, saa. Maize, crushed maize. Is vely, vely good. All African eat maize. It make you strong like a rion – you see, saa, you like nshima, me I know!" Isaac was busy unloading the wheelbarrow and storing its entrails inside the hut. He was becoming jovial again and this helped Bird deal with the situation.

"How often do we get rations?"

"Saa?"

"How long does this last?"

"Ohohhh. This one is for one month, saa."

"One month? You mean that's my food for the month?" Bird exploded, pointing with an exasperated breath. "You gotta be havin' a laugh, mate. You have got to be joking." He was now huffing and panting. "Where's the tea, where's the milk, where's the meat, the chocolate, the sweets, the pie, the pastry, the low-fat pastrami on rye, the bacon, the eggs, the chocolate mousse, the double chilli cheeseburger with large fries and a medium Diet Coke to go – where the fuck is all that shit?" His bleating whinges returned him to six years old as his frantically gesticulating hands eventually dropped to his hips, pausing momentarily before being thrown with a scream above his head once more. "Just what the fuck is going on here, man?"

He paced around in serious contemplation, pinching his bottom lip with his left hand and running his fingers through his hair with the right in a desperate bid to calm down and think rationally. It wasn't really working.

"I can't do this, I just can't. This is beyond the realms of acceptable human limitations, man. This isn't happening, it simply isn't happening. Why me? What did I do to deserve this?" He felt a lump building in his throat and tears well up in his eyes. There was pressure behind his cheekbones that burst a tear, releasing its budding load and transcending the vertical contours of his face. He buried his head in his hands and summoned any form of inner strength. He could cry on his own but not in front of Isaac.

"Don't worry, saa. I bring food for you from the kitchen. Madam, she not see. I bring milk and tea and all fings for you, saa. Don't worry, you see. Isaac help Bwana Berd. Isaac no let you suffer. You muzungu – muzungu always drinking tea. Same like Savongo. Him live like this too, saa. Savongo also sleep in muntu hut. You jost like Savongo, saa. Him strong, you strong, same like a rion. Evfing be OK, saa, you see."

Isaac's words were soothing like a tonic and they made him stop for a moment to contemplate his behaviour. He was being an arsehole. A selfish, Western, cossetted idiot, mistaking his man-made creature comforts for essential aspects of his survival. The neo-modernist's dilemma. Where's the TV and the hi-fi? Where's the internet and mobile phone network? Where's the loofah for the bath, the shampoo, the conditioner, the non-stick roll-on, the 'Giorgio Armani Après-rasage', the 'Drakkar Noir, l'essentiel eau pour homme'?

It's bullshit, a complete load of media-driven, marketing bullshit. But it works. We all believe it and our lives are meaningless and incomplete without such paraphernalia. Now, here was Bird with enough food to feed an African family for a month, and he's asking where the chocolate éclairs are.

If the Africans were able to survive comfortably like this, then why shouldn't he? Why shouldn't he also be contributing to the sacrifice for nature conservation? That was his resolve, wasn't it, to stay out here and learn from these people? Why shouldn't he be like Savongo – strong as a lion – half a sugar in his tea?

The tears dried up, and with each of these encounters the resolve that kept popping into his head to stay in Africa became stronger and stronger. He was amazed to feel the intensity inside him; it all seemed so natural. The spoilt child in his soul was screaming for attention and a strong, young man was emerging to cradle the fears that had held him back for so long.

Something was happening here. He was raising the dead from within his very own heart. That washed-up waster who gave a toss about nothing was graciously stepping aside, and a warrior was emerging out of his shell. Mr. Bird was sloughing his skin and leading himself down a path of discovery that would deliver 'Agent Green' to his environmental militia as they crippled the toxic giants of our world. The spirit of nature was free flowing and chilled, and his parched idealism drank heartily.

A new age was dawning, a new consciousness awakening.

13

FOR THE LOVE OF MAN

Isaac issued instructions to the children of the village, and a variety of implements slowly began to appear from within its depths. Before departing back to his duties, he gave Bird a thorough briefing on the concepts of African building maintenance and the individual functions of his assorted tools, then left him to rebuild the dilapidated shell that was to become his home.

The inventory of equipment delivered by the children included a broom made from bundles of coarse grass to sweep the walls and floor; a homemade feather duster bound with fibre to a long, wooden handle for removing spiders from the interior; bundles of grass and natural fibres to patch holes in his roof; a makeshift builder's trowel and holey basin for mixing mud plaster from a pile of fine clay silt; and lastly, water, delivered in a rickety bucket.

And so began the seemingly insurmountable task.

Never was much of a builder.

All the while, the children would watch with prudent trepidation from their den in the distant shadows, occasionally whispering hushed observations. They would see the bumbling white man struggle around this unfamiliar territory with clumsy form and elusive grace. They would observe the mutant as he covered himself and every surrounding surface with poorly-mixed mud plaster that cracked and crumbled almost as soon as he applied it to any of the walls. They would giggle as he tried to soothe his aching back from sweeping the ground with a handleless broom, and then they would turn to each other and say:

"What the hell is this white man doing here, anyway?"

And none of them would know.

Bird was aware of their amusement and briefly contemplated paranoia, maybe even anger, but his ego had been lost somewhere along the line and without it he soon warmed to their harmless cavorting pranks. He was a misnomer to them. A newcomer to a village back in England might receive the same kind of treatment from kids, only there it would be more malicious and intentionally damaging. These children emanated a virginal innocence that enabled one to understand their genuine intrigue. Time was yet to corrupt them with its media-driven shite. There were no computer games out here, no 'one-hit-wonder' pop stars, no reality TV shows searching for the next icon of the West, no devices or internet, no plastic bollocks that kids in his world seemed to depend on so much. There was just a melody of life that rippled through the trees and inspired these urchins into gyrating dance patterns at least six times an hour – and boy, did they love to dance!

Bird desperately wanted to communicate with them so they could help on the whole cleaning deal and save his throbbing back, but all his efforts at contact had been thwarted with their shrieking retreat. Even the delivery of his assorted tools and building implements had been to a neutral spot some twenty metres from where he worked, in a makeshift trolley bearing the name 'Titanic'. They then retreated to safety where they could analyse the beast moving in to pick up his quarry and speculate further on his devolutionary demise – Titanic's cargo safely conveyed.

Out here, children seemed to become adults very quickly. By the age of six, young girls were looking after baby siblings whilst pounding maize into nshima by hand. They were cooking, carrying, cleaning, watching, teaching – supporting their mothers and their relatives in the constant struggle for survival. Their homes had no running water so it had to be physically drawn in containers (themselves priceless commodities in such an environment) from the nearest available source. A lot of African villages have wells, but they are centrally located to service a number of homesteads, which could be as far as two kilometres away. There are no cars or buses, no trams or railroads – these people walked. They walked with their containers – ten, fifteen, twenty litres full of water. It wasn't such an issue in this particular village, as a well was centrally located, but water still had to be physically drawn.

This is the reason why African women have developed the unparalleled ability to carry huge and heavy loads on their heads for great distances. So long have they been the bearers of water, the hewers of firewood, the porters of numerous household utensils, that their backs have a strength that Western cultures can only dream about. Their natural sense of balance is intuitive and acute and focusses a lower centre of gravity, enabling them to perform the miraculous feat without breaking stride. The consequential curve in the spine also doubles as a rather comfy and convenient spot for a baby to perch, hence in any rural area of sub-Saharan Africa, most women over the age of sixteen will carry one, and mostly it's their own.

Whilst some of their strength is genetic, having been passed down through hundreds of generations, the rest is learnt on the job. These young girls are already making the journey to the well for water, to the forest for firewood, to the fields for maize, and a lot of them will be bearing siblings strapped to their tiny backs as they go. It gives them maturity at a very young age, brought about by the responsibility they have for their younger counterparts. The same can be said for young African boys, who themselves are not exempt from chores but are often conscripted to work in the fields, tilling the land and planting the crops for the forthcoming harvest, which exempts them from housework. It's not that this is the softer option because everything is done by hand, but it does carry with it a sense of the 'Hi honey, I'm home and I've had a shit day at the office' routine, enabling one to get home and put one's feet up, which of course they do. The women and girls, however, have had just as tough a day, sometimes tougher – but their work will not be complete until the last of their brood are asleep. The boys too young to work the fields sometimes help their sisters and mothers, but they are always safe in the knowledge that one day they will be men and their time will come to kick back, tune in and drop out. This time arrives for the women only in death.

Africa's women are the unsung heroines of the continent. Without them, the family unit on which all its cultures so strongly depend would crumble and fall. They toe the lines of inequality, they calm the storms of instability, they climb the metaphoric peaks of snow-capped glaciers then cross the windswept deserts of barren lands to work more hours than a day should contain – yet they are devoid of complaint. You will hear only the melody of an ancient rhyme pass their lips as they drift through the tidal wave they know as mortal existence with a smile and a prayer. African women possess a power of life that men of all cultures and creeds can only dream about. They are the silent warriors on whom the essence of life depends, the humble donors our charities cannot transcend, a calming force standing firm till the end – the giver of life and a man's best friend.

Women of Africa, we salute you.

As a young child, then, there are a few years of reprieve between a free ride on the back and the rendering of chores. This is the only time that the kids can be kids and they make full use of it, utilising any available paraphernalia for the amusement of play. Today just happened to be 'white boy' day and, seeing as this ridiculous being had somehow been thrust upon them, these urchins were going to make full use of its amusing possibilities, hence the game they played with the much-disgruntled Bird. Even they had to admit, this one was a real corker.

As the hours wore on, he found a kind of 'white boy, don't know no jungle shit' rhythm that began to kick the goat shed into some semblance of order. Sections of old wooden planks and bricks were delivered to the neutral refuge by Titanic and her crew, along with various other castoffs that helped to make shelves and surfaces inside his hut. He found some paint-tin lids, which were fastened onto stumps and dug into the ground around his cooking fire for stools. There was no room in the hut for additional furniture, so none was there to be found. The hut would serve only as sleeping quarters, as it was small and poky and barely large enough for him, his kit and his Robinson-Crusoe-fashioned shelves. Besides, it was dark and had a rank, musty smell of mud and untreated grass, so entertaining inside was virtually out of the question – of course, guests to be entertained within it were equally questionable.

Decorations would be superficial and unnecessary too, so all that was left was to lay matted grass on the floor inside as an underlay for his mattress – yes, the mattress – and fashion the rest of the grass to act as carpeting. Now, back to the mattress – he had forgotten that Jacob was having to beg for it and that there was the distinct possibility that this manger would have to be his bed for the next few weeks. That was fine, he would be able to handle that – Mike the landlord had donated him a sleeping bag so he would at least be comfortable. He bulked up on the grass and trimmed it off as neatly as he could against the event that Jacob was unsuccessful in his mission, then stared at the makeshift bed and smiled at the thought that all that was missing was a pillow and a teddy bear, and these kids would truly believe that a man from Mars had arrived.

With his accommodation rendered habitable and his kit squashed into the receding availability of his makeshift shelves, all that remained was to collect the debris that had been swept from its interior and dump it somewhere away from the hut. He threw it all into the mud basin and headed towards some bushes on the perimeter of the village. It was all natural stuff so he was able to just dump it anywhere in the bush, like where he was standing, next to some tall, bushy, green plants. And he was just about to, when a bizarre feeling of familiarity came over him. He put down the load slowly and deliberately, not shifting his gaze from the plants in front of him, and pushed his face in to further inspect the foliage. Once again, the unparalleled reward of scientific discovery swept over his aching limbs and he sighed graciously to himself.

"Holy Mary, Mother of God!" he exclaimed, pushing back his hair with both hands. "Beautiful, budding weed!"

He was standing next to a huge marijuana bush that was as tall as he was and as potent as a hurricane. At first he stood back and admired the entirety of the specimen, but then, unable to contain it anymore, he buried his head into the dense foliage and took a deep, exaggerated breath. It had been ages since he'd seen home-grown, and he savoured its rich aroma while examining the crystallised heads that sprouted from its stem.

There were about four plants, over six feet tall and clustered together, their limbs sagging from the immense abundance of buds spanning their anatomy. The leaves were large with seven, sometimes nine long, serrated fingers protruding from their spindly stems. They were a deep, rich and vibrant green, manifesting the radiance of health that blessed most flora in this region. The buds were tightly bunched and glistened as the fading sunlight refracted through their crystallised core.

This was good – it was better than good. Soon he would be smoking away on pure home-grown reefers and the trials and tribulations of the last two days would slip gently into euphoric oblivion, as Mother Earth's own remedy would once more soothe his aching body and calm his frantic mind. Life had suddenly got better.

In all the excitement of the discovery, what with the new abode, the mutant kids, Titanic and the whole traditional village scenario that was unfolding around him,

Bird had kind of overlooked one small detail that now became painfully apparent with the commencement of dusk.

"Hey, man, where the hell is the bathroom?" He looked around. "En-suite facilities here?" He looked around some more. "Nope!" No convenience to be seen.

A nice, hot, soothing bath to wash away the grime and sweat of severe exhaustion, followed by a cup of tea and a long, smooth reefer, would have sealed off his perilous day most beautifully, but there was not one bathroom in sight.

"Mr. Bird – good evening." That familiar African voice again, so totally different from Isaac's in its crisp and distinguished tone, yet so immaculately African. "Sorry I didn't get back earlier, but I have managed to secure you a mattress, mosquito net and pillow. Where should we put it? Have you prepared your hut?"

"Hey, Jacob, good evening to you too, mate. Thank you very much, well done, thank you. Yes, yes, I've been hard at it all day and I think it is suitable for habitation now. I'm a bit of a skank bastard myself so slumming it shouldn't inconvenience me too much!"

Jacob smiled. Luckily for Bird, he didn't understand the sarcasm in his humour, nor did he know the word 'skank', which had kind of thrown him off the whole scent of the conversation. If he'd understood the literal implication, he might have thought that Bird was referring to them as skanky for the way in which they lived, and he might have been the slightest bit offended. Bird, on the other hand, quickly realised his potential blunder and stuttered and stammered his way out of it.

"Ha ha, yes, yes, of course, this is much nicer than the gaff I used to have back in Blighty and I can tell you, it knocks ten bags o' shite out of the hole I slept in last night so I ain't really griping, man. Besides, I've got all you dudes here and it's an honour to be part of your scene, man – it really is, 'specially for a white boy – dig my groove?" He laughed some more.

Jacob afforded Bird a smile. He wasn't really getting what this muzungu was saying, but underneath it all he was sure that he was being complimentary. His own heart was sinking, though. The big lion man who was supposed to come and help him with the inordinate amount of work he was trying to get through was not forthcoming, and one thing was for sure, he wasn't this fool – not even close.

"You can eat with me tonight. Tomorrow, Isaac will organise your rations and then his wife will be preparing your food. My cooking hut is that side." He motioned to a rather smart area on the other side of the compound, where there were raised levels of activity around a building that had a corrugated iron roof.

Jacob was the headman and commanded much respect both here at work and back in his home village. As a result, he had the smartest accommodation, built with clay bricks and proper cement, twice as large as any other hut in the compound and with an iron roof that did not leak when it rained. Not only was his accommodation the smartest, but he also had the most of it. There were three substantial huts, one for each of his wives, and two large cooking structures in front – the hub of the aforementioned activity. He also had two bathrooms in situ behind his living quarters. Speaking of which...

"Um, Jacob, I'm very sorry but do I have a bathroom and if so, where is it?"

"Isaac didn't show you?"

Bird shook his head meekly "I'm afraid not."

"It is here – come with me."

Jacob led Bird to a paltry, thatched enclosure with no roof and a small slit for a door. Inside, grass sprouted through the mud floor and the walls were rotting and crawling with termites. It smelt rank, like a wet and rancid dishcloth.

"This is your bathroom," Jacob intoned, trying desperately to keep a straight face.

Bird said nothing. He was taking in the vacant scene with as much positivity as humanly possible while the fantasy of lying in that steaming porcelain bath loaded with bubbles, sucking on the end of a long reefer with tribal babes softly lathering his back, dissipated itself into his bowels and got farted out with his pungent gas.

What the hell have I done to deserve this? Alfred, I'm gonna kill you when I get home. Better believe it, old boy.

"Really? This is my bathroom?" He gazed at Jacob with a look that begged for sympathy. "Where's the bath?"

Jacob could hold it no more and blurted out his laughter. "No bath in Africa, Mr. Bird – only rivers, and you have to watch out for crocodiles eating your soap!"

The rank and rotting smell of the bathroom proved too much for Jacob's hilarious gasping and he made for the door. Bird was not expecting such humour from this man and it caught him right off guard. He stumbled out after Jacob and realised for the first time that they were surrounded by people.

"But Jacob, I haven't even seen a river and… and… there's n…n…no way I'm getting in one even if I do see it. Please, this isn't funny, I'm not bathing in no soap-eating-crocodile-infested river, man. No fucking way."

Jacob's hysteria set off the assembled crowd, who all howled with laughter despite the fact they had not one clue what was going on. They didn't really need to; they knew the state of the bathroom before the two men even went inside, so either the white boy was a total sucker or Jacob was having him on. They were of course right on both counts, which just amused them all the more.

"Don't worry, Mr. Bird. You can use my spare bathroom for tonight. My wife prepares the water for you now, and tomorrow we get your bathroom fixed up. OK?" He grinned a benevolent smile.

Bird felt like an ass but what the hell, the kids had been ripping the shit out of him all day anyway, and he was kind of getting the feeling that it would be some time before any of these people would be able to take him seriously – if indeed ever. At least they had a sense of humour.

Jacob's bathroom was no different from the shell he had taken Bird to, only it had a better calibre of grass on the walls, it was thatched very neatly and on the fresh mud floor was a large, aluminium bath tub – the portable kind with handles. There were also towel rails on the walls and fresh grass laid as a bath mat for when he got out. However, his long and gangly frame was not built to fit into such a contraption, and it was a physical impossibility for him to adequately cover his anatomy with water in one sitting. He was sure there was a knack to it and after a few days he would probably find it, but for now, he suffered and struggled to coat himself with the warm water, and his earlier fantasy of being lathered was clearly off all available menus.

More importantly, though, even Jacob's bathroom did not have a toilet, nor was there any sign of toilet paper in the whole establishment. A concerned look crept over his face as the realisation hit him that all such business might have to be conducted in the bush, maybe over a purpose-dug hole, maybe not – and toilet paper would have to be fashioned from the trees and the AK-47 plants that he had come to love and respect so much. The prospect positively frightened him.

It was getting dark as he strode back to his hut, now scrubbed and cleaned. As he approached, he saw a flickering glimmer emanating from his doorway. Someone had lit a candle and put it just inside the door.

Nice one, lads, I forgot there was no electricity out here.

It was starting to cool down quite dramatically and the flickering light was just enough to locate a warm, woolly sweater, which earlier that day he never would have contemplated needing. He paused momentarily inside the hut and looked around, following the skipping candlelight that danced across the walls and over the roof. His new mattress and the dreaded net covered a substantial amount of floor space and diminished the room even more.

He tried to comprehend this scene, but it was hard. He'd been working on the hut all day so it had become familiar in its own strange sense, but now that it was dark it took on a whole new perspective. This was home, and what's more, it was not terribly spacious. He hadn't exactly had the penthouse suite at the Wound, but this place seemed so primitive, so far removed from what he had grown up with. It should have scared him, but it didn't. He felt inspired by it, almost elated. It was awakening that warrior all the more, and that was really the purpose of his journey. This was all meant to be. He admired himself – he admired his courage for doing it and his resolve for staying. Nothing was going to be a problem – well, except perhaps for his door, which was a piece of cardboard propped against the opening.

Yes, I'll have to do something about this door; not really going to keep out any lions now, is it…

The sudden realisation of a forgotten thought – anxiety, that chemical shite again, in his mind, in his body – crystallised in his cerebral cortex and clammed up the neural message corridors of his brain – lions.

Fuck me, lions!

And suddenly he was grabbing his hair again, pulling at it like it was going to fix the next dilemma he found himself in. There were lions here and he was no longer locked in a concrete tomb for the night with a big, wooden door and a deadbolt – he was in a mud hut, sleeping on the floor. He rubbed his hands on his cheeks and wiped the sweat from his eyebrows as the paranoia consumed him like a parasite bursting through his veins.

What the hell am I gonna do if a lion starts sniffing around my hut? No… no… this is bad, this is very bad, yep, it's worse than bad, it's badder than bad – it's a bad, bad situation. I need a weapon, I need defence. What about snakes and spiders – scorpions, they have scorpions here. Oh shit, man, what am I gonna do?

He had done a fine job of winding himself up and was now in a state of extreme panic. He would have to hold conference with Jacob and make a plan – this simply would not do. He could not be dragged out of his hut by a pride of marauding lions and eaten – he just couldn't. That was no way for the Bird to die. Resolve or no fucking resolve, he was not going to be eaten.

As he approached Jacob's cooking hut, a man from the assembled crowd got up and offered him a stool. There were about four men with Jacob, sitting around the fire on rough seats carved out of timber, and they had been laughing and joking while kids shuffled around their perimeter and women crept in and out gingerly. He thanked the man for his courtesy and sat on the stool. Everything went quiet and the activity was momentarily suspended as all eyes rested on him. Even the kids stopped what they were doing and watched, although there was no need for the neutral zone as there had been earlier that day – their fathers were here to protect them now.

"Thank you for the bath, Jacob, I was very much in need of it." Jacob slowly bowed his head towards him in acknowledgement. "I'm afraid building maintenance was never really my strong point, so I think I have done a pretty shabby job of renovating my hut. As you saw, I got more mud on me than on the walls. Maybe I'll get some tips from the guys and smarten it up sometime?"

Jacob afforded half a smile. The other men said nothing – they just continued staring. The atmosphere was almost as tense as poker night back at DZ's, and Bird felt quite uncomfortable. He was an outsider in every sense of the word. He did not even know a greeting in their tongue, which would only be common courtesy for strangers anywhere else in the world. He was also not a lion man – maybe they, too, felt betrayed by him, as Sarah had done. This was their livelihood, after all. Did they hate him?

One of the men broke the ambiguous silence and spoke to Jacob in a low and soothing tone. His speech, like Isaac's, was passive and easy on the ears. The words seemed to roll off his lips in a gentle and sustained motion, and his voice sank and rose in pitch through exaggerated expression. It was no wonder English pronunciation was so difficult for these people, it was cluttered with such unnecessary expletives. English seemed otherworldly compared with this placid tone, and it instilled Bird with a tranquil serenity, diffusing any aggression from their intense stares.

The African man had motioned towards Bird as he spoke, and Jacob now interpreted.

"Orbut is asking why you have a picture on your arm."

"Picture? What do you mean, picture?"

Jacob forwarded the message and Orbut replied with a higher-pitched sense of urgency in his voice as he rubbed and slapped the top of his right arm with his left hand and pointed furiously at Bird. Jacob turned and spoke again.

"He says you have a picture of a bird on your arm and it is still there after you came from the bath. Why didn't you clean off the picture?"

"Oh… oh, that… ha ha… yes… ahem, that's a tattoo, it doesn't clean off. Would you like to see it?"

Jacob was unsure and consulted his entourage, who in turn consulted each other. It seemed that they had been doubting Orbut's eyes and did not believe his tales of painted birds. Now, confronted with the moment of truth, they had to decide whether they actually wanted to be proven wrong by Orbut or leave it as a mystery until another day.

"Yes, we will see," came the general consensus.

Jacob turned to a child sitting by his side and broke into his local language without drawing breath. At first, Bird thought he was still talking to him, and it made him jump. His tone had changed in an instant and he was rash and brazen, barking orders to the child, who leapt to his feet and disappeared into the darkness with haste.

Bird took off his jumper and pulled up the sleeve on his T-shirt. The light was not good, so he tried to get his arm down to the fire so they could all see the image.

"Sit!" barked Jacob, this time to Bird, who obediently jumped back onto his stool. Murmurs went around the gathered entourage, indicating that in the darkness outside the ambient glow of Jacob's cooking fire, more people were assembled to witness the stranger in their home. Bird sat and waited for his next instruction.

The child reappeared and gave a torch to Jacob.

"Now we can see."

Bird obliged, and the tattoo was illuminated by torchlight. It depicted a lanner falcon sitting on a perch, staring out from his shoulder. The artistry was of a very high quality and it contained sharp definitions of shade and colour, with intricate layered detail to the feathers. The people examined it and a series of clicks, tuts and whistles padded the air in amazement. They started talking and some touched it, tracing the outlines with their fingers and pressing his arm to see if the paint would smudge. They had never seen tattoos before and knew nothing of them, save the odd picture of a pirate or a vagabond in remnants of books that had made their way down the two-hundred-kilometre run from the nearest mission hospital. Even then, they were cartoon drawings in fictitious books that they were mostly unable to read, so weren't taken seriously. But now, right in their very midst, a white man stood before them and displayed his picture. Tattoos were real.

"Is this why your name is Bird?" asked Jacob.

"Maybe. My name is Bird because I love them. They are my gods and I worship them."

"Your gods say you must put their picture on your arm?"

"No, I say that. It's my tribute to my gods." Jacob nodded and translated to the troops, who in turn nodded their heads in understanding – well, as much as one is able to understand such a stranger.

"*Nikuyu.*"

"I beg your pardon?"

"Nikuyu. It's how we call lanner falcons in our language. They eat other birds. Sometimes they hunt alone, sometimes in pairs. They fly very fast, maybe one-twenty or one-thirty. Have you seen Nikuyu killing another bird?"

"No, I haven't. Have you?" Bird exclaimed, humbled by Jacob's knowledge of the creature.

"Many times. I will show you before you leave this place. Plenty Nikuyu here. We also respect Nikuyu. He is strong and fast and his eyes are sharp. He is good, but he is not a god."

"Ha… yes… well, that's all a matter of opinion, I suppose."

Jacob smiled and nodded. He wasn't about to get into a debate on spirituality with Feather Boy here. Besides, they would be spending much time together over the next few weeks – best not to kill all conversation topics on the first night.

There was a sudden flurry of activity. Women were moving in and out of the circle of men, busily placing enamel and wooden bowls on the ground in between them. In the shadows around the hut, people were milling about. Some were moving off to their own huts, while others perched on the edge of the light behind the five men gathered around the fire. It was dinnertime.

A bowl of water was passed from man to man, each in turn placing it at his feet and splashing water from the bowl onto his hands. The hands were thoroughly rubbed, splash-rinsed again and shaken off before sending the bowl on to the next recipient. Each man made every attempt to have minimal contact with the water and washed his hands away from the bowl to ensure minimal soiling. It was passed to Bird.

"I've just had a bath. My hands are clean." He looked to pass on the bowl immediately, but his neighbour would not accept it. He looked at Jacob.

"We always wash our hands before eating, Mr. Bird. We eat from the same bowls, so everyone has to see that your hands are clean."

"Right. OK. Sorry about that. I won't be a minute," he said, turning to the man on his right and smiling benignly.

The reason why water was splashed from the bowl onto the hands, which in turn were cleaned away from it, was that they were not only eating from the same bowl but also cleaning from it. If someone went and stuck their muddy paws in the bottom, everyone else would have to wash in their dirty water, negating the entire exercise.

Well, no one told Bird.

He merrily stuffed his hands in there and gave them a hearty rub whilst they were still submerged. Then he removed them, shook the excess water back into the bowl and happily handed it to the chap next door. He wasn't amused. He held the bowl and looked into it with disgust, then softly murmured a few words that held in the air for just a moment before everyone collapsed into fits of laughter. He threw out the water and handed the bowl to a young boy, then blurted out some words to Jacob in between bouts of his own hysteria.

Bird didn't have a clue what he'd done wrong but didn't think it boded well for his first supper with his new hosts. They were all laughing now, but what if that were just the humour before the execution? The calm before the storm?

The joker was trying to tell Jacob that the white boy should learn some manners, but his own comment had cracked him up so much that he was almost off his stool with laughter.

Jacob shook his head in disbelief. Some kind of cavalry this was.

For the past week or so they had been anxiously awaiting the arrival of the new scientist who was on his way to camp. Jacob had told them that he would salvage the lion project, which in turn would enable Sarah to get more money and keep the Institute alive. All the men had cheered when Jacob finally delivered the news that Mr. Lionologist had arrived from London and was at last on his way to camp. They had deliberated long and hard into the early hours of many mornings on what the new researcher might be like. Maybe he would be another Savongo; maybe he would have actually fought a lion with his bare hands or killed it with a knife. Maybe he had even slept in the lion's den. Who knows? One thing was clear: when Africans let their imaginations run wild, they can really run. By the time Bird arrived, it was rumoured that he was so highly regarded in the lion world that some thought he was even able to communicate with the beasts. His fall from grace was spectacular and free.

Bird had left all the planning to Alfred, who had always organised virtually every aspect of his life. Bird had trusted him implicitly. I mean, why shouldn't he? Alfred Weiss was a well-respected and world-renowned ornithologist – it simply wasn't in his character to lie. And Bird had just bumbled along with the plan as he usually did, expecting everything to work itself out – just the way he had bumbled along with Cracker's idea of having a leaving party that lasted two days. Was it his fault that he put his blind faith in the people he had known and loved since childhood? Maybe it was. It goes without saying that Cracker was a bad bet, but Alfred? He had always been there for Bird – a pillar of strength, a tower of knowledge, a foundation for healthy living and maximum utilisation of intelligence. Why had it fractured?

The roar of excitement reduced itself to a hum and everyone got down to the business of dinner, but Bird was now once bitten and twice shy. There was no way he was doing anything until he had studied his hosts in detail. He would do as they did, say nothing and try his utmost not to mess things up again. It was possible that within all the humour, he had actually offended them. He knew that Africans were sensitive and it was easy to compromise their good will by not adhering to their cultural traditions. He was on their turf now, and it wasn't like any turf he had ever been on. This is where mankind had originated. If he trashed it with this lot and they too threw him out, he really would have a very big problem indeed. This was his last place of refuge in a barren land devoid of reliable allies, and he wasn't exactly doing a good job of securing new ones. Conforming was essential.

The wooden bowls contained mealie meal, or, as Isaac had called it, nshima. This was the ground maize, which was cooked in water and made into a stodgy suet, like thick mashed potato or sticky rice. The enamel bowls contained a stew with large, fatty, bony chunks of meat swimming in opaque juice, a vegetable mush whose ingredients had been boiled so hard they were now reduced to a pulp, and the whitebait-type fish that he had been issued in his ration, fried in oil and heavily salted. There were two large bowls of mealie meal centrally positioned, with the three relish bowls being passed around frequently so everyone was able to get some. Bird observed. He would only strike when he was certain he was not being sabotaged and made a fool of. He studied all the men to make sure they were all doing the same thing, then lunged into his attack.

The nshima was scooped out with one hand and rolled into a cylindrical shape. This was then dunked into one of the relish bowls and eaten. If he wanted a chunk of meat or some fish, these were pressed onto the maize cylinder using spare fingers and the thumb from the same hand. One was permitted to pick out bones or fat chunks using the other hand, but they preferred using only one. The principle was fine and the texture of the maize lent itself very well to this style of eating, but what Bird had not taken into account was the fact that trapped within the stiff exterior of this maize was a core of latent heat that was yet to be released. As he dug his hand in to pull off a wedge, his fingers buried themselves into the heart of this scorching matter and absorbed most of its ferocity, which in turn forced a yell from the pit of his lungs.

"*AAAAAAAAGGGGGHHHHHHHH* – bollocks – get this shit off me!"

He shook his hand violently as he pulled away from the bowl, spraying all and sundry with the maize meal whilst still squealing like a stuffed pig. They took cover. A nearby water bowl seemed the obvious relief and he thrust his burning fingers into it instantly. But the molten tar was stuck fast and the water was slow to relieve his anguish, so he had to shove his hand into his mouth to suck the nshima off, then straight back to the bowl for cooling, back in his mouth to remove the last of the lava and finally back to the bowl with a deep and contented sigh. And in all the excitement, he had once again overlooked the small detail that this was the now-replenished water he had soiled in the first place, and it was here so that the assembled troops could wash their hands after dinner as well.

This very basic and simple fact hit him like a plummeting meteorite as he sat staring at the people around him, his fingers in the bowl and his eyes flicking intermittently from the soiled water to his astonished hosts. He felt like dying.

"Ah… huhum…" He slowly removed his hand from the bowl and cleared his throat. "Jacob, would you please tell these men that I am very sorry for being such an idiot and ruining their supper. I am also sorry to you for my ridiculous behaviour." He hung his head and felt pressure building behind his cheekbones again. Tears were not going to help his already questionable public image, and he thought he should leave before they began to consume him. "Please excuse me, I think I had better go. Thank you… I… I'm very sorry," he murmured as he got up to leave.

He was unable to make eye contact with anyone, and the tears were now running down his cheeks one at a time.

A lump formed in his throat and his nose started to block up. The darkness enveloped him as he started into the night and walked in the direction of his hut, biting incessantly at his bottom lip.

"Saa? Saa, wait. You no idiot. You muzungu. Muzungu no eat with hands – only muntu. You our friend and we not mind. You stay. You eat. Please, saa, you eat with us. Is no probrem, saa."

The words pierced Bird's back and shot through the cerebrospinal fluid flowing into his brain. He held his face in his hands and swallowed hard to fight back the tears. He was not even able to eat with these people; what use was he going to be if the simple act of eating with his hands was impossible?

Yet, did they feel malice towards him? Did they hate him? Did they reject him as Sarah had done? No. They understood that this was not in his culture – it was not how he had been taught – and they forgave him. These humble folk who had so little yet gave so much bore him no resentment for the way he had let them down – they took him into their homes and treated him as an honoured guest. Yet Sarah, who came from the so-called 'civilised world', had howled at him like a banshee on acid and thrown him out of her house with no regard for his well-being. What a hypocrisy it all seemed to be. These people knew the real meaning of community, and they always had done. These, the very same people that were labelled savages by the colonial regime and shoved into compounds and ghettos to rot or strung up in trees to hang until their death. These are savages?

It had been Raymond who had addressed him, but they were all now standing behind him as he swayed from side to side, trying to gain some composure. He removed his face from his hands and turned around to face them.

"Are you sure?"

Raymond nodded and motioned for him to come back and sit down. Bird stood for a moment and looked at the shapes of these men, which he could just about make out in the flickering ambience of light. They were his friends. They knew nothing of him except that he was a bumbling fool, but they were his friends. A shiver went down his spine. Could people really be so decent?

He followed them back inside and they all resumed their positions. A towel was handed to him to wipe the nshima from his face, transferred from his hands when he had buried them into it. They smiled and the conversation began in low tones, but once they were all into the swing of eating, the usual dinner-table banter took over.

Bird watched them intently as the firelight danced over the rounded contours of their faces. Their noses were flat and their nostrils flared. Their lips were large and almost connected to their prominent cheekbones. Their skin was smooth, dark and unblemished, and in the dim light there were no rough or sharp edges to their features. Even the way their jaws worked to eat and chew was a sustained and circular motion. They emanated a calm and gentle aura. There was no evidence of stress, no heart conditions, no anxiety attacks, no psychologists, psychiatrists or psychoanalysts, no animosity, no resentment, no negativity and no apparent hardship. They were constantly laughing. No one person was left out of the conversation – no one was picked on or abused. They all shared everything they had, from the water bowls right the way up. Everything about these people reeked of community and society, friendship and kinship, respect and love. Bird watched their interactions and felt honoured to be in their presence. Tomorrow he would ask about the weed – he would start to smoke with them and they would be able to share their experiences through the ancient tradition of spiritual levitation, not to mention the simple and beautiful act of just getting stoned.

But for now, there was the small issue of the toilet and the insubstantial door on his hut. The toilet information he thought could wait, but the door, well, that was kind of important. There were lions out here, after all – this was the African bush.

"Ahh, Jacob – I'm sorry, I don't mean to be a pain but… well, it's about my door…"

14

INTERVIEW WITH A LION

The now familiar and standard resonance of the robin's dawn chorus welcomed Bird to the morning. His first reaction was to check the makeshift door that Jacob had fashioned for him the night before – it was still intact. The action had become frighteningly familiar to him throughout the night, as numerous panic attacks had woken him from nightmares of lions and tigers breaking down his door and advancing on him with glistening teeth and slicing claws.

Tigers, sir? In Africa?

"Good morning, saa. Is Isaac, I make sum tea."

"Morning Isaac, how the devil are you, mate?"

"Oh, vely fine, saa. You?"

"Can't complain, Isaac, can't complain. Did you say you had some tea?"

"Yes, saa."

"You bloody star, mate. Thank you very much."

"Today you must go wiv Jacob to rooking ve rions. Him says you must take food because you stay out all day. I give to him already. Shadrack cooks for you, saa. OK?"

They're taking me out to the lions. What if Sarah has advised Jacob to lose the white boy? Would he do it? Would he throw me out when we're right next to them? They couldn't get away with that, could they? But then, who would ever know?

"Saa. You no go back sreep. Is OK for Shadrack to cook?"

"Yes, sorry Isaac, it's fine, no worries at all. I'll get up now."

"Yes, saa. I have plepared also some water for washing."

"Nice one, mate. What would I do without you, man?"

"Saa? You get up now."

This may not have been the lap of luxury and he may have had a paltry manger for his bed, but being woken up by Isaac sure beat being woken up by Maggie. As he stepped out to greet the dawn he nearly tripped over a large enamel bowl on the floor with hot steaming water in it. Isaac was trying to make Bird as comfortable as possible and his efforts were greatly appreciated. He hadn't been at the supper the night before when Bird had destroyed the banquet, but even if he had, this would still have been the treatment he would have administered. That was the kind of man Isaac was – it was the way they all were.

"Good morning, Mr. Bird, how was the night? No lions?" Jacob had a wry smile on his face as he greeted a wet-headed Bird.

"No lions, Jacob. Thank you once again for your help."

"Isaac's wife has prepared mealie meal porridge for you. Eat quickly and then meet me at the workshop. You will come with me today and I show you this place."

"OK, thanks, I won't be long."

The nshima of the night before had now transformed itself into a stodgy porridge, hot and steaming in its enamel bowl. It was coated with sugar and Isaac had managed to procure a spoon for Bird to eat with, much to his relief, as he was still nursing scalded fingers from the debacle of last night's supper. It set like concrete in his intestines and he was sure this would keep his hunger pains at bay for a few hours.

Bird trotted down the path to the workshop, binoculars, bird book and accompanying notebook in tow. Today was his real test. Today would reveal the meat and bones of this area and he would need to be alert and attentive at all times, taking note of everything in an attempt to learn as much as he could to facilitate a change in Sarah's disgruntled heart. The possibility of expulsion still loomed and if that time came, he would need ammunition to argue some sort of case to try to reverse the decision. It was what he wanted, right? He quickly checked his resolve and found that it remained intact, if not a bit stronger having survived his first night in the village.

As he neared the workshop, he could hear the gentle hum of a vehicle warming up and the voices of people. Work was commencing in the camp and everyone was starting to find their stride for the day. He hadn't expected to bump into Sarah, though quite why he was not sure. This was her camp and her home, after all, but he just didn't expect her to be there. Nerves tingled across his skin, sending electric impulses through his pores and inducing his neck hairs to stand on end. If he'd been expecting her, he could have played it cool and reserved all contact as he had been instructed to do, but as it was he issued a nervous 'Good morning' from his petulant lips and got duly reprimanded

"I thought I told you yesterday, I don't want to see you!" His eyes immediately lowered and he stared at the floor, his body motionless and his arms gently swinging by his side. "In the unfortunate event that I do somehow see you," she continued, "I do not expect you to talk to me. Is that understood?" He nodded solemnly, maintaining his defensive stare.

"Jacob, is this vehicle ready to roll?" she barked.

"Yes, Madam."

"Good, then get it out of here and take this bloody idiot with you."

"Yes, Madam. Thank you, Madam."

They got in the car and Shadrack jumped into the back as they drove out of camp and onto the dusty track that had been the downfall of his navigation two days earlier. It was only then that Bird realised he was sitting in an open Land Rover with no roof and no doors, going out into Africa's vast prairies in search of lions. This was complete madness.

It seemed somehow superfluous, though. Sarah's reception had deflated him somewhat and he sulked as they drove away. Why should he even care about this woman or this place? She had done nothing to accommodate him in any way and what's more, she had been downright bloody rude. Maybe he should just get on the next vehicle and get the hell out of here, get away from Tomb Raider with her foul mouth and disgusting manners. Why not? Just go home and be done with it. Besides, it was Alfred's fault that he was tasting her wrath; after all, he was the one who had prepared the fabricated resumé, he was the one who had applied for the job on Bird's behalf and he was the one who had told all the lies. The truth Bird knew inside his heart was that he was the injured party here, not Lara bloody Croft. She may be taking all the limelight, but his was the pride that had been hurt – he was the one doing time in the doghouse for a crime he never committed, so why not just say bollocks to the lot of them and go home?

That's why.

They drove out of the treeline and into the wide-open space that had awakened that sense of belonging on his first day. The track wound its way onto the plain and snaked into obscurity through the grass. Off to one side, the sun was just peeping its first rays over the crystal-clear horizon and shattering the morning air with laser beams of light. The battalions of antelope stood firm in their thousands as he had seen before, and again he noted the diversity, with large, horse-like creatures and groups of zebra and wildebeest milling about by themselves. Again, he was consumed by it all, but this time in a more secure way because he was heading out in a vehicle with Jacob and he wasn't lost and alone. His thoughts about Sarah dropped out of his head and tumbled onto the track behind him as they sped away from his negativity.

"What are those, Jacob? They look different to the others." He was referring to the horse-like antelope with their 'Mardi Gras' masks and huge, floppy ears.

"These are roan antelope. Very rare in other parts of Africa, but here we have many. They are relatives to sable antelope. Both live in matriarchal groups run by a dominant female. They're very shy – you never get too close – but they are clever." Jacob was almost shouting above the noise of the engine and the creaking bodywork as his vehicle lurched and bounced its way over the uneven terrain.

Roan antelope – matriarchal – small groups. Bird fought with his pen in a desperate attempt to note down the names of everything he saw. Jacob saw him struggling and offered a reprieve.

"Soon we will stop for lions, they're not far from here. When we stop I'll give you names of all the animals. For now, just listen to what I say and remember what you've seen when it comes time to write."

Bird acknowledged the remark with a casual nod of the head, seemingly more appropriate than screaming over the smelly, green contraption's din. His cool exterior belied the feeling in his stomach upon hearing the word 'lions', though. How could this guy be so confident that they would soon be with them? Were they in a cage – on a leash? How the hell do you just drive out and soon be with lions?

"These, they are oribi," Jacob continued, pointing to a pair of dainty animals that took off out of the grass at a hundred miles an hour. "Very small and usually in pairs or small family groups, and very fast. These are puku," now pointing in another direction. "They are different to lechwe, which you'll see just now. Puku are in big groups and usually at the edge of lechwe herds on drier ground. Those are warthog. August and September are when they drop young, that is why you see all the small ones – and look, Nikuyu." Jacob pointed to the sky above them where a lanner falcon was cruising at altitude over the savannah.

"How can you tell it's Nikuyu and not something like peregrine?" Bird screamed, his accent desperately British and alien.

"No peregrine here," Jacob replied without breaking stride.

The track wound its way out past the first clusters of islands and beyond, into the prairies, where the islands became less and less frequent. It was here that the major concentrations of antelope really began.

"These are red lechwe. See how the horns for the males are very big and the stomach is white?" Bird nodded and made a mental note. They looked no different from what had been called puku and oribi earlier, but he was sure Jacob knew the score.

"Over there is the river. This place is a delta, so when the rain comes it is all underwater."

"Where's the water now?"

"We are coming close to it. It's now just in gullies and ditches, but during the flood, water is everywhere."

"How do you get around in the flood?" Bird asked in idle but screeching conversation.

"We walk," came a pragmatic reply.

"You cannot be serious!" he yelped. "What are you, some kind of bloody Terminator? Who goes walking across water-logged plains looking for lions? When do the rains start, anyway?"

"Next month." A smile almost crept across Jacob's face with this last remark but as soon as it almost did, it did not.

Next month! Are you serious? How long was I supposed to stay here? Two months, was it? Bollocks to that. I ain't going walking after lions on flooded grasslands. No way, mate – resolve or no resolve, I did not come here to die and I did not come here to be hunted down by lions on foot in some smelly bog. When did the Tomb Raider say she would be getting me out?

"What do the lions do when there is water here? I thought cats didn't like water."

"Maybe cats don't like water, but lions, they swim. They even catch food in the water and sometimes eat it in the water. Sukula lions like to swim all the time. They swim for much of their life. It's something we think makes them different from other lions."

"What is Sukula?"

"It's the name of these plains. Sukula Plains, named after ancient people who used to live here – Sukula people. Sukula means 'place of water' in their language."

"They got that one right. Where are these people now?"

"Mostly gone. Some still remain but they have been mixed in with our people now, so very few true Sukula are left. Look, there is water."

Bird looked up. He could see a shimmering light in the near distance and then the flooded channels, which Jacob had referred to as gullies. The lechwe were more concentrated around the water, being highly aquatic, and as the vehicle approached, they took to the marsh en masse. Thousands of pounding hooves silhouetted a liquid chandelier against the backdrop of the rising sun, and as they gained momentum, bodies leapt metres into the air in random, streaking motions that defied their viscous environment. The scene's setting of a clear morning sun with its deeply-reflected light seemed only to exaggerate the already-incredible display, as if Sukula were juggling these beasts amidst a light-refracted spray of dropped catches. This place was alive with raw, untainted life that was free from marauding men and their ridiculous institutions. Mother Earth in her virginal state rotated around an invisible axis and cleansed the impure heart of this heathen disciple. Bird sucked in the air.

"See how these lechwe run," Jacob continued. "It is called the lechwe gait. They have hindquarters raised up above their shoulders and their hips are set high in the skeleton. They also have many muscles there to power them through the water."

The lechwe did indeed possess a rather ungainly stance and cumbersome motion. On hard ground, they ran with hindquarters raised, backs sloping towards the shoulder and noses pressed down to the ground, which seemed awkward and perilously slow. But in the event of danger, this clumsy parade transformed itself into an inextricably graceful stride that culminated in the angelic leap of faith that Bird was now witnessing. Their dependence on water, it seemed, was not only for the specialised grazing on aquatic grasses they had acquired, but also for protection.

The question of evolution manifested itself in Bird's awakening mind as he absorbed the scene, and suddenly the dormant intellect inspired by many years and numerous projects under the guidance of Alfred began to seep from within its permeable tomb. Were the lechwe already aquatic due to a propensity to feed on the associated vegetation, or were they ungainly on hard ground, which made them vulnerable to predators and forced them into the marshes?

As the questions arose, he looked around to the other antelope he had already seen and devised their stories, too. The dainty little oribi, for example – they seemed to hang out on the edges of the grasslands where the terrain was still wide open but the ground slightly harder and less prone to flooding. It would host different and maybe less nutritious grass species, but they still managed to eat. So what was their defence against predators? Judging by the speed at which they had taken off moments before, he surmised that an acceleration of zero to sixty in 2.3

seconds and a top speed of over a hundred and eighty miles per hour was probably it.

Load of old bollocks?

Well, just maybe, but then Bird began to question why one species grazed this lush, aquatic grass and the other ate the scraggy, weed-like grass on the edges. Both were surely ruminants, which meant that like cows, they had a four-chambered stomach and four digestive processes to extract the maximum nutrition from the minimum fibre. But why would two different animals feed in the same way on totally different grasses? Was it defence?

The vehicle was too loud to run any of this by Jacob, and now that they were approaching the marsh, he seemed to concentrate more on the job of driving than the evolutionary path of oribi and lechwe. Bird, however, was lost in his speculation.

Maybe natural selection has forced them into their respective habitats and they have taken the path of least resistance. Out there with a few million lechwe, the competition for food has got to be intense. To stay on the perimeter and remain smaller may have been a better adaptation to deal with poorer grazing so as not to compete with the rest – who knows?

The fact of the matter was that, within the space of just a few hundred metres on what looked to all intents and purposes like an open grassland, Bird had already seen five species of antelope exploiting five marginally different habitats. And something had started to occur to him.

He began to imagine how diverse the world's habitats must have been before man levelled them all with concrete. He thought of how many organisms might have exploited that diversity, and how many more each in turn would have supported. Then he tried to imagine how many might have been lost in this asphyxiation of our land, and to picture how it will be when the cancer of our creation has covered every available inch of this world.

He thought to himself that he could muse all night about why one animal has evolved in a slightly different way from another, but what was the point in that? What was the point of any wildlife research? He knew from Alfred that scientists had to relate their findings back to mankind and draw parallels with the natural world that benefit our species and teach us valuable lessons. But what do we actually learn about preservation in the grander scheme of things? What do we ever do about conserving our natural resources and their biodiversity?

Most scientists have to fight tooth and nail to get funding for their research projects, and they then have to justify it to their donors by showing how the project is beneficial to science, conservation, Man and their institution. But what about purely and simply benefiting the organism that is being studied? What about financing projects that will facilitate the study of some creature for the sole purpose of preserving it in its natural state on our Earth? What about compassion for the flailing plight of thousands of species that we threaten with our toxic wastes, our thirst for oil, our concrete jungles and our unequivocal desire to flatten the forests of this world, which we cannot replace with plastic?

"Is that a tree – out here by itself?" His thoughts were interrupted and his mind zoned back in to the present. "Wow, man, it is too. What kind of tree is that? It's enormous."

"It's a fig tree. Sycamore fig."

"It looks like it's in the middle of the flood zone. How the hell does it manage that without drowning?"

"It is on an island, can you see? The tree is very old, probably several hundred years. This tree was here before flood. That is how it survives. I wish the tree could talk, then we bring people to sit here and listen and she can tell of how many lions used to be here, and how many should be here. Then maybe the people would stop killing lions and I can go home."

"Do you want to go home?"

Jacob looked across at him, sincerity in his gaze. "Sometimes." He paused. "When I see another lion shot by hunters and my years of work are useless, I sometimes want to go home. Savongo taught us that it is better to have animals alive. Hunters and missionaries taught us that animals are more value when they're dead. Savongo is right because when many animals are alive, there is a future for my children and my people. When the animals are dead, the world is dead."

Jacob seldom looked at the track when he drove. His eyes were constantly scanning the horizon for lions and he handled the vehicle like a rodeo bull. Cars had to be 'driven' out here – one had to be aware of the revs, the gears, the vehicle's natural momentum, which if unchecked could hit a large hole and snap the axle. Jacob managed to make the whole thing look so easy, so natural – like he wasn't even trying – just an extension of his being. His mind was always elsewhere, but he had been driving these cars over this terrain for nearly twenty years and it was now an automatic response. Experience was everything.

"Have you seen many lions shot by hunters?"

"Of course. I used to be a tracker for the hunting company – I have seen many animals shot."

"Why did you stop tracking?"

"Savongo taught me a better way. He showed me the real value of animals. He saved me from the jaws of a lioness once, and all he asked in return was for me to work with him. I left the hunters."

Bird thought it rather touching how they continually referred to their god Savongo in the first person, as if he had been among them at some time or other. Fanatical religious freaks tend to do the same. They equate their gods in real terms as if they live side by side and it seems that, in their own minds, they probably do – that's the strength of the faith. Bird found it quite comforting and almost wished he could have a similar blind faith, but as yet he had found nothing tangible or real in any of these religions to warrant it. Maybe he could get close to the god Savongo out here.

The tree really was a magnificent specimen. Its trunk was gunmetal grey and fat enough for ten people to link arms around the base. It wasn't particularly tall, but the crown was huge and spanned many levels through an extensive branch network. There were blemishes all over the bark, which stood as testament to the many years of hardship she had endured but also gave an insight into the amount of time that she had stood here. When times were hard, the tree made her own plan and sacrificed limbs for the survival of the whole. When times were good, well, they were good for all. It seemed that the tree was refusing to lay down and die, no matter what nature's elements threw at her, so maybe this was the beating heart of Sukula.

"Hold on, we go through water now." Jacob took it all in his calm stride as he crunched the Land Rover into four-wheel drive, issued his instruction to Bird and hit the gully at 30 km/h, parting its water with the bonnet like Moses at the Red Sea. With his head still up and looking for lions, he powered the vehicle out the other side and onto hard ground.

"WHHHOOOOO YEEAAAH! Go on, my son! Nice driving, man, nice driving!" Bird wiped the mud and water splashes from his legs as he shrieked with excitement.

"Not finished yet," was Jacob's pragmatic reply as they hit the next and the next and then drove up onto the dryness of the fig tree's island. "You like to drive off-road?"

"Well, to be honest, I've never really tried it before. I have a driving licence but I'm not very good at driving and I've certainly never driven anything like this. But I like to drive off-road if someone else is doing all the work!"

Jacob parked to one side of the tree and used the elevated platform to view his surroundings while Bird examined the awe-inspiring specimen. Its huge limbs fanned out from the centre and could have housed a whole complex of tree houses, each unit complete with balcony, breakfast bar, car port and back garden. The crown, which spanned a radius of thirty metres or more, contained a large raptor's nest right on its pinnacle. Bird viewed it with his binoculars and could see no inhabitants, but he reasoned that it had to be an eagle of some sort. Various other fruit- and seed-eaters flicked about in the vast expanse of limbs as sharp reds and yellows flashed in and out of view. His bird book out, he jotted down a quick couple of names as he flicked through the pages.

The island was indeed almost centrally located in what was the heart of the delta's river system, made up of flowing gullies and streams. In the flood, the tree's island would be completely surrounded by water, but now, towards the end of the dry season, water was sporadic, mainly concentrated in a few of the larger streams. However, if the tree had been there first and they estimated the tree to be several hundred years old, then the flooding around the tree must have been occurring for less. The tree had to have been fairly well established by the time the floods started in order to withstand the water. But what was it like before? It would have been some form of grassland, but maybe there were a few more trees around. Was this river one channel or was it always a delta? And if it wasn't a delta, then where would all the lechwe have come from? Because from where Bird stood, all he could see stretching away from him in every direction were lechwe. And in the middle of these masses and this rolling plain stood a tree – one huge and lonesome fig tree. The whole area was bizarre.

"It's time to go," was all Jacob had to say on the matter, but Bird's heart was pounding with the excitement of where he was. This huge and defiant tree, the thousands of animals around it, the impressive raptor's nest inside it, the grasslands and the water, the dried-up gullies that would one day flow again, the sheer chaos of this area with its blinding contradictions and expanse of potential life – all had his mind racing with questions and his heart pounding in his chest.

But he was alone.

Bird had no one to share the joy of this discovery with – the energy of exploration, the excitement of facing new challenges and answering unsolved mysteries were his to indulge alone. Jacob had seen it all before and Shadrack could not speak English.

"Is that it?" Bird was still standing underneath the tree with his hands outstretched towards a perplexed Jacob.

"Is that what?"

"We just go?"

"Yes, we go."

"Dude, we're standing next to a geological phenomenon here and you say 'let's go'?"

"It is a tree, Mr. Bird. It is *mukuyu* in my language. There is no question here. The tree she grows, the tree she lives and the tree, one day, the tree will die. That is all. Nothing else. We go?"

"Nothing else, man – are you mad? There is a wealth of information here that if we just took some time to…"

"Why is it that white people always look for answers to questions that do not exist?" Jacob interrupted before Bird could finish expounding. "The most the tree can say is that the floods came here after tree was born, that is all."

"But you said yourself that if the tree could talk…"

"But the tree cannot, Mr. Bird, only man can talk and right now it's time for we men to talk about lions. They will tell us what we need to know. Please, let us go."

"All right, all right, you're the boss. I'm sorry I even tried to philosophise. I keep forgetting I'm just the lying idiot that's trashed the gig for you guys." Bird slouched into his seat with his bottom lip drooping like a child without candy. Jacob paused before turning the ignition key and looked across at him. His eyes were solemn and his face lacked expression.

"Just because Madam Sarah says you are an idiot, does not mean that you are. Only you can know the truth.

We are not botanists, Mr. Bird, we are lion monitors. In my culture, trees are very well respected; they tell of all things that happen around them – but we are not history teachers, either. The lions have answers for us and it is now time to find them. If you like, we will come back to the tree and you can learn of our tribal stories. For now, we are objective scientists, and African stories about trees that talk have no place in science. So – we go?"

Bird stared at him in a kind of excruciating bewilderment. Jacob had the habit of coming out with the most astonishing remarks at the most unlikely times and this had definitely been one of them. Underneath that brazen and traditional exterior was a profound human being, a gentleman of the highest order. He was striking the enviable balance between the science that was keeping him employed and the ancient culture into which he was born. Culture here was yet to be diluted by Western idealism – it was still relatively pure, and for him to ride the wave that bisected the two worlds required immense strength of character and a solid knowledge of his roots and who he was.

"We go, Jacob."

They drove off in the opposite direction to that whence they had come, and bumped and bounced over faint and undefined vehicle tracks. Their apparent heading was a small cluster of trees in the near distance, which they duly approached. Jacob slowed to a crawl and gently eased the car's engine off as it creaked to a mechanical halt. He looked at Bird, put one finger to his lips in a hush and then pointed towards the grass about twenty metres in front of them, motioning for him to look.

"Oh my God, oh my God!" Bird whispered, wheezing with excitement and barely able to contain himself as he put his binoculars to his eyes and savoured the marvellous sight. He had never thought he could get so close to one, and certainly not on his first day out here. Jacob sat back in his seat and smiled contentedly as he removed his notebook and pen and started noting down times and orientations. Bird was beside himself, sighing loudly with obvious gratification.

In his binocular view was one of the most perfect sights he could ever wish to have of a pink-throated longclaw – the bird that Alfred had so proudly proclaimed would be a governing force in his decision to go to Africa. At first he only saw its back, but now it turned and faced him full on, displaying the brilliant bib of pink across its throat. It moved up onto a prominent grass tussock and began calling a piping, fluting trill that echoed across the grassland.

"Oh, my life… oh my good God giddy aunt – that is just too beautiful," whispered Bird.

Jacob was still smiling smugly to himself. He loved showing people their first lion.

"Can you hear it, Jacob? Can you hear that call? That's why he's standing up on the grass tuft, showing his throat because he's calling his territory and displaying. Oh Jacob, thank you, thank you for bringing me here!"

The look on Jacob's face dropped as he registered the bird that this madman was getting all hot and sweaty about. He raised his eyes to heaven. Where the hell had they found this white boy and why the hell had they brought him here?

Bird was still consumed by the longclaw when, all of a sudden, a sharp movement behind it filled his binocular vision. He readjusted the focal length to get a better view. Something had flicked – was it the mate? The bird flew off but the entity that had flicked remained in his field of view. It was round and golden in colour with darker shading at its base. It flicked again – and then again. Bird stared hard in bewilderment, then the head to which the object was attached moved and an eye became visible.

What the hell?

The eye blinked and stared right down Bird's lens, through his eyes and into his deluded brain. It was orange with a black pupil, round like the eye of a human but with a far more intense stare. The shape moved again, and suddenly he was overwhelmed by the face of a lioness that completely filled his binocular vision and spilled out of its sides. She was staring into his soul, occasionally blinking.

"AAAAAAAGGGGGGGHHHHHH!"

He let out a loud yelp, making Jacob and Shadrack jump as the peaceful morning air was split by his shattering cry. Bird dropped the binoculars from his eyes as the heads of six adult lions simultaneously shot up out of the grass and stared in the direction of this obnoxious disturbance. The car was surrounded in a twenty-metre radius by lions, who all sat up and stared at it momentarily before raising their eyes to heaven and flopping back to their slumbers. Jacob and Shadrack allowed themselves a chuckle. Bird simply hadn't seen them.

"Lions! Jacob, these are fucking lions!" Bird wheezed out in a panic-stricken whisper. His movements now slow and deliberate, he tried to ease himself away from the gaping hole that was once a door on this vehicle. He wasn't sure where he was going; all he knew was that he had to get the hell away from this open side that allowed unrestricted access to these huge beasts. He eased himself towards the gear stick.

"It's OK, Mr. Bird. The lions will not harm you. They know this car very well. Have you seen? They are all lying down again except for Mia – she's sitting and cleaning. Have you seen?"

Bird was trying not to look at them. It was the thing he did as a kid: close his eyes and think that because he couldn't see the world, it couldn't see him. It really used to work, as well. Mia, meanwhile, couldn't really care less about him or his open-sided car. She had spent most of her life with this vehicle and to her, it was neither friend nor foe, it was just a smelly intrusion that occasionally coughed and spluttered in her presence.

"Look, Mr. Bird. Look at her."

"No, man, are you out of your fucking mind? If you look a predator in the eyes it's a sign of a challenge, and they'll kill you if they think you're challenging them. I ain't looking, man, I am not looking. Can we go now, please? Do we need to be so close to these bloody things?" Bird was still gasping as he spoke and now found it hard to even draw breath.

In his own very polite way, Jacob was kind of enjoying his discomfort. One thing was obvious to him, though: this Mr. Bird was certainly no lion man.

"We're not going anywhere. This is what we came here to see. They do not mind if we stay. We do this every day. You must look at them if you want to help me. Birds are no help to our project – people want to know about lions, and these are very special lions. We need to tell the people in Europe that Sukula lions are the most special and they must give us money to protect them. This is the job."

"It ain't my fuckin' job, man!" Wheeze, wheeze!

The young boy inside him was crying out again. The refusal to look was a defiance, the child that rebels against authority. The defiance was motivated by fear, granted, but with all the other encounters that had strengthened his resolve, the spiritual young man that cradled his fears and silenced the child was quick to emerge. Somehow, that young man had got preoccupied during this encounter and was nowhere to be seen.

"Either you look at the lions or I leave you here, Mr. Bird. I want you to see them. The choice is for you to make."

"You'll do what... leave me here? LEAVE ME HERE? Are you out of your fucking mind? What the hell did I ever do to you?"

"You are not the man they say you are. But I see in your eyes and in your heart that you have the spirit of a lion. I see that you want to stay here. No white man does as you do. No white man lives in a hut like a muntu – not since Savongo. I see the same spirit in you that was in Savongo – the spirit of a lion. Maybe you know nothing about lions and everything about birds, but in your heart you are a warrior. I will teach you about the lions, and you will tell the white people in Europe what I teach you and then they will give us money. But you have to look at them."

For the first time, as Bird glared across at Jacob, he saw life in his eyes. Before, his face had been blank and expressionless, almost bored with the proceedings, like he'd seen it all before – and really, he probably had. But now as he stared at Bird, there was a conviction in his gaze that beckoned Bird to do as he said.

Jacob was no fool. He may have been born into rural Africa and received little in the way of formal education, but he wasn't stupid. His only real downfall with the lion work was his command of the English language and his inability to write in a scientific way. He had never been to university, he had never learnt the Queen's grammar or arithmetic or algebra or any of the things that we all take for granted. He had taught himself to read scientific papers with a bit of help from some friends along the way, and he had taught himself to write monitoring reports. But preparing scientific journals for the donor community required a level of education that becomes research scientists, and Jacob was simply not up to the mark. He knew what had to be said; he just didn't know how to say it in proper English.

But Bird, this useless piece of shit that had been dumped on him for whatever sin he must have committed – well, he just might. He would know how to write and he would know about the English language – at least that was the theory.

Jacob had spent the night thinking of how to make the most of this situation with Bird, and he had decided that they didn't actually need a hotshot lion specialist here at all. Even if they did, time was running out for the project and they couldn't afford to wait for one. Jacob knew everything there was to know about Sukula's lions; all he needed was a scribe – an envoy to take his findings where they needed to go. And inside this blithering idiot next to him, he had seen the glimmer of something that just might have been hope. Sure, he was a klutz who spilled things and fell over things and generally made an arse of himself, but he had spirit. He had some form of courage and he didn't give up or shout or scream or moan like all the other white people Jacob had met – he was simply getting on with the job. Jacob recognised this as a strong quality, and he had thought of a way to harness that energy within the boy and use it to his best advantage. He had thought that by showing Bird the lions, he would instantly be converted to their cause and help Jacob realise his dream. The last thing Jacob had expected from this Braveheart was the reaction he was currently getting, and it kind of scoobied him for a moment, but he was determined to make the theory work. Bird had to look at the lions, he had to see how special they really were and join the ranks of this rather unlikely and quite extraordinary militia in their quest to save Sukula's lion population from extermination under the hunter's gun.

He's serious, isn't he? He's really gonna leave me with these things if I don't look at them and he's my only ticket outta here; I have to do as he says. Does he really think I have the spirit of a lion? Doesn't know me too well, does he?

The fear of Jacob's threat was enough to induce Bird out of his shell and off the gear stick, which he had slithered onto in a desperate bid to escape the lions. He slowly turned his head and looked at the lioness nonchalantly lying about ten metres away from his door. She was enormous.

15

SUKULA – LAND OF THE LION

Mia's front paws stretched out from her shoulders and cupped in towards each other. Her huge, tawny body sprawled away to her hindquarters, which lay on one side with back legs slightly overlapping, causing her muscles to twitch and writhe spontaneously like a serpent twisting beneath her coat. As she licked her forelimbs, her whole head moved in a long smooth motion, the barbed tongue scraping up skin and pulling it away from the bone. She was removing small parasites and dirt particles with each stroke, and occasionally she would lick the edges of her lips and swallow. Her eyes were calm and mellow, delicately concentrating on the job at hand and exuding a gentle confidence, profoundly enforcing the fact that nothing on this Earth was about to mess with her and she knew it.

Bird sat in complete awe of the creature, still somewhat dumbstruck by this outlandish transition that he had made. Five days previously he'd been off his face on Polish spirit, ecstasy and cocaine in the Wound and Bandage. Now, here he was enjoying an audience with the Queen of Beasts on Africa's great rolling plains. How the hell had it happened? How had he managed to end up here, in this predicament, with a psycho at the wheel of an open vehicle and six natural-born assassins lying not fifty yards away?

Something suddenly caught the attention of the lioness and she cocked her head forward, staring at the ground between her front legs. Her ears pricked up and wrinkled her forehead, and she looked somewhat like a puppy that had skin three sizes too big for its body. Bird chuckled nervously to himself – for a moment, she almost looked cute. She darted her face in towards the offending insect and tried to catch it in her powerful jaws, but it wriggled free and dug a hole in the ground to escape. She shifted her position and stuffed her nose into the dirt to sniff it out, but the bug was gone, tunnelled to subterranean safety.

The dust got into her nose and she let out a loud sneeze that made her whole body jolt, attracting the attention of another female, who sat up behind her. Both lions pulled back their heads and emitted simultaneous yawns, their mouths gaping skyward to reveal the devastating arsenal of ivory that had been the demise of so many through the years. The second female stood up and stretched herself out, first front, then hindquarters. Her lethal claws scraped, then anchored into the earth as she arched her back and pulled away to extend the muscles. With an athletic flick of the ankles and a quick shake of the head, she began sauntering, almost swaggering, towards Mia. They touched noses gently and rubbed the sides of their heads against one another. Mia remained seated but acknowledged the affection, emitting a deep, growling tone.

Bird sighed quietly and shook his head in disbelief. The two cats emanated a deep and sensual tenderness as they rubbed profusely, first one side of the head, then the other. Then, without warning, the second female just flopped her full hundred-and-twenty-kilogram body weight on top of Mia and held her pinned down like a wrestler. Mia's gentle growl transformed itself into a disgruntled yawl as she slithered out from underneath her assailant and leapt up, pouncing on the unsuspecting attacker and biting at her neck. The two rolled over and lay on their sides, padding gently at one another's faces with big, floppy paws.

A huge smile etched itself across Bird's face and he turned to Jacob as if searching for some kind of explanation. No one had told him that lions did this. He had no idea they showed such compassion or exhibited this kind of affection.

"These two are sisters," said Jacob calmly. "Mia and Alabama. They are now seven years old. Their mother is over there; her name is Kirsty and she is the 'in charge' of this pride. Another female is called Baby; she is a cousin of these two, but a bit younger – she is just five. Her mother died about two years ago in a fight with Kelongo pride females." Jacob was whispering quietly while the lions padded.

"What was the fight about?" Bird followed his muted lead.

"Same as always – territory."

"Wow, man, they have territories?" Bird did not take his eyes off the lions as he spoke.

"Of course. Don't birds have territories? Isn't that what the longclaw was doing just now, singing for territory?"

"Yes, but…"

"Lions are just the same. If they find other lions in their territory, they can kill them."

"Yeah, but the females? You'd think it was the males who would hold territories."

"Sometimes they do, but mainly it is the females. Lions are matriarchal. Females will usually live for their whole life with other female relatives in the territory where they are born. It is a female lineage, so it's also the territory where their mother was born and their grandmother, and so on. The males can move between the female ranges and try to mate with them, sometimes controlling more than one group at the same time, but the females nearly always remain in the territory of their birth."

"So, where are the Kelongo females now?"

"They are that side. After we finish here, we will go and look for other lions. We monitor four prides in this area, but there are others that we do not see so often. They are in the papyrus reeds and forest, in places we cannot get to. There are many lions in this place, Mr. Bird, many lions here."

"Yes, it seems so. Oh shit, what's she doing, Jacob? It looks like she's moving. Yep, she's definitely moving. Jacob, she's moving towards me. Jacob, what's she doing? Why is she moving? Where's she going? Hey? Jacob, can you hear me? Do you see her? She's moving, Jacob!"

"Keep quiet and keep still. No problem."

No problem? It's not your open door she's walking towards, mate – it's mine!

Mia had got up and was now ambling towards Bird's side of the vehicle. He flashed intermittent, paranoid glances between the lion in motion and the vehicle's non-existent door as a crippling fear bubbled up from the depths of his being and coagulated on his neck, forming little balls that sat like warts on his skin. His heart began to pound and he could feel droplets of sweat starting to form on his eyebrows. One inadvertently rolled over his eyelid and onto his retina, the saline texture stinging its delicate tissue. He blinked several times, momentarily obscuring his view of the advancing creature as instincts of flight and other evasive manoeuvres quickly materialised then dissipated inside his panic-stricken mind. But Jacob had told him to keep still and be quiet – instructions that proved difficult to bear, as even his breath seemed to resound with a church bell's toll.

It almost seemed like Mia was baiting him, as if she sensed his fear and was testing it somewhat. She moved to about three metres from his open door and stopped, looking into the distance beyond them without so much as acknowledging the presence of the vehicle. Bird had been too afraid to move his head, which still faced forward, and he now craned his eyes sideways to look at her. The strain became too much so he gently eased his head to one side, giving himself a better view and one less painful on the eye sockets. He had tried to be ever so slow and careful with his movement, but her instinctive awareness registered it like radar and she turned to look at him. The fearful warts on his neck began to expand with each minuscule infiltration of paranoiac molecular stress as her eyes held his gaze and seized his quivering soul.

And so it was that he found himself face to face with Mia the seven-year-old lioness, just three metres from where he sat, with nothing but pure Sukula air to separate them – their stares intertwined and locked, their paths now braided and bound. Her gaze seemed hypnotic though not intimidating; her eyes were placid, somewhat thoughtful, and she looked without intent or malice, even without intrigue. Her pupils were round, like a primate or indeed a human, and it seemed to give her an intellectual air that was somehow calming. She looked right through him to something in the distance and beyond. Slowly he began to relax, the fear starting to dissipate from his body. Her stare was enchanting; it was deep and enriching, totally captivating.

This was a wild lioness in her home territory – in her mother's territory and that of her grandmother. Her female lineage may have been more permanent here than the fig tree itself, yet she showed him neither malevolence nor spite for his intruding solicitation. He was a prowler at the window, an invader of her outlandish space, an uninvited, tasteless odour that aggravated her acute sinuses, but he was no threat to her. Not to her, her offspring or her food resource, so she was totally impartial to him. The sensation made him feel very small. If he had a million pounds in his pocket, it would have made no difference to the situation. She would control whether they stayed or left, whether the car was parked here or over there, whether he scratched his head or blinked an eye – she would control his very state of mind. And this power she possessed meant nothing to her, because she had no ego. There was no lion media telling her how to behave, what to wear, how to look or what to think. There were just instincts – pure survival instincts encoded as a blueprint in her mind that chemically controlled her reactions to different stimuli.

She eventually got bored of staring at the bemused creature in front of her and continued her saunter beyond the car to lie down. Bird exhaled a deep sigh of relief and his heart now began to pound again, as the anxious warts dissolved back into his skin and his body filled with pure inspiration. He was totally in awe of this animal for its unparalleled confidence and calm, and the unconditional acceptance of their presence had effected a change within him like no other. The rush from this experience was nothing less than super-celestial. It far exceeded any drug or stimulant combination he had ever tried in his quest for the ultimate high (and of these there had been quite a few), for this was the uncontrollable power of nature. This was Sukula.

"God, Jacob, that was amazing, what an awesome creature. I can't believe there is actually anything on this Earth that could threaten these guys out here. I don't know what use I'll be to you, man, but whatever it is you want me to do, I'll give it a shot. She is just too cool," he panted and gasped through an oversized grin.

"Right now, you just need to know who is who and where they are found. It will take some time for you to know these lions and where they live, so we will concentrate on that first. You will need to make reports that we must give to Madam Sarah. Then we will make a big report for the people in Europe when the rainy season comes. I think the first job is to make Madam like you again."

"Crossing the great chasms of space and time might be an easier task, mate, but we'll give it a go. OK, tell me who's who here. That was Mia – how do you recognise her?" His notebook was out and he began with his task.

Jacob began reeling off Mia's vital statistics – the notches in her ears, the scar on her spine, the shape of her face, the characteristic subtleties that separated her from the others. He explained how each lion has an individual fingerprint in their whisker spot configuration, and he taught Bird what to look for in the top row of whiskers that quickly and accurately identified each one. Then he moved to Alabama, revealing the same, and finally to Baby.

"Over there is Baby," he continued as Bird scribbled. "She has a scar on the left-hand side of her stomach, but her colour is much lighter than Alabama's and there are no scars on the ankles. She has blotches on her underbelly from when she was a cub but they have not yet faded."

"Should they fade?"

"Yes, all cubs have dark blotches on their underbellies when young but when they get older, the blotches usually fade. Not so for Baby. She still has them. Maybe she hasn't grown up yet. She is sometimes a problem and she likes to chase the car. She thinks we are the big, green lion." This was not intended as a pun and Jacob was not laughing, but Bird found it amusing for some reason known only to himself. He chuckled.

"Ha ha... yeah... nice one, mate... green lion... chase the car... heh heh."

"It is not so funny," Jacob frowned, "especially when you see her coming. We always have to be careful when she is around."

Bird's expression tightened and the humour left his face as he once again peered at the gaping hole that had once been the vehicle's door.

"Well, she's around now, right? I mean, you said she was just over there. Are you being careful now?"

"Now it is morning time. Lions like to sleep in the day. She is not active now. You will see tonight she will be more of a problem."

"Oh great, I can't wait till tonight then. Is there anything else like that I need to know?"

"Only Clearwater. He likes to lie in the shade of the car sometimes, very close to the door. You keep still if he is lying at your feet. It can be hard – he smells very bad – but you have to keep still if he comes."

"It gets better. What kind of a name is Clearwater?"

"I don't know. Savongo named these lions."

This Savongo character was everywhere. No doubt the inspiration for these names came from the great god himself and into the person who was naming them. They probably attributed all kinds of stuff to this god – well, they spoke of him in the first person so no doubt he would be with them at all times, helping to make all manner of decisions. Why shouldn't the ancient god Savongo name the lions? Gives them more credibility somehow. He probably just saved Bird from Mia moments ago.

"Did Savongo save me from Mia just now? Is that why she didn't attack me?" His thoughts spilled inadvertently from his dishevelled brain.

"No. You're not safe from Mia yet. She didn't attack you because you look bad and you taste bad. She has no reason to attack you. She sees you as part of Sukula, that is all." Bird wrinkled his face and scratched his head. "OK, that one there," Jacob continued with a sense that almost reached urgency. "See, she gets up now? She is the mother and auntie to these females. That is Kirsty – the matriarch," he proclaimed, somewhat triumphantly.

"Who the hell named these creatures and why?" Bird muttered into his notebook.

"I told you, it's Savongo and I don't know why, only he knows."

"Yes, yes, of course, my mistake, sorry."

Jacob cleared his throat. "Kirsty is the oldest. She's about twelve years now but that is just a guess."

"Wow, how long do they live?"

"Females up to nineteen years, males maybe twelve if they're lucky. Most males die before they reach ten. It is a hard life for male lions."

"Huh, that's not what we hear," Bird sniggered.

Jacob turned to look at him and paused momentarily. "You should not believe all things that you hear, Mr. Bird, maybe some are not true."

"Yeah, man, you got that one right."

"Now, Kirsty is a bit thin, not like the other females, and you can see she is lactating."

"Oh, yeah. Wow, look at that. She'll be easy to spot with those things hanging down."

"Be careful – cubs are quite old now, nearly six months, so her milk may soon dry up. Her face is longer than the other lions – their faces are round – and she has a scar on her front right shoulder, you see, there."

"Yes, yes I see." He didn't but he thought that he inevitably would soon enough, so why split hairs over the issue now? He carried on scribbling.

"She is much taller at the front shoulder than the others, so she is quite easy to tell from a distance. Ah, there is Creedence." Jacob smiled contentedly.

"Creedence, Clearwater – where's Revival? This guy had some sense of humour when he named these cats."

"The pride is called Revival – how do you know that?" Jacob looked at him perplexed, if not a little upset that this bumbling fool had pre-empted him and guessed the name of the pride. Jacob, of course, had never heard of Creedence Clearwater Revival. He'd never foot-tapped to Bad Moon Rising and didn't even know that there was such a thing as seventies rock. To him, all the white-man names were unusual so why should this be any different?

"You know, Creedence Clearwater Revival, the group?" Bird explained. "Holy shit man, who is that – what is that?" he spluttered, now somewhat derailed.

"That is Creedence, I told you."

"That's Creedence? But he's a male and he's a big fucking male, at that. Damn, he's huge. I didn't know there were males here. Look at the size of him. Why didn't you tell me there were males here, Jacob? Should I be worried? Forget it, I'm worried!"

Jacob raised his eyes to the sky and puckered up his face as if pleading with the heavens. What had he done to deserve this crazy, stammering white boy? Which one of those gods up there had it in for him, and why? Was it the God of the white missionaries who punishes the sinners with hellfire and damnation? Was it the God of the Indian shop owners who makes them starve for days on end? Was it the God of the American hunters who tells them to kill all the animals? It surely wasn't any of his gods – unless, of course, one of his was working for one of theirs? Now that was a possibility; it happened all the time on Earth.

"Creedence is a male," he sighed patiently, "and yes, he is very big. Keep writing. He is orange in colour and his face has many, many scars. There is a scar on his front left knee, and two canine teeth on the left-hand side of his mouth are wearing down. He's the dominant male of the pride. Clearwater is second."

"OK, I get it now, Creedence and Clearwater are the males and the pride is called Revival. Very clever. Savongo must have enjoyed his seventies rock, then?"

Bird was forcing the words out of his lips that were twisted around the end of his pen, and Jacob thought it bizarre that this clown should chew his pen when there was some of the finest chewing grass in all of Africa around them. He picked a stem and calmly slid it into the corner of his mouth to act as a subtle prompt that his pen was perhaps better utilised on the paper instead of his slobbering lips.

Waumfwa ami Lesa? (Why me, oh Lord?) Jacob thought to himself.

Bird looked up from his notebook, absentmindedly inserting the end of the pen back between his teeth. "OK, so we've got four females and two males and Creedence is dominant. I've got their ID tags in the book now so I can start practising with who's who in the zoo. You said Kirsty was lactating but I don't see any cubs."

"Maybe they're inside the trees already. All lions will soon go into the trees for shade and sleep for the day."

Behind the pride was a small grove of thorn trees, with sparse crowns and limited foliage but packed in tight, offering ample shade and refuge. The lions were all milling about in the grass in front, occasionally getting up and moving to another spot a few metres away, only to flop down again and resume sleeping. None of them paid the car any attention, and now that Bird was doing something fairly constructive, he was relaxed and removed from his earlier fear. He felt like he was being acquainted with a new foster family.

Clearwater got up and stretched out his huge frame. He was at least ten percent larger than Mia and he had a full head of hair around his neck and shoulders, which just exaggerated his colossal form. His body was more yellow, which contrasted with Creedence's orange and made them easy to tell apart. Creedence also looked older, with slightly sagging skin and a heavily scarred face, but they were both remarkable creatures. The barrelling wealth of body weight on Clearwater combined with his partner's psychotic demeanour made them a formidable pair. Bird thought it unlikely that any other males would want to challenge these boys unless they had more than two in their army.

"Do males ever get into groups larger than two?" he asked Jacob as his train of thought slipped from the subconscious to the conscious mind.

"Yes, sometimes as many as five adult males work together to control a group of females. They're usually brothers and cousins when there's five, though. In twos and threes, they can be unrelated. Females always stay with blood relatives. If a female separates from her family for any reason, she will usually live her life alone. She almost never makes friends with unrelated females."

"Some kind of freaky sisterhood."

"What is a freaky sisterhood?" Jacob asked.

"A sisterhood means they've got, like, some kind of clan where they all live together and look out for each other. Basically what this lot do is sisterhood-type stuff… I imagine?"

"Yes, clan is right – they have clans and they co-operate."

"Presumably they live together so they can hunt, right? I mean, don't these guys, like, lay ambushes and hunt in groups with plans and stuff? I'm sure I saw that on the telly once." Bird tried to appear informed.

"You know, Mr. Bird, I have been following lions like this now for eight years. Before this I was a hunting tracker for fifteen years. All my life I have lived in the bush, and a lot of time I spend watching the lions. I have seen many hunts and many kills, but I have never seen this plan that you talk of."

"Really? You've seen kills? Many?" Bird was now excited at the prospect of blood.

"I have documented more than three hundred. Most I have only heard at night when following hunts in the dark, but I have seen almost one hundred in the spotlight or in the day and I have never seen this plan. I sometimes see an accidental plan, but I never see a real plan. People think lions live together for hunting but this man, Mr. George Schaller from Tanzania, he proved lions live together to protect their cubs."

"Protect their cubs – really – from what? Hard to imagine that anyone would walk up to this lot right now and try to mess with their cubs."

"You see?" He smiled. "Plan of lion works. They live together so no one eats their cubs."

"Yeah, but what natural predators do they have besides man? None, right? I mean, no one eats lions, do they?" Bird was now talking as if he had become some kind of expert.

"Except other lions."

And in one swift statement, Jacob reminded him that he was not.

Jacob smiled. He'd had this discussion a few times with novices who thought they knew a lot about lions. Jacob knew his stuff. He had worked alongside one of the finest men in lion research for many years and he knew what was what with the Sukula lions.

"Other lions?" Jacob saw Bird almost gulp at the prospect. "You mean, lions eat lions?"

"Sometimes, yes. If a male lion has no females, he can come here and make a challenge to Creedence and Clearwater for their females. Maybe the other male is strong and he will defeat these two, then he takes control of the females. But he wants to have his own cubs, he doesn't want to be a father to Creedence's cubs, so he may kill them. Because females with young cubs are in oestrus, they have the instinct of a mother. This means they can come into season again very quickly – sometimes in one or two days – and then they mate with the new male."

"What, even though he's just killed their cubs?" Bird sounded incensed – outraged even.

Jacob chuckled quietly to himself. "A female lion does not care about death like a human. She just cares about being successful at raising cubs. If the new male has defeated the old male, he is stronger, so it means that he makes stronger cubs because he will have stronger genes. It also means that he is better at defending the females from new males who want to eat their cubs again. But the females can also make their plan. They live together in related groups and have cubs at the same time. This means it is more difficult for a new male to kill all their cubs so it's a warning to new males: 'Be careful, we are strong.'"

"But what if the new males are stronger, but they're discouraged because there are so many cubs in the pride so they leave them alone. Surely they're missing out on the strong genes. What then?"

"Better the devil that you know. Isn't that what white men say? The females know they are successful at delivering cubs, so they don't take the gamble that the new male is stronger. Maybe he is weak. So they stick with what they have until something bigger and stronger comes along."

"Fair enough, I suppose. It's all a bit intense, though – who would have thought that the King of Beasts could have such a rough time? And it's all with each other, too – there's no one else that is threatening them, just their own kind. Hmm, that sounds familiar."

"You see? We people are just the same, except that lions do have one enemy who is most fearsome of all – the hunters."

"Yeah, hunters. I still don't see the thrill. I can understand hunting to eat or to survive, but to come and hunt a lion so you can skin it and put it on a wall, well, I just don't see the point in that, man."

"The hunters, they say that it is for sport, but to me, sport is to play football or run a race. Hunting is not how we Africans know sport."

"Not much that's sporting about it, mate. To call it sport would indicate some form of challenge or fair play, but hanging bait in a tree and then building a hide doesn't sound all that fair to me. Tell me, are these hunters dangerous people? Sarah told me that the last scientist was chased away by the hunter – what did he do?"

"There is a hunter here called Mr. Visser. He came last year and did not know this area so well. I hear that he was chased from two other countries before coming here because he broke the law. Now that he is here, he claims that we do not know where the boundary for the National Park is, and he comes inside – me, I know the boundary too well and I know he hunts inside. We are powerless because he pays plenty money to the Chief and the government, so our complaints are never investigated. He shot two Sukula males already and one was inside the park. I found him with Mr. Baites and we started to argue, but he told Mr. Baites that here in Africa people can disappear in the night, so Mr. Baites became scared and ran away."

"What a wanker. I presume Mr. Baites was the scientist?"

"Yes, scientist from Canada."

"What about Sarah? Why hasn't she got scared and run away?"

"Haa… tsshhh…" Jacob rolled his eyes and sucked wind through his teeth, as Africans tend to do when they are bemused or overwhelmed. "You know, that Madam, she is very powerful. She has magic of the white lady to protect her. Mr. Visser came to camp one day and started shouting at her because I took down his bait hanging inside the park. He told her that she can dead and I can dead if we touch his bait, but Madam Sarah, she told him that for her to die is a good thing because she comes to Earth as a spirit and makes revenge for her death. Mr. Visser, he laughed, but the guys that work for him became very afraid and they didn't want to make trouble with the Madam. They are his trackers so they keep him outside the park for now because they know that she has the *muti* of a witch. They are afraid that her spirit will come for them, too, and they now keep Visser away. Since that day, Visser hasn't come to the park again – but now times are tough and there are no lions in his area. It is only time and that is all. The time will come when he needs to come inside the park again and shoot one of our lions. We are waiting. That is why the Madam needs help with lions now. There's only two more months before the rains really come and when rains come, hunters, they go, so we must watch out for the next two months. After that, there is four months of no hunting. It's the time for lions to become strong."

"Wow, Tomb Raider really is bad and not just to me, either. Tell me, what is muti?"

"Muti is the medicine of a witch doctor. African doctors are very powerful and they have medicine that cures sick people and makes sickness for healthy people. We Africans believe very strongly in the witch doctor.

White people, they also have muti of their own, but it's different to African muti. We don't always understand white muti but we know that some of it is very strong."

"Yeah, some of it surely rocks but some is also pretty dire, man. I know, the coke we were getting before I came out here was fairly lame but I tell you, I've had some blinding gear over the years."

"Your witch doctor makes you blind? How did you find a cure?"

"Ha ha, yeah, this is my cure – you are my cure, Jacob. Inside me there is a lot of pain from the white man's witch doctor and I have come here to Africa, to be with you people to heal me. My eyes can see but inside, there is a part of me that is blind. That's the white man's muti."

"Did someone put a spell on you? You sleep with another man's wife?"

"Not quite, but someone definitely put a spell on me and I have had a pretty harsh time of it over the last few years. I think I am fighting it well now, though."

"If you want I can make arrangements for you to see the African doctor – I think his medicine will not be powerful enough to fight the spell of your white men, but if you want I can try."

"No, thanks. You're all right, mate, but I'll let you know if I change my mind."

Jacob was flattered that the white boy thought he could cure himself by being with his people. He didn't know in what way they would help but, like Isaac, he had been around white people long enough to know that they had strange ways of going about things. If this was the cure his witch doctor had prescribed, then who was he to question it? What would be, would be. He certainly knew that the boy had courage and thought that this in itself would probably be enough to carry him through. His understanding and ability to absorb the science of what was going on here were encouraging signs for Jacob, and he hoped that at last he had backed a winner. Bird was asking the right questions and he was enthused enough to give Jacob heart that, between the two of them, they could formulate a plan that would help the floundering project and hopefully realise everyone's dreams. He just had to ensure that the bird talker 'Isamba Noni' didn't get too carried away with the feathered ones.

"It's time to go and find other lions, now. We know that Revival will stay here today and we'll come back later to see them. They'll go hunting early tonight because we have just finished the full moon, so maybe you'll see a kill. Hunting is always more successful in the early evening after a full moon because of the darkness. You think you are lucky, Mr. Bird?"

"Depends whether you call being witness to six marauding lions hunting down and killing some poor, defenceless animal lucky, I guess. If it happens, then it happens. I don't think it will be anything to do with me."

Jacob smiled at his modesty and realism. This man was not like the others. He was down to earth and practical, modest and pragmatic, unassuming and simple. Yep, he sure got that one right – this was one simple fool.

Jacob cranked the engine and they slowly lurched off in an easterly direction, following the flow of the delta's channels. The lions did not bat an eyelid as the car trundled off, except perhaps for Mia who half opened one eye as the vehicle rolled by, but it didn't warrant any more physical exertion than that. After all, she had a rough day ahead of her. Conservation of energy was a top priority in her preparation for the epic journey of thirty-odd yards from where she was lying to the shade of the trees when the sun became unbearably hot.

Lions – not many creatures on the planet with a greater propensity for sleep, and that's for sure.

16

SUKULA – LAND OF NIKUYU

Amid all life's confusion a bird sits on a wire,
Oblivious to the hate.
Like shadows on the bark we dance into a fire,
Blinded by our fate.

The lions had consumed Bird like a new toy enthrals a child. Everything in life now seemed peripheral to the encounter with one of nature's finest predators, and he gazed vacantly into the distance as the vehicle clattered and rolled down its awkward, ungainly path.

Jacob, on the other hand, had seen it all before, and he wondered time and again what it was about lions that induced such behaviour in men. They are fearsome creatures for sure, but when people viewed them in zoos in Europe, did they feel the same kind of reverence? Apparently not. So maybe it was nothing to do with the lions at all; maybe it was more to do with the place. After all, anthropologists now seem to agree that mankind did in fact evolve out of Africa, so to be confronted with wild lions on open plains would somehow put him back in the womb of his reality where he is just a babe in evolution's ancient wood. Ten thousand years ago he was nothing but a cave-dweller, and whilst he may have been a courageous hunter-gatherer and brave slayer of dragons, he was also a pathetic little creature huddled around the comfort of a flickering flame with only nature's walls for comfort. During the day, with his crudely fashioned instruments and in his micro co-operative groups, he was sowing the seed of undisputed governance over this world, but by night or by himself, he also became the predator's prey.

Now, maybe some paltry section of his bigoted mind still contains a relic from that prehistoric past. Maybe there is a renegade strand of reptilian DNA locked in the chasm of his chemistry, like some blueprint of horror, reminding him of how it was to be hunted down and murdered by a pack of wild animals. Maybe this is why lesser men are forced to hunt them – to avenge the fallen heroes of their yesteryear. If that is indeed the case, then he really should be asking himself whether he ever actually left the cave in the first place and, if he did, whether he is now busy devolving himself back into it.

Whatever it was, Jacob mused, something touched everyone in a deeply profound way when they were in the presence of lions, and even though he had met some who tried to deny it, he knew they all had felt it.

Bird's mental simplicity did not allow him to bury such feelings of insignificance, even if his ego had wanted to. His exposure to drugs and life's emotional mishaps prepared him to openly accept anything that Lady Luck threw in his path, and he was now getting the full effect of an initial encounter with Revival. Endorphins shot through his nervous system, making his whole body tingle with excitement, and in light of recent events, he embraced it with a solid heart. The change would do him good, and these new eyes with which to focus on his mission would deliver him from the despair that had begun to encase him like fabric around a mummy.

It felt good – the lions felt good. It was as if everything had been leading up to that moment, the final ingredient that would deliver this dormant Eco-Warrior into the casserole of life: seasoned, spiced, awakened and complete.

All this he pondered with a vacant stare, a wry smile and a sense of purpose that pervaded him more than the African sun penetrating his Celtic skin. For a moment there, he had almost forgotten that anything else existed besides the lions, and he was just dropping into lucid, encrypted tranquillity when a tremendous crash welcomed him back to reality.

He couldn't really expect to have this spiritual connection with birds and not have them send a wake-up call when his mind began to wander. After all, it was only his kind that were evolving into devolution; birds were too busy indulging their surf in the stratosphere to even contemplate such a thing. But as he had made it his life's ambition to develop the metaphoric wings that allowed him to taste their spiritual slipstream, so the fruits of his labour were realised as they shot it right back into his face and slapped him up with it.

Whhhhhhoooooooooooossssssssssshhhhhhhhh… thump!

"What the hell…?"

It had begun like the sound of an aircraft – like wind screaming over a titanium airframe – like a fighter jet breaking the sound barrier above him – like a space rocket heading out of Earth's orbit or a satellite re-entering it. These were all unlikely scenarios, considering his geographic location, but the options flashed across his mind as an incoming missile tore its way into a fluttering target with a resonating thump that rendered the guineafowl lifeless before its corpse even hit the ground.

Lanner falcons feed almost exclusively on other birds and are capable of speeds of over a hundred kilometres per hour in a stoop dive. Whilst they prefer to chase and catch their prey, they are not averse to a good old-fashioned mid-air collision at Mach 3 to procure larger quarries. A guineafowl weighs in at almost twice the weight of a lanner, which indeed classified it as larger prey, hence the explosive collision just metres from Bird's vacant door. The whole event had occurred in the blinking of an eye, but Lady Luck manipulated his blink in such a way that he registered the scene in retrospective slo-mo, recording each intricate detail as a precious memory to savour until his dying day.

Nikuyu came out of the contact in a barrel roll and circumnavigated the collision site with scepticism before making a final approach to consume his quarry. After all, this was a radical land with no shortage of scavengers to challenge him for the spoils of a good morning's hunt, so vigilance towards compromise was essential. The large green object concerned him somewhat and he continued circling until it ground to a dusty and mechanical halt in a zone he deemed to be neutral and safe. One final reconnaissance and breakfast would be his.

Jacob drove on far enough for the lanner falcon not to be disturbed by the car, and they sat watching it through their binoculars as it descended and began plucking feathers from its prize.

"You do have plenty of Nikuyu here, don't you, Jacob? Do you think it's a sign for me? Do you think this really is my place?" Bird was still gazing down his lenses as he spoke.

"Why do you think you can influence the kill of Nikuyu but not the kill of lions? Do you have a special power with birds?" Jacob quipped, as pragmatic as ever.

Bird glanced across at him momentarily. He was right, of course. Bird had said that if the lions killed it would be nothing to do with him, yet this lanner kill was somehow shrouded in mystic symbolism, trailing hallucinogenic banners across the sky. How was it that the lanner represented a sign for him but the lions did not? Would it have made a difference if his tattoo were a cat and not a bird, or were they simply reading more into the situation than they should have? Maybe.

"Yes, Jacob, you're right," he reasoned. "But what can I do? These things just flick my switch, man. Sorry for that."

"Isamba Noni. Soon you will become Bokwe Muchima and you will see into the mind of a lion in the same way that you see into the mind of a bird. You will see, lions will become so very important for you and together we will tell the people of Europe and America about them. You will see. Revival will change your heart."

"What are you talking about, Jacob?"

"You will see, Isamba Noni – only time will tell."

Bird was unaware that the men had given him the nickname Isamba Noni and was as much confused by Jacob's use of slang as the African was by his. But for now it was all rather superfluous, as he was wholeheartedly enveloped by the lanner falcon plucking the guinea's entrails in his binocular vision. The sensory overload from the morning's activity once again rendered his logical thought patterns void, and Revival, along with life itself, was temporarily submerged in the avian sea.

Jacob tried to take heart from the situation. If this kid could get so excited about a lanner kill, then surely he'd be equally inspired by his first lion kill. Maybe he just needed to satiate the avian desire so that they could close the chapter on birds once and for all and focus wholly on the job at hand – lions. Jacob reasoned that if he took the initiative now and showed the boy some of the waterholes that teemed with waders, then Bird could have his fill and be done with it. Yes, that would be a plan: they would go and find the Kelongos, then have lunch in the shade by a waterhole that was packed with birds. He would let this 'Isamba Noni' temporarily immerse himself in his feathered gods and quench this birding thirst once and for all.

As the lanner flew off with the remains of his quarry, Bird felt Jacob's eyes on him.

"You happy with Nikuyu?"

"Like you could never believe, Jacob. Thank you very much for that."

"It's better than being with the lions?"

"Not better, just different. I can't explain it – there's something about birds that appeals to me and Nikuyu is one of my favourites. To witness this is a very special event."

"One day maybe you say the same about lions. One day they, too, will become special like Nikuyu and you will have eyes open to Africa. This will be a good day."

"You have already opened my eyes to Africa, Jacob, and this is a good day for both of us. The birds do not compete with the lions, they are all part of the chain of life – the ecochain. Do you know about the ecochain, Jacob?"

"Yes, I know all things are connected in this world. I know that if you take out one link, the whole chain can break. This is what we do here. We try to preserve all links, and lions are the main link for me. That is my job, but I need help from you. The lions are our flagship and if we look after them then everything else will be protected as well, even Nikuyu, though it seems that he can look after himself." Jacob gestured towards the disappearing flapping of the lanner.

"I get the importance of the lions, Jacob," Bird pleaded almost defensively. "But that doesn't mean we can't have respect for Nikuyu – he is also a part of that chain. He is not directly linked to the lions but there is a connection. It may not be immediate – the ecochain is not about individuals, it's about a whole. There are many factors that influence the whole; there are many links to the chain. To neglect one small link may have a knock-on effect that ultimately each one will feel. The further down the chain you go, the more significant that effect might become."

Bird shifted in his seat to face Jacob. He was beginning to sound a lot like Alfred. "Where I come from, people have done immense damage to the chain. They have wiped out many species and we still do not know what the consequences of that might be. It is possible that we have done too much already. It is possible that we have activated the catalyst for a complete ecological breakdown. To respect all links in the chain of life is a start that may help us preserve enough of this world to survive. But hey, who am I to lecture you on shit like this? You've been fighting your whole life to preserve the natural world, man. If it wasn't for me and my fucked-up people, we wouldn't be in this mess in the first place."

"Yes, and I would not have a job." Jacob smiled. "What you say is right, Isamba Noni. People must respect all links in the chain. You know, we have a saying in my language: *Kabulwe sesa ma bichi kuwomo. Mwela, lubesha yavula – mambone abaya.* It means that the trees in a forest, they stand together side by side. When the weather is calm, the trees do not move and there is peace. But when the wind blows, the trees start to move, the branches begin rubbing against each other and sometimes they can break. The wind can be so strong that a whole tree will fall down and break other trees that stand around it. Many trees will die this way and it is all because of the wind. If there is no wind, there is no unnecessary death." Jacob paused for a second, as if in thought. "In this story," he continued, "the trees represent all the animals of our world, and mankind is the wind. If the wind does not blow, the trees do not die; the animals do not die. Is it possible for mankind to be still and respect all life in this world – be still and quiet like the trees in a forest? Do you think it can be this way?"

"Well, I guess we just have to hope, Jacob. For all our sakes, we just have to hope. How cool is that, though, man – great story. I should write it down to tell Cracker and the lads. Fat chance!"

"You are a good man, Isamba Noni. You are crazy about the birds but you are a good man. I respect your link and you respect mine, and maybe together we stop the wind from blowing." Jacob held out his hand towards Bird. "We try?"

There was a momentary pause of contemplation before their palms locked together.

"We try."

The feeling inside Bird was strange – it wasn't chemical or contrived, nor was it induced by drugs, but he felt a sudden high, a peculiar sense of the commitment that he'd had all those years ago. As he shook Jacob's hand, he realised that this was the calling that Alfred had been trying to instil, and he secretly pledged to do whatever he could to save the lions of Sukula. For the sake of Jacob, for the sake of Isaac, for the sake of Nikuyu and for every link in the ecochain, he would do what it took – even if it killed him.

Jacob kept his promise. They stopped for a lunch of nshima and dried fish under a tree near the waterhole. Bird experienced for the first time the volume of bird life that Alfred had described all those days before when he was first introducing the idea of Africa to him. It was not the spectacle it might have been because it was now the end of the dry season and water levels were low, but if this was how it was when the water was low, imagine how it would be in the flood. There were more than a thousand birds of various species milling about the receding mudbanks and Bird was duly in his element. Jacob and Shadrack made harmless fun of him, though Bird would never know, and amidst his excitement for the bird life, an expectant thrill was rippling up and down his spine for the evening he was about to share with Revival.

The Kelongos had been sighted earlier, but they were far off and across a large expanse of water that did not warrant crossing. They would appear again soon, and Bird would later become acquainted with them as he had with Revival. The Kelongos were the first to whet his appetite for cubs as he saw seven small fluffballs milling and jumping about their adult counterparts, all huge paws and fluffy, white potbellies. Jacob had told him that the three Kelongo females carried the same gene as the Revival girls, but a pride split about eight years previously had formed splinter groups of related females across Sukula. The Kelongos had been colonised by a large male who came in from the south a couple of years before. He was a park lion who differed from the Sukula males, now virtually wiped out by hunters owing to their huge trophy size, but his role was just as important for diversifying the gene pool and keeping Sukula lions strong.

As with any animal species, inbreeding reduces genetic diversity and propagates the expression of recessive traits found in the genes. The most common side effect is a reduction in immune system efficiency, leaving them open to infection from diseases they would normally be able to combat. Such diseases have been known to wipe out whole inbred populations in the past. Only the fittest could survive out here.

Jacob recounted a famous case in the Ngorongoro Crater in Tanzania where a resident lion pride once gathered its troops and became dominant over all rival prides in the area, eventually forcing them out or killing them altogether. He explained that Ngorongoro, as its name suggested, was a volcanic crater in the ground with a diameter of about ten miles and a floor so rich in nutrients that it contained its own Garden of Eden. As a result, there was an associated representation of most vegetation types, plus a healthy inventory of mammal species. Natural isolation from the outside world and ultimate domination on the inside one had made it easy for this lion pride to control their borders and stop any unwanted invasions. As he listened, Bird drew a disturbing parallel to the plight of his own species, whose insatiable greed had indeed put them at the top of their food chain – but at what ultimate price?

For a while, all was fine in the life of this pride, and their precious food stock began to grow in size and stature due to a distinct lack of competition from other lions. Jacob reasoned that they must have been the happiest pride on Earth to command such a rich and vibrant range, which undoubtedly would have left plenty of time for them to fully indulge the fundamental evolutionary cause of reproduction. But with no other lions to fraternise with, the resultant inbreeding was inevitable, and in the early sixties a plague of *Stomoxys* flies all but wiped out the whole crater lion population. With sufficient genetic variability, such a syndrome may have had less dire consequences. A handful of individuals did end up surviving the onslaught, but the rest never made it through. Of course, it didn't take long for word to get around that the crater was again up for grabs, and lions pulled in from all corners to stake their claim. The once-undisputed might of the crater pride was smashed in an instant by Mother Earth's militia – a plague of small flies.

Jacob had joked at the bizarre notion that such a powerful unit should be killed by something as insignificant as a fly, but he reasoned that the underlying message was perhaps not so humorous. Nature had a way of weeding out the weak, but she also had a way of weeding out the strong. She was ruthless and cruel, and her parameters would only bend so far.

"You see, Isamba Noni," he said, "maybe there was more than just one lesson to be learned in Ngorongoro. Maybe it was not just simply to say that you should not marry your sister or even your cousin. Maybe Nature is sending a message to men that greed will not be allowed in this world and if we continue, we can meet the same death as the crater pride from a plague of flies. Do you think it can be so? Do you think Nature can kill us this way?"

"Damn, man, I sure as shit hope not," came a philosophical response. "I guess our habitat can only support us to a certain extent and after that, the only way we're going is down. Let's just hope the big boys find out before it's too late."

"Anyway," Jacob quickly interrupted the silence that was about to enshroud them in worldly cynicism, trying hard not to dwell too much in the morbid arena of human annihilation. "What you think of the birds of Sukula, Isamba Noni – *kuwaama*?"

"I like them very much, Mr. Jacob. This place really is paradise, especially when I'm lying under a nice shady fig tree watching birds. But tell me, what the hell does Isamba Noni mean?"

"This is your name. You are the man who talks to the birds – bird talker."

"Hmm, I suppose I should be flattered?" quipped a frowning Bird.

"What is flattered?"

"Um, it means I should be appreciative of the name. It suggests that you believe I have a connection with birds."

"This you have. It was Raymond who saw you in the forest, talking to *Mabuki* – the honeyguide. He was most confused because he thinks Mabuki only speaks our language, but he saw you talking to Mabuki and the bird understood; he even answered you. Raymond thinks that you have taught the bird English, so you have now become the bird talker – Isamba Noni!"

"Ha ha – yeah – that's beautiful, man. How do you say beautiful in your language?"

"We say kuwaama."

"Kuwaama – that is kuwaama," echoed Bird.

They laughed together and for once, Shadrack laughed with them. His involvement in their conversations was limited because of his lack of understanding, but he had heard the white man use a word of his own and this had amused him. Apart from anything, the ridiculous pronunciation of the Englishman had tickled him pink.

"Jacob – is it true that Mabuki will lead you to honey?"

"Oh yes, Isamba Noni, this is very true. Mabuki is a much-respected bird in our culture. He has crossed the gap between birds and people. We use birds in many ways. Some will tell us that the rain is coming because they arrive from Europe for our summer. Others will tell us that there are lions on a kill in the distance, like the vultures. But none of them behaves like Mabuki. He finds you when you walk in the bush and he asks you for assistance with honey. This makes Mabuki very special for us."

"Have you ever followed Mabuki?" Jacob nodded. "Tell me about it. Tell me about one of your trips with him."

Bird closed his eyes and lay back in the shade of his tree. He could hear the oscillating calls of plovers and sandpipers, ducks and geese, stilts and stints, herons and egrets – all but a few of the many species jostling for position around the pool. Their frantic probing of the waterhole's mud kept their heads in the sand and left them vulnerable to aerial invasion. It was imperative that sentries be on guard for the ever-present Nikuyu, the stealth-bombing martial eagle, or the scavenging yellow-billed kite. The clicks and tuts, the chucks and woos, the kiwips and kleets were all contact calls from the sentries to the feeders, maintaining a constant communication channel that allowed the flow of information back and forth through these intricate and calculated societies. And against this backdrop of avian symphonies, Jacob unfolded his story of Mabuki, the honeyguide.

"If a man wants to gather honey from the forest," he began, settling himself into a comfortable position, "he can walk out and start to call Mabuki for help. The bird is always happy to lead the man because he knows that food will be there at the end. One day I went to the forest and with my axe, I started banging against a tree so Mabuki could hear that I was there. Then I started whistling 'whheeeooo whheeeooo', which is the sign for Mabuki to come, and soon he was there, flying around my head and calling to me like he was very excited. He was saying, 'Come, Mr. Jacob, come! Mabuki, he knows a very special place for you to take honey from today!'

So I say, 'OK, no problem Mabuki, Jacob is here to follow,' and then he flew. First to a nearby tree where he waited for me to catch up, but all the time shouting so I cannot lose him. When I reached his tree, he flew again to another one, this time some few metres further, but still calling. I reached that tree, he flew again, and so it went on. But Mabuki is very impatient for the slow man who has to walk on the ground, and he flew back again over my head and started shouting at me: 'Jacob, why are you so slow? The honey is there and it is plenty, but if you walk slow, we will lose the honey to the honey badger or another Mabuki. You must be fast!'

I told him, 'You Mabuki, you have wings and you can fly through the air. Me, I am a man and it is only my legs that can carry me through this forest. You will wait for me and be patient or I will find another Mabuki to take me to honey.'

He agreed, and he stopped fighting with me. He just carried on with leading me to the place of honey, but all the time calling to me – calling my name in his language of Mabuki.

I walked for many kilometres through the bush following Mabuki, who flew from tree to tree calling my name. Finally we reached a place where Mabuki flew in circles, calling very fast and very loud. He was now excited so I knew the bee hive must be nearby. When he saw that I started looking for the hive, he sat in a tree close by and for the first time in our journey, he was silent. He just sat on his branch and watched me, waiting for me to start with the work.

I searched. I looked here, I looked there, I checked in this tree, I checked in that tree. I stopped and listened to see if I could hear the sound of bees, but there was nothing; it was silent. I said to Mabuki, 'You Mabuki, where is this honey that you speak of? I cannot find it.'

But the bird remained silent. He just sat on his branch and watched me. I searched again because maybe it was my fault that I could not see the honey. Then I looked into another tree and I saw a hole that may have been the hive. I went to check closely and I found inside a piece of honeycomb, but it was dry and the bees had left this place many months before. I held up the dry comb to Mabuki and I said to him, 'You Mabuki, what is this? Is this what you have shouted at me for? Is this what we must hurry through the bush for? You are a mad Mabuki. Do you wish to eat this? Maybe you have been drinking *Kachesu*.'"

Bird sat up and looked at Jacob. "What is Kachesu?"

"Kachesu is alcohol that we distil in the village. It is a spirit made from maize and it is very strong. If you drink too much, you will lose the track to your house and you can be lost in the bush for many days. I think maybe Mabuki had been drinking Kachesu from his village and now he had become drunk – drunk and lost!"

Bird laughed loudly and slumped back into his somnolent position in the fig tree's shade. His laughter made Shadrack laugh out loud, too, in spite of the fact that he had not one clue what had caused the white man's outburst. It didn't really matter – Shadrack was laughing at Bird, not with him.

"So, what happened then?"

"Aggghh, tssshh. Then I said to Mabuki. 'You Mabuki, you have made me walk for a long time through the bush and you have told me to walk fast. I am now very tired and I need the honey for strength to return to my village. You must take me to another hive that is full of honey.'

Mabuki did not look me in the eyes. He became ashamed with his poor judgement and he started to think where to find more honey. After some seconds of thinking, he started again to talk, and he told me, 'Jacob, I am sorry. I do not know why I have brought you to this place. You follow me again and I find fresh honey for you. Come, we go.'

And then he flew once again from tree to tree, all the time shouting my name in his language of Mabuki so I don't lose him. This time we walked not so fast and not so far until, again, he flew around and around before stopping in a tree and remaining silent. I say to him:

'You Mabuki, this time you are sure there is honey?'

But he does not answer. He just looks as if to say, 'Stop talking and take the honey – it is there, above your head!'

I looked up and I saw the bees – so many bees, and a hole in the tree where the honey was. I gathered some sticks and made a small fire, which I started burning at the bottom of the tree. Then I took my axe and cut the hole a bit bigger so I could put my hand inside. When the hole was wide enough, I waved the fire beside it and the smoke made all bees move away. Then I put my hand inside and pulled out the honey.

It is very important to leave enough honey for the bees to survive, and it is also important to give some to Mabuki for showing you the place. I did these things. There were many pieces of honey inside, but I only took two. Then I broke off a piece and left it for Mabuki. We did not talk about his earlier mistake. It is better that we parted as friends, in case he finds me again next time and leads me to a hole that has a snake inside it. Mabuki is very clever like that and he will make trouble for you if you make trouble for him. I said 'thank you' to him as I left the honey and I cut a piece of bark to carry my honey home. That is the story of Mabuki."

"Wow, man, that's amazing. Will you take me to follow Mabuki one day?"

"Yes, I can take you. Savongo taught us how to follow Mabuki properly, because there are those who chop down a whole tree to reach the honey. He told us if we kept chopping the trees, one day they would all be finished and there would be no more honey. Before the missionaries came to this place, people respected nature very much. Now the missionaries have told everyone that God is the one who has given Man the nature so if we destroy it, he will just provide us with an even greater heaven. I also used to believe the missionaries, but now I see that God will not bring another nature when this one is finished. The rhino are dead in this land because foreigners offered Africans much money for the horn. Now all the rhino are finished and this God did not bring any more. The missionaries have lied. Savongo taught me that it is only Man who can stop the death, not God, and I believe him. I will take you to follow Mabuki, and then you must tell the people in Europe and America that their God is wrong. He cannot replace this nature that we kill. It is only Man who can stop the killing of the world, and to believe that a God will bring another is not true. You do this for me and I take you to follow Mabuki – OK?"

"Well now, Jacob, you might just have gone and got yourself a deal there, big brother. You might just have got yourself a deal."

As fireballs launch into space, some humbly sow a seed
As torment scars their aching face my heart will surely bleed
But this is me, I am alive and wired into this world
Brought here by the honeyguide, no flag to be unfurled.

17

SUKULA – LAND OF DEATH

The deep black of Sukula's night sky could have enveloped him like a womb, had it not been for a million perforations in the blanket of darkness. It was almost as if the sinking sun had drawn the curtains on their existence and parked their open vehicle inside Sukula's makeshift garage for the night. Bird was busy contemplating a multitude of philosophical ideals as he sat in his envelope, grappling incoherently with the concept of unadulterated space.

Man, I never knew there could be so many stars… and to think that each one is a sun with the potential to support galaxies just like ours – blows my pickling mind. I guess we'll never really know for sure. I guess we can only ponder through light-refracted lenses at what capacity of life may exist out there… hey, that's a good one, I should write that down… but who's to say that there isn't another world parallel to ours, with another parallel me on it? Who's to say there aren't a million such worlds?

Heaven forbid.

As he gazed into these heavens, the concept of space became more and more detached from his very human and finite mentality. In Bird's world there was nothing that could last forever, everything had a beginning and an end – everything lived and then it died. He reasoned that space could not be viewed in the same way as life on Earth, that it would need different parameters for contemplation because of its outlandish removal from our diminutive existence. Space, he thought, would not be one straight track with starting guns and finish lines; space would be cyclical.

"That's it!" he squealed as his thoughts pierced the semi-permeable membrane encasing his abstract mind. "Space is just a damn whirlpool!"

"Ssshhhhh!" came a hurried reply from Jacob.

"Oops, sorry," he whispered, slamming his palm over his mouth in exaggerated embarrassment.

The Revival females were some way in front of them, using the darkness of this late moon to conceal themselves in a wide-open land of opportunity. Up ahead, the hordes of lechwe huddled around receding water channels in the delta system, as yet oblivious to the presence of the lions, whose stealth could only be matched by their patience.

"Do the lions know that the moon will soon be rising, Jacob?" Bird whispered, having put the creation of the universe to rights and now wholly focussed on the job at hand.

"It is difficult to say what they know," he replied, gently. "They are instinctive. I think they take advantage of darkness and do not think about the moon. If the moon comes, they can still hunt, but hunting is easier and sometimes quicker if there is no moon."

Fairly logical, Bird reasoned. Lions were opportunistic creatures in perfect harmony with their natural instincts and the environment that supported them; they didn't sit around contemplating stuff like the rising moon. When they were hungry they killed, when they were thirsty they drank, when they got hot they moved into the shade. Lions, he thought, were nothing more than a chemical reaction to certain stimulants – that's instinct, a reaction to stimuli.

But he had also been told of their tight-knit sociability and had witnessed for himself an element of play that could certainly not have been chemically induced. And he was now aware of the 'plan' that females made: this synchronised birth syndrome, because the only natural predators to fear were other lions. Jacob had told him of instances where they would nurse each other's cubs, remain as sentries for them and sometimes assist in the feeding of their relatives' young when there was no direct evolutionary payoff. Scientists would argue that there is a genetic payoff in this communal behaviour because if their sister's offspring made it and theirs did not, then their genes would still be propagated.

Well, if they can think of that, who's to say they don't contemplate the rising moon?

Research in the Serengeti once recorded the case of a group of five adult related males who colonised a large group of females and began mating with them. The males had been together since birth and formed a coalition that, when they reached maturity, was to go out into the world and procreate their lionhood. It is uncommon to have so many males in a coalition for the very reason that competition over breeding rights would be fierce, resulting in a limited genetic payoff for some. Therefore, to split up and go their separate ways would give them all a greater opportunity to mate but, for some reason, this particular group did not – they stayed together.

Now, all the males contributed to the protection of their territory – they all patrolled its borders, they all called at night to advertise their presence, they all scent-marked and they all gathered together in any instance of trespassing that had to be dealt with – but they didn't all mate: only four of the five actually fathered cubs. The fifth was never given an opportunity, yet he still participated in the protection of the pride and its territory. His only genetic payoff, it seems, was that of his brothers.

It is one of those beautifully unique situations that sets lions apart. This kind of behaviour can be labelled with all kinds of scientific innuendoes, but the bottom line is that lions do not fit into a box and they conform to no one's specifications. There is an element of individualism about them and they exhibit behavioural traits that cannot always be explained. They are truly dynamic creatures whose position at the top of the food chain enables them a renegade freedom of behaviour.

As Jacob had explained, the co-operative hunting myth is really a myth and there seems to be no premeditated plan or strategy involved. But what about the simple factor of hunting together? If four animals go hunting after the same herd at the same time there has to be an increased chance of success, even if it is accidental. Scientists have found that the optimum number in a hunt is two. A pair of lionesses have the ability to successfully tackle prey as large as a buffalo and only have to share the spoils between two mouths. Compare this to large prides that specialise in killing buffalo. There have been instances where up to four are killed in one hit – impressive indeed, but considering the fact that the quarry is shared with as many as sixteen other lions, the payoff of meat per individual becomes considerably less than for the pair.

So, why not live in pairs and eat like kings? Because finding food is not the only presiding factor for survival.

They have to find a solution to the other influences as well, and that solution lies in sociability – co-operation of intentions for the good of the whole, no matter how base that co-operation might be. Bird had already recognised the parallel that these creatures ran with his own perilous race and reasoned that once a species had conquered all others and climbed to the top of the food chain, the only thing left to fear would be themselves.

"There. Did you hear that?" Bird's thoughts were punctured by Jacob once again.

"What?" Bird hissed.

"The alarm call of the lechwe. They know the lions are near. We wait."

Shadrack whispered some words in his local language to Jacob, who responded.

"What did he say?" wheezed Bird.

"He is asking if he should put on the spotlight, but I told him no. The chase will start very soon. We wait."

Bird felt a ripple of excitement tingle through his body. The lions were nearby and they were gearing up to kill some poor, unsuspecting antelope.

The build-up to this hunt had been excitement enough. They had arrived back at the clump of trees long before sunset and sat waiting for the lions to become active. As the heat of the day passed, Revival came lumbering out of their shade protection, defecating and yawning, only to find a new position in which to roll and then crash out. Kirsty's three cubs had come tumbling out as a combined unit of fluff with claws drawn and mouths agape. They had run around playing games of tag and ambushing one another, their hugely oversized paws seemingly a constant menace as they tripped and stumbled during chaotic manoeuvres to outwit one another's attacks. But once a victim was pinned down, the same dinner plate paws served them well to slap and subdue their opponent and inflict maximum blows on a multitude of body parts.

Bird had been enthralled by their antics. The games never seemed to end, and the cubs never seemed to tire. They would hide behind grass tufts and slink down low like a carpet, their back legs twitching in excitement as an unsuspecting victim drew near. The lightning pounce culminated in a tumbling hindquarter tackle as the hissing bundle of clawing fluff rolled and wrestled in a desperate bid for death and freedom. The amusing thing was, the victim was always aware of this impending attack but walked into it pretending to be oblivious. It was as if they knew it was their turn to get nailed and so played the part. They would be up on hind legs, their huge paws stretched out in a boxers' tussle as they slapped and thrashed at each other's guard.

Then there were instances when momentary boredom of attacking one another rendered the right time to launch a daring raid on a sleeping adult. It seemed that the greater the element of danger involved, the more satisfying the manoeuvre, and the more unconscious the victim, the greater the reaction. Baby was always good for a scrap, but she played hard and felt no shame in subduing the tiny creatures beneath a huge paw of her own whilst biting them until they squealed in submission. With ears pinned back in a disgruntled hiss, they would hobble away from an encounter with her, squeaking and squawking until the next ambush from a twitchy sibling subdued the embarrassment. This constant charging, jumping, rolling and wrestling left Bird speechless with awe, privileged indeed to have a ringside seat on this very real wildlife documentary with the gentle commentary of Jacob to explain its intricacies.

Play was of paramount importance to these youngsters. It prepared them for hunting and gave them invaluable experience in the art of chasing a moving object and jumping on it in full flight. It enhanced the bond between young siblings that cemented their link within the unit and gave them its vital security. It established a system of hierarchy that separated the weak from the strong and determined their destiny with regards to feeding and breeding. But perhaps the most astounding of all was the finale of every game, culminating with the jugular death clamp that lions employ in a kill: a genetic blueprint already encoded in their tiny minds.

It was difficult for Bird to grasp that this harmless infant activity could have such far-reaching ramifications with the hierarchy of dominance and survival of the fittest. They seemed so innocent, so oblivious to life around them. Nothing mattered, save the game and its participants. There wasn't even an end goal, there was just the here and now and the sheer enjoyment of life that typifies all young creatures of this Earth. Yet even within the fun of a youthful existence, there was purpose. He wondered if it was the same for humans – and if so, did the manufacturers of children's toys back in England think of the ramifications attached to their merchandise, or had the forces of supply and demand overridden this basic primal instinct?

The activities of Revival's cubs had also stimulated the adults. Mia stalked up on Alabama and leapt on her in a tumbling, rolling leap. Baby was busy nailing anything she could after a bout with the cubs had proved too easy, and a small, unsuspecting thorn bush was the object of her anger at one point, ripping the poor sapling to shreds and rendering it incapable of ever reaching maturity. It was then that Bird understood what Jacob had said earlier about watching out for Baby in this kind of mood. No sooner had the tree been annihilated than she looked around for something else to attack. Jacob had been watching her closely and all the while talking to himself in hushed tones, when he suddenly cranked the engine and retreated twenty metres or so. The movement stimulated her and she stared intently, tail flicking vibrantly as she charged a couple of steps. But the big, green lion was too far away for a successful ambush, so she left it alone – it lived to fight another day. It was years of practice and an intricate knowledge of lion behaviour that enabled Jacob to pick up the signs long before she began her charge. It was almost as if he had pre-empted her very train of thought.

Within this chaos of feline utopia, the unwritten laws of cohesion drew them like a magnet towards the common goal. Amongst the growling tumble of harmless combat, a silent order was issued and the unit slowly moved out. One by one, they had filed in behind Kirsty, their slow and methodical leader, as she trudged off into the murky light of dusk with one purpose on her mind. As she moved, the other three females ceased all activities and gravitated towards her with a nuzzle and a reassuring rub against her flank that told her they were there, right behind her, every step of the way.

The fluff-balls were not so quick to respond, but the game of catch-up was one well known to them. Their lolloping great paws paddled awkwardly through the grass to under Kirsty's advancing belly where the games would once again commence, leaping onto her massive rump and attempting to bring her down in mid-stride. But an effortless flick would send them tumbling into the golden, wisping grass, ginormous paws fumbling over their exposed bellies and disgruntled squawks emanating from their tiny mouths. Kirsty was unimpressed. She had seen it all before and barely broke stride to expel the jittering parasites from her side. Mia, Bama and Baby seized any opportunity to effect their dominance and pounced on tumbling cubs as they grappled the forces of gravity and tried desperately to right themselves after ejection from their mother. Squeak, squeak, squawk, squawk!

The Land Rover trudged on behind, a hundred metres or more away so as not to compromise the advancing hunt or interfere with the group dynamics on constant display. And when the kill was finally made, Creedence and Clearwater would appear to claim their share of the prize. They wouldn't be seen and they wouldn't be heard, but they would always know when dinner was served, and out of the darkness they would loom like angels of death beneath a cloak of dominant despair. Until that time, however, sleep was still the order of the day for them.

And so it was. The blanket of darkness had slowly cast its shroud over the Sukula Plains and Revival's four females sat patiently in the grass, downwind and a safe distance from their oblivious prey. Jacob had tried to anticipate the direction of the charge and positioned himself in a direction that would make no impact on the hunt but would allow them a ringside seat on any action. It was not uncommon for the females to manoeuvre themselves in behind the car and use it for cover to gain extra yardage on their prey without detection. In these instances, Jacob would sit with his lights and engine off and behave like a chunk of granite, waiting for them to move on and try their luck without him. They always did. The big, green lion was neither prey nor threat to Revival – it just was.

"There. Do you hear that? The snorting. They are moving in. Be still and be quiet."

Bird could hear the snorting, but he was clueless as to what it was – momentarily. The once tranquil darkness was suddenly engulfed with an almighty sound of snorting alarms and fleeting feet as five hundred lechwe took to the watery marsh for safety.

"What the hell…"

"Ssshhhhh! No sound!"

He was silenced once again, his heart racing like a greyhound and sweat breaking out on his brow. His fists were tightly clenched, and he strained to try and make sense of what was unfolding in the darkness around them. The charge was halted, save a couple of late hooves dancing in the water, and alarm calls resonated through the black night as if the regiments of antelope were calling in casualty evaluations within their ranks.

"Chase, but no kill. Be silent but remember, chase number one failed." Bird acknowledged the remark without making a sound.

Then once again, a symphony of hooves commenced their ballet across the glimmering stage of Sukula's waters as her lechwe hoards danced the ritual of survival and pitted their wits against the dice of natural selection. It was only a matter of time before one fatal mistake would serve a veritable banquet to the madding crowds, and the fortunate few would feast with the deity of malevolent desire.

I can't believe I'm sitting here, waiting for death. These are lions, man, real-life lions on the rampage, in Africa!

And then Jacob was shrieking in a whispered tone. "There! There! Kill! *Bika pa kyeya! Bika pa kyeya!"*

A high-pitched, spine-chilling scream ripped through the darkened arena and there was no mistaking the cause. Even Bird, a vestal virgin to this sensation, knew that a kill had gone in and an unsuspecting victim had fallen prey to one of these mighty beasts. The spotlight went on and illuminated a flurry of golden bodies tossing and tumbling through the water in apparent mayhem. Jacob switched on the engine and cautiously approached the scene. Kirsty's cubs were running in from one side and intensive growls of the killing females echoed around invisible walls in this deathly chamber. The sound was heart-stopping to Bird, for the first time endorsing his fears of just how fucking hard-core these creatures were.

"They have two. Look, there are two kills. Mia has one and Kirsty has one. Alabama doesn't know which one to join."

But her mind was soon made up, as Creedence leapt into the foray and charged Mia off her kill with a ripping roar that made Bird literally leap into the air. Clearwater was right behind him, grappling with the animal's hindquarters amid a flurry of resonating growls and flying fists. They agreed to disagree for now, and both sat on their respective halves of the prey with a view to feeding first and fighting later.

Meanwhile, Kirsty had delicately sunk away with her kill intact, and she sat to one side of the vehicle, away from the fracas, feeding peacefully with her cubs. She growled and remonstrated at the inevitable advance of her pride females and they duly submitted, bowing their heads and keeping their distance for a second or two before advancing cautiously and starting to nibble on the lechwe's hindquarters. But it wasn't long before a feeding frenzy ripped the once-majestic antelope apart, spraying up crimson blood and exposing its inner core amidst a flurry of bloodied jaws. Then it was heads down and tearing flesh on all sides.

Jacob was frantically scribbling down notes, referencing his GPS and scanning the horizon with the light to search for landmarks and clues as to where they were. As he swept the spotlight over the grassland, something caught his eye and he brought the beam to rest on a female lechwe lying down close to where nine lions were feeding on two of her fallen kin. He spoke to Shadrack, who responded in a low and humble tone, and Jacob then mumbled something incoherently to himself. The lechwe was injured and tried to stand, but it appeared that its back leg had been broken, rendering its flailing attempts to move useless. Jacob scribbled some more.

"Baby is the last to join the others here to feed. I think she has caught this one but let it go because she saw the others had also caught. Maybe she didn't catch it so well and instead of chasing again, she just came here to eat. She didn't realise this lechwe is crippled. Maybe adrenaline helped the animal to get away from her at first, then it collapsed."

"What will happen to it?" Bird asked.

"They will find it. We take off the spotlight, but they will find it."

And find it they did. It was as if an inaudible signal had ricocheted through the air, and the heads of all four females lifted out of the bloodied carcass simultaneously.

They all pointed their noses to the sky, testing the air, then returned to their feeding. All except Mia. Something had got her attention, and she was up and moving like a sniffer dog in the direction of the wounded animal. Jacob followed her with the spotlight, its dim glare illuminating her rump at the very edge of its beam. She suddenly broke into a gallop and charged at the animal, which saw her at the last minute and made a desperate, bleating lunge away from her advancing frame. Mia's front paw came out and bowled it over with one mighty glance, and she was upon it in a flash, gripping the head in her powerful jaws and sitting on its body.

The animal's crying pleas alerted the other females, who ran at her in a bid for seconds, Baby and Bama leaping onto its rump and frantically ripping at the exposed rectum and belly, chasing the prized entrails of the kill. All the while, Mia sat on its shoulders and gripped the animal's head with her teeth. Blood ran in lines down the lechwe's face and into its gurgling mouth as the other two ripped out the intestines. It died slowly, amidst a flurry of nerves kicking out the last of their neural messages as blood gargled and spluttered through its muffled screams.

The lions feasted on, apart from Mia who held firm, sitting on the animal's shoulders and gripping its lifeless, bloodied head in her jaws. It was as if this was her prize and she wanted it to remain intact for her exclusive use. Alabama and Baby tore at the last of her prey's hindquarters and all three began a tug of war that would eventually rip the carcass three ways, leaving the lions to shrink into the darkness, each with their share of the spoils.

Bird was unable to speak. He had no opinion that he could offer on the situation and seemingly no conscious thoughts going through his mind. He felt a full mixed bag of emotions in his body. This was his first day out in Sukula, and already he was on first-name terms with a majestic pride of lions who had just served up a triple kill before him. He had seen them love one another, clean one another, fight one another and play with one another, and now this. Three animals had died in one gripping Sukula moment with the obligatory social role-plays being enacted right before his eyes, and he was left totally astounded. There was simply no way he could leave this place without making his mark on the conservation of its dynamic environment and unassuming people. No way at all.

"What do you think, Mr. Bird? Lions amazing creatures or killers without hearts?"

"I think they are both, Mr. Jacob. I think there can be no place like this on the whole Earth and I think that we are very lucky to be out here witnessing it. I still don't know what you want from me or even why I'm here, but I guess I just have to count my lucky stars that the pontoon is down. You guys are truly gallant for living out here and doing this shit, Jacob, do you know that?"

"What is gallant?" he enquired benignly, still writing in his notebook by torchlight.

"It means brave like a warrior. I guess you're an Eco-Warrior in the truest sense, and right on the front line, at that. Gotta hand it to you, dude, you sure know how to rock your world."

"Thank you. I think our job is done here. They will all be friends again soon and they will start to lick and clean each other. I think now is time for us to return to camp and eat some food for ourselves. You hungry?"

"Wow, hadn't really thought about it. Yeah, I suppose I am. How the hell are we gonna get back, though? I don't see any road."

Jacob reached across and tapped Bird twice in the middle of his chest, right on his solar plexus.

"Inside here, all people have a map. They have a map of the place where they live, and if they listen with the heart instead of with the ear, they find answers in that map. It will always direct them home and tell them what the heart is hearing. If all people listen to their hearts, maybe we have no more problems in this world. The mind talks in language of greed and hate, the heart talks in language of kindness and compassion. These will show us the way to get home, Isamba Noni – every time. We go?"

"So you won't use the GPS then?" They smiled at each other in the darkness. "Yes, Mr. Jacob. We go."

The spotlight swept one last time over the bloodied spectacle. Revival were spread across the carnage site, each with a share from the evening's hunt. The atmosphere was now serene and placid; they all had their bone to chew on and the hunger that had inspired this onslaught was satisfied and silenced. All that was left to do was the mutual grooming of one another to remove blood and guts from their faces, and the cohesion of feline utopia would once again preside over this frenetic and intense family – paradoxed by their unequivocal love for one another and the constant struggle for survival on Sukula's outlandish prairie.

Long may you live, dudes – long may you live!

18

AND THE BEAT GOES ON

The journey home had taken them back past the old fig tree, through the river crossing points, over the floodplains where the thousands of lechwe were and back into the maze of islands that stretched towards the forest. Jacob had managed to retrace his steps right the way back to the workshop, and as he parked the car and killed its lights, Sukula's dark and moonless night once again consumed them. It took a few seconds for Bird's eyes to acclimatise as he hung his book and binocular straps around his neck, but eventually vague shapes began to emerge out of the darkness.

"You have everything, Bird? Ready to go?"

"Yeah... yeah, I think I'm OK. I'll be right behind you. Hang on a minute." He paused, glancing left and right in the opaque light. "Where are you?"

"I am here, behind you."

"Yes... ha ha... yes, of course you are. Lead the way, skipper."

They bumbled and fumbled their way out of the workshop and up the path towards the camp's staff village – at least, Bird bumbled and fumbled; Jacob and Shadrack walked quietly and purposefully. For them this was all very natural, engraved into their senses through centuries of survival in a volatile environment, but for Bird, it was about as far from natural as he could get. He reeked of the

Western world with his awkward obtuseness, and he would fast need to learn the way they behaved and emulate it to stand any chance of survival. There was no awareness in his footsteps, no idea that they may compromise others and no anticipation for uncalculated events.

In his world, a walk at night was illuminated by glaring streetlights, and a paved walkway was always provided. The only other traffic he was likely to encounter would be occasional pedestrians who, like himself, would walk with their heads bowed, collars upturned and eyes focussed only on the floor. There would be no need to keep quiet or be aware of his surroundings because there was nothing to disturb outside the concrete tombs. He was so protected and so pampered in his world that the element of survival had been diluted to just one allelic variation, fixed to a nondescript chromosome that floated randomly in a sea of genetic deviancy.

In nature, however, those who can't survive will die and that is all there is to it. The survival of the fittest – you eat what you kill. In spite of the harrowing day he had just been privy to, Bird was still painfully unaware of the dangers that lurked in the shadows, and had it not been for Jacob and Shadrack then this would surely have been the last walk he ever took. Jacob had already told him of the natural compass lying within his chest, and perhaps he was delivering a subliminal warning to Bird by doing so. It had not been well heeded.

It is reputed that the San people or 'Bushmen' of the Kalahari were so in tune with the compass in their solar plexus that they could feel the padding of distant feet in the desert sand up to five kilometres away. Their barren habitat was so devoid of readily available assets that they had to tap every obtainable resource for survival, and to 'feel' those that were around them with possible access to water and food was essential. It also gave them the ability to track animals for hours on end across monotonous landscapes and still find their way home. Unfortunately, the very same gift that granted them life for so many centuries would ultimately serve as their undoing when great white hunters came to their land and shot them for sport.

Perhaps the same recognition of his own surroundings, and to learn from those who were trying to teach him about them, would have been the safer path for Bird to tread right now. But his callous Western upbringing with its 'hard day at the office' routine rendered him temporarily oblivious to where he was, or indeed what was out there with him, and all he wanted was to get home and put his feet up. His night vision had acclimatised enough to make out large objects around him, such as the trees, but he was so busy walking with his head pointing at his thumping feet that he did not register the two men in front, who silently stopped in their tracks. He walked right into Shadrack, who was duly shunted along into Jacob.

"Wooaa... sorry, dude!"

"SSSHHHH! No sound. *Nzovu!*" came a hurried response from Jacob.

Bird froze. He had come to understand the urgency of these hushed tones and once again his heart pumped loud, long and fast. He stood motionless and tried to absorb as much as possible of the ambient light to make out the cause of this disturbance, but he could see nothing. All he heard was the loud huffing and snorting of what he thought was Jacob in front of him. Had he stopped to think about it, he would have realised that a man like Jacob simply did not make such sounds, and even if he did, they would not be blowing up dust, as was happening a few yards in front of them.

"Jacob – what is it?" Bird hissed his whisper once again.

"Nzovu – elephant. Just here. Ssshh, be still."

Did he say elephant? Just here? Holy shit!

That vital gland delivered a healthy dose of adrenaline into his surging bloodstream and his pounding heart echoed from his bowel to his chin. He looked around and squinted at the darkness to try to get a view, but there was nothing. He tried to see where the other two were looking and squinted there as well. Again, nothing – just black night. But then, with another one of those dust-blowing snorts, the blackness moved, and behind it he could see the distant glow of cooking fires in the village. With the grace of a ballerina and the silence of a majestic fruit bat, the colossal form moved away and into the darkened trees, huffing and blowing as it went.

"Nzovu, Mr. Bird," whispered Jacob eventually. "Elephant often come around here and it is always important to look where you are going and be silent when you walk. Nzovu does not see very well. He only smells. If the wind is like tonight, he won't know you are coming until you step on him. This can be very dangerous because Nzovu can step harder on you than you can on him. Next time, you look. OK?"

"Yes, OK. I'm sorry. It never occurred to me that there would be elephants here. Especially not so close to the camp, I mean, we're only in fucking Africa, mate!"

Bird's sarcasm tried to hide his genuine fright and he chuckled nervously at the end of his ridiculous statement.

"Yes, they come looking for our vegetables. Some of the guys have made warnings for Nzovu to stay away, but they still come. They like sweet potatoes very much."

"What kind of warnings?" Bird followed Jacob's example and kept his voice to a whisper as they waited to make sure the animal had gone.

"They make wires around their gardens. If Nzovu breaks the wire, pieces of the tree fall on his head and he runs away. But Nzovu has learnt about these traps and he steps over the wire or puts his trunk through the fence, and he steals vegetables without the tree falling on his head. Nzovu is very clever. He is also very peaceful. If you do not trouble him, he will not trouble you, but if you scare him or his children, he can kill you. You take care when walking here. OK?"

"Yeah, man, don't you worry, message copied. Fucking elephant, right here!"

An elephant was the last thing he had expected to find on his short trek from the workshop to the village at nine o'clock at night, and really, who could blame him? Where Bird grew up, he didn't just bump into elephants on the road home. The only danger in his sleepy little town would lie in the shadows, where his paranoiac thoughts constructed demons and sorcerers to carve out his very finite and mortal existence. Out here, people didn't have time to be paranoid about imaginary stuff in their minds because the danger was so real. It may not have been witches and leprechauns but there was no shortage of life-threatening perils hiding in the bushes, of which he was now painfully aware.

By the time Bird reached his hut, his nerves were on the threshold of their bearable limit and he almost staggered to his abode. The subdued and intimate atmosphere around the cooking huts was a calm welcome to his homecoming, but altogether too much shit had gone down today for him to relax. Once again, a candle had been lit in the doorway of his hut, and in the glimmer of its flickering light he could see that a new door had been hung. He admired it.

"Oh, Bwana Berd. Welcome. How are you? How was ve day?" Isaac's beautiful voice rang out of the shadows and soothed him instantly.

"Isaac! How you doin', matey?"

"Oh, me, I am just fine. Same, same in life of Isaac. How is Sukula? You see many rions?"

"Yes, Isaac, I see many rions and they even made a kill. Three, in fact."

"Oh, oh, oh, oh. Those fings – vey rike to kill too much. Always ve rions wanting to chase ve lechwe. Them eat so many lechwe. Maybe one day, all lechwe get finished, then ma rions become starving!"

"Ha ha. Yeah, not likely to happen in the near future that, mate. I must have seen more than two thousand today. The buggers are everywhere."

"What mean bugga?" He straightened his gaze momentarily.

"Oh, nothing. It's just an expression in English."

"Oh ho – I see. Rook, Bwana Berd, have you seen? Ma guys make a new door for you."

"Yes, I see. Thank you very much. Who did it?"

"It is Ba Compass. Him make door for you. But other ma guys, them make nice bafloom and toilet for you. Come, I show you."

He led Bird with a swinging hurricane lamp towards the rank ablution shack that Jacob had showed him the day before. The walls were freshly thatched and a second, smaller structure had been erected next to it. He could see that the floors had been laid with mud, which was yet to harden.

"You not go inside because mud on floor still wet, but you rook."

"Wow, man, it rooks really cool," he teased, half caught in Isaac's own dialect and half sarcastically. "Check it out, they've even put up towel rails for me. This is awesome, man. But where's the bath?"

"Oh, Bwana Berd, you no wully 'bout tings rike vat. Me, Isaac, I negotiate with Madam today and her give me baff for you. Is by my house. When mud is dry, we put. But rook, toilet is this side."

Next to his bathroom, the second structure's doorway faced that of the bathroom to make them almost interlinked. He could see no porcelain bowl of a toilet inside, but instead a hole in the ground with smoothed mud around it. It was a long drop and Isaac had even procured a conventional toilet roll for him, which hung on a makeshift holder protruding from the wall. Next to the door, a rough stand of sticks and poles held an enamel hand basin, which was set at about waist height. Built into the stand was a rustic towel rail tied on with fibrous binding, with a hand towel neatly hanging over it. Above the basin, tied on to the thatch, was a small piece of mirror about head height.

"Have you seen, Bwana Berd? Ma guys, they put milla for you for shaving. Is good?"

"Ah, mate, it's totally awesome. Thank you very much. Tell me, Isaac, did you really talk to Sarah about me today?"

"Yes, saa." Isaac nodded enthusiastically.

"Well, what did she say? Is everything OK now?"

"That one? Ohhh, she is vely, vely angly about you, Bwana Berd, but me, I tell her, 'No, Madam. This one not the fault of Bwana Berd. Him a good man and someone, they make mistake for him. Is not the fault of him.' Her say to me, 'Is it how you fink, Isaac? You fink he is a good man?' I say, 'Yes, Madam, this one he a good man, and Jacob teach him so many things about Sukula rions and him become rion man, same rike Savongo. You will see.' Me, I am Isaac. I tell Madam this Bwana Berd, him come good and him learn all things about Sukula and him help us to make money from the muzungu. That is all."

"So, what do you think – does she like me now?" Bird asked, ever hopeful.

"This Madam Sarah? Oh no, saa. She hate you vely, vely much!"

"Oh, great."

"But you know, Bwana Berd. The woman, she is just like that. One day she rike you, another day she hate you. This the way of all women. We men, we no undastand. Better we just leave them to be alone when it is day they not rike you, otherwise they make a big, big trouble for the men. Vely big trouble! We leave alone, they make no trouble. You see?"

"Yeah, man, I see. I guess it's the same the world over. Women – I sure do love 'em but like you say mate, I sure don't understand them. Thank you, Isaac – for everything."

"This no problem, Bwana Berd. You a good man. The suppa is leddy for you. Come, we go. You take bath after suppa. Is OK?"

"It's OK, dude, I'm famished."

"Oh, and have you seen? Isaac, him get extra food for you. The meelk, the tea, some tin of bake beans and some honey from Mabuki. Is inside the house for Bwana. This good, yes? I get food for you, yes?" Isaac's smile shone like a beacon in the night.

"Yes, this is very good my little friend, but please, be careful. I don't want Sarah to catch you and make a big, big trouble for you, OK?"

"You no wully, Bwana Berd." He chuckled. "Me, I am Isaac. I rook after kitchen. Is only me who knows where all ma food is kept. Isaac, he very careful, he no get pluned."

"What is pluned?"

"Pluned – is mean fired. Me no get fired."

"OK, but you just watch yourself, mate. All right?"

Isaac smiled again. It was a knowing smile, as if to say: I know what I'm doing, white boy. You concentrate on your gig and I'll concentrate on mine. Look after the lions and I'll look after the food. Or was that just his interpretation?

Bird dropped his kit in his room and saw the extra rations that Isaac had procured for him. He smiled to himself and shook his head slowly. Why did this cat look after him so – why did all of them? What had affected Sarah so badly, but not them? Did they just not care as much as she did for the whole affair? Were they more used to disappointment than she? Or was it the fact that they simply didn't read into the situation the same judgements that she did? Maybe they just accepted people for who they were and not who they were supposed to be. He didn't really know, but one thing was for sure: whatever the reasons, he thanked his lucky stars that they were different. Had they had the same reaction as Sarah, he would be up a creek with no paddle right now.

Dinner was a much more subdued and intimate affair than it had been the night before. Aside from Isaac and Bird, there was another man dining whom Isaac had called 'Ba Compass'. He was the carpenter responsible for Bird's new door and he spoke not a word of English. His hair was matted into tight curls and tinted with the off-grey colour pertaining to his ageing years, and the lines in his forehead added a wisdom that the elderly in these parts carried so graciously on their faces, but his story was not a usual one.

A man in his mid-sixties, Compass was considered ancient by the rest of the staff in camp. Even Jacob was only thirty-eight, and the majority of his men were under twenty-five. Compass had been contracted into the Research Centre by its founder eight years previously, and together with Jacob and Isaac, he was among the first employed to dig the foundation that was now the Sukula Research Institute. He was employed on account of two main factors:

Firstly, he was one of the most notorious poachers in the area. He was rumoured to have shot the last black rhino with a homemade weapon back in the early eighties and apparently had been the demise of many an elephant, too. And secondly, as one of the most notorious poachers, he knew where all the animals were most of the time and was able to navigate through the bush with astounding ease – hence his name of Compass. The Institute's founder deemed that by giving meaningful jobs to poachers, it would hopefully deter them from their activities and put a slightly more profound value on the heads of their animals. It was Compass' job, then, to establish a road network that would enable researchers to get where they needed to go in the quickest time possible and hopefully open up new areas for them to study in the process. He had excelled.

Out here a man could lose his mind in search
of truth he'll never find,
Just like the mad who lead the blind, this the
fable of mankind.

The art of road-making in these parts was indeed a profound skill to be cherished. The forest was thick, irregularly interspersed with open grasslands superseding an array of habitats from sparse wetlands and riverine thickets through to scrub bushland and the primary forests that surrounded Sukula itself. These improbable breaks in this dense mass of trees looked all too similar in makeup, and for a man to recognise one from the other took years of walking experience that most did not have.

Compass' father was of the last generation of true bush people around Sukula, untouched by the inappropriate spattering of an education system the colonialists had thrown at them and also unchallenged by the preachings of nearby American missionaries. His generation were hunter-gatherers who understood the dynamics of their environment and recognised the delicate balance of the ecochain within which they lived. Colonialism, along with its insatiable desire for trophy hunting and the onslaught of religious conversion from the missionaries, had compromised many of the ancient tribal traditions that had held these communities firm through centuries of time, and Nature had fast become a gift from the white man's God to exploit at will, as opposed to a power and force of its own. If all the animals died, it was no longer an issue because the people had already been saved.

Most of the population were left at sixes and sevens regarding their place in this new world community, thinking that the way to salvation lay in a pair of jeans and a Bible. The ancient gods that had given them wood for their fires and meat for their pots were now gone – mere creations of a more formidable force that would 'strike down with grave vengeance and furious anger those who tried to oppose it', but one that never revealed itself. Confused and bemused, they trudged along in a spiritual slipstream that left a loophole in their folklore, allowing them to consume and exhume the natural resource that had perpetuated their existence for years without reprisal. The ride had begun, and the spiral went only one way.

In weeping forests ablaze with green as if
awakened from a dream,
Just like a God that's never been, these the
things a man has seen.

Compass had been taught the way of his father and the elders of their tribe. He knew of no greater God, he knew of no glittering prize and he knew no other way than to hunt for his gain. If someone wanted the tusks of an elephant or the horn of a rhino and they were prepared to trade him an automatic weapon or a bicycle for the quarry, he was in no position to refuse. He worked with these traders for a number of years and killed many animals to placate their insatiable greed, but the riches they had promised and the prize they once assured seemed never to actually materialise. He reasoned that some kind of anarchy had broken out in the peaceful world his father had shown him, but he couldn't fathom why. The ancient traditions of respect and accountability were gone and great white trophy hunters paraded through his land one after the other, each paying small fortunes to kill everything that moved, so why shouldn't he get rich off it, too? Why was it that they were labelled heroes and he a worthless poacher?

A time of peace, an age gone by, a hole burnt
in the deep blue sky,
Just as you pause to wonder why, there's a
bomb the man let fly.

Compass, then, found himself feeling disillusioned and betrayed, torn between the ancient culture his father had taught him and the potential material gains of his unruly profession. He knew the rhino population was being decimated because of the demand for its horn, but he had reasoned over the years that at least he was making a living to provide for his future and family. However, once the numbers got low and his quarries harder to find, he started questioning the foundation of this unprofitable enterprise and sought alternatives to his most unsatisfactory lifestyle. He soon learned that this white man, with his bizarre desires for horn and hide and his furious and mighty Bible, had destroyed the culture that had formulated the very foothold of his society and every belief they'd ever held true. The ideal world and ancient creed of his ancestors was gone, so who would actually care if he killed the last rhino that lived here? Who would even know? Only the traders with their lies and deceit – and if they stopped coming, then maybe life could resume the beautiful harmony his father had once told him about. But it was not to be. After the demand for rhino came the elephant – then the meat, then the trophies, and finally even lions themselves. The truth was the traders in their various guises would never stop coming, and one way or another they had actually been coming for centuries.

Whether out of guilt for the slain animals or a fundamental hatred of the people who had deceived him, no one knows, but the day arrived when Compass laid down his weapons in the face of a dwindling trade in ivory and simply refused to carry on killing. His fellow poachers were outraged at his decision and even tried to oust him from the community, but his resolve stood firm. He tried to make them understand that the continuation of their sordid occupation would ultimately effect its demise on them all, but these were futile words that paled into insignificance alongside the supposed glittering prize. Without him, though, their hunts became less successful and the supply of ivory to the traders of the area slowly dried up, forcing them to move on to more lucrative domains. Two years later, Compass began work at the Institute and the last of the elephants lived to fight another day.

Bird passed on his gratitude for the new door, using Isaac as a translator, and Compass acknowledged him with a humble bow and sat quietly while Bird and Isaac talked through dinner. There were no bloopers to send Bird off in tears tonight and it was starting to feel a little more natural to him. He ate heartily and quickly, his appetite strong from a day in the African sun, and when dinner was finished, the three men moved their stools and rested their backs on the poles supporting Isaac's kitchen.

Compass rummaged through his pockets and produced an old piece of newspaper, from which he tore a strip. He then removed a small, plastic packet from his person and plucked some of its entrails into one hand. He seemed to pick through the form and discard unwanted sections onto the floor, pouring the remaining contents of his hand into the newspaper and rolling it into a long, fat cone that he licked and sealed then tapped on his knee to tidy up loose ends. He lit it in the fire and sat back, inhaling a huge well of smoke.

Bird looked on, salivating with delight. This had to be home-grown weed, and, sure enough, the rich aroma of marijuana soon filled the air and illuminated Bird's pleading eyes. Compass said something to Isaac in his rough and croaky voice, bringing a smile to both men.

"Compass say you rooking rike you want a *jamba*. Is it so?" Isaac asked.

"What is a jamba?"

"Is cigalet he smoke. It make strange things in the mind."

"Yeah, I know all about the jamba and yes, he is right, I would love some."

Isaac passed on the message and Compass wrinkled his face into a knowing smile. He handed Bird the packet and issued some form of instruction as he did so, staring long and hard, straight into Bird's eyes. He looked to Isaac for assistance.

"Compass say he grow jamba for many years. This one from the camp. It vely strong. He say white man must be careful when smoke the jamba cigalet, or you can run into the bush with no clothes and be eated by rion. Is it so?"

"Ha ha, yes, it is so! Tell Compass not to worry. Tell him where I come from, we also smoke very strong jamba and I am used to it. And thank him, as well. How do you say thank you?"

"Is *twasanta mwan-eh*. I say for you, then you follow." Isaac looked at Compass and bowed his head slightly forward while clasping his hands together in front of him. "Twasanta mwan-eh." The words almost melted from his mouth.

Compass responded by gently clapping his hands together and growling out the words: "*Mwan-eh, Sakyo mwan-eh.*"

Bird followed suit and bowed his head similarly towards Compass with his hands clasped in front of him. The action was easier than the words and his pronunciation must have left something to be desired, but Compass got the gist and afforded him the same response.

"Twasanta mwan-eh. Twasanta mwan-eh. Twasanta mwan-eh…" Bird whispered out the phrase to himself over and over as he sat back and inspected the weed.

It was home grown, that was for sure – full of bud, sticks and seed with some dust in the bottom of the packet. Large, glistening, dried-out heads bobbed around in his hands as he tried to extract some of the prize, and before long he had laced up a similar sized cone to the one Compass was now merrily sucking on.

Compass squinted at Bird, intrigued by the cigarette papers he had used. With a gesture of his hand, he beckoned a closer inspection.

The lad offered an explanation in his language as he passed him the papers to examine. Through Isaac's translation, he showed Compass that they had a glue strip along the top for ease of sealing, and he pointed out the texture of the skins, which gave an even burn and meant that the bare minimum of paper was inhaled into the lungs.

Compass cocked his head to one side, then laughed quietly. The technicality of it all amused him – it was a good day if he even had paper to roll with. Usually he smoked a hand-crafted pipe, but with the frequent movement in and out of town for supplies, newspapers were becoming more readily available, which in turn gave him more spliffs to smoke. Bird, on the other hand, was not content with the fact that there was an increase of newspaper here; he had to bring his own with fancy glue on them as well. White people were definitely as weird to Compass as they were to Isaac, no two ways about it.

Isaac chuckled inwardly as Compass, through his chortling grins, expressed his derision of the cigarette papers that he now handed back to Bird.

"What did he say, Isaac?"

"Him Compass, him say muzungu have many fings in their life. They always having special tools for every job. We muntu, we just making the plan but muzungu, him have plan already. Compass, him rike your papers."

"Thank you." Turning to Compass with his hands clasped together and a belittling exaggeration of his bad accent: "Twasanta mwan-eh."

Compass once again responded, but with puzzlement in his eyes. Isaac guessed he was wondering why the white man was thanking him – he certainly hadn't been complimentary; quite the opposite, in fact. He had abused him for being a lightweight who had to use special papers with glue on them, and he had described his people as weird because they couldn't smoke a good bit of wholesome newspaper. Why on Earth was he being thanked?

Bird sat back and examined his spliff in a divine contemplation of its emphatic prowess. The last smoke he'd had was probably on the train with the lads when they took him up to the airport, but he couldn't really remember. His last two days at home were a barbituated whirlpool, and quite how he had managed to leave England at all was something of a mystery. It might explain the fact that he had arrived so badly prepared for a stay in the African bush, and it was definitely the reason for the filthy condition in which he had arrived a few days earlier.

The art of lighting joints from an open fire was not as easy as Compass had made it look. It was too hot for Bird to put his face near the flame, so he kind of wafted his spliff aimlessly through the fire, hoping that it would eventually ignite without melting his hand first, but it just wasn't happening. Every time he removed the joint and put it up to his lips to start drawing, it went out, forcing him to repeat the ridiculously painful process over and again. Compass chuckled quietly to himself and once again barked some words at Isaac.

"Him Compass, him ask if you need help with jamba ciglet?" Isaac enquired.

"Ha, yes, ha ha! Ow, fuck, that's hot. Huh, yeah. Not really got the hang of this yet, have I? No, it's all right, tell Compass thank you very much..." turning to Compass once more, "Twasanta mwan-eh... but I have to learn myself." And he returned to his agonising task.

Compass was once again amused by the fool's insistence on thanking him for the abuse, when what he had said to Isaac was, "Let's see how long it takes the dipshit white boy to burn his fingers and trash his spliff." He shook his head in disbelief as he reached down and removed a glowing stick from the fire, which he handed to Bird.

Bird accepted the stick from Compass. There was a pause as he once again realised his lunacy and gazed incredulously at the purpose-built lighter, as if trying to fathom its blinding simplicity.

Compass leaned in and stared long and hard at Bird. The fire's glimmering reflection danced over his face and illuminated his eyes against the black night, suspending Bird's reality for an instant and making him feel like a child bumbling through an antique shop. The simplistic wisdom of a thousand lifetimes resonated from these staring eyes.

> *A tribal hunter counts his dead, so many*
> *thoughts pass through his head.*
> *Just as you lie awake in bed, this the force a*
> *man will dread...*

"Twasanta mwan-eh." Bird took the stick but kept his eyes fixed on Compass indignantly. He rolled the glowing timber across his spliff and chuffed out smoke plumes from the other end.

"You are wise and I am foolish, Mr. Compass – this I know," he said, eventually, with smoke trickling from his lips. "But at least I am trying. Most of my friends would have given up long before now, mate, and that's a fact. If I cause you amusement, then the prize is mutual, for I have no wish to ever cause you pain. I laugh when you laugh, even if it's at my expense." He sat back and sucked at his joint.

By way of reply, words grumbled and wheezed their way from Compass' mouth in his local tongue as he stared intently at Bird. He bowed his head, then leant back against his pillar and resumed negotiations with his own spliff, inhaling a deep well of smoke. Bird looked to Isaac, who wasn't smoking. His interpretation now adopted an air of sombre sincerity.

"Him Compass. Him say you are Isamba Noni, the bird talker. You have the heart of a hunter and the spirit of a rion. Him respect you. That is all."

Bird said nothing – he merely bowed his head in the direction of the wise, old hunter and leant back in a similar manner. He was getting the hang of this now. He was earning the respect of people like Compass whilst sharing the age-old tradition of smoking mind-altering plants for the purpose of spiritual meditation. It gave him acceptance, which in turn gave him purpose, and this thing called resolve was setting like concrete into his being.

The heart of a hunter and the spirit of a lion? I'll take that!

As the smoke enveloped him, he reflected on his harrowing day and felt the warmth of the herb cradle him in the womb of its presence. What prospects would tomorrow hold in this strange and distant land? What encounters would he have to face and what challenges must he overcome in the simple action of existence in Africa? What would Revival be doing and how many more priceless gifts would Sukula bestow upon him? No one could know. One thing was for sure, though: this home-grown weed was now starting to kick his little white ass – real bad.

Out here a man has lost his mind in the
endless quest for abandoned time,
Just as this fuse ignites the mind, this the
failure of mankind.

19

CRANE DANCE

Bird blinked three times at the comatose reflection in his broken mirror. His eyes were heavy and throbbing and black stains hung like rain clouds underneath them, dripping ingrained sleep onto his face. He pulled them open wide and stared at his reflection.

Mutant bud, man, I slept like the dead – look like it too. Mum?

He inadvertently skipped down memory lane for just a second and saw the image of his mother's face smiling with that feigned belligerent sincerity she always carried to disguise her torment. She was sitting at the kitchen table in their old house nursing a bottle of hard liquor with an empty glass, rocking back and forth with that customary ill ease as a garbled drone tumbled from her blue and lifeless lips.

His face crumpled into a searching stare, looking for his own reflection, but the mirror was consumed by this image of his mother – a wretched tomb encasing her former self – and he was nowhere to be found. She stood up from her table and moved over to where he sat, wearing her smile like a mask. She was still speaking but nothing made sense; the sounds were not audible enough to comprehend. There was no aggression in this image – she was just moving towards him with her arms outstretched in a motherly embrace – but he hid his face and prayed for redemption as her expression contorted into that of a demon and she lashed out at his quaking, infant form.

He screamed out loud and pulled himself away from the mirror as nervous ripples caressed his skin. His arms were wrapped around his torso, his body shivering in the warm morning air. Around him, the unfamiliar sounds of his environment began to register, and he could hear the muffled tones of men and women talking in this unfamiliar tongue, then the shriek of a baby somewhere off in the distance. He looked around and gathered himself together, moving back to his enamel basin and splashing warm water over his face.

Bloody hell! That was my mother – what am I thinking about her for? God knows how long it's been. Maybe it was the weed – I did get very stoned last night. I haven't slept like that in years. Compass was right, that Sukula bud really did kick my ass! My mum… I wonder if she's still alive…

"Good morning, Mr. Bird. I believe your porridge is ready from Isaac's wife. Are you going to be long? We need to be going soon."

"Good morning, Jacob. Thank you; I won't be long. Same routine as yesterday?"

"Yes, same, only today we look for other prides. We will stay out for lunch again, but I think we'll come back a bit early tonight. No need to see if Revival kills. I think they'll do the same as last night. They do the same every night at this time of the month, while the moon is late and the early evening is dark."

"Oh really? You don't watch them hunt every night?"

"No. Just last night because it was important for you to see how they behave. Today the men will make a table and chair for you underneath this old cooking hut. I will get hurricane lamps from the Madam, and you can start to write reports every night about what we do with the lions and give them to Madam. Today you must take notes to remember for the reports. Is it OK?"

Bird felt like he'd just been given a horrendous assignment at school, and a lump of concern globulated in his trachea. He swallowed to try to remove it, but the psychological paranoia of his assignment gripped him like a fever.

"Reports? Yes, I guess so. I don't know if I'll be any good, though – I don't really know what goes into a report on lions. You'll have to help me."

"It's no problem. I have some old reports from Savongo which you can read. You just copy what he said but you tell of our story and not his. I'll see you at the workshop."

"Savongo wrote reports? Are you sure?"

Jacob had turned to leave, but he glanced back over his shoulder, his face registering mild confusion. "Yes, I am sure. What makes you ask?"

"Nothing, really." Bird started to stammer with the insanity of what he was about to say. "It's j…just that I thought S…S…Savongo was some kind of god. How would he write reports?"

Jacob's stare confirmed Bird's suspicion. "Savongo was a man. That was the name we gave him – Luke Templar was his real name. In our language Savongo means 'the unworried man'. Mr. Templar was very brave, and his heart was extremely tall. It was he who started this place. Three years ago, he disappeared in the night and we have not seen him since that time. No one knows what happened to him. Some say he became mad from living with the lions and ran away, others say it was the hunters who put a spell on him and he died in the bush. We do not know."

"Really? That's what some say? What do you think?"

"I think he is dead. I'll see you at the workshop." And with that, Jacob melted into the village – pragmatic and realistic as ever.

"You know, Bwana Berd, Savongo, him also smoke plenty jamba," a voice suddenly echoed from the other side of his hut. "Me, I think the jamba have turn him crazy." The edges of Bird's eyes crumpled in a perplexed intrigue as he turned to look at the man who spoke. "Savongo, him love these rions so much. Him know evryfing about rions. The rions were his life. Some, they say Savongo smoke so much jamba him turn into a rion and go out to Sukula – the prace where all ma rions do live. They say that one day, him come back and make fight with Creedence and Clearwater and him take females for Revival. You will see, one day another rion, him come and him be very, very big. Him take females for himself and when him come, you will see, this is Savongo."

Raymond had been standing nearby, listening to Bird and Jacob's conversation. He was peeling a raw sweet potato with a homemade knife, whittling the skin as if it were timber. Every so often he would snap a piece off the root and put it in his mouth, crunching it like an apple and chewing loudly with his mouth open.

Unlike Isaac, Raymond was tall and gangly. He had longer, unkempt hair and his uniform was bedraggled and worn. His gum boots were ripped at the top and patched with old tyre rubber, making them uneven and cumbersome. He fitted the persona of Africans that Bird had envisaged from his paltry media stereotype back home, and for a moment, Bird stood mesmerised by the concocted apparition.

"No one know what happen to Savongo," he continued amidst a mouth full of yam. "But the witch docta is telling me that him have seen a new rion in the dream. This rion is too big and very powafool. The hair is golden like the sun. Him telling me this rion, him not born of Sukula, him come from another place. Somewhere very far from here, somewhere too far for the rion to walk – somewhere in world of spirit. This how the rions they used to look here. Them all very, very big. The body is blue like the sky and the hair is golden like the sun. The hunters, them kill all Sukula males who looks like this. Now, all are finished, but the witch docta say him have seen this rion in the dream and him bereev it is Savongo."

Bird stared with deep intensity at Raymond as he recounted his tale and whittled his yam, the tune from *The Twilight Zone* echoing through his mind. This god called Savongo was actually Luke Templar, the founder of the Sukula Research Institute who disappeared under strange circumstances three years ago. No wonder Sarah was having trouble keeping this place afloat: its driving force had gone – vanished in the night. And now there was talk of a new male lion, a Sukula male, the last of whom had been shot by hunters however long ago. A new male from the spirit world to challenge Creedence and Clearwater and bring back the extinct Sukula gene.

So, that's why he took half a sugar in his tea. He wasn't a god at all – he was a bloke all along. A mere mortal dude.

"When did the witch doctor see this lion in his dream, Raymond?"

"Him see just now – maybe two weeks ago. You will see, Bwana Berd. This ma witch docta, him know evryfing about this place. When he say he have a dream and him see image of rion, this rion him come. You will see." And with that, Raymond spun on his heels and sauntered in the direction of camp, the rubber on his gum boots flapping up against his shins as he moved.

What a weird morning, man. Anything could happen today.

Bird was more prepared for Sarah this morning and he clocked her presence long before he was in sight of the workshop. The voice of her barking orders drowned out the perpetual dawn chorus like a Megadeth concert over Beethoven's Fifth at the Albert Hall as Bird lurked ominously in the shadows, waiting for his ride. Jacob reversed the car out of the workshop and Bird swung into the front seat as it passed by without so much as a glance.

Sarah saw the manoeuvre and felt a twinge of anger in her gut, but it soon passed. He was doing as he was told – he was staying out of her way. Jacob had asked her for hurricane lamps, stationery and a chair so they could start compiling reports, so maybe there was hope for this fool yet.

"Tell me about the Sukula lions, Jacob. Large, blue bodies like the sky and golden manes like the sun?" Bird asked as they clattered down the dusty track.

"You have been talking with Raymond. Better you don't listen to the men when they talk of the witch doctor's dreams. Can it be that a man can become the spirit of a lion and come here from another world? These males are gone, Mr. Bird, and that is all we can say."

"Well, you can at least tell me about them, can't you?"

Jacob was once again synchronised with his machine as they lurched through the forest and out onto the plains where animals in their thousands dotted the horizon. Nothing is reliable and permanent in Africa. It is a dynamic environment subject to massive changes at the drop of a proverbial hat, but sunrise on a clear summer's morning never fails to illuminate the heart and lift the spirits of mortal men. Its molten glow lit up the air and painted a golden world in the grasp of its Midas touch.

"Yes, we used to have big males in this place," Jacob yelled over the sound of the engine. "Much bigger than Creedence and Clearwater. Their faces were round and their shoulders strong, standing higher off the ground than an average male. The mane was concentrated around the head and neck, and not onto the back as you find in other parts of Africa. The body was more grey than blue, but this is because of the soil in Sukula. It is called black cotton soil. You can see it is very dark and this affects the colour of the lions' coat. It gave them a colour of blue, but they were not actually the colour of the sky. Their mane was very light and you could say it was golden. When the light was shining right on them, they had a very strange look, and in our tradition, we have stories of these males who came from the god of lions in the sky. We say that these were the spirits of our ancient warriors who turned themselves into lions after they died. Because they are spirits and they live in the sky, these are the colours they have, which makes them different from all other lions in the park. But these are just stories, Mr. Bird, they are not the truth. Sukula males were bigger because the food resource is very good here. They also swim from a very young age and they climb trees. This is why they have big shoulders and stand a bit tall. They are not the spirits of our ancestors, but you can see how the stories began?

"The last male was shot just four days before Savongo disappeared. We caught the hunter and wanted to prosecute him because he was hunting inside the park. A big fight happened between hunter and Savongo, but we had proof that the hunter was in the wrong place, so he was definitely going to lose. The day before Savongo was supposed to go to town for court case with the hunter, he disappeared. Everything else is just stories about what happened to him. We are scientists, Mr. Bird, we have to remain objective."

"Yes, yes, of course we do. So, no one knows what happened to the man? He simply disappeared?"

"Yes, just disappeared."

"But come on, Jacob, you obviously knew the guy well – what do you really think happened to him?"

"You know, Savongo was born just near this place. He knew everything about the bush. He could speak our language and, like us, he grew up in this area. It would be very difficult to take him from his house at night because he was a brave warrior who knew this land, but even so, I think the hunter killed him. I think he came in the night and put a muti to make Savongo sleep, and then he took him into the bush and killed him. If a man dies out here, you will never find any remains. The hyenas and the vultures, they eat everything, even the bones. You will never find him."

"Fucking hell, mate, it all sounds a bit heavy. What happened to the hunter?"

"Madam Sarah, she took on the case and the hunter was prosecuted – but not for the death of Savongo. We found no body and police have no case without a body. They say it is possible that Savongo ran away, maybe everything became too much for him to stay, and he ran. But me, I knew Savongo well – this was not his way. He was a soldier, a fighter like I have never seen. He had the heart of a lion. No one can know for sure what happened. But for the hunter, his hunting licence and business were taken away and he returned to his home country."

"Which was where?"

"South Africa. He came from South Africa. You remember I told you we have a new hunter here called Mr. Visser? It was his brother. Maybe he has come to get revenge for what we did to his brother."

"Holy shit, man, the plot thickens. Now his brother has come back to avenge the situation? I don't really know if I am up to this task any more man, it's all getting a bit hectic. This place is worse than fucking Baghdad!"

"We have to make the hunters understand, Mr. Bird. They have to see that if hunting is controlled and the area is made safe for lions, there can be plenty for them to hunt. Savongo was trying to tell the government people in town that with control, this place can be best for all people. They just have to stop for two or three years and allow lions to settle. After that, there will be plenty lions here for hunting. This is what we must continue to do. We have to make the place safe for lions to breed. They are quick to recover, and if we leave them alone then they will make plenty lions for all – same like it used to be. Maybe this new Mr. Visser is better than his brother, maybe he learns from the mistake of the brother and he will work together with us. This is all we can hope for."

"Yeah, but you said yourself that he is already coming inside the park and he is telling you that you don't know where the boundary is. It doesn't sound to me like this guy is here to co-operate."

"Maybe so, but maybe not. I think he just gets desperate because it has been a bad season for him. Soon the hunting season is over and maybe next year, after the rains, we can make a change. We have to fight, Mr. Bird, and you have to help us." Jacob almost shouted this as an instruction and Bird had to wonder how bad it was.

"The situation must be pretty dire if you are looking to me for help," he quipped. "Look, I'll do what I can, but I'm still not convinced that I'm the cat for the job – you dig?"

"Dig what?"

"Hey, check it out, wattled cranes – starboard bow, eighty metres – pair! Oh my life, they're amazing. I didn't know you had wattled cranes here."

Jacob threw a glance in the direction of Bird's frantic gesticulation. He didn't much like being interrupted during such an important discussion and he was desperate to make this young white boy understand the situation – these distractions simply weren't helping. Wattled cranes were plentiful out here; they could see them any time of the day. There was more pressing business to attend to and it certainly didn't involve bird-watching. Jacob afforded him the courtesy, though, and reasoned that the way to this boy's heart was definitely through the birds and not the lions – first damn white boy he'd ever met who was like that, in so many ways.

"Yes, there are many. Sukula is one of the best places in Africa for cranes. We also have crowned cranes here."

"Why didn't we see any yesterday?"

"I think we did. I think you were just too concerned about Mia eating you yesterday. Anyway, today we are in a different place looking for other lions. You like cranes?"

"Well, this is the first time I've ever seen them in the wild, but yeah, I'm a bird man, I love cranes."

Jacob stopped the car and Bird watched in awe, astounded by the elegance of the cranes and deeply moved by the experience of seeing them wandering free across an open African floodplain. They had brilliant white necks, long, slender bills with red wattles dangling beneath them and grey skullcaps on the tops of their heads. The feathers on their bodies were a silvery grey that extended into long and drooping tail plumes, and their underbellies were dark – a deep contrast to the brilliant white of their necks and shoulders. They moved across the plains in pairs and occasionally small groups, gently probing at the soft soil for their food of small reptiles, frogs, tubers and grain.

"God, they are amazing – so graceful, so elegant. Have you ever seen them dance, Jacob? Do you know they have an intricate courtship dance that is seldom seen?"

"Maybe in your country, Mr. Bird, but out here, they dance all the time."

"No, man, you must be mistaken. When do they breed? Dancing is only for courtship during breeding."

"I don't know when they breed but I tell you, out here, they dance because they love to live in Sukula. They dance all the time."

Bird dropped his binoculars and looked across at Jacob, slightly perplexed. Yes, he did have the advantage of local knowledge and he had lived here all his life, but this ritual that Bird referred to was not something that one just nonchalantly spoke of – this was one of the many fascinating marvels in the avian world. It is an intricate and complicated courtship display, not some wild expression for the love of life in Sukula. He must be mistaken; the dancing that he had seen must be some freaky adaptation of gathering food, not the elusive ritual that Bird spoke of.

"Are you absolutely sure, Jacob? I mean, I know this is your place and you should know better than anyone what goes on here, but are you really sure about this?"

"Yes, I am sure. Look, see them now – is that not the dance you are speaking of?"

Jacob pointed across to the pair, motioning at their display, and Bird could hardly believe his eyes. The male had instigated the routine by stooping his head and picking up an offering of food in his bill, which he tossed in the direction of his partner to begin the heart-stopping sequence. His neck gyrated up and down, moving the head close to the ground and rhythmically raising it to its highest elevation repeatedly. Then his wings came out in huge fans on either side of his body as he circled his female. The wings were extended and folded in a rhythmic unison with his gyrating neck as his feet skipped the light fandango in circular motions. This built into a circular, quivering crescendo that culminated as he threw his body into the air in short, fluttering leaps, exposing his legs and belly. The female acknowledged the dance similarly, splaying her wings and skipping around, until both birds were continuously leaping into the air with wings outstretched and necks waving in beautifully sustained motions.

The display was breathtaking and Bird followed it in amazement through his binoculars. They pranced around for a few minutes, continuing on and on in perfectly balanced circles, each complementing the stunning grace of the other before gradually slowing to a perfect halt. At its termination, both birds stood facing each other and shook off the plumes in their tail feathers to signify the end of the show. This performed, they casually resumed feeding, gently probing at the ground again for food. Wattled cranes have been known to pair for life and their bonds are as solid as rocks on the ocean's floor.

"Wow, man, that was freaking cool – did you guys see it?" Bird turned to face the passenger in the back of the car. "Did you see that, Shadrack? Kuwaama?"

Shadrack laughed heartily and looked at Bird. "*Mwane ehh. Kikatampe kyawaama!*"

"He says yes, this is very beautiful," said Jacob, interpreting the obvious.

"And what do you think, Mr. Jacob? Even though it is not scientific and they are not lions, I see that even you appreciate the dance of the wattled cranes."

"You know, Mr. Bird, if I had the choice to be any animal in the world, this is what I would choose. They are always peaceful, they are always beautiful and they are always happy. They just dance because they are happy to be alive here in this place, Sukula. They know no enemies and they fear no evil. They always move with the wife, never fighting, never arguing, never complaining. If the food is little here, they spread their wings and fly to another place with the wife next to them. They realise how lucky they are, and they give thanks every day to the world for being alive. This is why they dance.

"You white people always like to make simple things complicated. You travel all over the world, spending much money to see this dance which you think only happens for courtship. What you do not realise is that this male always has his wife with him. Why does he need to dance to win her love? He dances because she is here, by his side and they are together in the place of much beauty – Sukula Plains. If the white men never see this dance, it is because their eyes are not open. They are blinded by what they call intelligence, but sometimes this intelligence makes things to happen that are not supposed to happen.

"This is Shadrack, he is a simple man but he has seen the dancing cranes every day of his life because his eyes are open. There is nothing in his mind to cloud his judgement. He knows they do not do it for courtship, they do it for happiness." Shadrack nodded in agreement, despite having no clue as to what he was agreeing with. "This is why you will always see people of our tribe dancing – whether there is music or not, we will dance," Jacob continued. "The reasons are the same – we are happy to be alive in this land of Sukula, nothing more and nothing less. I am glad you have seen this. I like to show you things that make you happy. Now is the time we need to go and find more lions. We go?"

Bird sighed a deep and contented breath. His life was now complete. This image would stay with him forever and lighten his heart any time the inconsequential rot of human existence invaded his psyche. This was where he wanted to be, on the Sukula Plains with wattled cranes that danced every day just for the hell of it. Could there really be a heaven up there in the sky when Sukula was real and alive on this earth?

Is there really a stairway?

"Yes, Mr. Jacob, we go. I guess my witch doctor was right to send me here, after all."

As Jacob cranked over the starter motor and the engine purred into life, Bird caught sight of something way off in the distance and stared hard through his glasses to identify it.

"Jacob, what is that?" he asked rather deliberately.

"Oh no, that is Visser," came the reply, and both men stared intently through binoculars at the distant image of a vehicle snaking its way over the Plains. "We are close to the boundary here and Visser is hunting. Better we go, I don't want to see him."

Bird looked over the vehicle and was filled with unfamiliar repugnance at its sinister intrusion. He could see a man standing in the back with a rifle in one hand. There were others, trackers and spotters scanning the horizon for prey and a very large, rounded man driving the vehicle. His hat was brown and wide-brimmed, and it concealed his face from Bird's view. It reminded him of Butch Cassidy and the Sundance Kid when they were being chased by that posse that they never saw clearly, they just loomed behind like some putrid disease. Such was the hunting vehicle, a venereal sore on the face of this beautiful landscape. Jacob started off in the opposite direction and drove purposefully away. Bird suddenly experienced a pungent, rotting taste in his mouth.

Jacob and Shadrack shouted at one another over the hum of the vehicle, negotiating the direction in which they needed to head. They may have been in a different place from yesterday but it sure as shit looked the same to Bird. How these guys managed to navigate their way around here during the day was a marvellous feat in itself, but to do this at night with the excitement of lion kill running through their veins was quite exceptional. Bird kept looking over his shoulder to see if the hunting vehicle was still visible, but only a distant dust plume rose over Sukula.

Visser was gone – the question was, where? The taste in his mouth remained.

They followed a faded track that seemed to peter out and reform at intermittent intervals. They were obviously running parallel to the delta system, as hordes of lechwe stretched to the horizon and beyond alongside them. In the near distance, the similar-looking puku were closer at hand, indicating that the ground was a bit higher and drier than where the lechwe were.

There were also islands of vegetation in this area, springing up like icebergs from the golden sea. Their long palm fronds waved and wisped in the breeze, brushing against tall trees in random, floundering motions – slaves to the wind. A group of the 'Mardi Gras' painted horse-type creatures that Jacob had called roan antelope, startled by the vehicle, came crashing through an island, scampering onto the amber-tinted grasslands where they broke into a gelding's gallop and disappeared.

Myriad birds twittered, flickered and danced through the islands' treetops, their grassland compatriots darting in and out of the meadow as the vehicle flushed them from their grassy lairs. Brightly-coloured grasshoppers flashed in and out of view as this machine, this terrestrial vessel, wavered across the anatomical sea of life. They were like dolphins at a ship's bow, leaping and flying with graceful ease.

"Look, there, lions! Must be Kelongos, and the cubs are with them," Jacob yelled.

"Wicked, more cubs. How many in this pride?"

"Seven and one big male. I don't want you to say like yesterday that no one told you about the male, OK? Today there is a male." Jacob afforded a wry smile from the side of his lips but didn't made eye contact with Bird.

"OK, OK! I'll try to control myself today, just as long as they don't come sniffing around the door again."

Bird was laughing and joking, almost complacent about the fact that he was on his way to meet his second pride of lions. It seemed as though he'd been out here forever after yesterday's events, but the reality of his situation began to take its grip and his chest tightened with anticipation as the lions loomed into view.

They were out in front of a huge island with a large fig tree in its centre. Around it were acacia trees similar to the ones they'd seen the day before, along with the obligatory spattering of palms, but there were also two long and lean trees with gunmetal grey bark. One was a striking red in its leaf colour, the other a deep green. The colour contrast from the fig through the acacias, into the palms and around the gunmetal trees was striking.

"They are called leadwood," Jacob explained. "In our language, we say *Mutokwe*. The wood from this tree is very strong and it makes good coals for the fire."

"Why are their leaves so different?"

"You know, Mr. Bird, in this place we have plenty rain and we are close to the equator, so the trees do not need seasons for growing. Sunlight and water are always here so they don't need weather to change. The red one is losing the leaves and making way for new ones. The green one has already made new leaves and this is its colour."

"Wow, autumn reds and spring greens all in the same place, that's incredible."

The Kelongo pride's seven cubs were now ten months old and about a third larger than Revival's. There were four males and three females, all born in close proximity to one another thanks to their mothers' synchronised maternal clocks. The mothers, three sisters about five years old who had never spent a waking moment apart, had teamed up with their male, 'Ivanhoe', eighteen months previously. With his help, they had set about extending the borders of their range to secure a suitable habitat for their impending offspring. Initially this had been a fairly trouble-free exercise, as Revival were four females who roamed free and hadn't burdened themselves with youngsters just yet. The Kumato pride had three sub-adult cubs but no male so they relented without a fight, too, but the Jilambo pride acquired their male at roughly the same time, with the inevitable clash of interests.

As Jacob had explained before, lion territories were primarily matriarchal, incorporating the help of transient males when it was time for breeding. The problem in Sukula over the years had been the neighbouring hunting concessions and the activities of trophy hunters to lure big males off the plains, so none had managed to last more than a couple of seasons before coming under the hunters' gun and being exterminated. The disruption to the prides was obvious and the subsequent definition of home range and territory size was changing all the time. With no cubs to consider and the abundant food resource, bands of females and their sub-adult cubs ranged far and wide across the plains, generally avoiding one another and simply getting on with life. But as males introduced themselves into the equation, the jostling for supremacy became a heated affair.

Lions actively mark their ranges with scent, threat displays and calling, and it is the males that seem more preoccupied with this activity because this is their role within the unit; they are the transient ones, so it is they who have the largest claim to stake. However, if a male lion can sit in the middle of his territory and call out a formidable roar audible from five miles away, then half the job is done without having to lift a finger. Other males in the vicinity will hear the call and be wary of its strength and ferocity, hopefully forcing them off to greener pastures with fewer monsters. But it could work the other way, too.

It has been proven that lions have the ability to count. The roars of different numerical combinations of male lions have been played to lions holding territories and their reactions observed. With a one-on-one situation, the males were prepared to get out there and fight their challenger. When the odds favoured the home team, i.e. two defenders and one challenger, there was no question about it and they advanced on the loudspeakers with urgent intent. But when the odds slightly favoured the away team, i.e. the lions that were calling to challenge them, they gingerly approached to just 'survey' the scene before weighing up the options for attack. When the odds greatly favoured the away team, i.e. three on one or four on two, some of the defending lions actually ran for cover.

And this is why calling could work against a male lion if he was alone and there were two potential challengers out there spoiling for a fight. With their ability to count, they would undoubtedly know that the odds were stacked behind them to kick his ass and steal his females. This is possibly why lions adopt a number of forms of territory marking and why they actively patrol the borders of their range in groups – females and sub-adults included. If intruders are found, they are liable to be killed.

In the context of Sukula, four new males arrived within a couple of months of one another and were met by a selection of willing females controlling undefined sectors of this vast food resource, which they were only too willing to share. Creedence and Clearwater came in from the west, Ivanhoe from the south and Tyson, an ageing phenomenon reaching the end of his years, came from the east. All these males were what they called park males, which did not possess the attributes that Raymond had spoken of found in Sukula males.

With the abundance of females and lack of resident males, there existed some kind of feline utopia. This point had been illustrated many times when Jacob had witnessed prides hunting within visual proximity of one another, making congruous kills, feeding in the vicinity then going their separate ways without incident or battle. Similarly, though, he had witnessed Revival stealing kills from neighbouring prides using sheer weight of numbers and cunning wit to acquire their quarries. But territorial battles were few and far between.

The astonishing dynamic of these activities involving seven known prides that incorporated more than forty individuals, plus any number of vagrant lions that passed through from time to time, was the scientific anomaly that Sarah wanted to illustrate to her donors to justify the continued existence of the Research Institute. Their unusual behavioural traits of swimming, tree climbing and apparent tolerance of one another would all be angles with which to approach the peculiarity. Of course, the fact that Sukula males were so striking in appearance and huge in form was the emotional string that she hoped to tug by publicising their extinction under the hunters' gun. If only one such male still existed, the task would be so much easier.

Jacob had parked at a safer distance than the day before and had been explaining the delicate intricacies of lion territorial dynamics to an intent and note-taking Bird. The Kelongo adults were, as one may have assumed, dead to the world and sleeping like babies. They had chanced upon an early morning kill just before sunrise, which the cubs were now devouring the last of, and minor battles raged for pieces of the animal's hide, gnawed bones and chewed ears – all that remained of it after half an hour in session with the pride.

"The male over there is called Ivanhoe, but we say Ivan for short. He arrived about two years ago from the southeast. He's a park lion, not a Sukula male."

"All Sukula males are dead, right?"

"Maybe. We have not seen one since Savongo disappeared but there is plenty place for them to hide here – maybe one still survives and will come out when the time is right."

"Fair enough. Maybe Savongo himself has evolved into one and he'll come and kick Creedence's ass, just like the witch doctor said?" Bird smiled into his notebook, trying to get a rise out of Jacob, but all he got was the hint of a frown.

"Keep writing. Tonight you start your reports, remember that. You must remain objective."

"Yeah, I know, it feels like I'm about to sit a radical chemistry exam. You know I only helped on reports for the research paper, I didn't write them? Alfred reckoned I wrote well but it was quite a while ago now. I was also only eighteen at the time, and I was working with one of the best ornithologists in Britain. A lot has happened to me since then – I've taken a lot of drugs and fried a good portion of my brain. I don't know if I can reproduce the same sort of quality you cats need – dig?"

"Don't worry, we have reports from Savongo for you to follow. Just make sure the information is correct."

"OK, man, we'll give it a whirl. Hit me with it."

"First tell me, Mr. Bird – when you take drugs to cook the head, does smoke appear from your ears?"

Bird mused over a mental caricature of Cracker distorted into a red dragon with smoke pouring out of his ears and nose, and laughed.

"Jacob, thankfully for you, you will never meet my friend Cracker, but the answer to your question is yes. If one hangs out with Cracker too long, one gets all kinds of shit coming out their ears – and into them."

"I see," Jacob replied, vaguely and politely, before returning to the business in hand. "OK, these females are all sisters and they look very similar. You will draw the whisker spots another day because we already know them. The obvious marks to look for are on the ears and the faces. That one there, she is Quatro and the sister next to her is Vega, then the third one there is Hinde. She is having a big scar on the right cheek from a fight with Ivan when eating. He punches her hard like Muhammad Ali. You know Ali – the boxer?"

"Yeah, I know Ali, how do you know him?"

"Him float like a butterfly and sting like a bee, and that's why they call him Muhammad Ali!" Bird collapsed into fits of laughter as Jacob chanted out the age-old rhyme. "Who do you think can win between Ali and Tyson? Me, I think Tyson. That one, he is strong like a gorilla. I think he would even beat Ivanhoe in a fight."

"Yeah, man, Iron Mike is strong. I wouldn't get in the ring with that psycho, mate. Not even for a million bucks."

"Yes, maybe you can die, then you have no way for spending the money." They laughed together, momentarily relieved from the enormity of their task.

"Anyway," Jacob continued, "Vega is very easy to spot because she has no tuft on the end of her tail. She lost it in a fight with Revival girls many years ago. You remember I told you that the mother of Baby died in a fight with Kelongos? It's the same time."

"Vega, Hinde and Quatro. Sounds like some freaky car assembly plant. No, wait, hang on, they're all female vocalists. Suzi Quatro, Suzanne Vega and Chrissie Hinde. That's it, yeah, nice one Bird, see how clever I am? Savongo liked his music, then?"

"Oh yes, Savongo listened to music all the time, but why do you think you are clever?"

"Because I guessed where the names came from. That makes me clever, doesn't it?"

"OK, if that is what you say. You also like music?"

"Yeah, man, music is my middle name. I love it. Not sure that mine and Savongo's tastes are too similar, though. I'm a rocker at heart and a raver in spirit but I can dig seventies rock."

"OK." Nonchalant as ever, Jacob returned to his lions "Now, the cubs, they don't have names yet. We like to wait for one year before naming them because they are likely to die. Lions don't have big success with raising cubs and usually they start strong and then die. We recognise them by whisker marks and refer to them as male one, male two and such like."

"How come they die?" Bird asked, still pondering whether he was more of a raver than a rocker, bearing in mind all the ecstasy he had done.

"As they get older, they start to eat more and more. Sometimes life is hard for the lions and they don't manage to kill enough food, especially when the rainy season comes. Lechwe spread out very far when this place is wet and it makes hunting more difficult. Cubs then become prey to disease from malnutrition or other predators, like the hyena. Many will die like this, maybe only thirty percent can survive."

"Thirty percent, is that all? These creatures really do have a rough life. You know, Jacob, everyone in England knows about lions – we all know they exist and that they're some kind of King of the Beasts – but in reality, nobody really knows anything about them. I mean, you can watch as many documentaries as you like, you're never really gonna get the gist of how life is for these cats until you come here to appreciate it. I wonder if anyone will even care."

"This is our job, Noni. We need to convince them to care."

"I agree, I'm just not too sure exactly how we're going to do that."

"For us, it is easy. We just do the fieldwork and prepare the reports. Madam Sarah, she will do the rest. I told you, that one is strong – she is a lioness and this place is her cubs. She will die before she lets any people take her cubs away. She is strong, and that is all. It's up to us to provide assistance for her. She'll do everything else."

"Well, if it's as easy as that then bring it on, brother."

Bird sat with his notebook and Jacob went on to explain the history of the Kelongos. They had been cubs when he had first started on the project, and part of a much larger pride, but the nature of the prey being lechwe and not buffalo dictated that smaller splinter groups were more effective in Sukula, and so the pride split.

The Kelongos were related to Revival – distant cousins and a product of one such split. Kirsty, her sister and their three combined youngsters went one way and Kirsty's cousin with her three offspring went the other. For a while, things were rosy between the two groups but as their meetings became more irregular, encounters got more hostile. Eventually, the inevitable occurred and a vicious battle ensued after a hunt where Revival's girls had made multiple kills, which the Kelongos tried to muscle in on. In the skirmish, Kirsty's sister and the Kelongos' mother were killed and much damage was inflicted on the survivors. It seems that both groups received a severe wake-up call with the whole incident, as they now steered well clear of each other, both showing more tolerance for non-related groups than for one another. Maybe the fact that their blood was linked bore some significance in the animosity of the event, but they now seemed to hate each other with a passion.

Bird listened with intent and marvelled at the complexity of this unfolding scenario. Lions are instinctive creatures with basic, fundamental reactions to a variety of stimulants, but that's not all they are. It can't be labelled personality, species variety or ethnic variation, but something else definitely induces sporadic exchanges in their behaviour. They're not at the evolutionary intelligence levels of dolphins or elephants and they do kind of trudge along in that 'eat what you kill' mentality, but they seem to operate on some kind of emotional level as well. And as this analogous phoenix began to emerge from the ashes of Sukula's lion story, the angle that Bird was groping for started to raise its metaphoric head.

There is an emotional level there that we, as people, can relate to. Here are creatures at the top of the food chain, in their natural habitat, with nothing to fear but their relationship with one another. The complexities of these associations create enough of a strain on their livelihood without man interfering further – I mean, a thirty percent survival rate for their offspring is nothing to write home about but if Man's interference is jeopardising even that, then surely they deserve more from us.

If he could gather enough information to illustrate the struggle that goes on in their natural lives and somehow evaluate the damage that this professional hunting is doing to the population, well, he might just have a case. And if he has a case, well, he might just be able to stay here a little bit longer and get the psycho Tomb Raider on his side. It was worth a shot.

For now, he would keep quiet and allow this idea to fester in his mind, to evolve into an admissible form, which he would present to Sarah when enough groundwork had been done to substantiate it. He needed to ascertain as many facts as possible before preparing a report that he would submit to her with his proposals, before that damn pontoon righted itself and she sent him packing back to where he came from. The initial daily reports would supersede it and pave the way for success, and he would prove to her that he was not a piece of shit – he would prove that there was another level to his being, too, something else worth conserving. He was not just the fucking barman. His name was Bird and he was here doing his bit for this beautiful world he lived in – he was here, and he could be somebody.

20

CLARENCE – ENTER STAGE RIGHT

Days rolled into nights, dawn into dusk like the relentless clatter of the Midnight Express. Out here, the weeks were not punctuated with weekends – there was no mid-week music chart show or weekend ball game on the television to indicate where one stood in the grand calendar of life. His daily reports contained dates but these were just numbers at the top of a page, more like a filing system than a chronological log, and before he knew it, he'd been in Sukula for over a month. The pontoon was now restored to a semblance of order, and two supply vehicles had rolled in with rations and fuel and returned to town without him. Sarah had issued no marching orders.

He had begun submitting monitoring reports, which at first were meek and bland, the words of a desperate soul clutching at the far reaches of redemption like a blind man in a room full of sound. Sarah wasn't too impressed by them, but she reasoned that he was just the fucking barman after all and let it ride. However, as time went by and he became more acquainted with the other lion prides, his reports became more comprehensive. Parallels were being drawn between the clans, GPS waypoints plotted onto the map to show pride ranges and territory overlaps, theories surmised as to why they lived in their separate areas and what the chances were of any expanding to the degree that they may force out rival units. It seemed unlikely – for the most part they seemed to respect one another's boundaries and the larder was always full.

Bird hadn't realised that two vehicles had come and gone across the now-restored pontoon and was still awaiting his imminent fate. To be honest, he had become so consumed by the lions of Sukula that he didn't even know how long he'd been out there. To him, it felt like a week and a lifetime all rolled into one. He knew the dreaded day would come when Sarah would put him on that bus home and he wanted to glean as much as he could from the place before it happened, so just focussed all energy into Sukula and her lions and tried not to contemplate that blasted pontoon. Not surprisingly, it was a mixed bag of feelings that he experienced whilst sitting with Revival on a clear and sunny morning when Jacob told him of the supply runs. They were talking about fuel, as Bird had asked where it came from to service the project.

"The pontoon is *what*?" he squealed as Jacob explained that two vehicles with trailers came in with supplies once a month from town, and that these two had recently come and gone across the pontoon without his knowledge. His outburst attracted the attention of a couple of sleeping lions, who raised their heads; one flicked a sleepy paw at the rude interruption. He looked over to the huge cats and apologised before returning his speech to a wheezing whisper, as if the librarian had just asked him to keep it down for the last time.

"It's fixed? Are you sure? Then why am I still here? I thought I was going as soon as it was repaired?" He looked around in paranoia, as if he were doing a sketchy drug deal on a busy street corner. The lions ignored him –

they couldn't really care less what he was up to as long as he kept his voice down and didn't disturb their slumber.

"Yes, the pontoon is fixed and supply vehicles have come and gone. I am sure." Jacob seemed to get caught up in the charade too, flashing paranoid glances into the distance and whispering in the same urgent manner – as if he were the dealer in this imaginary scenario. They both looked at each other and, on registering their bizarre behaviour, cleared their throats and looked around innocently.

"So, why am I still here? Why didn't I leave on those vehicles that went back to town?"

"The Madam says she gives you another chance. She likes the reports we are writing and she thinks if we keep going, there will soon be a case that we can prepare. She thinks you are OK – dood?"

Bird laughed at Jacob's mockery and sat back in his seat, propping his two feet up on the windscreen-less dash in front of him. "She likes me. I don't believe it, she actually likes me."

"No, I don't think she likes you," Jacob reassured him. "She just thinks you are OK and that is all. That Madam, she doesn't like any men. I am sure she thinks men are bad creatures. She has no husband and she has no boyfriend. She lives out here for many months at a time and she never goes to visit a man. The guys, they think she has something wrong with her. Maybe she cannot have children, we do not know and we never ask her. Mr. Baites, he once asked her if she had a boyfriend and she just told him no. She never spoke about it with him again."

"Well, in our culture, Jacob, that isn't so strange. There are women who refuse to get hitched with men for a number of reasons. These days, girls are more into their careers and making something of their lives than getting married and having a family. Time is moving fast, my friend. In England, we have women who are in the army, they are airline pilots, they drive trucks, they run big factories – they do everything and anything that men can do, and they often do it better. People these days sometimes even prefer to employ women. It isn't so strange that she has become like this after living out here on her own for so long. Did she ever get together with Savongo?"

"Ha, Savongo, that man. You will never meet a man like Savongo. He stayed in the bush for many years and never was with a girl. I think maybe Madam Sarah, she wanted to be with Savongo, but he was not interested. He just thought about lions and Sukula Plains and nothing else. He had a wife when he first came here, but she died. Malaria got into her brain and turned her crazy. She died in the car on the way back to town. Savongo, he drove like a soldier to get her to hospital but it was too late. There was no more time for her. She died on the road. He was very sad. They were only married for a few months. Malaria can be a problem out here. Many of our people back in the home villages die from malaria every year, no way you can stop it."

"Hectic, man, hope these drugs I'm taking hold out for me, it doesn't sound like a fun disease – wicked dreams, though. Hey, check out the cubs, what have they got? It looks like a stick."

While Jacob and Bird had been discussing Sarah's marital status, Kirsty's three fluff-balls were busy tumbling over one another like steamrollers. They each gripped a piece of the same stick in their tiny mouths, frantically trying to break it free from one another, which in turn threw them all over the playing field. Hindquarters were toppled over forequarters, back legs tossed high into the air as squawking heads disappeared into the grass and massive paws paddled in a limbo lambada. Bird looked on, taking intermittent notes and shaking his head, grinning constantly. These things never ceased to amaze him. They had so much life, so much character. One could never guess that they would evolve into the slobbery beasts their parents were, who had more inclination to sleep than hibernating polar bears. It is estimated that an average adult lioness rests for approximately twenty hours a day, and it's probably even more for a male – now that's a lot of rest. Their cubs, on the other hand, never seemed to stop.

As the fluff machine waddled, paddled and pawed its random direction over Sukula's majestic savannah, a bewildering sight caught Bird's eye and gripped his stare in an instant. His face wrinkled and his head twitched erratically, caught in supreme disbelief at what he was seeing – could this be real? He looked to Jacob for some form of explanation, but was met with a similar expression of confusion, only confirming Bird's earlier perplexity. All at once, the cubs also got wind of the misnomer and simultaneously ceased their activities as a gripping fear paralysed their tumbling, furry bodies. This invisible exchange stimulated the adults, and suddenly all heads were up and staring in the direction of Bird's quandary. The proverbial bomb, it seemed, was about to drop on Sukula.

Sitting in a clearing in the most casual of manners, with his head upright and his bright blond mane flowing in the morning breeze, a huge male lion had appeared out of thin air not more than fifty metres from where the rest of the pride lay sleeping. He wasn't there moments ago, they were sure of that – someone would have seen him, specifically Revival. These alert and attentive creatures so in tune with their natural habitat would normally have registered his presence miles away and taken effective action to deter him from encroaching any closer than two kilometres from their cubs, but this cat simply hadn't been clocked – not by lions and not by people – not even by life itself. The first sign any of the assembled entourage registered of his presence was the combined rolling fluff machine coming to a dramatic halt just metres from his colossal forepaws, which stretched out in front of his grey-blue body. By then, it was too late.

With a cry that ripped Sukula in half like napalm on a forested hillside, the beast was upon these tiny beings, swatting two with his powerful paws and seizing the third in his mouth. He gripped it by the head and shook the body free with astounding ease. The small animal was decapitated in an instant, so quickly that its legs still kicked and jolted as the meagre, headless form thumped and bounced into the grass. He was on the other two quicker than Bird's human eye could follow and had administered the same demonic treatment by the time he was able to fix his stare upon the beast once more. And all in the space of one terrified heartbeat, the fluff-balls were dead. Decapitated, bleeding, headless and jolting.

The first of the adults to move was Clearwater, stumbling in sustained slow motion in comparison to the beast. He was a formidable sight, hurling himself headlong at the intruder with claws drawn and teeth bared in a fierce display of aggression, but his challenge was met by an upright bipedal stance that swatted him to the ground like a cockroach. Clearwater rolled away with agile ease, suggesting this contest might be an even one, but the tank was on him in mid-motion, smothering him with his huge bodyweight and biting deep into his neck. Clearwater thrashed relentlessly beneath his assailant in a desperate bid for life, snarling, scraping, twisting and scowling out his insurmountable rage. He'd been in scraps before – he was a survivor, a warrior – he wouldn't go down without a fight, and his deep, resonant growls seemed to shake the very core of this Earth.

Creedence was always the slower of the two Revival males, his ageing form lacking the agility it once exhibited. He lumbered across to his flailing ally and took a giant leap of faith at the psychotic assailant, who seemed to anticipate every move these two bumbling fools tried to make with astounding ease. Rolling away underneath Creedence's aerial advance, the attacker spun to his feet just in time to witness the impact of Creedence onto his bleeding brother-in-arms.

It had all happened so quickly for poor Clearwater, and the adrenaline was pumping so hard through his veins that he had no idea it was Creedence who was now above him. He spun frantically to meet the impending figure with a rush of slicing claws and ripping canines. Creedence yelped, trying to free himself from this wretched assault, but Clearwater was too fired up to release his grip and sunk his deadly jaws into Creedence's throat as he carried this leonine momentum to the ground amidst a barrage of reverberating growls.

By the time he had realised what was happening, Clearwater was once again under attack as the intruding male hit him from behind like a speeding freight train. The impact shunted his jaws deeper into Creedence's throat and snapped his own spine like the twig of a blackberry bush laden with fruit. His body lashed out in desperate death throes as he released his grip on Creedence, twisting and contorting through the grass, writhing like a serpent trapped beneath a rock. Spinal fluid seeped through his ruptured vertebrae, depriving his nerves of any feeling as his senseless body crumpled into the earth.

The beast then fastened his own grip on Creedence's jugular, shaking his head frantically and ripping at the throat as it tore away from his body. The cries of pain ceased in an instant as his throat came loose and detached itself with the force of those gripping jaws, leaving a spasmodic, convulsing Creedence in a similar state of disrepair to his now-dead comrade, Clearwater.

But Creedence's fate was not so merciful. His suffocating lungs slowly filled with blood that pulsated from his torn jugular in a sustained and rhythmic oscillation. After hundreds of gradual convulsions that squeezed the fading life from his ruptured corpse, his dying eyes fixed themselves finally upon the Land Rover. And as a chilling silence crept across the morning heat haze, the two creatures lay motionless and detached in the bloodied, windswept grassland of Sukula's barren plain.

Creedence and Clearwater were dead.

In the foray of battle, Revival's females had bolted for cover and were hidden in an island, watching this barbaric assault on their family. They huddled together and observed the assassin from a safe distance as he walked around the death site. He picked up the body of a cub and began to eat it, ripping its tender fur, crunching its infant bones and exposing the young flesh to the morning sun. It was shining pink.

With blood on his mane and death in his eyes, the male walked with an erect posture and pointed his nose towards the delta system, still teeming with antelope. He let out a devastating roar, heaving the formidable call from the depths of his groin as a terrifying warning to any out there who would dare challenge his passage. For over an hour he called and called and called without ceasing. It was sapping the energy from his colossal form, but this was his way – this is how they do it. The adrenaline was pumping through his veins and Dunkirk was his. He had taken on the biggest and baddest pair that Sukula had to offer, and now what had once been theirs was rightfully his. The females would soon come out of hiding. He had killed their cubs and terminated their males – he would be the new king and all would bow before him. He called incessantly, occasionally changing his stance so that the far-reaching cries could be heard across the distant landscape of the Sukula Plains. He wanted everyone to know that this place was his – his – his – his.

The rotten stench of death slowly permeated the air, but not the familiar scent of an antelope captured for a feast. There was something more profound about this smell – putrid, yet profound. It was like no aroma Bird had ever experienced. The only word that kept ringing in his mind was *death*. This was the angel of death if ever there had been one, and by his mighty hand, the legacy of Creedence Clearwater Revival on the Sukula Plains had been extinguished.

The end of an era.

21

KINGS AND CONQUERORS

Bird took a moment to examine the new lion and noticed immediately that, in spite of the ferocious battle he had just witnessed, this creature had not a single scar on his face. The striking contrast between the gold of his mane and blue of his body meant only one thing – the Sukula males were not dead. He was at least ten percent larger than any other male on the plains, which was emphasised further by his perfectly rounded face and massive front shoulders. This was exactly the creature that Raymond had spoken of all those weeks ago; this was how they had described the old Sukula males. It may have only been in the people's folklore that these were the spirits of their ancient warriors from the sky but, after the display he had just witnessed, Bird was in no position to argue the point. Nothing was about to mess with this cat and live to tell the tale.

During his battle and ensuing bouts of territory calling, the lion had not registered the presence of the vehicle, but now that he was starting to calm down he eyed it with disdain. Jacob recognised the signs immediately and backed up, far out of his reach. The beast lunged at the retreating object, but seemed to have a certain respect for the gesture and quickly lost interest. Bird's heart missed a beat as this angel of death advanced on them momentarily, and then skipped into a foxtrot when the half-hearted charge dissipated.

"He is not used to vehicles and he is very angry after the fight. We should give him plenty of space and allow him time to accept us."

"Yeah, good idea, man, he looks like a bad motherfucker and I don't think we should mess with him. Is he a Sukula male?"

"Yes. He is one hundred percent Sukula. I told you this was a big place and one could still be hiding somewhere. I knew they could not all be dead. Do you know what this means, Mr. Bird? It means we have our story for the people in Europe. It means there is proof of our unique lions and they must now give money for us to protect them. This lion has killed Creedence and Clearwater, but he might just have saved us. This is a good day."

"Yeah, I'll confirm that when my pulse returns to normal. My God, I've never seen anything like that before. Have you?"

"No, this is my first time. I have seen males fighting for food but never this. It is called infanticide. This is what I was telling you about when I talked of lion territories. It is why they roar at night and patrol their boundaries. I don't understand how he got here, though. How he managed to get so close without anyone seeing him?"

Jacob turned to Shadrack and fired a string of questions at him, to which he replied in the negative on all counts. He was obviously asking if Shadrack had seen him coming, but he hadn't – none of them had. The angel of death had simply manifested itself.

Jacob was perplexed. The most bewildering thing was that Revival themselves hadn't sensed their killer. Jacob had witnessed their intuitive senses of direction and awareness of each other on countless occasions. There were times when a kill had been made just before dawn and he had arrived at the scene after the feeding frenzy had subsided at around sunrise. The lions would clean and groom, then perhaps go for a drink and a crap before sauntering into an island to sleep off the meal. Jacob would sit and watch them disappear over the horizon one after the other. Sometimes they would walk more than two kilometres from the kill site, until they dropped off the end of the Earth and out of his binocular vision. The males would always be last at the kill, licking bones and crunching cartilage, oblivious to life around them and seemingly unconcerned about monitoring the direction their family had all departed in. Sometimes more than an hour would pass before they got up and lurched off to join the others, but each time they made a beeline for the direct spot where the rest of the pride had holed up for the day. There seemed no communication between them that was audible, the males would not sniff the ground for a scent trail and many times they would be walking with a trailing wind so could have no windswept scent to work on. They just walked in a straight line and always re-joined the pride, even if they were two kilometres away.

This behaviour in itself had presented something of a mystery to Savongo and Jacob during the many times they had witnessed it. Why bother going so far to rest in a specific island when there were others, seemingly of equal adequacy, nearby? Did they have favourites? Was it something to do with territory patrol?

They had conducted a study of islands utilised over the years and tried to ascertain seasonal patterns, but none emerged. Sure, some islands were used more than others, but there was no consistency or linear correlation to their use. They just used them. Water also seemed to pose no threat to them. On many occasions they would swim great distances, leaving the pursuing scientific vehicle stranded at a gully as they watched the lions disappear onto the opposite bank and into an island of inferior quality to ones nearby and on this side of the water. What was the attraction, and why swim to get there?

They also tried to determine if perhaps the leading lion chose the site and had some personal reason for doing so. Again, the only pattern to emerge was one they already knew – that mainly Kirsty, sometimes Alabama and less often Mia led the charges to hunting grounds or resting sites – but again, the islands did not correspond to any personal preference. They concluded that perhaps they were searching too deeply into an issue that really had no far-reaching ramifications at all. Perhaps these chemically-instinctive beings did just trudge along with no real purpose in their minds until they eventually got hot or tired and found the nearest island to crash out in.

Maybe they were reading too much into it, but why did the males follow the same path hours later to be reunited with their females? What was the point of following their family night and day, and walking vast distances to be with them? There are always times when lion prides are apart without incident, so what drives them to be together most of the time? Could this be another example to illustrate the fact that lions really are just instinctive creatures that follow the whims in their prehistoric minds without will or purpose? If this is the case, then why is it that they are able to organise themselves into co-ordinated groups when the occasion calls for it, and how are they able to communicate intentions, such as which island they will be sleeping in today? They didn't know.

Whatever it was, this hugely intuitive olfactory sense that allowed them to track one another down or sniff out intruders at vast distances had simply not been there today. The beast had unleashed itself on an unsuspecting Revival, and Creedence and Clearwater had paid the ultimate price.

The new male calmed himself down after two hours of incessant sniffing at the corpses and territory-marking. His calling was becoming more and more sporadic as he wound down the aggression. His objective had been achieved.

At one point, he sat close to the bodies of his victims and licked their heads continuously. Then something attracted his attention and he stared into the distance momentarily, before getting up and moving to the border of his battle site to call for all he was worth with that chilling howl that was to become his hallmark. Eventually, he stood up and began to walk. He strode away from the carnage and crossed his tiny boundary for the first time in three hours.

His huge frame swaggered from side to side with the momentum of a swinging pendulum as he walked purposefully across the grassland, heading for an island. Unbeknown to Bird, Jacob or Shadrack, it was the island where the Revival females had taken refuge during his assault. He circled it three times, stopping and staring into its core every so often. Low growling sounds were emitted from the bowel of this haven, a desperate and instinctive plea from the females facing a situation they had never before experienced nor had any knowledge of, but the male did not respond – he just stared inside. Then he sat in the shade next to the island and surveyed his new land. It was just a matter of time. These girls weren't going anywhere, least of all without him.

In a world of hate and greed it's hard to learn to trust,
In a life of haste and speed your love could turn to dust.
But something stirred me deep inside, I know you felt it too,
There's nowhere left to run and hide, so here I'll wait for you...

"It is up to you this time, Mr. Bird – what name should we give this lion? It seems he is not just passing through, it seems he has come here to stay and I think we will be seeing a lot of him. What name do we give him?"

"I think we should call him Clarence, Mr. Jacob," Bird said, without so much as a thought or contemplation.

"What kind of name is this? Is he another singer of muzungu music?"

"No, he's just a lion called Clarence. Clarence the lion."

"OK, this we will do. His name is Clarence. We must take down whisker spots and ear notches and open an identity card for him. We have to stay out for about three days now and see what happens. It is going to be hard, Isamba, but we have to do it. We must stay with them for three days and three nights and see if he starts to mate. I will radio the camp and get them to send a vehicle with food, water and blankets. We will take it in turns to sleep and watch what they do, day and night. Is this OK?"

"Fine by me, mate. What about Shadrack?"

"Oh, he is tough. He has done this many times with me, he knows what happens."

Jacob radioed in for extra rations and blankets while Bird started noting down the beast's vital statistics. First the ears. He examined each one and made rough sketches of the notches and scars. He then examined Clarence's body for visible marks that would help identify him, but after careful inspection found none – no scars, no blemishes, no scabs. In his binoculars, with the animal in the shade, the tinge of blue was ever more apparent, and his mane was now a deep yellow out of the sun's glare and concentrated around the neck and shoulders, exaggerating his size all the more. Bird moved his gaze to the animal's muzzle and started to sketch his whisker spots.

The Institute had drawn up identity cards of each lion ever surveyed, and these were updated on a regular basis as new scars formed and old ones faded. Every lion in turn had a file that detailed the prides in which they lived, family associations, home ranges, pride dynamics, births, deaths and so on. Jacob went out daily and gathered ongoing information on all of these factors, keeping the Institute up to date with who was who in the zoo and what they were up to. Within the main files at camp were the vital statistics of eight males, similar in form and stature to Clarence, that were now marked deceased – shot by the hunters' guns. They had gone to Texas.

The supply vehicle arrived with water and ready-made food to last the rest of the day and that night. There were three blankets and a couple of cushions, and Isaac, being the considerate soul that he was, had managed to snaffle a flask which he filled with freshly-brewed tea especially for Bird. There were treats such as homemade cookies and fresh fruit, and some mosquito repellent that the courier had informed Jacob came directly from Sarah.

"They say the Madam has sent this for you. She is very happy that this has happened and maybe now she likes you. What do you think?" Jacob asked.

Bird paused a moment and scratched at sporadic whiskers on his stubbled chin. "Naah. I don't think so."

"No, me neither."

They all laughed together, including Shadrack (who was still unsure of why but reasoned, 'What the hell, the white boy's still an idiot!') They had backed up out of sight of the awaiting Clarence to meet the supply vehicle, and it allowed them a moment's relief from the day's shattering events. They were in for a long haul, though as yet Bird was blissfully unaware of just how long and uncomfortable it might get. Jacob knew the drill and felt it better not to inform him. He had been on all-night follows many times, doing hunting analyses or speaker call-outs or waiting for females to deliver cubs, and he knew what they entailed. This one would be hard.

Once back with Clarence, Bird poured himself a cup of tea and tipped the brim on his wide and haggard safari hat. It had once been jungle green, but the years of shade provided from the sweltering sun had faded away the pigment and left it a putrid brown with white sweat-marks around the bowl. The hat had belonged to Savongo and Jacob had obtained it after his disappearance, along with a few other meagre possessions. In Cracker's haste to get wasted with Bird on his final days in England, he had overlooked the fact that Africa was a place of immense heat and completely forgotten any sort of solar protection. If it wasn't for the consideration of the likes of Mike the landlord and Alfred himself, Bird would not have come away with suntan cream or malaria pills, either. He often wondered why he ever placed any semblance of trust in Cracker and marvelled at the fact that the two of them had survived so long on this planet relatively unscathed. Jacob had lent Bird the hat on his third day as sunstroke was starting to affect his judgement and threatened to fry the remaining brain cells left alive in his skull. It was definitely helping.

Sukula's midday sun was now starting to swelter and the meagre offering of shade that Jacob had found was quickly receding. Clarence was feeling the heat, too, and shifted his pose to a more comfortable spot closer to the island's core. He was now only partially visible to them, but Jacob hesitated before moving for fear of creating any disturbance in the already-delicate situation. He had habituated lions to the vehicle before and knew that all it needed was time and patience, both of which he had in abundance. Ultimately, the beast would become as nonchalant and accepting as the rest of Revival, though hopefully never quite as familiar as Baby.

Clarence was a true Sukula male, and an impressive specimen at that. Revival were in turn true Sukula females, and between them they could carry on the lineage that had been systematically erased by hunters. Somewhere along the line they may even be related, but how closely was anyone's guess. With the extra funding this event could attract, blood could be taken and DNA analyses conducted by their friends in the University to ascertain exact genetic diversity. It could even be that the link was perilously close, threatening the gene pool for their offspring, but even if that was the case, there was nothing anyone could do about it now. The damage had been done and the beast had staked his claim – there wasn't an animal alive that would want to contest that.

"We must be very careful now, Mr. Bird. This Clarence, he has a price on his head. He is the biggest male by far in Sukula and if this Mr. Visser finds out that he is here, he may come looking for him."

"No worries, man. How do we keep it quiet, though? It's not like we ever go around there and socialise, is it?"

"No, but we must monitor this pride daily and see what their movements are. If they start heading towards the hunting area, we must remain with them at all times and make sure there are no baits close by. This is very important. We cannot lose Clarence."

"Like I say, no worries, man." Bird gazed at the beast through his binoculars, still marvelling at his immense size and towering strength. "Amazing that a little shit like me has been assigned to protect a monster like you, man. Like, how the fuck does that happen? Beyond me." He let out a deep and resonant sigh. "Long may you live, dude – long may you live!"

Birds and animals possess a variety of attributes that help them regulate body temperature and allow them to tolerate extreme climatic conditions. Man relies more on his habitat for this and as the heat intensified, Bird marvelled at the lechwe and puku, the zebra and wildebeest all melting into the acrid haze of Sukula's shimmering grasslands without so much as a hint of discomfort. His, on the other hand, was very real. Jacob had parked in the scattered shade of a measly acacia tree and the sun poured through every gap in its paltry foliage. Unlike their animal counterparts, they were equipped with nothing to fight the heat and so they sat, like Romans in a hot bath, sweating profusely and sighing intermittently for hours on end. But as the sun began its final descent for the horizon, so the heat began to fade and relief slowly came to the three observers hidden inside the belly of their big, green lion.

Clarence stirred himself and sat up once again, surveying his surroundings. He had been lying on his side, but he wasn't sleeping. There was still work to be done in this takeover bid and he knew all too well that losing the females now would negate all his earlier effort. There was no sign of movement from within the island, but he was in no hurry. Vultures were busy gorging themselves on the remains of his morning exploits – soon, all that would be left of the legacy of CCR would be bones and skulls. If Jacob had not been there all these years writing everything down, it would have slipped away unnoticed by man, lost in the chasm of nature.

The easing of noon's heatwave seemed to trigger the impulses of Revival's females. In spite of the terrible events earlier that day, bodily functions remained intact, and the call of nature would start forcing them into the open any time soon. The first to appear was Mia. Gingerly and with caution strapped across her eyes like a kidnapper's blindfold, she stepped from the confines of her refuge. Clarence turned to look at her for a brief moment before returning his gaze to the wide-open expanse of his new home.

Mia was not happy. She stepped with the feather-like grace of a ballerina and manoeuvred herself into the open without taking her gaze off the beast. She squatted and defecated, all the while facing the formidable form of Clarence, who paid her no heed. When she had finished, she scraped her back feet along the ground as if kicking dust over her excrement and then skulked several metres to her right and sat down. She didn't shift her gaze from the lion – not once.

Her successful completion of the mission seemed to inspire confidence in the others, and soon Bama and Baby appeared from the island, adopting the same tentative footwork that Mia had used. Once again, Clarence offered them a quick glance, then looked away. Baby met his stare with a snarl, emitting a low cautionary growl in his direction as her face creased and exposed her pristine incisors. Any other animal in the world might have shown her the respect that her powerful limbs and gleaming teeth rightfully deserved, but Clarence didn't seem too bothered. He looked on without even affording her a fleeting glance. She was not his target – well, not yet anyway. The two girls moved over to Mia and sat close by, all three staring at Clarence with intent, not to mention a touch of concern. His gaze remained peaceful as he nonchalantly viewed his lands. In time, their attitude would change, and he knew it. His main concern right now was Kirsty.

Infanticide in lions is undoubtedly a shocking experience, for the lions that experience it and the people who happen to witness it. It had hit Bird in a place that only humans can feel, and the emotions shot through him like missiles across an Afghan skyline. Clarence was simply responding to a primal urge to perpetuate the genetic lineage of his species on this Earth, but as Kirsty emerged, it struck Bird that the one individual who should have been most affected by the day's events was she – a lactating mother who had watched as the beast butchered her three young cubs right before her eyes. He had ripped off their heads and eaten their bodies, and it should have been Kirsty who chose to ignore the stranger or treat him with the disdain that he might have deserved, but instead she stepped from the island, saw to her needs and sat down close to Clarence. She did not watch him as her daughters did. She did not growl, nor snarl, nor show him any form of aggression – she just sat quietly.

The beast knew that this was his prize. Her lactating femininity was alive with oestrogen as a result of her cubs, and this in itself would induce her into season almost immediately. She knew she would be first to mate with the intruder, as hers was the loudest calling. She did not fight the urge or try to escape the inevitable; there was no time for mourning or sorrow. Her purpose, like his, was to perpetuate her genes, and here was a bad motherfucker who would be unlikely to suffer the same indignation as her previous partners due to his colossal form and outstanding prowess in the ring. If she was to have any chance at procreation, this was her best option.

Clarence remained motionless. It was as if he understood the predicament of these females and chose not to cause them further grief. He was allowing them to get used to his presence without forcing the issue, and this behaviour seemed amazing to Bird. Admittedly, he was not an expert on lions and parallels were difficult to draw, but he had expected further expressions of dominance by the male to assert his authority over these newly-acquired jewels, as they do in the feeding frenzy. But Clarence saw no need. His confidence was astounding. He had not a care in the world.

Sunset washed the Earth in its characteristic glimmer once again, and the horizon began to absorb a molten glow that slipped from the western sky as darkness crept in from the east. Jacob knew that the first night would yield groundbreaking discoveries in this new alliance, and the prospect of interference with the spotlight concerned him somewhat. How was the beast going to react to intermittent light showers coming from the now-familiar green and smelly lion? Would it have any serious implications on their behaviour? More importantly, would it discourage any activities? Only time would tell, but his sensitivity to the delicate situation was of paramount importance.

"We follow at a distance and use the spotlight as little as possible. We get as close as they will allow us and use our ears for sound. You will operate the light, Mr. Bird, but it is very important not to make this Clarence scared of our spotlight, OK?"

"Yeah, man, I'll try. I'll point the beam into the sky and use the very edges of the light tracer to illuminate them, how's that?" He shone the light to the heavens and dipped the outer edge of its beam onto the ground, partially illuminating the grass. Jacob approved.

Tonight, it was Alabama who initiated the obligatory move towards the delta system's abundant prey. This was not unusual, as she often led the charge, but tonight's atmosphere was very subdued. There was no physical interaction as had been witnessed so many other times – no rubbing of noses, no licking or mutual grooming, no jumping on each other and rolling around, no lying on their sides gently pawing each other's faces. Just a quick rub of bodies and off they went in single file behind Bama towards the killing fields. For once, Kirsty was bringing up the rear, flicking her tail over her back, and Clarence padded silently along behind her.

Tonight, Jacob found following the pride unusually hard as the Land Rover bumped and bounced its mechanical form without the slightest hint of subtlety. The lions moved with their customary methodical precision until they reached a safe distance from the lechwe, where they sat down. Clarence sat close to Kirsty, watching her like a hawk – clearly he did not want his prize to be stolen in the night. It was difficult for Jacob, Bird or Shadrack to make any close observations on the pride because of the distance they had to keep, but that spine-chilling squeal soon split the night and they knew once again that a kill had been made.

The usual feeding frenzy was a subdued, almost tranquil affair, and all eyes, both human and feline, seemed to be focussed on Clarence. Normally, males immediately attack females with kills and steal the quarry for themselves with no regard for sharing, even with their own cubs. Mia had caught tonight's dinner and the other three girls were quick to join her at the table, with the usual grunting and growling over feeding rights. They all kept a watchful eye on the beast who had followed Kirsty in to the kill, but he sat a couple of metres away and allowed the girls to feed without interference. The suspense of his impending assault seemed to eat away at their conscious minds, but the element of survival overrode the emotion and kept them ripping at the animal's carcass. They repeatedly looked up from their feeding and checked on Clarence, but he showed no sign of any interest.

After a while, he got up and quietly moved across to the feeding fray. The females ceased their activities for a second and looked at the towering form standing above them, but there was no aggression here. Lightly and gently he eased his way in between Mia and Kirsty and started to feed. The girls looked at him as if he were on some kind of mind-altering drug, seemingly confused by his behaviour and unsure whether or not to trust his placidity. Maybe he would erupt at any moment and start slaying them all as he had done earlier in the day – but he didn't, he just fed quietly, minding his own business.

After some minutes of this subdued feeding, Kirsty began to lick his neck at the point where his mane met his skin, and Clarence responded with a low grunt. All the cats began to feed once again, and for the first time ever, Revival ate without slapping, biting, growling or hurting one another. Was this the influence of the beast – the monstrous savage that had eaten their family before their very eyes? Was his influence calming their own savagery? Only time would tell.

Clarence was the last to leave the carcass and stayed chewing on its bones for more than an hour. There was no tug of war tonight, no garish contest for bone and sinew. Everyone ate their fill and then casually moved away to start cleaning themselves and drinking heartily from a nearby gully. The females mutually groomed and, for the first time that day, they began to show the affection for one another that had become so indicative of their loving bonds.

The three men sat in the darkness of Sukula's black night and talked quietly to each other, occasionally casting a tranquil glow over their study animals. Clarence had moved close to Kirsty after his feed and another intense bout of territory-calling that ripped across the night sky. Once he was done, he received some gentle grooming which he also indulged in himself, licking Kirsty's neck and face.

It was only at about three o'clock in the morning, amidst the whine of mosquito wings around the scientists' ears and the cramp of suppressed muscles in their legs, that the inevitable occurred and the unmistakable yowl of mating lions rang out across Sukula's vacant grasslands. Kirsty had finally relented, and the drawn-out process of sustained copulation had begun. This, in time, would also induce the other females into season and mark the start of a new beginning.

"You think we still call the pride Revival, Mr. Bird? Do we need a new name for a music band now that Clarence is here?"

"Naa, Jacob. The pride have Revived themselves after a potentially catastrophic day and I think Revival is probably the most appropriate name for them. I tell you what, though, I don't know if I can take three nights of being out here like this – it's killing me and we haven't even finished the first one."

"Maybe he will finish mating with Kirsty before three days and we can go home early. We have to see how it goes, but when they sleep tomorrow, we will get a good position and take turns for sleep. For now, we have to stay. Don't worry, Mr. Bird, this is where you will find the action. There is nowhere else a lion man would want to be at a time like this – is there?"

"I guess not. Does that mean I'm a lion man, then?"

22

STAYING POWER

Sexual reproduction in lion populations is an extremely long-winded affair. Males have a traditionally low sperm count and females' fertility is linked to their food supply, which can be erratic and affect conception. To counterbalance this, they mate very frequently during female oestrus seasons. Bearing in mind their huge propensity for sleep and clinical avoidance of physical exertion, it can get tedious and tiresome for the courting couple, even emotionally distressing.

They mate on average once every ten to twenty minutes, with insemination occurring within about sixty seconds of penetration. This activity can last for anything up to sixty hours, sometimes all day and throughout the night. Obviously, as the hours wear on, the pair begin to tire and not only are copulation times reduced but the number of sexual encounters decreases as well. It is not uncommon for the pair to leave the pride when mating in order to wholly concentrate on the job at hand, which denies them the opportunity to hunt and feed. It is for this reason that Jacob wanted to stay with them for at least three nights. He intended to count how many times they mated and compare this to previous records of known males in the area. It would also help gauge fertility and give them an approximate due date for cubs – about three and a half months later.

Once the mating began, he allowed Bird and Shadrack to get some sleep while he stayed up to count. It was easier for him because he knew what copulation sounded like so there was less chance of making a mistake.

Bird wasn't going to complain at the chance of a rest, but sleep would not come easy. Getting comfortable was in itself a mission; what's more, mosquito activity around the delta's now-stagnant gullies was a thousand times harsher than it ever was around camp, and his insect repellent was having little effect. He was sure they worked on force of numbers as the Zulus had done against the British. The first wave of mosquitoes would sacrifice themselves for the cause and absorb as much of the repellent as they could, smearing away a clearing on the skin where their compadres could penetrate and suck his blood.

Bastard parasites!

Apart from the potential life-threatening disease they carried in their deadly hypodermics, the sound they made annoyed a fidgety Bird and the sensitivity of his Celtic skin meant he couldn't get rid of the itch, no matter how hard he scratched. He became so obsessed with where they were and which side he was going to be attacked from next that the option of sleep was slipping ever further from him. He decided a spliff might help proceedings – maybe the smoke would drive the bastards away long enough for the potent bud to distract his mind from their incessant buzzing and send him off to sleep once his brain was sufficiently pickled.

"Is it OK for me to smoke, Jacob?"

"Yes, no problem. Mosquitoes not let you sleep?"

"Yeah – little fuckers."

Over the weeks, Bird had become well acquainted with the staff back at camp, and endless supplies of jamba had been rolling in from all over the village. Luckily, Cracker's head was switched on enough in the smoking department to have helped him organise many packets of rolling tobacco and even more skins. He had enough papers to last him a year, let alone two months, and they took up more luggage room than his books had done, but maybe that's because he only possessed one.

He laced up a big cone and lit the end, sucking the smoke deep into his lungs as he slumped back into his seat. It tasted sweet – sweet and fresh. The effect upon him was instantaneous and a lightness emerged in his neck, making his head feel detached, like it was floating on air as his mind drifted off into unrelated thoughts, none of which he was able to hold for any length of time. The night sky was now a milky blue with the late half-moon and his smoke illuminated the opaque light, making him feel like he was in an old black-and-white movie. He was still wearing his hat and a Humphrey Bogart caricature entered his thoughts, standing beneath a lamppost with his hat cocked over his eyes and a plume of silver smoke emanating from his mouth against the creamy night.

I'm so far away from old movies. I'm so far away from any kind of life I know. What day of the week is it? I wonder what the lads back home are up to. All still the same I'll bet, and here I am sitting in the middle of the African savannahs at night with hunting, mating, sleeping lions. Madness. I wonder if they still think of me? Do I think of them?

He hadn't really had time to miss home. The heat applied by Sarah had got him off his arse and into some semblance of upward motivation that kept him focussed on the job at hand. In his efforts to capitalise fully on the experience and hopefully avoid catching that dreaded bus home, the clatter of his modern world had suddenly become obsolete. Even music, the food of life that had satiated his escapist hunger for so many years, seemed inappropriate out here. The alter-ego jukebox that inspired relentless waves of tunes from various artists that used to roll endlessly through his mind now occurred as fleeting guest appearances when out in the bush or sitting around a campfire with the guys.

There had been such a pressing need for escapism back in England due to societal cloning and political institutionalisation, and refuges like the Wound and Bandage, drugs and rock and roll were essential for survival. But here, there was no need for evasion – nature was everywhere he turned. The fundamental issues of pure survival had consumed him with such a fervent desire that it fine-tuned his senses to focus only on the task of Sukula and her lions.

To let his mind wander for even the briefest of moments could result in missing some momentous event or, worse still, could threaten his very own existence. It wasn't as if music were forgotten, it was just that it had its place, and out on safari following prides of lions wasn't exactly the ideal stimulant for Sid Vicious' rendition of 'My Way'. Africa demanded concentration in its entirety. Mother Earth in her raw and untainted state beckoned the heart into the present and filled the soul with a spiritual nourishment that could never be ignored. Africa was real. Musicians will always be the prophets of our time, but in this place, where Nature's spirit is served on tap and chilled, that once-parched idealism can be baptised in the river of life and step forth revitalised and complete.

The way he looked at it, the day would soon be coming when he would have to saddle up and ride out of here forever. Once he was gone, there would be plenty of time to consider the outside world, but this place – this Sukula Plains with its many lions, thousands of antelope and huge aggregations of stunning birds – well, this would be a once-in-a-lifetime gig. Better to make the most of it while it's here – besides, this was also for Alfred, a man amongst men.

His thoughts were put on pause as Clarence once again ripped out his concerto of unprecedented terror, advertising his presence and prolific power to all within his range. Lion calls traditionally have little variation between populations. A standard territorial roar generally consists of a few heaving groans followed by a series of growling grunts, the only real variations occurring in combinations of the above – groan to grunt ratios. As Bird had come to expect, this Clarence, who had a unique way of doing things anyway, did have a kind of individual call, one that separated him marginally from the others. It was more in the strength and the pitch, his range being wider than most though his combinations were also different.

His rendition would typically commence with four or five crashing groans starting at a tenor's cry, tumbling through an alto's groan and yowling into a bass head's growl. These would then be followed by a dozen or so ripping grunts, shunted in short succession as if to push the short, sharp, pungent sound through any obstacle that stood in its way. However, midway through the grunt concerto, a huge 'heave-ho' would emanate, like a forgotten bar in the earlier movement, slipped in discreetly to inform listeners that, in spite of the grunts signifying the end of his repertoire, there was still spirit within him to heave out one last big one. Bird surmised in his semi-stoned state that this might be like the old metal bands accused of working on the subliminal evil within the subconscious by recording demonic vocals backwards. Or maybe that was just the weed?

His fearsome symphony complete, the beast returned to the tedious job at hand – courting Kirsty. Could this animal really be the reincarnation of Savongo?

Bird's bud had done the trick and a grey light of dawn draped itself over the landscape as he opened his eyes to the world. It was a bizarre feeling waking up in the middle of the Plains with no Isaac and no camp noises around him. The chirping and chirruping of small grass birds such as warblers and cisticolas offered a poor rendition of the Heuglin's dawn chorus, but the unusual meowing of crowned cranes could be heard in the distance like the call of domestic cats. Then the bizarre, screeching honk of a pair of wattled cranes rippled across the landscape as they passed by overhead, gliding with fleeting ease and swaying flight feathers. A fish eagle threw out its resounding cry. Sukula's daily ritual had begun.

The lions were off to one side, scattered within a hundred-metre radius. Baby slept and Clarence was very close to Kirsty, both crashed out and dead to the world after their night of leonine passion. Bama and Mia surveyed the scene, sizing up the chances of a morning's hunt and evaluating whether it would actually be worth getting up for, which it probably wasn't. Baby slept on. Thousands of lechwe grazed peaceably all around them as the dawn drew ever nearer, and as the sunlight crept quietly across the grassland, Baby still slept.

Bird poured a cup of tepid tea and felt the faintest sense of warmth as he slugged it. He passed it around and saw the other two wince as they sipped at the plastic cup – it had no sugar, and Africans like sugar in their tea.

Kirsty got up and stretched, immediately inducing a reaction from Clarence. She moved over to him and rubbed the side of her head against his before manoeuvring her posterior to his face and walking off with a flick of her tail that brushed his cheeks. No doubt this movement emanated desirable pheromones, which she tantalisingly washed over his nasal receptors to entice the beast into action once more. He obediently followed, like most bumbling males in this situation, as she walked seductively for a few metres before delicately squatting in front of him, offering the evolutionary prize.

He clumsily shifted his great form and straddled her from behind, his pelvis pulsating in short, sharp bursts as he tried to find the penetration point somewhere around the base of her tail. Once in, he started yowling and howling like a deranged alley cat, but the resounding hum of her gentle purr was deep and resonant and he bit greedily at her neck without force. Fifteen seconds later, he pulled out as she violently twisted onto her back, swatting his face with her front paws before rolling uncontrollably through the grass. She writhed left and right, over and over before coming to an abrupt and motionless halt with her huge paws cocked in the air above her. Clarence collapsed – first his rump, then his mid-rib and finally rippling onto his great loping side, his body pursuing its limbs as though someone had taken out his legs. His final position was once again beside his amorous partner, who watched his every move with seductive intent.

"So that's how it goes," remarked Bird, now having actually witnessed the event for the first time. "He doesn't have much staying power, does he? Reminds me of the old days back home!"

Jacob looked across at Bird in bewilderment. Most of the time he could understand the white boy, but then there were times when nothing he said made sense. How could he have witnessed this back in his country in the old days? Maybe it was lack of sleep and he hadn't quite heard right. He wasn't sure – but he was just about to turn and ask him when instinct took control and he cranked the engine. Baby was awake. She was awake and looking to kill. Jacob sensed her intent and, in a single motion, slammed the vehicle into reverse and out of her line of fire. She charged a few paces and then stood, tail flicking, head up, surveying the land around her.

Once Bird's heart was beating normally again, he cracked out some fruit and soggy sandwiches for breakfast and prepared for the long and wearisome day ahead of them. Jacob had already recorded fourteen copulations in the last four hours. During the daylight hours, he would assess how many were instigated by Kirsty and how many by Clarence. Bird practised his whisker-drawing on the other females and Shadrack caught up on some well-earned sleep now the mosquitoes had surrendered for the day. Both Jacob and Bird kept an eye on Baby. They were in for a long haul. The day could not be broken up by going to see other lions or chilling around a waterhole watching thousands of birds. Soon, the monotony of mating would far outweigh the initial excitement of first-time viewing, and the only break they had to look forward to was sleeping lions in between bouts of prematurely-ejaculated sex.

Great! Lion research is not all guns and glory, man. These things can sleep – boy, can they sleep. I wish I could!

Then a chill shot down his spine as he remembered Kirsty's cubs and the terrifying scene of their slaughter. How would he ever be able to explain it to people back home? He gazed off into the distance again, consumed momentarily by thoughts of England. Sukula was so much a part of him now that it almost seemed like home had always been here.

The supply vehicle arrived once again with fresh rations for the day and a camera from Sarah, with instructions to photograph the new male and as many mating attempts as possible. A plan was formulating in her mind and she needed to start gathering data in as many different forms as she could for the donors. This was the trump card they had been waiting for – the appearance of Clarence was going to give them something tangible to take back to the holders of the purse strings. He was proof that Sukula lions were different in appearance and behaviour, and therefore that they required further investigation, for which cash would have to be sourced. Once it was secured, DNA testing could be done, radio and satellite collars could be fitted, and mapping could begin, along with food analyses, scat analyses, computer models to ascertain the longevity of Sukula as a wildlife resource with current levels of consumption, and on and on.

If she could get funding for the lions, she could introduce a whole host of related projects on soils, vegetation, hydro analysis, parasites, diseases and more.

For this, extra scientists would be employed; they could get a real institute together, a real field research station conducting ground-breaking studies but more importantly, drawing the plight of Sukula's diminishing resource to the attention of the donor communities. Once they found out what was happening, they could get some serious muscle behind them and start to implement real schemes that would curb the hunting and subsidise local meat poaching to a negligible degree.

The rainy season was fast approaching and Sarah would go back to England for the worst six weeks of the flood, as she did each year – only this time, she would have something real to show them. She would have a case like never before and they would see that she had not been struggling for nothing all these years. There really was such a thing as a Sukula lion and their males really were as formidable as folklore suggested. They would see that she was committed to finishing what Savongo had started, because he had inspired her in the way he inspired everyone and even if the body was dead, the spirit lived on regardless.

After his disappearance, everyone had been so supportive and sympathetic. They held ceremonies for him, revered his work, praised and decorated him, then consoled his family over their tragic loss. He had been a brave young man, indeed an irreplaceable asset to the donors, and they were sorry to have lost him. There was lots of that – you know, meaningless, polite bollocks that comes out of these situations by people who are obliged to be sympathetic but really just long to get out and get cracking on the workload which has now tripled because matey boy's gone and died.

But once the pleasantries were over and they were seen to have done their bit for the poor deceased lad, it was back to politics and balance sheets. Savongo was not there anymore – the driving force was gone. In the interests of a positive public image, the bizarre notions of this rather eccentric female who stood before them with preposterous ideals of unique and unusual lions were entertained in a civil and 'equal opportunities' manner, but she was never really taken seriously. They had kind of hoped she would just go away and afforded her as much plastic courtesy as their frail egos would allow, but the charade could not go on forever and sooner or later, someone was going to have to tell her straight and get her out of their hair once and for all. The time was drawing ever nearer and she knew it. Of all the people to jump in and save her decaying plight, who'd have ever thought it would be that fucking useless barman?

The instruction Bird and Jacob had received was to do a detailed analysis on the physical appearance of the male, drawing as many comparisons as they could to other Sukula males. In the absence of tranquillising equipment, exact weights and measurements could not be taken, but photographic comparisons were to be made between Clarence and the remaining park males left in Sukula. Everything about his physical attributes was to be recorded, including all scars, blemishes and unusual markings, as well as mane structure, colouration and body weight ratios. The same was to be done for the females.

"Sarah needs to come out here and see for herself. Clarence doesn't have a single scar on his body, nor a blemish, nor a mark. What do we tell her, then? And how can we do any of this stuff accurately without drugging the cat first? It doesn't make sense," Bird moaned as he read Sarah's list of instructions.

"We already have this information on the females. Better you update all their cards today and tomorrow so she can see all information is current and correct. Take as many notes as you can for the reports when we get back. I will give you the information again and you can start to compile the big report about what happened yesterday and today."

"Roger that, big man."

"Who is Roger?"

"Oh, huh huh, no one. Just some strange military radio talk. It's not really important man, you just have to remember that I use a lot of slang when I talk, that's all. You'd be best to ignore me half the time, I know most of the people I grew up with do." He shrugged.

"Yes, Isamba Noni. I have seen that you talk a lot with slang. Much of your English makes no sense to me. I think I will also ignore you when you start to talk this nonsense. It is why we call you the bird talker – you speak another language which maybe only the birds can understand but we Africans, we cannot."

"Ah well, can't win 'em all, mate. Look, they're at it again. Don't they mind mating with the other girls right there?"

"Sometimes they move away but most of the time they just do it there and then. I think when the others find an island for sleeping, these two may stay on their own. Maybe they will also eat tonight, maybe not. Many maybes with lions – they are instinctive."

The now-familiar coital experience kicked off once again, this time instigated by Clarence. He had sat up and shuffled close to Kirsty in a meek and humble manner, gently resting his head against hers then licking her neck amorously. At first she gave no response, gazing into the distance with that forlorn 'please lechwe, come and die in front of me so I don't actually have to get up and kill you' look. Clarence was quite incidental to any thoughts she seemed to be having – if anything an intrusion on her lucid tranquillity.

This was her one moment of power and they were few and far between for Kirsty, so why shouldn't she capitalise on it? The Women of Orange, or the Suffragettes of the early 1900s, spoke only against the oppression of human females; there was no representation for lionesses, whose fleeting plight was not given cognisance. This would be one of the only times in her life when he would allow her the right of choice and would answer to the call of feminine authority that males of every species might do well to hear once in a while – with the exception of spiders and praying mantises, of course. In lions, males normally dominate their females to an extent that would please the most militant of dictators. For Kirsty to get one back was an all-important moral victory, and it seemed she would savour it.

But in the fullness of time, she and the others would come to understand that things would be different with Clarence. He was to be like no other male lion – a Renaissance cat, a new-age man, a styling millennial. His behaviour at the banquet the night before was proof of a new beginning. A new leonine order, a new state of mind. His way would secure the future for all to come, and a brighter day would emerge in the East for all of Sukula's lions.

Clarence was obviously ready to get busy again, but Kirsty did not respond to any of his advances. She would not be enticed off the ground and into a squat, and she was damn sure that no mating would take place until she deemed the time to be right. When she finally did relent, she played a cruel teasing game with the beast and dummied the squat to get him excited before pulling away at the last minute and walking off, flicking those desirable pheromones from her swishing tail. Clarence was like a bumbling buffoon behind her, but the taste of that sweet love emanating from her carnal form proved too enticing to ignore and he just ambled along regardless.

By the time 10 a.m. arrived, the sun was beginning to swelter once again. The other three females had crawled into a nearby island to sleep off their rough night of rest and the honeymooners had moved perhaps twenty metres all morning. The research crew were starting to heat up beyond the levels of reasonable acceptance and they unanimously agreed that the shelter of a nearby fig tree was imperative. It didn't give them the greatest view of the young feline lovers but it offered an equitable alternative to being out in the hot sun, where only mad dogs and Englishmen might be – Bird knew which he was, so what did that make Jacob and Shadrack?

Now that it was daylight, Jacob reasoned he could clock off for a while and try to get some well-earned rest, leaving Bird with the unenviable task of monitoring copulation times and intervals – not to mention instigators. Five hours later, when Jacob woke up, copulations were hovering around the thirty-plus mark and shade seemed to be of no concern to the lions. Bird was humming the tune of "Love is in the Air" by John Paul Young, occasionally throwing in a word from the lyric, when he caught the movement of Jacob as he stirred from sleep.

"Dee dum dee dum dum dee foolish... Jacob me old mate, did ya get a good nap? Wicked! I think the sun and this lack of sleep have gone to my pickling mind, man – I'm starting to sing 'Love is in the Air'. My legs are trashed too, and if I smoke another one of these reefers, I may never come back, dude."

Bird's eyes were sunken and drawn. He looked like he'd gone two rounds with Mike Tyson, which was enough for the optical sun to set on his irises and force them into a sea of white forever, leaving him Stevie Wonderfully visionless.

Jacob sighed despairingly. He knew there were better things in life to wake up to than this deranged specimen singing bad seventies covers – he was sure he had woken up to better things many times before, so why then did he have to have this? Why him – why now?

"You know, Mr. Bird," he huffed through a sigh, "I believe that everything that happens to us in our lives happens for a reason. There is a force out there that makes these things. I don't know if it is God or Nature or our ancestors or the birds or the trees or what – but something is there to guide destiny for us..."

"That's cool, man." Bird gazed into the distance, silencing Jacob with his interruption. "I can dig spiritualism at a time like this, I really can. I get your angle, dude," he said, tapping his fingers rapidly on his leg.

"...What I am failing to understand," Jacob continued, "is why I have got you. I think maybe this point would become clear if I knew who the god responsible for this destiny was, but I do not. Maybe if that god revealed himself to me, I would know why you have been sent to me, but for now I do not, and it troubles me."

"It was Savongo, man," Bird quipped without breaking stride. "God of the lions – god of Sukula reincarnated into the stupendous form of Clarence the man – butt kicker and lady lover extraordinaire. Don't you think it's somehow weird that this cat decides to reveal himself now and not when Butt-cheeks Baites was here?" He at last turned to face Jacob and ceased his finger tapping for a moment. "I mean, it would have made a whole lot more sense for this cataclysmic revelation to have occurred when a reputable scientist was here to record it, but it didn't, mate. It happened to little old me – Captain Birdseye who doesn't have a pot to piss in or a window to throw it out of. Little ol' Featherhead is granted the eternal gift of Clarence's long-awaited revelation to the world, and do you know why, Mr. Jacob?"

Jacob's cheek was buried into his right palm with his elbow resting on his knee, somewhat in despair. He shook his head and wrinkled up his closed eyelids again, searching the stars for a sign, a message that could reveal to him why he was having to deal with this half-wit fool going off on some demented head trip.

"I'll tell you why…" Bird was completely oblivious to the man's anguish, but quite frankly he was unconcerned. He had been sitting for five hours, continuously counting lion fornications in the African heat whilst smoking vast quantities of home-grown reefer and reflecting on his bizarre situation. Shadrack had seen no purpose in staying awake and joined Jacob in a peaceful siesta, leaving the white boy alone to get wrecked. Jacob had had no idea that his mildly humorous remark was going to send the boy off like this and was starting to wish he had never woken up.

"…'Cos I fucking get it, mate," Bird carried on regardless. "Yep, that's right, I get it and Mr. Institutionalised Butt-cheeks Baites didn't. It wasn't his fault, man, that's just the way it is. He was part of the wheel – part of the wretched system that had become his all, his reason for being, which wasn't open to events such as these. You think this cat is dumb?" he quipped, pointing across to Clarence. "Think he don't know the score? Wrong, man, he knows exactly what cuts here – this is his fuckin' war and we are his fuckin' infantry. He didn't want Butthead fighting in his trenches, he wanted us – you, me and old Shaddy back there. Maybe Raymond was right, maybe this is Savongo after all and he has chosen me to be his messenger because he knows I'll get it. He knows that no fucked-up regime has got me running in a hamster's wheel – I'm a free agent. Hallucinogenic, cat-agenic, open to the catastrophic annihilator of Nature's heart, free from artificial colouring and flavouring. This is me, dude – take what you see, give what you get. I will tell the story in its fullness without prejudice or bias because this is when divine inspiration is at its finest – through the eyes of a drug-crazed heart… YEAH!" He leapt up onto the bonnet of the Land Rover and punched his victorious fists into the air, throwing back his head and ejecting the hat.

"Do you see me?" he screamed. "My name is Bwana Bird and this is my place!"

Shadrack threw his arms up and cheered, echoing the words "Bwana Bird". He didn't understand the sentence but it didn't matter – Bird's enthusiasm and zest for life had shot a ripple of excitement through his body and meanings of words were totally incidental. This was raw.

It was happening here and now and he felt it – like a jackhammer in his chest excavating the casing around his soul and exposing the clandestine shell that encapsulated his being. This was Bwana Bird.

"Maybe you are right, Isamba," Jacob relented at last. "Maybe what is needed here is spirit and strength of character. Maybe this is why you have come to me. I am getting lost in science and failing to see the humour in life. I am discounting our ancient tribal beliefs because I cannot prove them with a scientific theory, but maybe these beliefs are as real as the science we are trying to achieve. Maybe because enough of our people believe in them, they happen. Can this be so? Can it be that a white man called Isamba Noni has come to show me the way back to my culture? You say your witch doctor told you to come to my people for healing – well, maybe our witch doctor also called you for the same thing."

Bird was still standing on the car's bonnet with arms aloft like William the Conqueror. He had been pirouetting slowly as Jacob spoke, and his face twisted in a bizarre confusion when the statement hit him, bathing his desiccated idealism in spiritual nourishment that washed the scales from his eyes. They were now wide and attentive, their pupils no longer setting into the grey-black clouds of deception hanging below them. He was listening to a word from the wise guy and feeling a sense of purpose stirring within his loins.

Maybe he was the prophet that went into the wilderness for sixty days and sixty nights to find his true spiritual purpose; maybe he was the envoy summoned for the glory of Mother Earth's enlightenment to sanctify the ills of materialistic prophets; maybe he was the misnomer who would carry the torch of our environmental goddess while she preached to all mankind. Yes, maybe he was that Agent Green after all, and this had been his spiritual realisation – just maybe.

"Long may you live, dude – long may you live."

It was four o'clock the following afternoon after another night of mosquito hell when they all decided enough was really enough and the pair of mating lions were all loved out for now. One hundred and forty-six copulations had been recorded over thirty-seven hours of intensive sex. The record would undoubtedly belong to Clarence. He had stamina – which was more than could be said for Bird, who had slept off the last few hours of the afternoon sprawled across the back of the vehicle like a sack of rations. The lack of sleep, the intense heat, the mundane nature of his waking tasks and the sheer quantity of marijuana consumed over his fifty-eight-hour ordeal had proved too much for the lightweight white boy. Cracker would have admonished him severely for his limpness and he would have had to take it like a man. When Jacob had awakened him to give him the good news that it was all over and they were going home, he felt like John McCarthy when he was released from five years of illegal and immoral kidnapping imprisonment.

Jacob fired up the vehicle and they lurched in a homeward direction. The lovebirds were dead to the world whilst Revival's three rejuvenated females looked on, rested, revived and alert. They would organise dinner for their exhausted mother tonight and maybe, just maybe, they would reflect on the encounter and ponder their own fate when the menstrual clock struck twelve and Nature's pheromonal machine swished the desirable scent of carnal enticement off their own flicking tails.

Then again, maybe not.

23

TURNING THE FEMININE TIDE

To everyone's complete surprise, Sarah was among the gathered crowd of Sukula Research Institute's finest to welcome home the battered and beaten field crew after their shattering ordeal. This was not an unfamiliar situation for Jacob – he had endured many long-term stays on the plains and was held in the highest regard by his peers, who welcomed him like a hero every time. And it was the same in their homelands, too. When any of the men returned home for leave, children would flock around them like United fans on Ryan Giggs, groping and grappling about their beings for an awe-inspiring touch of these great men. Women would fuss over them, bringing food and water, and elders would greet them with a warm embrace. For Jacob and Shadrack, this was all very natural – for Bird, however, it was something of a phenomenon.

The very presence of Sarah sent him into spasms of shock and he shuffled about the vehicle, pretending to gather belongings in a desperate bid to look busy and avoid eye contact. The men were speaking loudly and congratulating their heroes, shaking hands and slapping shoulders amid shrieks of excitement. Isaac appeared at the back of the car where Bird was scurrying madly and held out his hand.

"Bwana Berd, Bwana Berd!" he yelled. "Welcome, saa, welcome." The customary smile etched itself across his face and distracted Bird momentarily from his attempt at invisibility. "You see, saa, Isaac tell you when you first arrive – you are the rion man. So many rions here on this prace – is how I say. Now, have you seen? You are the rion man that we bling from England. I'm telling you so. You have spirit of the rion and all ma guys have seen it in your eyes. Bwana Berd, the rion man – same like Savongo!" A cheer went up as the gathered crowd chanted their native rhyme:

Isamba Noni – mupashi wa bokwe,

Isamba Noni – mupashi wa bokwe... (The Bird Talker with the spirit of a lion.)

Jacob looked across at him and smiled. "This is how we receive a lion man in this place, Mr. Bird. I think now you are becoming one."

Bird smiled back and bowed his head towards his mentor. The feeling that his words inspired felt better than scoring a winning try in the county rugby championships. He hadn't but if he had, this would have been the feeling – bloody marvellous.

"Congratulations, Mr. Bird. I guess I was wrong about you, after all."

Sarah.

His mind immediately flicked to the night with Miss Cleavage back in the Wound when she'd teed him up so beautifully by the bar and then shot him down with a heat-seeking missile. He wasn't going to get caught out like that again. He'd already got a taste of the Tomb Raider's wrath and he sure as shit didn't want any more. His heart raced in his chest as he searched for something to say – something that wouldn't ignite the fuse – but nothing came out. He just nodded in agreement and looked to the ground as he stood fumbling and frozen.

"I understand if you don't wish to talk to me. It's all right; I probably wouldn't talk to me, either. Well done anyway, and thank you." She made as if to go, leaving Bird still looking at the floor in a paranoiac paralysis, and then turned to him once more.

"By the way, a letter has arrived for you. It's in my house. The supply vehicle came and went some days ago. I'm sorry I didn't give it to you sooner but it kept slipping my mind. You are welcome to come and fetch it if you like or I can give it to Isaac to take to you, the choice is yours."

She looked to him for some kind of response, but none was given. He remained motionless, gawking at the dirt and wishing she would just go away. It wasn't that he didn't want to talk – I mean, the opportunity of winning her trust and sorting out this whole rancid affair was a dream for sure – but cloaked in fatigue, his tongue was tied up firmly and no appropriate words sprung to mind. Women were mysterious creatures to him and he never had been that good at handling them. This one was his boss and held the key to his destiny; to screw up with her again would assure him a place on the wagon out of here and blow this gig forever. He had come about as close to that parameter as he ever wanted to – blowing the gig now would almost certainly be too much for his fragile ego to cope with, and so reclusion offered the only sanctuary in this encounter. So he remained staring at the ground until, with a meek shrug of the shoulders, she walked off, congratulating and thanking Jacob and Shadrack.

Isaac's voice sounded behind Bird and he looked up. "Bwana Berd, you must go to pick the letter. Maybe it is the wife from home who writes for you. You must go."

"I don't have a wife at home, Isaac, you know that. It's probably from Alfred, he'd be the only one to write to me."

"Still, it is you who must go. Make the peace with Madam Sarah, become her friend. You are muzungu and she is muzungu. You must learn for friends. We all must be friends in this prace, same like us. Evbody to be friends. You go, Isamba Noni, you go."

"Do you think so?"

Isaac nodded at him with a purposeful sincerity traversing in truth waves across the veins in his eyes.

"What do you think, Jacob?"

"Isaac is right. There is no place for hatred here. We live very far from other people. We are not like the people in cities who can ignore each other. Out here, we all know who everyone is and we all need to be friends – there is no place to hide. You must go, make your peace with the Madam. You will see, her heart is good – she keeps the job going here for all the guys, she gives them something to work for and she loves Sukula very much. It seems that now you have some things in common with her, so there is no need to fight anymore. She does not think you are a fool now and you have shown that you are not. Go to her, Isamba."

"Yeah, you're right. You're always right, Jacob. I wish I could be more like you – wish I could be wise."

"Wisdom is not something a man is born with, Isamba. Wisdom is something a man must learn. You have learnt about the whisker spots of lions; maybe you can learn wisdom, too. Now go, I have to sleep."

"OK… yeah… OK. Go… go to Lara. Yeah… I'll go to her, but whatever happens I can't get her pissed at me again."

He walked off, muttering to himself about defensive positions, evasive manoeuvres and high tackles. He would have to play this by the book. He didn't want any intimidation to go on here – he would play fair and square, make his apologies, hear her reasoning, shake her hand, grab the letter, give a quick smile and thanks and get the hell out of Dodge. It was imperative to remember that this was the Tomb Raider – she could slice him up in a second and throw his wretched remains to the lions. Tact was of the utmost importance.

"Oh, Mr. Bird, you came? I… I wasn't expecting you." She was talking to his distorted image through the gauze of her screen door. He quirked a sharp smile out of the side of his mouth and looked down once again. She was a step or so higher than him, as she was inside the house and he was out, and she stared at him a moment with something akin to pity. The moment seemed to last an eternity for Bird and anxious thoughts flashed through his senses.

She wants to make me sweat a little. She likes the power of being taller – she's keeping me on the step on purpose. I can feel her staring at me… don't look, dude… don't make eye contact… just follow orders and keep your head down.

In truth, Sarah had locked her gaze on him for no more than a couple of seconds, and it was feelings of guilt rather than abusive power that consumed her. He had a way about him that she had identified in their first meeting. There was something very unassuming, something profound. He had no airs or graces. He made no pretences. There was a confident lack of confidence within him that shone through like a beacon in the night – he was mysterious, a man of secrets, hidden agendas and social role-plays that defy the whole. That was how Miss Cleavage had perceived him, and she was right. But Sarah was more intuitive; she was not part of the big wheel of life that Miss C played into. She was on her own mission; she created her own life and therefore had more of an insight into what was around her – like manners, or lack of them.

"God, I'm sorry, I've lost my manners, please come in. I've left you standing there like a prune." The door creaked with a weary groan that indicated it had slammed home once too often on its unoiled brass hinge, and it slammed home again behind him.

"I'm used to being a prune. I think it becomes me." He'd intended this to be a joke but the meekness with which it had been delivered made him look like he was fishing for compliments – and who knows, maybe he actually was.

"We can all be the things our minds tell us we will be, Bird. You can choose prunehood if you want, but I don't think it becomes you." This was the best he was going to get if he thought that compliment fishing might sway her. She'd played that 'poor old me' game before and it didn't inspire her. She turned and shuffled off to the office in search of his letter.

Bird almost forgot he was in the Tomb Raider's den as he quipped back in a casual manner, "I think if I have many more days in this African sun then prunehood will not be a choice. It's all right for mating lions – they are covered with fur, but we have to sit it out in the sun and wait for the inevitable, then count it. They should be more considerate of us, don't you think?"

Bird looked up and realised that he was talking to himself. Sarah had disappeared from view, leaving him standing in the doorway of her kitchen, speaking aimlessly into a void. As she reappeared, her outstretched hand wafted a blue airmail envelope in front of his nose, clasped between her fingers. A huge smile illuminated her face and those piercing blue eyes once again bathed him in sincerity – not to mention a touch of desire.

Her hair was clean and sparkling, not like the first day they had met. It perfectly matched the deep brown complexion of her tan and reflected waves of cherry-red light through its auburn body. There was neither blemish nor wrinkle on her beautiful skin – the concept of prunehood appeared so totally irrelevant when confronted with this angel. She seemed to ebb and sway around him, like the ballad of a mermaid gently caressing the last surviving mariner from a sunken ship's crew. She really was a peach, and he had to prise his eyes away from her for fear of sparking that aforementioned intimidation again. The last thing he needed was her thinking he was some kind of letch and sending her cataclysmic ballistic on him once more – besides, any lustful thoughts would undoubtedly be met with the inferno that had ruined the night of passion with Miss Cleavage. Best to look away.

"Would you like a drink? Some tea, perhaps?"

"No. No, thank you. I am very tired. I think I must be getting along now. Thank you for the letter."

"Please, Mr. Bird, don't go just yet, there are a couple of things I'd like to talk to you about and now is probably a good time. Please, just five minutes. Will you at least sit?"

"Um… well… yes, OK, five minutes."

"Thank you."

She took a deep breath as they sat in two mismatched armchairs facing one another. She perched herself on the edge of her seat and clasped her hands in front of her, resting them on her knees, which were locked together. The skin on her long legs was smooth and tight around the limbs. She looked sleek and well defined, like an athlete. Even her knees had no wrinkles. Bird's eyes shot around the room taking evasive action from her mesmerising stare, the words 'don't get her pissed' resonating through his skull like the sphere of a yo-yo ricocheting from the hand of a child.

"I just wanted to apologise for my behaviour when we first met," she began. "I think I was out of line. I have since found out that it was Alfred Weiss who wrote your CV and applied for the job on your behalf. He said he was afraid we wouldn't take you on if we had known you only had experience with birds and not lions, and he would have been right, too. However, he did say that he knew you could apply your mind to anything and that all you needed was a chance and you would be able to prove yourself worthy, which you have. I didn't know that at the time, and I apologise."

The edges of Bird's lips creased into an acknowledging smile and he bowed his head groundwards, hoping that she would soon be finished and he could get off to bed. Unfortunately, there was a bit more conscience left in this high-interest account and she was doing her best now to clear it.

"Look, Bird, your reports have been fantastic. The parallels you are drawing between the prides, the theories put forward for pride distributions and range sizes, inter-group dynamics, the proposals for extra equipment for blood and faecal sampling – they're all exactly what we need. This is the sort of work I have been looking for out here and you are delivering the goods. It's brilliant. And now, with the advent of this new lion and the pride takeover, well, this is a gift sent from heaven – you do know that, don't you?"

"Well, I don't know about heaven but it is a significant result, yes." He looked at her momentarily and then shot his eyes away once again.

"Well, whatever it is, these events are of vital importance to the Institute. This is exactly what the donors have been asking me to produce and now I have it. In the past, my arguments have been based on animals that are dead and we've never had enough viable data on them to substantiate the theories of species dimorphism. I'm not sure whether you know, but in the early 1900s, well over twenty subspecies of lions were thought to have existed throughout Africa and the Middle East, but most of their differences were attributable to skull shape. Nowadays, with advances in genetics and DNA to separate subspecies within a whole, those theories have been thrown out and lions in the African sub-Saharan region are said to be monotypic – i.e. all one species. Physical variations between populations have been recorded but the genetic differences have never been enough to substantiate a taxonomic reclassification of any lion population. Are you getting all of this?"

"Yes, yes, I think so. Savongo spoke a lot about this kind of stuff in his reports. He seemed convinced that Sukula lions were actually a subspecies, but the blood sampling he did never reached any testing laboratory in a suitable state to prove it, and he never managed to sample enough individuals for it to mean anything. But what exactly makes a subspecies?"

"Well, it's a number of things mainly to do with skull formation, cranial cavities, dentition and bone structure, but nowadays they can tell everything from allelic variation in DNA. You see, in the past, scientists believed that for an animal to evolve in a slightly different way from others in its species it needed to have made some anatomical changes to its physical makeup. To just have a different colour coat or longer mane can be accountable to all kinds of things, but for an animal's bone, cranial or tooth structure to have changed, some kind of genetic variation has to have taken place – hence a subspecies. As I said, these days it's all done with DNA, and allelic variation on chromosomal loci seem to be among the most popular determining factors. Genetics has opened a lot of doors with taxonomy, but there are also those who believe that genetic scientists are looking too intricately at minute details, so some are reverting back to the old morphological theories of brain, bone and tooth."

"Wow, if you say so! But why didn't Savongo just send off some bones to clarify the whole thing if the blood sampling wasn't working?"

"Well, this is where the argument flared up. Hunters were taking the whole trophy animal away with them, bones and all, and none of this kind of work could be done. He did manage to procure the skull of a female that died in a territorial battle, but the Government were not happy about this being taken out for analysis and the paperwork proved too difficult to export. We were trying to get the funding to bring a team out here to do the analysis onsite, but no one really wanted to know because as far as they were all concerned, no subspecies of lions exist. So when the technology became available locally we wanted to do DNA sampling to show variations, but by then, all the true

Sukula males were gone. And then, in the middle of all this, Templar goes missing and is presumed dead. That's why the appearance of this lion is of vital importance."

"Yes, yes, I see. OK, well, you have my word that I won't let Clarence out of my sight and I'll try and stop the hunters from nailing him."

"Excellent. Now, how about a drink?"

"Are we going to be much longer?" As the words tumbled from his lips, he caught a glimpse of the Tomb Raider peeking out of the corner of Sarah's eye. She was being nice and hospitable. If he compromised that hospitality now, she could unleash hell at any stage. He stuttered on, "Well... um... OK... ahh... I'll just have some juice, please. Thank you."

She stopped in mid-stride across the room and looked at him again. He felt her stare burning into his head like the imaginary fans in his rugby stadium, and he kept his head down and eyes fixed on the trees outside her window.

"I don't bite, Mr. Bird," she said calmly with a smile. "You can look at me. I am human, you know."

He raised his head slowly and looked at her, another one of those embarrassed smiles crumpling the edge of his lips. She was human – a very beautiful human at that – but she was wrong about one thing: she definitely did bite. Yep, she bit like a rottweiler on PCP.

"Yes, I know you're human," he murmured. "You're a very beautiful human indeed, but you have the defence mechanism of a lioness and I don't want to be the cause of arming that again. It's better this way."

Maybe it was the tiredness; the most heartfelt truths are often uttered when defences are down, and extreme fatigue brings down those guards as surely as ten pints of Guinness at the Wound. He kind of knew he shouldn't have said it, but the temptation was just too much and the words were out before he had time to check himself.

Sarah was left speechless for once in her life. She stood and looked into his eyes and for once, he held her stare and felt a twinge of lust in his gut. If Tomb Raider didn't get him, he knew the burning image wouldn't be far behind, but the moment was heavenly.

A million thoughts crashed into Sarah's psyche, but none of them materialised into action. She was genuinely flattered. No man had been this honest with her in ages, let alone one that she had treated this way.

"Yes... well... umm... I'll... I'll just go and... um... and get the... uhh... the drinks. Yep... the drinks... I'll just... yes... shan't be a minute." Her hands were fumbling and bumbling self-consciously in front of her, matched only by her feet, which danced like a hyena running over hot coals. She had been caught out of her crease and was now standing mid-wicket like a buffoon, waiting for the inevitable finger from the umpire to send her marching back to the pavilion.

Never was much of a cricketer!

The last thing she had expected from this man was a compliment. It wasn't just that, though, it was the sincere honesty in the way he had delivered it. He wasn't hitting on her, he wasn't fishing for something, he didn't have to prove anything, he just said it because he meant it. He meant that she was too beautiful to stare at because he didn't want to intimidate her. As she poured the drinks, thousands of combined connotations raced through her mind about the words he had said. At the end of the day, he was being honest and that was about all she could really ask for.

Bird accepted the cup of juice that Sarah held out to him. He felt like he'd just come off a thirty-six-hour rave having done a multitude of pills and acid. They always dropped acid when coming down from big Ecstasy sessions – either that or get monumentally pissed, but that always meant parting with hard-earned cash unless they got Cracker to steal it. Either way, the washed-out feeling was the same, and he seemed to huddle in his chair in spite of the afternoon's heat.

"Mr. Bird..." Sarah began.

"Please, call me Bird."

"Yes, I'm sorry, it's just such an unusual name."

"Could be worse, I could be called Cracker. Cheers!" He took a sip from the glass and cupped it in both hands in front of him.

"Bird, you know that I will be going away soon? I always leave for a couple of months in the rainy season – not much happens and we can't really get around. Jacob sometimes does foot follows but even those are seldom successful. The lions see him coming from miles away and he can't make any meaningful observations. He does go on anti-poaching patrols with the rangers, though, and kind of monitors them; it's an activity left over from the Templar days. Meat poaching increases in the rains because we are not around and neither is the hunter, but it's been going on for years and the area can sort of sustain it. There are a couple of tourist lodges that use the vicinity but they generally operate further south, away from the hunting area, and they are all closed for the next few months. Not much goes on but I do like to keep a presence here. In the past, we have had university students who come out and do work on plants and trees. They basically sit out the wet and potter about camp." She paused and looked across at him. He was trying to be as attentive as he could, but the fatigue was taking its toll and he wondered what she was getting at with this little speech.

"Well? Go on, what does this have to do with me?" he prompted.

"Well, I was kind of wondering if you wouldn't mind staying here and looking after the place during the rainy season. I'll give you your old room back or you can even live in the house here, if you want – it has a flush loo and a proper shower. What do you think?"

"If I stayed here, Sarah, I would find it hard to move out of the village – it's kind of my place now and besides, I think the guys would feel a bit disappointed if I moved." His right hand moved up to his chin and stroked his whiskers as he stared off into vacant space. "How long will it be before I go home, then?"

"Home? Oh, yeah, sorry. Umm, well, we are sorting out a work permit for you now to enable you to stay for the next two years – if that's what you want, of course. If it comes through, you can go home when I get back and have a couple of weeks' leave. We'd need you back here for the dry season to start on the programme again, but it would give you a holiday and let you see your family and friends again. Would you like some time to think about it? I'm not going for at least a month so you can have a couple of days to mull it all over, if you wish."

Mull it over? Are you nuts? This is my place and my name is Bwana Bird. What's there to mull over? There's only Cracker and the lads at home and we'd just end up getting wasted again and reminiscing about old times. None of them would really want to know about this place, except Alfie, and it wouldn't really faze him not to see me for a while more. Shit, man, consider it mulled, I'll do it.

"Consider it mulled. I'll do it," Bird chirped as his thoughts tumbled from his mouth. Sarah was taken aback.

"What, just like that? You don't need to think about it?"

"Nothing to think about, really. There isn't much waiting for me back home and besides, there's no lions in England – you heard the staff, I am becoming a lion man now. No problem, I'll stay."

"Oh, Mr. Bird... I mean Bird, that's wonderful. Thank you, thank you very much and once again, please accept my apologies for my behaviour when you first arrived. I can't make you understand but at least I can apologise."

"I think I understand, Sarah. I understand that you care so much about this place that it has almost consumed you – it's your passion. I see it too, man, I see it too."

"Good, then that's settled. OK, plan of attack for the next four weeks is to get as much information as possible on the new lion. I'll need your reports to continue and then I'll need a fairly comprehensive final prognosis just before I go, detailing what resources we will need to substantiate genetic lineage of this chap and what the implications might be if he really is a Sukula male. We have to document as many unique behavioural traits as we can, and hopefully they will tie in with Templar's behavioural analysis, which will enable me to pick up the reins on his line of thinking. Oh, and photographs, as many as you can get. I've got a spare so just hang on to the camera and shoot at will. OK?"

"Yeah, man, no problem. Now, can I go and sleep?"

"Yes. Yes, of course you can. And you can read your letter. From a girlfriend, perhaps? A loved one back home? Or is it your mother?"

"No. No girlfriend, no mother. It's from Alfred."

"What, no mother? Are you telling me your mother doesn't miss you just a tiny bit now you're out in Africa and so far away from home? Come on, Bird, all mothers worry about their sons, even yours I dare say."

She had intended this to be a joke. Sarah wasn't the street ghetto type who cussed people's mothers for fun – it just wasn't her style. But his reaction put an abrupt halt to her march for comic prosperity and sent queasy shockwaves through her stomach. He stood there staring into her eyes and biting his bottom lip in restraint. For the first time she saw real emotion there, like he was burning up, and she didn't know how to handle it.

"Are you OK, Bird? I was only joking."

"Yeah, I know, it's not your fault. I'm OK. I'll see you tomorrow."

"Wait Bird, I'm sorry, really I am. I didn't mean any harm. Are you sure you're all right? Was it something I said?"

He looked away for a second and then returned his stare to hers. His lips moved as if trying to vocalise words, but nothing seemed to come out. He sighed and swallowed, sucking air through his teeth, and his eyes squinted into a hard glare.

"You know, I haven't seen my mother in over twenty years," he said, in such a casual manner that at first Sarah thought he was joking and almost giggled. "My father is a convicted criminal. He drove the getaway car for a robbery that went wrong and ended up killing two policemen. He got a life sentence for each one."

And then she realised there was no humour in this tale at all.

Bird continued his story. Normally, he never mentioned his past, but now it was hard to stop himself – the words just formed independently and then began to drip like remorseful stalactites from his lips as he delivered the cold rendition of his unfortunate history. It had been a while since anyone had wanted to know and so it had remained bottled inside him like a vintage wine that had long since turned to vinegar. This seemed as good a time as any to get it out of his head and clear some space on the dusty wine rack in the back of his mind.

"I couldn't tell you where my mother is right now. I don't even know what she looks like anymore, how much she's changed, if at all. She was always a bit of a drinker, and after the conviction she took to the booze big time – it was the only way she knew how to deal with it, I guess. We lived together for a while – just the two of us in a small council house – though I spent most of my time with mates or at Alfred's place as she was impossible to be around when she was drunk. Then, this one day I came home from school and found the place empty. There was a note from my mother on the table and ten pounds in cash. The note was some form of apology for being so crap and that she would always love me and think of me and stuff but for now, she just had to get away. I was nine years old."

There was no display of emotion as he told the story, just an analytical portrayal of cataclysmic events. He had actually memorised her words and held them in his head every day since she left, but Sarah didn't need a recital. In his own way, he had dealt with it and he didn't need to cry anymore – the tears were long gone but the silence was still with him. What remained in that silence were questions. Questions with no answers. Why had this happened to him? Why had she left? She was all he had, and he her. Why would she run out on the last thing she had in the world? Her own son? He never knew but he asked the question over and over, almost every day of his life, in a bizarre quest to try to silence the silence.

"I haven't heard from her since – I don't even know if she's still alive," he went on, unprompted. "I packed up my things that day and Alfred came to collect me. I gave him the ten bob and he never asked for another bean in rent again. He took me in like I was his own and raised me, and now he's all the family I have. The prison board recommended that I stop visiting my father, as his behaviour was deteriorating and they didn't think he was a suitable role model for me anymore. I haven't seen him since my mum left and he never writes. The only person who really gives a monkey's about me these days is Alfred – Alfred Weiss, the famous ornithologist – the same one who lied on my CV to get me here.

"You see, Sarah, I am a lost cause, it's in my genes. They even have to lie in order for me to get these opportunities. It's a good job the pontoon went down and you didn't send me home at the start of this gig, else it may well have all been over by now. I was slipping in England, I was slipping away. When you're young, you deal with these things in your own way but as you get older, you start to question them more and more. The only answers I found were closed doors and rejection. Silence within the silence. The lifestyle I had gave me a kick and kept those hounds from my door for just a little bit longer, but coming out here has really saved my life – this place and these guys. It has given me something to fight for, a reason to live – and more importantly, a reason not to give up.

"All mothers should worry about their sons, Sarah – you're dead right there, especially if they're in Africa. Alfred is my mother – he's my mother and my father and everything I will ever need and he probably does worry about me, you know, but I dare say he's not as worried as he was before – it's better here and he knew it would be. He always knows what's right, does Alfie." He paused for a second as he remembered Alfred, and then he turned to Sarah once more with half-glazed eyes. "I gotta go man; I'm beat. I'll see you later. Thanks for this."

And then he was gone.

The gauze door creaked and banged home once again and he was back into the evening light, breathing that sweet, sweet air of the hardwood forest. The Sukula Plains were away off to his right, with Revival now under the new patronage of the most awesome creature in this land. The hunter was ready to pack up his things and leave, and Lara Croft would be back in her tomb and off his case forever. The sanctuary of his little village lay ahead in the trees, and a good night's rest on a comfortable mattress beckoned his weary bones.

In the east, storm clouds gathered and lightning flashed out its warning of impending rain. The seasons were about to shift and Sukula would slip into another domain. He only had one month left to gather all the information he could on Clarence the destroyer, and to send his envoy back to the mutant lands with a message to the distorted race about the priceless jewel on which they stand. He would embrace this challenge with an open heart and a head full of desire as Nature's chronology ticked and turned, hands pointing to the hour that beckoned him to fulfil his dream. The Eco-Warrior was here, on the front line of life – locked and loaded, ready to fire at will.

Long may he live.

I wonder what Alfred has to say for himself. There better be an apology in there!

24

POACHING PATROL

Cordite.

The word kept ringing in his head like the incessant chant from some rhythmic revolution. Cordite. Running round and round in there like a rabbit in a warren. Cordite. What did it mean, where did it come from, was it even a word? As if there wasn't enough real shit going on in this situation, he had to go and get all hung up on a word racing through his mind – a word that might not even exist.

Cordite.

Well that's how it smells, man, it smells like cordite. Word or no word, the shit that's in my mouth is cordite. End of story.

The smell was so prevalent that it was in his mouth. It had dripped down from his nose and melted into the back of his throat. He could taste it and he could feel it; he could even hear it. Can you hear a smell? It's unlikely, but his whole being was completely consumed and this cordite stuff was so intoxicating that it was starting to devour his very soul.

He lifted his head from the mud and strained a view at what was happening. He could see a pair of boots lying in the brown, shallow water a few yards ahead of him. To one side was the obscured and partially hidden view of a camouflage jacket, more boots were further ahead, and on the other side, poking through the grass, was what looked like a rifle barrel.

And then he was burying his head in the muddy water once again as another burst of gunfire rang out from his left, the high-pitched cracks piercing through his ears.

He had never known how he might react in a surreal circumstance like this. He'd seen the movies a thousand times, acted out the role as a child – even as an adult here and there – but when confronted with it up close and personal like this, everything changes. He had never had to consider what he might actually do in a gunfight and he was still somehow detached from it all.

They had walked into a sort of ambush, though this was not a war. Had it been a war, they'd have been killed in seconds – but the people who were, by default, their adversaries were not military, nor were they mercenaries. They were men – normal, average village men forced into a situation that scared them senseless.

The patrol had chanced upon them with their quarry of a buffalo carcass that they were busy hacking up. Sure, two of the poachers had automatic weapons – AK-47s to be precise – but they were not soldiers. Commercial meat poachers with no regard for wildlife preservation, but not soldiers. As the patrol burst into view, one of them got the shits and squeezed off a few rounds that sent both parties diving for cover. The patrol rangers immediately returned fire and pinned the shooters down, giving them no option but to burst off rounds every now and then to keep the officers at bay. The situation had been going on for a fair few minutes now and all Bird could think of was this word *cordite* that was bouncing around his skull, because he was sure that was what he could smell. The smell of spent cartridges and small-arms fire.

The rainy season was now full steam ahead and a lot of the area was covered with surface water and mud. The once-dormant grass had found a new lease of life and tall strands shot up from every available surface, providing ample cover for wildlife and ideal breeding grounds for a million or so insect species. During the three days of mind-numbing trudging through the saturated terrain, Bird had got so wet that he was now soaked to the bone. Some kind of trench-foot fungus had colonised his feet, a rash had appeared in his crotch where his shorts rubbed against his skin, a multitude of bites and welts that had adversely reacted with his skin formed mutant lumps and blisters, his lips were cracked and dry, skanky sweat and dirt had formed bulges in his matted hair and as if that wasn't enough, he was now lying face-down in the mud with cordite penetrating every pore in his body. Something had to give.

A series of shouts and screams rang out as the patrol rangers served their opponents with some form of surrender ultimatum. Bird lifted his head to see if he could glean the gist of it, only to be met with another burst of gunfire that peppered into the grass around him and sent his face back into the dirt where it belonged. Then scuttling and shuffling, more shouting and screaming, another crack of small-arms incendiaries, and suddenly all went quiet.

He lay motionless for a second with his arms wrapped around his head and for the first time in the whole confusion of this moment, he felt afraid. Too much had happened for fear to have registered before and he had really just been acting on pure survival instincts. But now that a plan was being formulated and some kind of counter-offensive being launched, he felt very alone, as he had not one clue as to what the offensive might be or whether he was even involved.

This ain't my fucking war, man!

He sneaked a look towards the boots that had been in front of him before, only to find that they had since vanished from view. He looked left and right, but the rangers either side had disappeared as well.

Where is everyone? They better not leave me here, man, I doubt whether I'd find the way home. Hey, what's that up ahead?

Curiosity killed the cat, or so they say, and it very nearly killed Bird, too. He scrambled up onto his knees and peered over the top of the grass towards a dark brown lump that stood about twenty metres ahead of him. It looked oddly out of shape and somewhat alien to the whole setting until it turned and faced him, fixing him with a glare of indignance that implied he owed it money.

The male buffalo had bolted from the trees with the excitement of gunfire around him, and as the rangers and poachers had charged off in pursuit of one another, the only safe refuge, oddly enough, was the site of the original contact where the poached buffalo was being dismembered. This very alive and now very pissed twelve-hundred-pound animal suddenly found itself at the death site of one of its brethren and, to add insult to injury, was now confronted with a most bedraggled-looking Bird, who just represented 'human' in the animal's eyes.

It's difficult to say whether buffalo have any sense of emotion that compels them to avenge the death of their fellow kind, but what they do have is an incredibly low tolerance for intruders and virtually no sense of humour whatsoever. Couple this with relatively poor eyesight and a pair of razor-sharp, pointed horns, and a potentially catastrophic situation could present itself.

The beast squinted its eyes and huffed a snort through its nostrils before advancing a couple of steps towards Bird for a better view of him. The action caused a slight bowel movement in Bird's pants and then sent him howling and screaming into the nearest thicket to get away. This motion then caused the buffalo similar bowel-related concerns and he shot off in the opposite direction. It's possible that if he'd had the capacity to squeal in the same way that Bird did, he may have done it. As it was, they both charged off at divergent tangents and before Bird knew what was what, he had climbed the nearest tree to the highest point and was now clutching to it for dear life with his eyes tightly shut, his mouth vocalising remorse for his current situation and every muscle in his body strained to breaking point.

The sense of relief that he felt when he finally heard Jacob's voice asking him if he was all right was quite overwhelming.

"No, no, not really all right, Jacob, but thanks for asking anyway."

"Well, what are you doing?"

"Getting the fuck away from that monster, what do you think I'm doing?"

"I am not really sure."

As Bird opened his eyes, he could see Jacob, but something was slightly amiss. At first, he couldn't quite pinpoint it, but something definitely wasn't right. It took a second to adjust to his viewpoint but once he had, he realised Jacob was upside down. How the hell had this happened? He craned his head sideways and saw that the ground was only some three feet away from him, and indeed it was he who had been inverted, not Jacob. He released his grip on the tree and crashed face down into the mud once again, which seemed an all-too-appropriate end to this whole sordid affair.

"May I suggest you find a stronger tree to climb next time the buffalo is chasing you?" quipped Jacob as he grinned across to the officers.

"Yeah, very funny, mate. It was the first object I saw, and I just scaled it. How was I to know it was a sapling?" he asked, dragging himself to his feet.

The tree was tall, Bird could be granted that, but it was still very junior in years and its number one priority in life was to grow towards the nearest available light, which was straight up. It hadn't wasted time with branches or excess foliage or even spreading a wide girth. This tree's only mission was to get up into the canopy and grab a share of that light. The extra weight of Bird's scrambling body didn't really cause the tree too much concern, but it wasn't going to stand up against the leapfrogging jerks that propelled him up its stem. Consequently, the further up he went, the more the tree sagged until he was back, not three feet from the ground, eyes shut tight and holding on for dear life, thinking that he was safe in the forest's canopy. That was how Jacob had found him.

"So, would someone mind telling me what the hell just happened here?" Adrenaline was now pumping through his veins and fear was still surging through his heart, as confusion raged in his mind and the trace of skid marks lay in his shorts. Bwana Bird was angry, and he demanded answers.

"Meat poachers, Bwana," came the reply from one of the rangers. "They have killed a buffalo and it is a female."

"Well, did you catch them?"

"No, they have run away but we get a weapon and the meat, so I think they have now gone."

"I don't think I'm up to this, Jacob. I didn't come here to get shot at by meat poachers, man. What's that shit all about?"

"You knew there may be risks, Mr. Bird. I told you that we go on patrol looking for poachers, and now we have found them. This is very good. We may have lost a buffalo, but they know that we are here patrolling and it means they will move to another place for poaching. I don't think they wanted to kill us."

"Whether they wanted to or not is totally fucking irrelevant, mate – they were firing at us with live ammunition. It only takes a stray bullet… damn, I don't even want to think about this anymore, man, it's not funny. I'm not laughing."

He sat on a log and pulled out his tobacco packet. His hands, covered in mud and water, were shaking uncontrollably. Rolling the smoke was not going to be easy but in light of recent events, raising the Titanic would have been a walk in the park.

Compass was among the ranger patrol group and he took a seat next to Bird. He looked at him expectantly and Bird duly handed over the tobacco packet, this now part of their unspoken bond. At one point Bird thought Compass might have come to console him but alas, it was just the tobacco that he sought.

"I think we must camp here tonight and finish cutting up the buffalo meat. Tomorrow we will carry it home and use it for rations for the next patrol. I think it will take about one and a half days to reach camp and there is much meat to carry, but at least we can drop you back at home and then we don't need to hear your complaining for the rest of this patrol. Is it OK?"

"Yeah man, it's better than OK. Just get me the hell outta here – please."

Jacob had advised Bird not to come on the patrol. He had told him that all kinds of stuff could happen and that, aside from the obvious dangers with poachers and hunters, it was incredibly uncomfortable sleeping out in these conditions and there were any number of insects and monsters that roamed in the rains. Bird had now been out on Sukula a good few months and had let his little ego run away with him. He thought he was 'Jack the Lad' and could handle anything. Besides, if it was good enough for Jacob, he reasoned that it should be good enough for him, too. Jacob had relented to his constant pestering and thought that this patrol, being a fairly local and low-key one, would be a good and safe option. The last thing he had expected was to encounter poachers, and certainly not ones that were prepared to have a gun battle. In retrospect, however, he was glad that it had happened, as now 'white boy' here would be off his case for the remainder of the rainy season and stop bugging him to come on patrol.

At that point, the dark clouds that had been gathering in the east opened up their valves and poured raindrops the size of tennis balls down on the bedraggled unit. Camouflage-patterned sleeping tarps appeared from backpacks and everyone took meagre refuge under his own roof. Bird's smoke was long since history and the advent of rain just made him pout up his lips and huff a disgruntled sigh.

It's not easy being a lion man.

He stared out from beneath his canopy at nothing in particular. At this time of year, the rain came so heavy that visibility was reduced to less than negligible and dormant rivers began flowing in seconds. The ferocity of the rain had caught Bird clean off guard when it first began, flooding his hut and washing out his few meagre possessions in its wake. Once the initial tide had been stemmed and adequate drainage dug around his abode, round two was ready to commence, which it did at around three o'clock the following morning. The second torrential burst of rain fell in the night and sprung every available leak within his thatched roof. Such things had not to be considered in the dry season and it is only at such times, when one is snuggled up in bed, sound asleep, that nature calls one to consider them. It was also at this point in his day (or night, as the case most definitely was) that he was at his lowest tolerance for emergency situations and indeed that his sense of humour stood the greatest chance of failing. There are those who think that the world revolves around their own pathetic axis and such an act of nature is sent specifically to annoy them, which just aggravates the situation further. Such was Bird.

He had failed the sense of humour test many times since Sarah had departed for England and the rains had come, and indeed had been forced to question his commitment to the whole damn affair on more than one occasion. Had it not been for the fact that he had no choice but to remain in camp, he might well have packed his bags and left. Unfortunately, or maybe even fortunately for him, no roads were passable owing to the sheer amount of water that had fallen, so the option of flight was non-existent. It was this very sense of being trapped within the village that had urged him to pester Jacob into taking him on patrol.

Maybe by some bizarre notion, the patrol would chance upon a helicopter about ready to depart for London with one spare seat aboard, or perhaps a hovercraft bound for Amsterdam, or maybe even a Harrier Jump Jet just on its way back to base in England. Who knows, maybe the patrol would stop at a motorway service station halfway through and he could order a Whopper with cheese meal and go large for just 50p extra. Whatever his reasons, he needed to get the hell out of camp and go somewhere – anywhere – just to know he was alive and there really was a world out there.

When science takes on a routine of maintenance on old findings and the pioneering exploration is gone, the likes of Bird become totally disinterested. He had done the geeky boffin thing of marching around camp with tree books, plant books and bird books. He had referenced about as much of the flora as his little mind was prepared to accept and worked out all the summer avian visitors, ascertaining what they were doing here and where they had come from. So, sitting in camp with just the books for stimulation, frustration had begun to set in and, bearing in mind the fact that they were unable to go out onto the plains to see the lions (kind of negating his newfound status of lion man), he was, all in all, not a happy camper. With no supply vehicles coming in and out of town, there was very little change in his daily diet and treats were few and far between. Most of his special rations such as chocolate, cookies, cornflakes and Coke had been consumed within the first two weeks, and now nshima and kapenta (the whitebait-type fish) was all he ate three times a day. The buffalo meat would be a welcome change.

Three days into the patrol that was to offer him absolution in this hamster's wheel that he found himself trudging, they walked into what was, to all intents and purposes, an ambush – and for the first time in his life, someone was taking potshots at him with automatic weapons. Once that little fiasco was under control, a psychotic buffalo had charged at him full steam ahead, and then it began to rain. This, coupled with all the other ailments he had, such as the trench foot, all added up to the fact that Mr. Bird had definitely seen better days.

"Who were those guys, Jacob? I mean the poachers – where did they come from?"

"Luchange, I think. It is a town to the west, very far away. There is an old refugee camp there, which is where they got their weapons, and the refugees have money, so they can always sell the meat."

"Really, they're selling meat to refugees? Heavy shit. Were those guys military?" Bird tugged on a smoke while he watched Jacob and the men dismember the remainder of the buffalo carcass with axes, the rain having temporarily abated.

"No, they were not military, but they are not afraid to shoot."

"You don't say?"

"Meat is not only sold to the refugees. There is big market in this country for bush meat – it is much more prized than beef. As you can see, the butchery is very simple and the meat tastes completely different. There are many people who trade in this meat all over Africa. Anyone who wants to make money is involved with meat poaching, and this buffalo could have been sold all over the country if they had finished the job. Can you see, they dry the meat on these smoking racks and that preserves it for many months. It also makes it easy for transport, and it goes all over the land from trader to trader. Our people are starving, and we will never stop the poachers from coming. The best we can do is stop them from coming here, to Sukula. We can patrol and chase them, that is all."

Clandestine drying racks made from cut branches had indeed been erected all over the site, and half the patrol were busy stoking fires beneath them and arranging the strips of freshly-butchered buffalo on top for smoking. The other half were dismembering the carcass, and Bird was sitting on a log, smoking a jay and firing questions in to Jacob. A thousand vultures loitered in nearby trees and on thermals above them in the sky, and the whole scene seemed like some surreal Road Runner cartoon set. It seemed that dinner was served not only for the rangers but also for the scavengers. Bird wondered if it would attract hyenas in to the position, and he contemplated for a moment the prospect of sleeping under the stars in the African bush next to a rotting buffalo carcass and drying racks full of meat.

"Have you ever caught any poachers, Jacob?"

"Yes, once or twice."

"And what happens to them?"

"It depends on the poacher. If they have shot an elephant for the ivory, then they are serious and to catch them you must be clever and also very brave. Ivory poachers will kill you quickly. We send them to town for trial at court, but transport is always a problem and the rangers cannot keep them safely at their camp. We do not have too many problems with ivory poachers here because elephants are few and there are better places for poachers to go, but if they come, better you run, and don't climb a tree like with the buffalo, this will not help you." A giggling ripple traversed through the men, all knee-deep in buffalo meat, and Bird shifted his pose on his log and cleared his throat. He kept thinking how glad he was that Cracker was not here to witness these events of stupidity or he'd never hear the end of it.

"Yes, yes, of course. Cheeky bugger," he added under his breath. "So what about the other types of poachers, then? What would we have done if we'd caught this lot, for example?"

"These hunters were probably from Luchange but the rest, their carriers, would have been local guys. We may have sent them back to their villages and asked the chief to discipline them, and then the hunters would have gone to Kamache for trial with the local magistrate."

"And what sentence would they have got?"

"Usually a fine, but it depends on amount of meat and guns they have – they can also go to prison. But this is Africa, Isamba – if you know the judge or you are an important member of your community, you can get away with no sentence."

"Really, you can bribe the judge?" He sounded surprised but reasoned that he shouldn't be. Judges can be bribed all over the world, it's just that in some countries it takes more money than in others.

"Of course, you can bribe anyone. Is it not so in your country?"

Bird stopped and contemplated this a while, and then thought about those church deacons and bishops back home that abuse their altar boys and never seem to get prosecuted; maybe they were bribing judges, too. Then, of course, there's major corporations and politicians literally getting away with murder, and large sums of money had to be involved. It seemed corruption was not just an African thing, after all.

"Yeah, I guess there is bribery at home. You know, we have important men in the church who do bad things to little boys and always seem to get away with it – I guess there's some form of corruption going on there."

"What do they do to the boys?" Jacob seemed somewhat perplexed, if not a little shocked at this remark. The church was held as a bastion of propriety, so what were these acts and how could the lines have become blurred?

"It doesn't really matter, mate, it's sick and if you don't know about it, Jacob, then you truly have been spared one repulsive aspect of our society. What sort of sentence do ivory poachers get, then?"

"It also depends. Maybe they are selling ivory to politicians and they go free, but usually they get about five years in prison. There is plenty pressure from the outside world these days to stop ivory poaching, so they have to be careful. It is the same for a rhino, but all the rhino in this place are gone."

"So, what about some little dude from the village who whacks an antelope or a warthog for his family, what do you do if you catch him?"

"Nothing, we let him go. People have to eat and he is not killing plenty, so why should we stop him? For some of the elders in the villages, hunting is all they know – it is part of our culture. Anyway, it is better for community relations if we overlook some of these poachers and let them have meat from Sukula. At least then, Sukula is providing something for them."

The weed was coating Bird in its customary blanket of oblivion once again and he was starting to wind down from the events of the day. The smell of incendiaries had long since vanished, washed away by the rain, and was now replaced by the combined smells of the buffalo carcass, its stomach and bowel contents and the waft of the smoking meat. The sun was sinking into the west and the men set about making camp and bivvying down for the impending rain. A number of fires were being prepared around their perimeter to dissuade any scavengers from chancing their luck in the night, and no setting around Sukula would be complete without the obligatory call of a Heuglin's robin.

What a day, man... what a fucking day. Is anyone going to believe this when I get home? I'm questioning whether I even believe it. Better work out where I'm gonna sleep to maximise safety and minimise hyena threat, hmmm.

He laid out his mat and sleeping bag and then slung his mosquito net and rain tarp over some crudely-fashioned sticks to make a tent. It wouldn't keep him dry, but he was now beyond caring. He hadn't been dry in over three days, and at least tomorrow they were going home – it was the end of the road. The patrol had done one thing for Bird: it had made him glad to be getting back to camp, the very place that had driven him out here to begin with. Isaac would be there with his customary joviality and excellent hospitality, the other guys would all be milling about doing their assorted jobs, laughing, joking and tormenting each other, and the kids that at first had been so scared of him would be running around his feet squawking and shouting – probably abusing him in their own language so he couldn't understand.

The children had come to accept the white man now, in spite of their initial fears and the inevitable language barrier. Their English was non-existent and his command of their language confined to a few words and crude sentences, but they were always good for a game of tag or to kick about a ball made from bound-up plastic bags and rubber – and to dance. The kids would always dance, whether there was music or not – their little pelvises would thrust and gyrate and their faces would sparkle at the excitement of it all. Occasionally drums would be beaten and within seconds the whole village would spark up into an impromptu concerto of thumping percussion and wailing voices, inducing every creature alive to step out to a little funky groove.

This had become his life and these people had become his family. He was Isamba Noni, the bird talker, and they had come to respect him. When he was first thrust upon them, they had felt a certain pity for his predicament and so took him in and gave him shelter in spite of the fact that he had betrayed them. He was not the man they had expected him to be, but Africans for the most part are very forgiving people and this minor hitch in the grander scheme of things could certainly be overlooked. Besides, Jacob had decided that he actually was the perfect man for the job, simply because he knew very little about anything, so he instructed all the men to make his stay as comfortable as they possibly could. All that 'heart of the hunter and spirit of the lion' bollocks was just intended to entice him to stay. None of them had really believed he had those attributes, but it seemed that, as time had gone by, he assumed that very persona and those accolades became him in a manner that demanded their manifestation.

All the previous scientists that had worked at the Institute came with their fancy degrees and grandiose theories attained from research conducted elsewhere in Africa, which Jacob just had to politely entertain. He always had to take a back seat by the very nature of their importance within the scientific community, and all too often his theories and reasoning for events in Sukula were completely overlooked. But Jacob had been studying lions out here for more than eight years now. Just because he didn't have a PhD or an MSc didn't mean he couldn't make a valuable judgement about behavioural dynamics or the like. Jacob knew what his abilities were; he knew what was going on in this corner of Africa, and what's more, he knew that time was not on his side.

With Bird, he could present his own story to the donor community. He could deliver his theories and his reasoning for what was going on and the boy would never question it. He would not need to justify anything as he had done before, and consequently they could get the job done a hell of a lot quicker and minimise the risk of losing further male lions. Jacob had seen the worth of the white boy's stupidity within seconds of their first meeting, and that is why the men had been so quick to accept him, and also why Sarah hadn't shipped him out at first light – Jacob was fighting his corner for him. Under normal circumstances, acceptance by the men would have been more gradual and, in Bird's case, maybe even non-existent; but on Jacob's instruction, they all took him in and gave him the rite of passage in spite of their own feelings towards him. In any case, they soon learned that this Isamba Noni was actually good entertainment and worth having around – the guy was fucking hilarious without even meaning to be.

Jacob had secretly thanked his lucky stars when Sarah went all ballistic the first time she met Bird; he quickly realised the opportunity that now presented itself. Here was a scribe sent from the very land where his voice needed to be heard the loudest – an envoy from the west, summoned by Sukula, that would be converted to sanctify the ills of his society, guide this poetic prophecy and save our floundering earth. Had it not been for Jacob, Bird might well have slipped back into obscurity forever.

It was a fact that Bird would remain completely oblivious to, but perhaps that wasn't such a bad thing. After all, his sense of self-worth was teetering somewhere on the edge of just about nowhere, so why threaten that tentative position any further? Best to make him feel needed and wanted, though to strike the balance between that and the reality of his incompetence had at first proved harder than Jacob had ever thought. Now, though, the metamorphosis of his envoy was just about complete, and the future had delivered him here on the front line of salvation.

Man, I can see the stars. First night since we've been out on this godforsaken walk, too. I hope that means no rain tonight – that would really impress me.

But then, a flash in the distant sky, closely followed by the obligatory rumble and resonance of thunder, soon put paid to that little idea. It should have filled him with dread and remorse, but instead it rocked him gently off to sleep. By now, there was no situation that would be too heavy for him to handle. He had been taken into the cradle of his existence and shown his rightful place within it. For this was Sukula – out here, even Bird could be a hero.

Is there really a stairway?

25

A NEW BEGINNING

The first real glimpse they got of Kirsty's three new cubs filled both Jacob and Bird with a rippling excitement. At eight weeks old, they were just venturing out into the world for the first time, stumbling over their tiny legs and grappling with saucer-sized paws. Their little ears were not yet fully formed and the delicate bumps on either side of their fluffy heads gave them something of a mutated air.

The rainy season had come and gone, leaving behind its legacy of burst gullies and flooded plains, and this was the first time they had managed to get close to Revival since the rains had departed, all other encounters having been at a distance across swamped grasslands. Whereas before Jacob had floored it through the waterlogged gullies, now just getting out to where the delta system began was a mission on its own. Access was limited to the east side of the system only, and crossing to the fig-tree island and the west bank would be impossible for another few weeks.

The advent of water had attracted wading birds in the astounding numbers that Alfred had spoken of all those months before. Herons, egrets, ibises and storks probed the mud in their wet vehicle tracks searching for insects, amphibians, invertebrates and molluscs. Larger expanses of water accommodated birds in their thousands, from waders to terns and even inland gulls.

Flocks of openbill and yellow-billed storks, five hundred strong, performed intricate dance routines as subliminal messages transcended their ranks, instigating erratic colour changes with the shifting light. Above them, squadrons of great white and pink-backed pelicans filled the skies with incoming waves of V-formationed aerial ballets as they descended upon the abundant food resource. Sandpipers and plovers, stilts and stints, ruffs and geese, ducks and teals, in flocks, in groups, in families and in gaggles, came pottering, probing, diving and jabbing – where there was water, there was life. At a good feeding spot, over two thousand birds would gather and excavate their treasures. Around them in the grasslands, the pipits darted, the warblers burbled and the cisticolas twitched. The ever-present cranes danced their life dance with a familiarity that almost bred complacency, and amongst it all, Nikuyu rotated through intricate thermals identified only by the eagles, vultures and marabous who used these invisible elevators to survey their colossal domain for food. Such was the spectacle of Sukula as her floodwaters once again inched their way into a dry-season recession.

The rains had descended upon them much more quickly than Bird had initially anticipated, and the final four weeks before Sarah's departure had shot by like an express train on a highway to hell. As per her request, they had spent the maximum time with Clarence and acquired as much information as humanly possible for her to take back to the donors on the annual fundraising visit to England. Their daily routine back then seemed to comprise only Land Rover, cooking hut and bed. More than half the day was spent with lions in the searing heat of pre-rains

Africa, and Bird had often found himself longing for the comfort of his rustic hut at the end of each day.

But coming home after a day in the field was not quite how his infant career stereotypes had led him to envisage it. There was no loving wife at the front door with a cup of cocoa and slippers at the ready. There was no comfy armchair to melt into whilst catching up with the day's events on TV. There was no steaming bubble bath to soak away the toil of modern living, and there was no rum-and-raisin ice cream for dessert.

Instead, there were Isaac and Compass talking shite on rickety wooden stools, and mountains of stodgy nshima, and plenty of blinding home-grown. The dank and musty smell of his hut had engrained itself into the very core of his senses. Whilst it might not have been the epitome of luxurious comfort, it was home, and sitting out on the baking plains, watching Revival sleep hour after torrid hour, had him longing to return. The constant smell of wood smoke around camp, the shrieking children and their calloused, padding feet, the gentle harmonies of women while they worked and the constant sense of dust that congealed in his mouth and nose were all gratifying mementos of what had now become his domestic abode.

And then the rains had begun.

The rudimentary excitement of metamorphosis as the village shifted into its wet-season dimension had spurred the irrepressible desire of broadened horizons and willingness to learn, and Bird, at first, was a keen and eager recruit. Waterproofed insulation was not a statutory requirement for these huts and he fervently patched the leaks as they occurred. The drainage he installed was also somewhat patchy and unplanned, and on those magical occasions when a hundred millimetres of rain fell in one night, Bird had often found himself bailing the water from underneath his very bed, laughing like a madman. Mud had become so much a part of his life that shoes had been sacrificed for the common good and bathing became wonderfully superfluous. Yes – the initial excitement of this paradigm shift and awe-inspiring display from Mother Nature had had him shrieking with delight, but all too soon the reality of dealing with extreme weather in an unsheltered environment had lost its allure and found his sense of adventure sorely wanting – not to mention his sense of humour.

Days of endless flooding had left them huddled around flickering flames under their paltry shelters, conversations whittled to primeval grunts as they concentrated on elusive warmth and getting stoned. Bird thanked his lucky stars each day that he was back from patrol as he took refuge in the meagre shelter of his hut from the torrential downpours that drove on and on for days. The patrol had at least instilled in him some form of gratitude for simple luxuries. Had he known quite how extreme the rains were going to be, the option of leaving with Sarah would definitely have appealed to him – but as it was, he did not, and besides, that option never presented itself.

With the dry season washed away and the increase in rain, their trips onto the plains had become shorter in distance and longer in time. Many hours were spent digging the car from its treacle-like lair that sucked in its wheels and sapped at their energy – altogether too many to justify further trips. Their final endeavour had lasted twelve hours for a six-kilometre round trip and required a second vehicle to pull them out, and it was then that Jacob threw in the towel, parked the car for the duration of the rains and began to prepare for his routine foot patrols conducted with wildlife rangers.

At first, Bird hadn't been particularly upset when Jacob had advised him not to accompany them, what with tales of gunfights in the mud and endless hours in the relentless rain with a million jungle critters biting, stinging and crawling about their bodies. He would be content to stay in the locality of camp and watch birds from a safe perch, compiling lists and referencing habitats with the aforementioned zest of unadulterated enthusiasm. Armed with books on plants, trees and birds, he was like some kind of nutty field boffin as he skulked around the locality of camp, notebook in hand and binos around neck, observing and marvelling as he had done with Alfred all those years before. The only difference now was the accompanying team of research children, scuttling and shrieking in his wake, eager to discover more about the strange beast that now inhabited their own shores. It was somewhere around week four that the excitement of discovery had finally worn thin and he had decided to annoy Jacob for a chance to go out on patrol. Had he known the outcome, he might well have kept his big mouth shut – and once he'd returned with a fistful of buffalo meat, that's exactly what he did, content once more with the plants and the birds.

He amended the Institute's bird list, which contained over four hundred species, and consolidated erratic information on breeding migrants and their nesting habitats as and when he could. The local flora had been scantily referenced in the past and he endeavoured to bring the plant records up to date and into line as well, correlating the data into a linear, usable form. He even managed to identify the glorious purple flower that had created that blinding contrast on his first morning after breakfast with Isaac when he got lost in the woods. *Adenodolichos punctatus* – of course, how could he ever forget?

His work on plants not only gave him a valuable insight into surrounding habitats, associated soil types and geological influences, but also kind of opened his eyes to the absurdity of Latin. When compared to the native tongue of this area with its flowing viscosity and audible tranquillity, Latin seemed almost alien to the planet. The language of these people, whilst based on a Bantu dialect, had roots that were just as ancient, yet its simplicity was as glaring as the Latin's complexity. Their speech had the consistency of dew running through a mountain spring, soothing to the ears and calming to the soul, but this Latin and its derivatives were harsh and brazen, complicated and clouded with grammatical innuendoes that needed qualifying and quantifying in order to be understood.

Somehow, the generics of it all seemed to detract from the fundamentalism. He had become strung out on names for a while there and may well have drowned in a labelled database of bullshit, had it not been for the simple rationality of one man's thoughts on a fine January afternoon.

Jacob had given Bird a vehicle and told him to pick up firewood a couple of klicks down the road from camp, in an attempt to get him out and about and away from the paperwork for a while. Raymond and another man named Stetsonn were to accompany him, as they knew the way. The rains had been particularly harsh just days before and water had bogged sections of the road. The two-kilometre journey took them the best part of three hours, mainly because of the mud and water but also because Bird was so crap at off-road driving – or any kind of driving, for that matter. Naturally, once in the mud, he thought that the more juice he gave the throttle the quicker the car would come out, and marvelled benignly at it all when his axles sunk further and his wheels spun deeper while the vehicle remained motionless, trapped in its lair. An hour of jacking, packing and pushing later, not to mention screamed commands from Raymond, the car would crawl out, creep down the road another fifty metres and sink monumentally once again. And so it went on, hour after painful hour.

His two assistants had been stuck many times before and knew the drill backwards – all they were lacking was an actual ability to drive which, had they possessed, would have cut down their journey time significantly. It was no real bother to them, they had nothing better to do that day and a day out with the crazy Isamba Noni to fetch a bit of firewood seemed a good alternative to just sitting around. For Bird, though, the fun of his endeavours soon began to wear off when, into their sixth hour on the job, they had still not reached camp and the task of unloading and repacking the collected firewood for the umpteenth time in the mud became laborious and painful. Hunger burned in his stomach like an arc welder on steel and it seemed at one stage that the reality of camp was becoming ever more illusory.

He was a broken soul as they finally turned onto the track that would lead them home, mud-free and close enough to walk even if they did get stuck. A feeling of profound achievement was stirring in his bones as the end drew near and he triumphantly rounded out the final bend onto the home straight for camp.

It's difficult to say how or why it happened – with so many erratic influences on a single action in Africa's untamed lands, one can never pinpoint rhyme nor reason for accidents that occur. But whatever it was, it caused a jolt on the car that shed his load and sent all the firewood flying from the back and the three-man team reaching for the skies. In a moment of unprecedented rage, Bird leapt from the vehicle and screamed at the top of his voice:

"Aaaaaaaaaagggggggghhhhhhhhhhh!"

Just like that.

Calmly and serenely, his two gallant infantrymen stepped from the car and began repacking the cargo without uttering a word. They could see the white boy was pissed enough without their wisecracks to antagonise him further, but Bird continued in his tirade, kicking the car and jumping on the firewood.

"Fuck this!" he shrieked. "Fuck this place with its water and its mud! Fuck you, rain!" he screamed, raising a finger to the sky. "You want my firewood, you take it – take it all – see if I care. Bollocks to you – bollocks to it all." The tantrum seemed to alleviate part of his rage, which just left him with one final, profound rationalisation:

"Shit, man, why the hell is this happening to me? *WHY ME?*"

And it was then that one man's simplicity opened the door to a sea of compassion and a lifetime of understanding that was to change his whole attitude towards the rains. It was Raymond who felt compelled to break the treaty of silence.

"No, Isamba Noni," he calmly interjected. "This is not happening to you, it is just happening."

And that was it. That was all Raymond had to say on the matter.

Bird was stopped in his tracks, mid-kick on a piece of firewood and suspended like a statue in a *Star Trek* episode. The ray gun of life had stunned him right between the eyes, highlighting his absurdity and relieving his soul of this outlandish self-absorption. He was the centre of his universe and everything that went on there was directly linked to that ideal. In releasing this importance and following the words of Raymond, he was suddenly absolved of a multitude of sins. The paranoia of prophetic existence rested no more upon his shoulders and life could take its natural course, oblivious to his existence. He became just a part, and not the whole itself: a simple molecule in the organism of life – no longer the ruler of the planet.

"You're right, Raymond," he remarked in astonishment. "You are so fucking right. It's just happening, that's all. It is just happening, and I will just have to deal with it. I am not the victim here, it is just my circumstance."

Had he adopted this fine attitude five hours earlier, the whole episode might well have been an enlightening experience to strengthen his resolve and not the punishment that it had now become.

The rains gave Bird plenty of time to reflect on the how, the where and the why, just like the hallucinogenic drugs used to back home. Out here, death lurked in every corner of the African bush, from massive rainclouds high above him firing laser beams of light and torrential floods onto the Earth, to tiny mosquitos harbouring deadly parasites in their lethal jaws. Elephants roamed through camp, buffalo gathered in huge numbers on the grasslands and lions ranged far and wide with the scattering of their prey to the abundant water sources. During the dry months they never heard lions from the research camp, but in the rainy season, their calls would ring out in the dead of night as fringe prides jostled for the scattered prey. Potential death was everywhere, yet he felt no hostility, even against the trigger-happy poachers on his unfortunate patrol.

In the so-called modern world, danger of a different kind ran high with the volatility of evolution's unchallenged humans. Stripped of their will to survive, people fed the vacant chasm in their souls with misdirected aggression at their fellow men and the wilderness that supported them. Man, he thought, has made a world where nature's ferocious elements have been tamed and all there is left to fear is himself. He is like a virus. He devours the very resource that perpetuates his existence and shifts the molecular structure that encases his soul each time the environment tries to control him – and, one day, there may be nothing left to consume but himself.

These simple events – the reassuring words from Raymond, the fundamental aspects of survival such as drawing water to bathe and fetching firewood to heat the boiler – had illuminated to Bird the radical insubordination of 'modern man' to his environment. We live within a chain – an ecochain. We are but one link in the mystery of life that surrounds us, yet it seems we do not know it. The glorious, purple flower that perfectly contradicted all that surrounded it that first morning in the forest was a prime example. Shining out like a mirrored ball on the disco floor, *Adenodolichos punctatus* advertised its presence to the world. When most of nature deals in the concealment of camouflage for the element of survival, here she was shining like a beacon on the high seas. She had painted herself in a striking mauve against a backdrop of parched browns to advertise the treasure she bore in her bosom. She recognised her dependence on a mobile source to sow her seed far and wide, and she beckoned a thousand insects into her womb to carry that genetic code. And she was not alone.

Plants may not build metallic structures that scrape the sky nor send rockets to the moon or steel ships floating on our rolling oceans, but they have the intelligence to recognise that an insect can be contracted to pollinate their flowers. All that is required is a simple exchange – a sip of their nectar for the carriage of their genes. They recognise the interdependence of all life on Earth – the links in the chain, the vital need that we have for one another – and they exploit it. But do they enslave the insect and persecute its soul to fulfil their need? No, they trade with it – for if they were to jeopardise that relationship, the messenger would be gone.

As the inspiration of this new beginning unfolded around him, Bird reflected on the life he had gleaned during his first six months in the bush. That prying mind that alerted his teenage revolutionary militia to the toxic giants of our planet was once again awakened. The decaying tissue of his drugged-out remorse was now replaced with the vibrance of knowledge and a piece of understanding about the volatility of the ecochain. His own mother had abandoned him just when he needed her most and, in her absence, the source of life had gently intervened and taken this lost babe to his rightful existence in the jungles of her womb. He was her envoy, her spiritual representative, for there were no fabricated ties that kept this boy in the grip of mankind.

Once back with Revival, the job at hand limited any spiritual philosophising to the confines of camp amidst reefers of home-grown weed. The unusual tenderness that Clarence displayed around kills at feeding time had become commonplace and predictable. He never once challenged his females for food or showed any signs of aggression towards them. Boundary patrolling was done as a unit, and territorial calling, whilst instigated and predominantly performed by Clarence, was embarked upon by all. When Revival's five-man army began its repertoire just metres from the vehicle, paintwork would peel and chassis bolts would loosen with the reverberating echo. Bird would feel the calls rattling into his rib cage and penetrating his heart, filling it with a profound fear and astounding reverence that made him thankful to be human for once in his life.

As predicted, Mia had come into season just before Sarah left for England, and once more the procreatory endeavour had shattered the loins of Clarence the beast. Four months later, Mia was seldom around, which meant that her endeavour had been fruitful and she was holed up in some lair, nursing her progeny.

"Are they big enough to sex yet, Jacob?" Bird asked, referring to Kirsty's newborns.

"No, they are still very small. Another few weeks and maybe we will know. But they are two and one. Have you seen how these two are always close and that one there is apart? Maybe the two are males, maybe females. Time is going to tell. They are very white, though; they have the look of Sukula lions and this is a good thing."

"Yep, sure is. Mia is not here again so she must have been successful, too. I wonder who will be next, Baby or Bama. Care to make a wager, sir?"

Jacob looked across at him and shook his head. It had been six months, but this kid still spoke double Dutch to him sometimes. "What is a wager?"

"It's a bet. Care to make a bet as to who you think will come into season next?"

"Why need to bet? Alabama is older, it will be her." Jacob huffed out a chortled laugh through his nose. "You see, Isamba, you are still foolish. I could have taken your money with this bet very easily; I could have won when I already know the answer. You have been spared this time. It is important that next time you are more careful when you wish to lose the money that you do not have."

He had a point. Bird wasn't exactly the most flush when it came to cash, though Sarah had taken the liberty of forwarding some meagre funds to Alfred when she was overseas as a token gesture of her appreciation for the boy. His speech on how he had lost his parents had tugged the emotional strings that were hidden in the depths of her soul, and she found herself obligated to do something. When more cash came through, she would start to pay him properly, which could be any day now.

Initially, the donors in England had taken well to Sarah's newfound enthusiasm and drive for the project. She was received like a real scientist and her presentations had been thorough and professional. An interim grant to keep them running on their existing shoestring budget had come through almost immediately, with the promise of more funding to follow. Proposals for genetic analysis and satellite tracking collars were approved in principle, and enthusiasm for the lion project was strong. But an overzealous accountant fresh out of college had somehow picked up on the fact that Bird was just the 'fucking barman', and his scientific integrity once again came under great scrutiny. Two weeks after her return to Sukula, Sarah learned that the proposal had been denied for lack of credibility with her staff and, unfortunately for Bird, this had unleashed her anger on him once again just when he thought he was at last off the 'hated' list.

It did have the positive effect of putting his mind back on the job, though, and the appearance of Kirsty's earless, fluffy claw-balls had once again ignited the fire of scientific discovery. But it was Clarence's behaviour around the kill that had now become the focus of their behavioural analysis. His resolve to never show dominance over his females, to quietly share the meat and calmly feed alongside them, was a mystery to all. As far as Jacob was aware, this kind of sustained amiability had not been documented before, and they were interested to see how it had evolved. Quite how they would do this was still unclear, but one question they were working on was how he would react to his cubs once they began to take meat. Could it be that this was some kind of Romeo revolution, inspired only by his desire to perpetuate the genes of an ailing race, and that once the job was done and the family born, he would revert to the Philistinian ways of his counterparts? It would be a few weeks before the answers materialised, if at all.

In the meantime, life in the pride carried on as normal. Kirsty nursed her new brood of cubs, Baby and Bama offered periodic support to Mia with babysitting duties that gave her time to go and feed or get a well-earned rest from her own cubs, and Clarence just surveyed all that was his in his unique and trouble-free way. The scientists (dare they be called so) had even once caught a fleeting glimpse of Mia's newborns as they were transported between lairs in the massive jaws of their mother, and Bird was once again struck with awe. This enamelled machine of razor-sharp precision and deathly clutch was so gentle when wrapped around the neck of her young that it was hard to quantify the wrath it had inflicted upon so many other less fortunate creatures over the years.

Lions, thought Bird, are the ultimate paradoxical beings. The violent squabbles around the dinner table juxtapose their love and affection when it's all over. The mutual grooming, the tender physical touching, the soft and gentle contact calls between one another – yet, in an instant, the angel of death possesses them, unleashing hell's fury and laying waste to all that stand in their way.

And somehow this glaring paradox seemed ironically indicative of his own connection with the mighty beasts. As he marvelled at Mia's crushing jaws stooped in tenderness, the parallels of his quest for existence became ever clearer. Shunned and outcast by his own family, he had been forced to make an alliance with a most unlikely partner of distant blood relation. The coalition with Alfred had allowed him to colonise the most vibrant of females – Mother Earth – and together with her, he was now setting about securing the range of his entity, that it may be safe to harbour the manifestation of his soul. Sukula provided his means and allowed him to propagate the genes of his existence whilst giving him pride of place within her heart. He was, in effect, a true male lion who had now come home.

Africa had offered him untold bounties that could never be found in his western society. It had enabled him to lift his head from the despair that surrounded his mundane quest for survival and smell the fresh scent of existence that overrides the balance sheets and trading accounts, the profits and losses, the production and distribution of bollocks that constituted the outside world. Yes, Sukula allowed him to feel the essence of the ecochain and establish his link within it. Isamba Noni – the bird talker who, when all is said and done, might actually have the heart of a lion after all.

26

PSYCHO PEACHES

"So, what do you think, Jacob?"

"I think you are right."

"I'm often right these days, have you noticed that?" Bird paused, as if giving Jacob time to respond, then fired in his next question. "Is it time to name him? The lone male cub?"

"I notice that your observations about simple things are correct and that you write very good reports, but I do not notice that you are often right," Jacob quipped defiantly. "Yes. What name shall we choose?"

"Elvis."

"Elvis?"

"Elvis. In memory of Savongo."

"Who is Elvis?"

"*'Before anyone did anything, Elvis did everything.'* That's a quote from John Lennon, though you probably don't know who he is either?" Jacob shook his head almost apologetically. "Elvis was the first great rocker of our time. Savongo loved his music, so we should name this lion after the greatest. Don't you think? Elvis the man – the new Clarence."

"Yes, if it is as you say then I agree, this Elvis could be *'the man'*." Jacob mocked Bird in a forced and pompous accent. "He is the firstborn male, which means he will carry the lineage of Clarence, providing he

441

survives, but this does not mean you are right about everything." He shuffled in his driver's seat and faced Bird. "You are Isamba Noni, yes – the talking bird? It is you who should know about all things with feathers in the sky, yet the other day, you tried to tell me that a red-necked falcon was Nikuyu. This is one thing I do not expect you to get wrong."

"Oh please, the thing was up on a thermal and I hadn't had time to get my binos on it. I was making an educated guess using local knowledge."

"But you were wrong. It is you who must teach me about birds and I teach you about lions. So far, I have not made a mistake with the lions, but you have made many with the birds. I have to say, you are not right all the time." Jacob seemed insistent on making his point and keeping the boy in his place. "You still have far to go, Isamba," he persisted. "Your progress has been good, much better than I thought when you first arrived at this place. You are a good man and lucky for you, the spirit of a lion is inside you, but you are not Savongo. Maybe in some years this can be, but for now, you are still my assistant – my worker!" Jacob chortled out loud.

"There you go! You need to take a reality check, man, it's the twenty-first century and there's a new sheriff in town. Just because that last report had your name blazoned in stars all over it, don't let it go to your head, mate. Be sure to remember how you got there when it's all champagne and cocaine parties to celebrate. You'll be thinking about getting into politics next."

"I am not a politician." He snorted indignantly. "Politicians are liars and thieves and they do not live in the bush. They live in big houses in the city and they are fat. Even if you ask me to become president, I think I would refuse, because a president cannot spend all day out here with the lions. This is my place and that is all."

"Amen to that, mate. I think you should feel proud, Jacob – you'll be getting the recognition you deserve at long last and that report highlights the fact that not all lion specialists have to have PhDs. You are proof that experience can pay just as many scientific dividends, if not more, than academic qualifications. They'll recognise your work, you'll see. And I'll recognise you as a righteous brother for getting Sarah off my back – I owe you for that."

"Yes, you owe me for many things but I think you will never be a rich man, Isamba, so as you say in English, I have backed the wrong horse."

"Yeah, yeah, whatever. Just remember who helped you out of the relegation zone, mate." They laughed together and crashed fists, even though Jacob didn't have the first idea what a relegation zone was.

The cubs had indeed been sexed correctly, a male and two females, and the prediction on Clarence's behaviour around the kill with his young, who were now eating meat, had also been right. His extracurricular activities of babysitting and gentle play with his offspring just intensified his unusual demeanour and ignited a thousand questions behind many closed doors, prompting an urgent report to the donors.

By now, Mia's cubs were also starting to waddle out of their lair to join the rest of the family from time to time. They observed their cousins closely and often emulated their behaviour. On occasions, there would be six little lions jumping all over Clarence, pulling his ears, hanging off his mane, clawing their way onto his colossal back and rolling off his rear flanks. But the giant cat never once flinched or showed any untold aggression towards them. He simply lay there and let the whole thing unfold, occasionally offering a playful paw or a gaping jaw to continue the show without irritation.

At night, he was left with the crèche clawing and climbing all over his frame whilst the females went off to hunt. Once dinner had been procured, a shining pair of optical beacons would appear in the beam of their spotlight with six smaller such pairs bouncing around below them. They would approach ever nearer until the lion came into view with tiny cubs dancing in and out of his massive stride, occasionally ambushing and attacking his padding paws. The three older cubs would go immediately to feed, the three younger sitting to one side, perhaps chewing on a mother's tail whilst Clarence sat on the edge, quietly awaiting his turn.

On one bewildering evening, he had stood virtually submerged in a flooded gully and goaded his cubs one by one as they squawked and paddled madly, reluctantly forging the miniature river with the help of this leonine bridge. Jacob had found this so extraordinary that it prompted a draft report to go in to the donors as an emergency plea for assistance to investigate this bizarre trait further, and perhaps ascertain how and why behaviour like this could have come about. He thought that if it came directly from him they might start to listen; after all, political correctness was rife overseas and here was an African man working on an internationally-funded project who needed help with his studies. Surely, after what Bird had told him about the donors' desire to give aid to underprivileged Africans, they would hear his appeal and start the money tap flowing again.

A comprehensive report on this behaviour was drafted and submitted to Sarah out of the blue, along with a proposal detailing the required assistance in manpower and equipment needed to investigate it further. A supply run took it into town and David, the systems co-ordinator, was quick to get the document off to London. It meant that if they were looked upon favourably, not only would a grant be forthcoming with extra funding, but hopefully some zealous lion specialist would pick up this unique behavioural scent and offer his services, adding weight to their ailing credential status. If it worked, an ongoing project would be formulated and Sarah's dream would be fulfilled – not to mention Jacob's. Of course, the minor issue of where Bird would then fit into the equation was somewhat in the balance, but no one had thought of that until it was too late – least of all Bird.

"You see this Clarence," Jacob continued. "Now he is starting to have many cubs, he wants to make his home range bigger. We are so close to the camp today. He has seen that when there is water, the lechwe are spread out very far, and he wants to control as much of this land as he can. Do you remember how it was when you came last year? The lechwe were just in the middle of the delta – now with all this water, they are spread very far."

"Yeah, I remember. But I think I prefer it like this because of the birds. You might not see thousands of lechwe but man, are there ever a lot of waders. Not too sure how happy I am that Revival are so close to camp, though. They're so familiar with the vehicle, you would think that one of these days they might just follow us all the way home."

"Yes, this happened once before. That is when Savongo saved my life." Jacob laughed at first, then paused for a moment and looked into the heat haze starting to shimmer off Sukula's grasslands.

"He was just starting to work with Revival at that time," Jacob reminisced, "and one day they were close to the camp, same like this. It had taken time for the females to accept his vehicle but once they did, they became very curious. Then, one morning when he had been following them to an island where he thought they were going to sleep, he turned to go back to camp, thinking all lions had finished their activity for the day. But without him knowing, it was they who started to follow – all the way home.

"I was the first to see them. I was standing next to the office where the road goes into camp. There was another worker with me, a man named Lackson who had never seen a lion before. As we looked down the road, we saw more than eight females and sub-adults heading in towards us. Three of them were the Revival females from today. Baby was not yet born, and in those days they were part of a much bigger group that we called the Sukula pride.

"Lackson became very afraid when he saw the lions and started to run inside the camp to escape. He did not know that you are not supposed to run from lions, and his movement made them start to chase. They charged straight towards us, and for some reason I stood still and watched as two females came running in with their teeth bared across their wet lips. It is true to say that I thought my time to meet God was going to be then. I was unable to move because fear had gone into my legs and forced them not to work. I was very afraid." Jacob paused and shook his head as he remembered his fear, clicking his tongue against the roof of his mouth repeatedly.

"I stood and watched as the females came closer – there was something like excitement in their eyes and hunger on their lips, and I was sure of death. But as they came, Savongo appeared from the other side of the office. The females had not seen him there and he was running very fast, shouting loudly and waving his arms in the air. He was charging straight at the lions and he took them completely by surprise. They had never seen a human in this way before and they became very afraid. Mostly their prey runs away from them, not towards them. They turned quickly and ran back through the forest and onto the plains. The look on their faces must have been as fearful as my own. The tracks where they turned were five metres from where I was standing – just one leap.

"Since that day, they have never come around the camp, and since that day, Savongo has been very much respected by our people, for never before have we heard of a man doing such a thing. He had the spirit of a lion and the heart of a hunter. He is dead now and his spirit is in the sky, together with all the great warriors of our people. This is why you thought he was a god when you first heard stories of him, because our people love him. Never has a white man come to this place and done such a thing.

"When he saw that I stood still and did not run from the lions, he said that I had an understanding of these creatures and so he began to teach me about this job. He saved my life, and that is why I have to continue his work until my days are finished, for if it was not for the bravery of Savongo, I too would be dead now and my spirit would not be with our warriors in the sky. At that time, I was not a good man. I had helped the hunters to kill many of our animals and I think the gods would have looked to me unfavourably. I do not believe in hell, Isamba, but the place where my spirit would have rested would not have been a good one."

That half smile adorned the side of Jacob's lips again but there was no doubting his honesty. However, the concept of such an incident repeating itself, with these lions being again so close to camp, did weigh rather heavy in Bird's mind. Would he be expected to do the same?

"Wow, man, what a tale – what a guy. I see why you all feel the way you do for him. I guess I'd feel the same. You must have soiled yourself that day, mate! I can't say that your story fills me with confidence, though. What if they get that sudden curious urge again and come skulking into camp tonight? You and the men can't expect me to go charging into marauding lions on foot. I may have their spirit inside me but I assure you, with death looking me in the eyes like that, I think I would take my chances and run."

"Then you would be sure to die, Isamba. Four legs of a lioness will always be faster than two legs of a man."

"Fundamentally I agree, but adrenaline is a strange substance and with enough of it pumping through my veins I reckon I could give Linford Christie a run for his money. Anyway, I don't have to outrun a lioness, I just have to outrun anyone else stupid enough to take their chances running with me!"

"I think it is time to go. The lions will remain here and shouldn't move too far tonight. You can come back tomorrow to find them. Do you know that I have got the next few days off?"

"No, I didn't know that. Where are you going?"

"I am going back to my home village. One of my wives is having another baby soon and I have to take her home for the birth. Tomorrow you will come out with

Shadrack. The lions are close, so you will have no trouble finding them. Come, it's time to go – I need to start off back to the village before the sun sets. You can take the rest of the day off and smoke jamba and watch birds – the favourite pastime for Isamba Noni."

"Amen to that, big Bwana. Show me the way to go home and let my fingers do the rolling!"

Once back in camp, Jacob swapped vehicles amid a flurry of jabbering excitement. Three men were going home with him for time off and they were almost uncontrollable with their banter. After helping them sort out the car and load their kit, Bird bade their snaking dust plume a fond farewell with an exaggerated limp wrist and then turned to lock up the workshop.

As the vehicle melted into the distance and its dust began to settle, the customary unfurling of an African evening cloaked itself on his senses once again, but somewhere off in the distance, he also picked up on the voice of Sarah. She seemed to be going off at someone again, though her tone was unusually calm – almost subdued. She was some way off, perhaps by the office, and whilst her assertiveness was apparent, there was an unfamiliar submission about her pitch that he did not recognise. She had a way with her staff that exuded confidence and calm, a control she always managed to maintain that somehow was lacking here. Then came a man's voice, with a white man's accent – not English, but white – harsh and monotoned, a South African perhaps. It warranted further investigation.

"I don't care who you bleddy torked to missy, you have no right to inturfearr with my bleddy quotas. Who tha 'ell do you thunk you arre? This is not a bleddy joke, I am

449

trrying to rrun a busnus yere. You an' yourr bleddy bleeding hearts is always trrying to unterrvene in matters you know nuthing about. Why can't you jest leave me alone?"

His dialect was brazen and harsh, as if English wasn't his first language. He left out pronunciations at the beginning of words, but not the way Maggie did; his was more through an inadequate understanding of the language he spoke, so unfamiliar with his natural vocalisation methods that restricted his mouth from affording certain words their full pronounceable quota. He also rolled his Rs at every available opportunity, which became rather irritating to an eavesdropping Bird.

"Mr. Visser," replied Sarah sharply, "you know as well as I do that the quotas are unreasonable, and since this new lion has arrived, it is well within my interests to ensure he doesn't suffer the same fate as all the other Sukula males. I am also trying to run a business here and I am trying to conduct a scientific analysis of the predatory diversity within this area. If, for whatever reason, we lose this male as well, I will have no more Institute to run. We have a conflict of interests here and I am hardly going to lie down and let you steamroll over me just because you pay more money to the Chief than I do. All I have asked is for the quota to be reduced by twenty-five percent, and judging by the unrealistic consumption by yourselves in the past, this does not seem unreasonable."

"And what about George – my client? What will he do if there arre no lions to shoot?"

"I couldn't really care less what he does," she shot back, flashing a glare across at George. "He can go somewhere else to shoot a lion, just not in my back yard."

"But we have 'ung baits in the concession for overr a week now and there's been bugger-all interest. George has paid a lot of money to hunt yere, you know."

"That does not mean you can drag my boundary road. Look, Mr. Visser, I appreciate that you have taken the time to come here and 'inform' me of your intentions, but I have to say that if you bait for this male, I will have no option but to call in every favour I can, both in town and in the donor community, to bring this to the attention of everyone concerned. I'm sure you understand where this might lead in light of your brother's unfortunate incident here. The Vissers are not well respected for that."

Bird was unable to see Sarah. He was hiding around the back of the office and they were standing in front of it. But he could picture the psychotic Tomb Raiding glint adorning her angelic face as she offered these acerbic jibes to the hunter, and he would have been glad to see a more deserving victim receiving the wrath she normally reserved for his skinny, white frame.

Sarah was uneasy. She hid it well behind a front of derisive sarcasm, but Visser was clearly not amused, and neither was George. Their vehicle reeked of death and guns, and George sat in the passenger seat wearing bad Desert Storm camouflage castoffs and a camo hat perched on top of his rounded face. His fat paunch of a belly rested on his thighs, and his face bore a look of disdain that made her feel somehow apprehensive. Evil resentment was written all over him.

The hunter had come to inform her that he was having no luck hunting lions in his concession and so was going to drag a bait along the boundary road to entice males out of the Park. This sordid practice was not only one hundred percent legitimate in the eyes of the law but also totally acceptable to the hunters' 'sport'. Sarah was painfully aware that Clarence was their target and so was trying her damnedest to dissuade Visser from carrying out his plan, but it just wasn't happening.

"Well, if that is all we Vussers are not rrespected forr, maybe I should make it morre wurrth our while and do something they can rrurlly hate us for. Do you know what I mean by that, missy? Ut's been a long time for me out yere in thu bush and muy patience has run thun." Visser motioned towards Sarah with an evil glint in his eye as he eased his bloated frame towards her. She flinched momentarily, almost sliding away from his impending form. It was important she showed no signs of intimidation or else he'd get the scent of fear and then who knows what might happen? She wished someone would walk around the corner – anyone – just someone to take his vile attention away from her.

"You lay a finger on her, fat boy, and I swear I'll take you out where you stand – where you fuckin' stand, man."

Well, OK, anyone except Bird.

Now there's warlords in the East
And hunters in the West,
Wage their bloody wars and incarcerate our
best,
They kick away the blocks
And the feet on which we stand,
Nothing left alive in this international land.

He had appeared around the side of the office and was casually leaning against the corner of the building, inspecting his fingers. It almost seemed like he was picking his nails, treating this offensive recipient with apparent disdain. He looked like a Millwall fan about to sing: "Come an' 'ave a go if ya think yer 'ard enough!" And a glint of sheer psychosis adorned his unconcerned eyes that put Tomb Raider to bed with a dummy and a dolly. It worked.

The overweight hunter stood staring at this apparition in complete disbelief. There was a sidearm holstered on his hip, a hunting knife hanging off his belt and three high-powered rifles strapped to his car less than five yards from where he stood. And yet, in the face of this prolific arsenal, here was a bleddy pommie standing not ten yards away, making inane threats at him. No one could quite believe it. The sheer surprise of his shattering audacity had even forced George out of the car where his massive gut was now left to sag on its own, somewhere below his waist – bloody gravity.

"And who the bleddy hell arre you?" scowled Visser, after a pause of unreal contemplation.

"I'm Bwana fucking Bird, mate, but that don't really matter. What does matter is your apology to the lady, which might just about excuse the lack of manners within that Neanderthal frame of yours – know wot I mean?"

His accent shifted to sharp cockney with this final remark and a self-assured smile curled across his lips. He'd had his head kicked in so many times in drunken brawls that the famous British football hooligans' last stand of dementia was now a mere formality.

George couldn't quite work the guy out. He'd had the odd fist fight in a bar and fucked up many a frat boy freshman back in college, but he'd never encountered an enemy quite like this. Was he for real? He wasn't sure, but one thing he knew: scum like this, gotta take 'em out first and question their skinny ass later. George was getting ready to rumble.

"I don't apologise to bleddy bleeding hearts and I don't take orders from skellums like you. Do you think I even care about your rrudiculous threats, boy? You'rre nuthing to me. I could kull you so fast you never know wot hit you. Poes," Visser snarled.

"Yeah well, that's the whole point innit, fat boy? By killin' me you'll be doin' us a big favour, won't ya?" His answer came fast and hard, fired in before Visser could even draw breath. He'd pushed himself away from the building with his shoulder and begun sauntering towards the man, scuffing his feet in the gravel and seemingly more engrossed in his fingernails than anything else.

He was now talking matter-of-factly, as if he were explaining a football match he'd seen on TV the night before, and it was only when he'd finished his statement that he actually made eye contact with the hunter, smiling sweetly.

"You see, I'm here to test myself," he continued, oblivious to the hunter's glare. "I'm here to find a conviction that I know I have. I'm here to prove something to myself and the rest of the world – something I never thought I was capable of." Pause... shrug of the shoulders... gaze into the distance... theatrical, like that Millwall fan. "Well, in death," he shrugged, "the proof is absolute – the point is crystal. You will have realised my dream and I will have your fat arse to thank for it. 'Course, if I'm goin' down, that same said arse is coming with me and there ain't no negotiating that one, pal – it's just the way it is – know wot I mean?"

He had now slipped into full-blown cockney, heavily laced with the aforementioned shoulder shrugging and vacant glares. He gave off an air of extreme confidence in his ability, like he didn't have a care in the world – and who knows, maybe he didn't.

Sarah just stood and absorbed this diverting display of verbal testosterone. Visser, meanwhile, was quite frankly confused. He didn't say anything, but he looked at the slight frame of Bird in complete bewilderment. What favour could he possibly be doing for the fool?

"Well, I got a cause, in't I?" Bird ranted on. "My cause is right here and right now. It's this place and these lions, yeah? That's my cause. If you take me out and I take you with me, you'll be proving that at least I had the fucking conviction to die for my cause and that, mate, is very special – it makes everything worthwhile. I actually feel good about the fact that I'm ready for it – for death, like. Know wot I mean?" Pause… vacant stare… quick shrug… then glancing at Visser with a persistent stare. "The question is, mate – are you?"

The hunter wrinkled up his face in complete disbelief at this kid. I mean, who the hell did he think he was? This was Visser, Marius Visser, a great white hunter. He killed lions and hippos and buffalos and elephants for a living. How could this streaky length of piss even think he had a hope in hell with him? Surely he knew how tough Visser was. I mean, he worked so damn hard at trying to prove it to everyone, it should be elementary by now – why didn't this little shit get it?

As the neurones flashed messages across distorted synapses within Visser's simple mind, George was having his own kind of Neolithic difficulty keeping up with it all. He knew that Visser had just been abused pretty badly and this kid had a lot of nerve to talk the way he did, but George didn't quite understand why. They were both much bigger than he was and they had lots of big guns to prove their manhood – he must have been even a little bit afraid, surely? Maybe the kid was bluffing, who knows – or maybe he wasn't? Either way, neither hunter quite knew what to do about it. Luckily for George, Visser came up with an answer first.

"Well, boy," he huffed. "You might jest get the answer to yourr bleddy question sooner than you think. You might jest be seeing me before you've yad tyme to make yourr peace."

And that was it. He strode over to his car, hopped into the driver's seat and sped off in a cloud of dust, George's parting cry of "Ya mama!" fading inaudibly into the distance.

So run rabbit run
From the bullet and the cage,
Man is breaking out from the prison that he
made,
And it don't matter
About the wars he wage,
As he march on through this international age.

Bird and Sarah stared off at the dusty sunset as Visser's car disappeared into the trees and a strained silence cloaked itself around them. Soon the noise of the car would be completely gone and one of them would have to say something. If it was to be Bird, the concept of what he wanted to tell her weighed heavier on his mind than the confrontation with Visser. As it was, he needn't have bothered – Lara Croft was back.

"When I need your help, Mr. Bird, I will ask for it. I had that situation firmly under control before you strode in here like Ronnie fucking Kray! There's no telling what he might do now – you might just have blown everything. When are you going to learn to just stay away from me and stop messing up my life?" And she spun on her heels, stamping a purposeful march in the direction of her house. This was always her defence, not giving him a moment to answer back, having her dig and then leaving before any repercussions could be felt.

Well, not this time, Tomb Girl. It's do or die – with Visser and with you.

"I don't think you had anything under control, Sarah," Bird hazarded as he scuttled behind her marching form. "I think he came here to hurt you – to scare you, at least. He wasn't listening to anything you had to say – he was going to do what he would do anyway, but now he might actually stop to think about it. I had to take the gamble, I couldn't just stand there and let him hurt you."

"You are not my father, nor are you my protector. I can look after myself and I don't need you to do it for me. I've survived twenty-nine years on this Earth without any help from you so far, thank you very much."

She stormed into the house and the old screen door slammed and creaked as she disappeared inside, but Bird was not done yet. This time, he steamed in there after her, demanding an explanation – an end to this madness.

"Can't I stick up for you, just once?" he snorted.

"No!" screamed the reply.

"Can't you let someone help you, just once?"

"No!" Once again.

"Why do you have to be this rock, this island? Why do you always have to be so damn independent? What is it about me that makes you so mad? Did you lose it with the hunter? No. You just stood there and took his shit. But me – I try so fuckin' hard to help you and this is what I get? Why? What have I done?"

They were now in her lounge at opposite ends of the room. He was pacing up and down, ranting like a jackhammer with his arms flailing in the air and his hands intermittently clutching at his matted hair as he searched for some reasoning in this lunacy. He wasn't looking at her as she turned, exhibiting that Tomb Raiding glint that had kicked him in the pride once before.

"What have you done?" she hissed in a low and resonant whisper. "You want to know what you've done? Well, I'll tell you. Nothing. Fuck all." This outlandish statement stunned them both momentarily and an eerie silence clattered into the room around them.

"What?" Bird said quietly. "Nothing?" He gazed about the room in disbelief, dazed and somewhat confused, that fragile ego teetering once again.

"Nothing. Just fucked it all up, didn't you? Like you've done your whole life. When I needed real help, a real scientist, someone authentic and recognised, you were what I got. Nothing."

"You wot…?"

But before he knew it, she was storming across the room at him with a shriek resonating off her lips and a demon rampaging in her soul. She was onto him like some demented druid – kicking, punching, biting, scratching – and all the while her chilling war cry echoed through this deathly chamber. He was up and grappling in an instant, not because he'd gone mental himself, but more out of sheer defence from this potentially fatal assault. He locked her arms and managed to subdue her legs just in time to eliminate a stumble onto the couch where gravity could roll the ultimate dice on his mortal being.

Her momentum was suspended for a second and all she had left to move in this paralysed artillery was her head, now locked and loaded with gleaming white canines in this unequivocal display of latent fury. She began head-butting him like a drunken Glaswegian, craning her neck and exposing her deadly, snapping jaws as she fired her head in time after time. He'd never been in a situation like this before, so could only have been acting on primeval survival instincts that deemed the only defence here was to subdue the mouth sufficiently to avoid bite injuries, but like Sarah, his only free body part was his head. There was no other way but to clamp his lips onto hers and suck for all he was worth – tongue and all.

Oh shit… what am I doing… what have I done… are we snogging? Burning cars… get her off me…

Yelping with fear, he pushed her away and reeled backwards, closing his eyes tight and trying to hide from the vision that was about to ravage his psyche. The defensive lip clamp had suddenly reinvented itself into a full-blown kiss and luckily for Bird, the adrenaline pumping through his heart managed to intercept his impending euphoria just before it went too far – this was far enough. He bent himself double and thrust his face into his hands, preparing for his inevitable doom, but the head was bare and the image non-existent.

Come on – where are you? I know you're there, come on out…

But there was nothing. The image of the car that had haunted him for so many years, every time he had a romantic encounter with the opposite sex, was suddenly gone. He peeled his face away from his hands and slowly raised himself up.

"It's not there," he whispered. "The car is simply not there – why?"

Sarah stood in the middle of her lounge listening to him talking to himself as if she were some incidental bystander in a cataclysmic charade. Confused and self-conscious, she glared at him in complete disbelief. She was sure he had just kissed her but wasn't quite sure how she felt about it. It had been a while since she'd had any kind of romantic involvement herself, the last boyfriend being unable to compete with her transient lifestyle, but this boy had just kissed her, tongue and all, and in a strangely bizarre way she felt kind of aroused.

"How dare you try and kiss me? What do you think I am, some kind of slut?" she said, touching her lips.

"What do you think I am, some kind of loser?"

"I don't know… I don't know what you are, but you can't just stroll into my house and force yourself on me. Who do you think you are? Stop that, stay where you are."

"No. I gotta see if the image has really gone."

And again, he advanced himself towards her, cupping her face in his hands. She tried to move away but her efforts seemed futile. She, too, wanted another taste – just to see how the first one had felt, just to know whether they should continue. It was all a bit confusing, but her defences were weak and she quickly relented as he pressed his lips up to hers.

Bird's hand clasped the back of her head as the kiss rolled itself into a euphoric embrace, their arms wrapped around their bodies as they ebbed and swayed through one another's rhythm. His tongue performed a delicate symphony with hers, and all the while his head was filled with desire and longing and the image of the car eluded him.

This is amazing, no burning car. Am I set free?

He broke away and stepped back a few paces, running his hands down her arms and releasing his fingers from hers in a lingering clasp.

"I can't believe it," he said. "The image has really gone."

"I can't believe it, either. What the hell is happening here? What image are you talking about? How dare you force yourself on me?"

"Yes, how dare I?"

The innuendo just stirred his loins again and he was onto her, kissing, embracing, darting, stroking. It felt like heaven. Cyndi Lauper's 'True Colours' rang in his ears like the bells of Notre Dame – her beautiful ballad of unconditional love that had ignited his virginal teenage lust all those years ago – and he immersed himself in the dream, the gift of feminine liaisons reborn in his soul.

"Bloody hell, who would have thought that Lara bloody Croft could release me from this prison? The Tomb Raider turns out to be an angel in disguise. Ain't that a thing?"

Sarah stood a few feet apart from Bird, her hand still entwined with his. She was in something of a daze – nothing about this situation made any sense but there was an unfamiliar yearning deep inside her. He was talking, but his words were meaningless.

"What are you talking about? Who is Lara and what prison are you in? This is madness, it makes no sense to me. Perhaps you should go."

461

She should be breaking away and sending him home, but something had stirred deep inside her and in truth she wanted to know more. The whole thing was confusing, his banter and her own paradoxical feelings. What was he on about? Here he was, standing in her lounge with a massive smile etched across his cheeks, talking about Tomb Raiders and prisons whilst forcing himself upon her. What was going on – and why did she enjoy it so?

"You know," he murmured, "my last girlfriend left some years ago and I haven't heard a peep from her since. We'd been together since we were teenagers."

Sarah hadn't actually wanted an explanation and she certainly didn't need to hear about this fool's past love life, but she looked at him, somewhat enthralled, somewhat appalled by his bolshy confidence. Their hands were still clasped together and she stared into his eyes as a thousand thoughts ricocheted through her mind. He released his grip and strolled away from her as he continued his tale, and for once, Sarah was speechless.

"I really thought we had something. I thought it was something you could never have again, like the one chance you get to find true love. My life used to be pretty perfect, you know?" he said, glancing at her though the statement was somewhat rhetorical. "I was a regular Sunday Joe. I played rugby for our club, I was involved with conservation and bird projects, I was getting offers to go to university and study ornithology – I had mates, prospects, winning teams, a beautiful girl – the lot – the full nine yards."

"That's whole," she interrupted.

"You what?"

"It's the whole nine yards, not the full."

"Whatever," he chirped, ignoring the remark and then chuckling to himself at the irony of it all, like these things constituted normality.

"Anyway," he sighed, "I got this friend called Cracker and he's been into drugs for a long time. He's the world heavyweight champion at getting fucked up and no one can really touch him. In the beginning he did drugs for their mind-enhancing effects, you know, all spiritual like? He knew the risks with every concoction he tried and he avoided them, making it all look so easy. Huh, not anymore," he snorted with a malignant smile.

"I used to smoke a bit of pot now and then – just a bit, mind you; my rugby meant too much to me in those days to get really involved. It was always just an extra kick at the end of a piss-up – know what I mean, when we really just wanted to get out of it? But as we got older, the kicks needed to get stronger. I started smoking more and more, then I moved on to other things. Kelly wasn't happy about it, she thought I would lose everything if I got into the scene, but I was almost beyond caring. I've sort of got this fucked-up gene that likes to tear it all down, as you rightly pointed out, and I was reaching that point. I'd achieved all my accolades, and really, going to university didn't thrill me that much – it never has. The high I was chasing kicked much better. Besides, it didn't seem to matter how much she smoked, just me."

He huffed a sarcastic snort through his nose at this last remark, as if the girl had treated him unjustly. Sarah wasn't really sure if he was even talking to her anymore. He seemed so engrossed in his past that she was completely incidental to the whole affair. She listened, though – something was compelling her to give him audience, and politely, she did.

"Anyway, we had this all-night beach party one summer when ecstasy was at its peak. We all did loads of pills and had a right old bash as it turns out – all night on this old smuggler's cove – gettin' wasted – corker really – one of the best. As the sun came up, Cracker and I dropped acid – not just one, like – a whole stack. I still don't know how many I did, he just handed me this stuff and I swallowed it." He grinned cheekily to himself. Sarah shook her head in amazement, having never touched illegal drugs even once in her life.

"So, Cracker and I go AWOL for a while, seemingly a good few hours. When someone eventually found us, Kelly was doing her nut, going off on one about how irresponsible I was and how I didn't care about anyone except myself. I was in no state to argue and just stood staring at her, nothing to say, trippin' me nuts off.

"She bundled me into her car and started to drive home. My incoherent state didn't allow me to think about seatbelts or anything and she was too mad to even care. I just remember her screaming and shouting at me and I was having all these hectic hallucinations about shit dive-bombing us and people jumping out the hedges and onto the car. I kept ducking to get away from the images and lashing out at nothing. I guess it made her lose concentration and she went off the road and through a hedgerow. The car flipped and rolled." He paused and stared away for a second. Teardrops welling in his eyes made them sparkle in the light and he blinked a couple of times.

"The next thing I remember, I was on my knees in a field with the car some way in front of me. It was burning and exploding like TNT was igniting throughout its interior. I could see Kelly in the flames. She was trapped by her seatbelt, banging on the window and screaming my name. She was begging me to save her, but I couldn't move. I was rooted to the ground. It was like my knees had grown into the grass and I was part of the field, unable to shift them. I watched her until she melted into the flames and disappeared. She kept fading in and out of the fire, hammering on the glass, and I just sat there and watched. There was nothing I could do. Eventually, the whole thing was consumed by fire and smoke and she was gone. I watched my true love burn."

Sarah clutched her hands together and rubbed her palms self-consciously. She hadn't expected that. Her middle-class upbringing was so full of love and life, so easy and normal compared to this tragic existence. It seemed like everything this boy ever held pure either deserted him or died in front of him. Why was it that Lady Luck rolled uneven dice? Why were some born into heaven and others to hell? And why did some just float along in purgatory, where neither seemed an option? She was horrified.

"I never saw Kelly again. Her family had to move after the accident to be near facilities that could help her. You see, the car was never on fire. I had been thrown out when it rolled and somehow escaped injury, but Kelly was strapped in and my seat had crushed her seatbelt buckle. She broke her back in three places and was paralysed from the waist down. She didn't get out of the car until the firemen and ambulance dudes came and I don't know how long she banged on the window, but it must have been a fair old while – couple of hours, perhaps.

"She could see me, on my knees in the field, staring at her. She was banging on the window, begging me to help, but all I could see were flames. The acid was running riot through my head and I physically couldn't move. As far as I could work out, the thing was on fire.

"So there I was, her boyfriend of almost seven years, her true-coloured rainbow, and I just sat, staring at my girl as she begged me for help. I just sat there staring at her like a fool. Is it any wonder she hates me?

"Apparently, she's in and out of hospital the whole time now and still confined to a wheelchair, no feeling from the waist down and unlikely to ever walk again, let alone have kids. I tried to visit her once, but the family threatened to kill me if I ever went near her. That was more than three years ago, and I haven't so much as kissed a girl since without that image tormenting my mind and bringing it all back. For the first time, now, I am able to hold you and all I can see is Kelly's smiling face. She's smiling as she fades away. She has set me free – you have set me free. Bizarre, isn't it? I mean, you're a badass Tomb Raider, but today you have saved me. Weird."

Sarah said nothing as she moved across to him. Like Kirsty out on the plains, this time she was the instigator. Her hand reached up and touched his cheek. She closed her eyes and kissed him gently – lovingly. He felt right for her, it all felt right. Not for eternity – I mean, there was still a job to be done here – but for now, this boy had tugged the emotional heartstrings inside her and she felt something for him.

"I'm sorry about all the grief in the beginning. If I had known… well, I don't know what I would have done. I'm sorry. What more can I say?" she whispered.

"Nothing. It had to be this way, man. If you had known any of this earlier, you would have put me on that first ox wagon out of here and sent me packing like some kind of loser. Time alone knows when she is right, Sarah, we just paddle along within her."

"That's beautiful."

"I'm sorry too, Sarah, I'm sorry you didn't get your real scientist."

"Yeah... me too. Anyway, what's done is done." She paused and looked away, then turned to face him with a naughty smirk crumpling her lips. "I still could have taken care of Visser if you hadn't come around the corner, you know – I have a gun."

"You have a what?" he squealed.

"A gun. Look, I'll show you." She moved over to a cabinet and opened the top left-hand drawer. An automatic nine-millimetre pistol emerged in her hand and she held it up triumphantly.

"Eight in the mag, one up the spout. Accurate up to a couple of hundred yards, depending on how good a shot you are. I could have taken him out."

"Holy shit, I believe you. Damn, girl, you're armed. All this time you've been screaming at me and you're fucking tooled up. You could have taken *me* out!" His mind raced to their first encounter when she had launched at him on the porch, just outside this very room. She'd gone in to get his CV – she could have collected the piece as well and shot the shit out of his lily-white frame right here that very night. A chill of fear rippled down the back of his legs as he thought about it. Lara could have iced him any time she chose.

"Will you stay with me tonight, Mr. Bird?" she begged. "I promise I won't shoot you and I'll try to be nice." She was swaying from side to side whilst holding the weapon in two hands and gently caressing her bottom lip with the end of the barrel. She was a peach, an absolute psychotic peach.

"Whatever you say, man, you got the gun."

…They're beautiful… like a rainbow…

27

ELVIS REAPS THE WHIRLWIND

The Heuglin's robin was familiar. As long as the sun rises on the Sukula Plains, the Heuglin's will be there at dawn to perform his delicate recital to the world, but that was about the extent of Bird's familiarity this morning. The usual sounds of a village preparing for its day were absent, and aside from the dawn chorus, all was very silent – very peaceful.

Nothing was the same here. The smell was different; the touch, the feel, the whole aura of wherever it was he had just woken up wasn't right, and the unmistakably sweet scent of a female engulfed him. It was on the bedclothes, in the room, in his nose and in his hair – everywhere – she was all around.

His groin ached, too – that was a first in a long time.

Wow, did it really happen? Did I really spend the night with Tomb Raider? Where is that precious little flower? I can smell her, she must be here somewhere.

But the bed was empty – the room was empty. Sunlight streamed through her curtainless windows like a morning waterfall and the dawn chorus tumbled in with it as if every paradisiacal feature of Mother Earth was craning to get inside this little piece of Nirvana he'd found. Heaven was indeed a place on Earth.

He rolled over and sat up. The bed was bare but for his naked self and Sarah's beautiful scent. The thought of waking up with her had been a precious fantasy for many months and now that at last he had, she was nowhere to be found. Was it all a dream? Had he walked in his sleep and got into her bed? Would she be bursting through the door at any moment with a nine-mil in her hand and a Tomb-Raiding glint in her eye? Could this be Judgement Day?

"Get up and get dressed." And just like that, there she was. "I don't want any of the men to know you slept here last night. Come on, up." She tossed his clothes onto the bed and strolled out, turning on her impetuous heels, leaving Bird confused.

"What's wrong? Are you embarrassed? Was I no good? It has been a while."

"I don't need a post-mortem about how the sex was and we don't need to analyse what went on. We both needed some form of intimacy last night and we got it, that's all."

"Do I at least get a cup of tea?"

"Isaac will be in soon, he can do it for you. Now please go, I am on the radio to David."

He'd been following her around the lounge, hopping and skipping into his clothes as they spoke, and she had just deflated that old male-ego thing and everything else about him with one effortless swoop. Here he was thinking that at last he'd met his true love in his true place of destiny, and she was carrying on like it was just some clinical need they were fulfilling. It wasn't on – this simply wasn't cricket. He knew it had been a long time but he couldn't have been that bad, could he? It's like riding a bike, isn't it? He sat down on the porch and rolled a smoke as he contemplated both the dawn and his predicament.

Maybe she's just not a morning person, maybe she'll come round by this afternoon and we can do it all again? God, I hope so.

"Oh, Mr. Bird, wonderful news." She burst suddenly onto the porch and danced around in front of him as if Santa had just brought her a snazzy new dress.

Weird, man, this is all too weird.

"They've accepted the funding proposal! David will be getting a bank draft through in the next few days and better still, a lion specialist will be coming from Minnesota to work on the project with us. Isn't that fantastic?" She grabbed his face and kissed him a smacker on the lips, then hopped up and down madly across the porch. "Oh, thank God, we've done it. There's finally a future here for us all – fan-bloody-tastic!"

"All except me." Her euphoria was suspended momentarily as she turned to face Bird. "If a hotshot lion man is coming here from Minnesota you won't be needing me around anymore, will you?"

"Oh yes, I hadn't thought of that. What about you?" She placed her fingers on her chin and drummed one against her lip. "I think I'll have to work out my feelings for you before I make any kind of decision there."

Bird stood up and flashed his own psychotic glance at her for once. "Work your feelings out? What do you think this is, Sarah – a game of fucking chess? What about *my* feelings? What about the work I've done over the last few months? What am I? Some pawn in your mind game – tossed aside when you have no more use for me? That's pure fuckin' evil if I am."

He thrust himself off his chair and stepped on his cigarette butt as he made his way to the door. He didn't have his shoes on yet and the cherry burnt the base of his foot, but he tried not to flinch.

"No, Bird, I'm sorry, I didn't mean it like that. Let me explain what I meant. Of course there's a place for you here, we couldn't have done it without you, please, let's have a chat about it."

But they were both suddenly cut short by Isaac, whose banshee-like howl pierced the air from outside Sarah's door.

"Bwana! Madam! Come quick – it's Clarence!"

Isaac's footsteps thumped up the path to the house as he hollered for them in a stricken panic. They stopped their bickering and looked at each other in bewilderment.

"Clarence?"

Bird was up and running for the door as fast as motion could take him. He tore it open to reveal Isaac, banging and screaming like a man possessed.

"It Clarence, saa. The hunters have put the bait. Is jost here, close to ma camp. Please, you must come quick."

"Holy shit – Clarence!"

Instinct took over, sending adrenaline surging through Bird's arteries while his heart thumped frantically. As he passed Sarah's desk, he threw open the drawer and grabbed the nine-mil, cocking it like he'd seen so many times in the movies; surprisingly, it worked.

"Bird, wait! Don't go out there! Wait, please!"

But he was gone, sprinting barefoot up the road and into the forest towards the plains before Sarah had even got out of the house.

"BIRD, WAIT!"

Her voice receded into a distant echo until all he could hear was the pounding of his feet on the sandy track and the resonance of his gasping breath deep inside his chest. Isaac was running alongside him, panting out directions as to where the bait was, shouting about how he'd seen the hunting vehicle manoeuvring into position while Clarence was inspecting a carcass they'd strung in a tree.

"Where are the others?"

"They com, saa. I call all ma guys."

"Not them, where are the other lions – the females?"

"I donno!"

As they burst into the clearing, Bird caught sight of Visser's vehicle up ahead, close to an island on the edge of the plains. He couldn't see the lion yet, but George was perched on the vehicle, resting his face on a rifle that was tucked firmly into his right shoulder.

The deep and resonating thud of a .375 high-powered hunting rifle cracked through his very soul as George's body ricocheted with the absorption of its kick. Clarence suddenly burst into view, twisting and spinning from behind a tree, just yards in front of a racing Bird, bellowing a ghastly yowl. His body spun two or three times in random, jerky motions as he howled out his unparalleled anguish. The shot contained so much power that it seemed he would never stop spinning, but the energy was absorbed and eventually he was bowled over his back and onto his side. The agonising howling subsided into hollow shrieks until his body finally crashed to a dusty halt, twitching at first and then motionless.

The sight tripped Bird into a virulent frenzy and a fearful wrath exploded inside his gut, sending shockwaves of horror through his distorted mind. In full stride and screaming like a deranged private bolting from the trenches of World War I, he raised the nine-mil up in one hand, slowed to a purposeful gait, steadied the weapon like a gyroscope in both hands and started squeezing off rounds.

BANG—BANG—BANG—BANG—BANG—BANG.

Bullets peppered into the truck and bodies flew in all directions as the trackers were sent diving for cover, streaming off the vehicle in a tremor of dishevelled panic. Visser barely had time to draw breath before a projectile smacked him straight in the face and sprayed crimson blood across the dashboard of his vehicle. The round entered just below his left cheekbone and burst off the back of his skull, taking half his brain with it and crumpling his body into the steering wheel, jolting like a cardiac victim receiving full wattage from a defibrillator's charging pads.

George was taking his time. This was a gift from heaven, and a song spontaneously ignited and rolled around his mind, blocking out the carnage of their incoming fire. He gazed purposefully down his scope as the Four Seasons' tune 'December 1963 (Oh What a Night)' rang out, forcing him to hum and sing along as he tucked his rifle into its familiar position.

"Breathe."

The crosshairs of his sights rested on Bird's bouncing chest. Everything went into slow motion for a second and he could even see the delayed flame spurting out the barrel of Bird's pistol.

"Nice an' easy naw, boy. Come home to Pappa. Breathe." He exhaled, held the pose and then gently squeezed the trigger as the satisfactory jolt of his weapon's kick struck his shoulder once more.

The shot caught Bird somewhere on the right-hand side of his chest and passed straight through his lung, spinning him like a top as it exited his back. He pirouetted like a ballerina on one leg, the force of the blow throwing his other up at the knee and sending him into a perfect twist before dropping him onto his side just yards away from where Clarence's body lay motionless.

The opportunity was too good for George to miss, and he was up and cocking before Isaac could say 'More tea, Vicar?', slamming a round into the chamber and fixing the boy in his sights. Live bait – something he had always dreamt of. Another deathly thud and the body in his scope crumpled as it spewed backwards, breaking Isaac's neck on impact and dropping his lifeless form to the ground in a cloud of dust.

And then suddenly, all was quiet. The carnage of seconds ago melted into an acrid haze. Even the morning breeze and ever-present Heuglin's robin had ceased. Nothing but death lingered in the air.

George was alone in the truck. Visser's body was draped over the wheel, the remains of his tongue lolling lifelessly from the side of his mouth. Remnants of his skull and brain spattered the vehicle behind him as flies began to gather on his bloodied face and saliva bubbled off his lips. A tracker was bent double over the rifle rack in the back of the car, bloodied and motionless. Any others that had accompanied them were long gone – they had taken flight from the nine-mil assault and scarpered into the bush, their loyalty to the hunter as fleeting as their care for the animals he killed.

George slapped another round into the breech and went out to inspect his work, throwing his overweight frame off the vantage point mid-section in the vehicle. As he hit the ground, he froze and cupped his rifle at the ready in case of impending assault, but all was quiet. The emotion of the situation was overwhelming him somewhat – he'd never had a crack at human targets and this was something of a dream come true. His father had refused to let him join the army as a young man because he was required at the helm of the family business, and since then George had never quite been able to fulfil that primal urge that stirred within him. The anger he possessed was deep and true. Gratuitous wealth helped, but there was a chasm inside that grew like a cancer. Killing animals only offered a temporary reprieve, but this – the power he felt here from taking these lives – this was what his aching soul had been yearning for all these years. This was true redemption. His whole body tingled with excitement.

The song burst into life once more and he held up his rifle as if it were a dance partner, a beautiful girl reminiscing about days of old when times were good with him. The end of his barrel reeked of shot-powder and he nuzzled it with his lips as he embraced the stock. His sordid waltz began and he sang whatever words he could remember from the song, humming and bumbling when he couldn't.

He stepped gracefully, left then right, back then forth with his rifle held gently in his arms. He stared at the barrel and caressed the stock as if it were Aphrodite herself sharing the last waltz with his distorted reality. His footwork left something to be desired, but he stepped and turned away from the car and out into the open, twisting and weaving, engrossed in his nostalgic trance of a time when women could share space with him free from ulterior motives. They were few and far between. These days it was just Mr. .375 who could bear that pleasure.

Then suddenly there was motion and he was immobilised mid-stride, frozen like a deer in the headlights. Something was moving in the long grass off to his left – he couldn't see it but it was there. Perpetrator, bleeding-heart scum, some other lower-than-life form trying to outwit him on the left flank. But this was George H. Rhymski – Special Forces? Corporate assassin? Slayer of all bleeding hearts? It didn't matter. Out here, he could be anything he chose. Everything his father was not.

BOOM.

The heavy thud of the .375 hammered home at the movement and a piercing squeal split the air as an animal was jettisoned out of the grass, tumbling and rolling from the force of the impact until gravity pursued it no more and an adult warthog lay bleeding and contorting, her legs twitching out their last rites. It was a female, and three tiny hoglets scurried about her corpse in jolted starts, sniffing and pressing their tiny snouts up to her skin, testing for life. All three suddenly froze together and snorted into the air with their little noses. Something was not right. They scuttled into the grass, tails in the air and confusion in the mind.

"Fuckin' hoags!" George mumbled to himself as he checked the ammo pocket in his jacket. He only ever kept four in the magazine so as not to stress the spring, but there were normally plenty in the pocket. Today, though, it was empty.

"Damn, left the boax in the car. Weren't expectin' no militia to hit me. Thoaught it were just me an' this oal' lion here. No bother, evryun's fuckin' deed anyhows. Gonna check the boadies."

His pirouetting feet stepped into life once more, the thrill of another kill stirring those loins into a rhythmic trance that had vacated them years before, the unloaded rifle once again his beautiful partner and the song gently cascading off his lips as he reminisced about that night – and what a night it was. Not sixty-three though, more like seventy-eight.

George had been part of an elite fraternity in college, but it wasn't his prowess on the sports field, in the lecture hall or on the thespian stage that put him there. His was a right reserved only for the privileged few – the *nouveau riche*. The jocks couldn't quite figure him out, the brains found him intellectually wanting, the socialites only engaged him so that he paid for all the booze and the cheerleaders steered well clear, his obsession with guns and military paraphernalia seemingly too hot to handle. But he was always around – always on the edge of the spotlight, lurking in the shadows, his profile low enough to be inconspicuous but visible enough to belong. He paid his dues and stumped up the coin every time he was asked, and that kept him just within the madding crowds and around the frivolities.

George was part of the fraternity, but he was not in the fraternity in the way that others were. He didn't need the human contact they seemed to crave. He was happy on his own and comfortable with his role on the edge. But the anger was there, lying beneath – infant and untainted – manifesting its loathing that would become the chasm he was unable to fill until today. This violation of human life reminded him of that night back in the frat house, that one night of pleasure that he would take, the only time he allowed the anger to surface.

It was just another typical Friday night and the place was crawling with wild ravers. A freshman girl new to the scene had seen him on his own and ventured to talk to him with the gallant bravado of slightly too much beer flowing through her veins. Her small-town upbringing gave her impeccable manners, and the reality of college life that had always been a precious fantasy had the excitement racing in her stomach. She had seen George on the edge, tapping his foot to the classic Frankie Valli vocal but speaking to no one. She struck up a conversation and he bumbled along at first in his usual ungainly style. But it didn't take long for him to sense the opportunity, and he soon steered the conversation to boyfriends and sex.

She had made the mistake of mentioning that her friends were getting sassy with some of the jocks and that was when George pounced, suggesting to her that they do the same. She wasn't comfortable with his advances, but he kept plying her with alcohol and she quickly became disorientated and confused, trying to palm him off but unsure of how to do it. They ended up in George's room, though she didn't know how. All she knew was that she didn't want to be there, but those manners kept tripping her up, her polite obligation keeping her in check and in the moment.

Something about him didn't add up, and it made her uneasy. His breath smelt of stale liquor and she tried politely to resist, but he persisted with relentless intent. It wasn't so much that he forced himself onto her, more that he weaselled his way into her in a clumsy and unsolicited fashion. She felt violated after the sordid affair and he picked up on that, savouring it as a little victory and feeling some kind of degenerate satisfaction as it filled a small void within the chasm. With his coital urge satisfied, he had kicked her out without so much as a thank you and goodnight. She found herself alone in the corridor, angry and a little afraid, and had gone on home without her friends. Meanwhile, George lay back on his pillows with smug content.

Human violation was hard to come by back home, but its bounties were endless. He had learned it that night, but nothing could top what he had achieved out here today. This was indeed a great day for George.

He prodded Isaac's body with his foot. It was still soft. Half his entrails dripped from the gaping hole in his chest, and the buzz of flies was now becoming intolerable. He would inspect the lion, then the boy, and what the hell, he may as well head into camp and look for that pretty girl they had been talking to yesterday – it wasn't far from here. The stench of death in the air was whetting that old appetite again and she sure was a pretty one.

"Damn pity I can't take this lion home with me. He's a beauty," George murmured to himself as he strolled over to where Clarence lay.

Bird was on his side with his back to the hunter, but he looked pretty lifeless as well. George's view had been clear, the shot had hit him somewhere around the heart and it was unlikely this boy would have survived the impact – he was dead for sure, there was blood everywhere. But

George hadn't even reached the dead lion when a sudden movement froze him to the floor and a chilling fear rippled down his spine, standing his hairs on end.

The boy was moving – he was moving, and he was alive.

Bird spun around to face the hunter, blood all over his chest and face, with the nine-mil in his hand, pointing straight at George. There was no ammo in the rifle and for the very first time in his life, George was looking down the wrong end of a barrel. His bowels shifted and putrid liquid bubbled into his pants as he whimpered like some lost puppy dog, the sweat breaking out on his eyelids and running over his cherry-red, rounded face. Bird had the look of a demon in his eyes and he was panting like a jackrabbit, but the pistol remained motionless and focussed on its target.

"Take it easy now, boy. Can we talk? You got a name? What's your name, son? You need money? I have plenty of money I could give ya. Please... please don't do this. I'm a good man, I'm a very good man. People, they respect me, I do good for them and I could do good for you. We don't need to do this, son, please, come oan now, what d'ya say, huh? Why don't you just put down that there gun and we can talk. What d'ya say, huh? You need money? I got money – plenty. C'm oan, boy, what d'ya say?" George was begging and pleading, trying to appeal to any glimmer of decency within the wounded boy, but something in his heart was quaking at the glint in his assailant's eye.

Bird said nothing. He held the moment in divine silence, allowing the angels of death a moment's contemplation before they indulged on the remains of this misguided soul. George could only pray that the boy's silence was his redemption. He could smell that liquid in his pants now.

"What d'ya say, boy? We got a deal? C'm oan, son – how 'bout it? We gonna talk? What's your name?"

A large smile caressed his sweaty face as it made a futile effort to appeal for some form of reprieve. His whole body seemed to gyrate as he paused for a second to entice an answer out of the boy, his palms outstretched and lines furrowing across his gleaming brow.

"I'm Bwana fucking Bird, fat boy."

BANG!

It was the last round in his magazine, but Bird wasn't to know that. He'd been lying there, trying to count how many shots he'd got off, but it was impossible to tell. The concentration had been hard, but it was a good way of ignoring his pain. The pistol's kick had spun him onto his back and he was now sprawled with his arms and legs out in a star shape, looking up at the sky. He could see vultures circling on thermals above him, fluently gliding on outstretched wings as their heads twitched in surveillance of the carnage site, safe in the knowledge that dinner would soon be served and there was now plenty of it.

The round had caught George in his throat and pushed it out through the back of his neck, taking the top of his spine with it. The momentum of his legs staggered him back five or six paces, but the hunter was dead before his cumbersome corpse hit the ground.

Bird tried to call out for Sarah – she must have been on her way – but his breath was lost, escaping out of the hole that had once been his right lung. Blood pumped out of his body faster than it pumped into it, and he hoped that lying on his back would stem the flow enough until Sarah got there. She wouldn't be long.

Thoughts were crashing around his mind like a pinball ricocheting across obstacles in its cabinet. Each one clicked up a multitude of points and sent bells, chimes and buzzers off in his ears. There was so much going on that he almost couldn't hear the sound of scraping earth behind him, but the sudden realisation that Clarence was still alive and moving sent spasms of fear down his spine. He craned his neck sideways and saw the beast clawing and heaving his huge frame across the dirt towards him. The animal was looking into his eyes, and within seconds he was only a few feet away from a paralysed Bird. Even if he could have run, he wouldn't have had time to get up before the monster was upon him. As it was, half his chest was missing and the option of flight was non-existent.

But the look in Clarence's eyes was not one of malice – it was not even one of fear. Bird was facing death in all her gripping fury, and although it should have filled him with dread, he felt a sudden calm. The beast lifted up his huge head and tried to lurch his body closer to where Bird lay. It was as if he was summoning his energy for one final battle with mortality, one last stand for leonism, one ultimate thrash at revenge. Their stares locked for a second as Clarence's head craned upwards, towering above a defenceless Bird. The time was right, and his elevation could have carried him onto the boy if he had focussed all his attention at once.

But the beast just sat there, looking down his nose at Bird as he squeezed the last gasp of breath from his ruptured lungs. Slowly, he exhaled a deep sigh of defeat and his body deflated, lowering his head and releasing what was left of his soul.

He sank to the ground and stared at Bird as the remains of his earthly being slipped from his colossal form. His energy drained away and seemed to excavate itself into Bird's diminishing strength, shifting all his pain into latent obscurity. Everything he stood for was here in this lion: the conviction for his cause, the fire in his spirit, the will to survive a human assault on his beautiful world, the very reason for being. Here, in the dying heart of this lion.

And then he was gone.

Bird's staggering eyes suddenly rested on Isaac's body. He had been too engrossed in his own desperate situation to even remember that Isaac was with him.

"Isaac?" he wheezed, but there was no acknowledgement. Isaac's face stared blankly at the sky and his body lay motionless. "Oh Isaac, what have I done?" The despair numbed every sense and he lay back hopeless in reticence.

Images flashed violently in and out of his mind. First his family, their faces looking at him as if he was in some sort of crib. They were distant and unfamiliar but family all the same. There was no malice in the image, only peace.

Then he was racing – Cracker and Iceberg were up ahead and they were pounding through the forest. There was a fight – they were all tumbling and rolling through the leaf litter – everyone was laughing. Alfred's face faded in and out, and his image was like a sedative that calmed the boy down and filled him with hope.

He was hit by a wave of light and sound, and in an instant the forest became his stadium. His body was numb from the pain and feelings were relegated to a mere memory of subconscious demise, but he remembered the chill of excitement with the screaming fans. He remembered how badly he had wanted it – to play for England at Twickenham and score the winning try in the corner – but destiny had drawn another course and that childhood dream would lie in the womb of his mind, never to be realised. Some dreams remain that way for life, while others choose to manifest themselves. Sukula's calling was louder.

Then there were birds. Hundreds of species flashed across his mind – in trees, on the ground, in flight and in dance. Wattled cranes as they stepped out their rhythmic unison of undefined love. Squadrons of pelicans gliding in V-formations, synchronised into aerial ballets. Egyptian geese with their bickering and squabbling. Yellow-billed storks cascading through gentle river currents with an outstretched wing reflecting delicate shades of pink through their plain white feathers. And then the vision of waterholes with hundreds and thousands of birds all prodding at the water's edge. Nikuyu was circling and bee-eaters were probing. Birdsong filled his translucent thoughts and the beauty of life was exonerated through their mortal beings. Alfred's face was constantly appearing and fading away – the one constant in his life, all he could ever really trust.

Then he was on the cliffs and the ocean was pounding away at their base, relentless in its onslaught of reclamation from the mainland. Fishing boats were dancing around the surface and fishermen waved across at him from their vessels. He was waving back, smiling. The imagery was calm and reassuring – seagulls bobbing on the breeze and coastal flowers swaying at his feet. He was on the viewing rock with Cracker, and a procession of boats was snaking its way below them, sailing out to distant shores. They were waving – waving, but not drowning.

Suddenly, there was a movement. It caught the corner of his eye, jolting him into real time – there was something in the grass. His pupils twitched to one side and rested upon the form of little Elvis sitting some way off, underneath a shrub. He was watching Bird. He was alive and well, gazing at the scene that had been his father's demise. He was looking at Bird, fixing him with that stare that Mia had done all those months ago, but now there was no danger for Bird – it seemed to him like they were all a unit, a motley family of sorts.

"Long may you live, little dude." The words wheezed out of his panting chest, barely audible to himself, let alone the tiny lion.

The lineage of this great beast was not dead. His might have been the ultimate sacrifice for survival, but the Sukula male gene lived on and the Institute that was born to save it looked stronger than ever before. Visser was dead. An inquest into the carnage of this day would highlight the gaping hole of moral injustice where man sells the souls of wild animals to be hung as trophies on his walls. Maybe the carnage would yield a brighter day, and man would see that the ecological value of a living lion can far outweigh the cash in its wholesale slaughter.

Lions then filled his mind. A thousand images peppered his thoughts: hunts, kills, matings, affections, ambushes, fights, slaps and pats. Visions of clawing, biting, leaping, loving, chewing, yawning, squatting and playing. Rolling fluffballs of cubs, jumping and slapping sub-adults, grooming and amorous females. Their rounded ears, their primate-like eyes, the look of bemused excitement as they gazed at insects that scurried around their massive frames. Lions. Beautiful beasts in their entirety. Paradoxical yet constant. A simple reflection of our very selves upon this Earth. The King of Beasts. Celestial beings whose spirits make up the stars in our sky and the reverence in our hearts.

Lions – long may they live.

"Bird… oh my God, Bird… you're bleeding. Are you OK?" Sarah had followed them out to the plains and just caught the tail end of the slaughter, unsure what to do as gunshots echoed through the air. She had been rooted to the ground behind a tree, watching the tragedy unfold, but she hadn't seen Bird get hit and now that she was there, she knew it didn't look good.

"Raymond is coming with the first-aid box. Hang in there, Bird, just hang in there, please. *RAYMOND!*" she screamed over her shoulder, as her hands pressed onto Bird's chest. She took off her shirt and wrapped it into a bandage, smothering his gaping wound and trying to stem the blood.

Sarah's voice pierced his frozen pain, and despair gave way to hope. Her face was looking down at him as she wiped the sweat from his brow.

"Hold on, Bird, hold on, please."

He gazed up at her and was filled with a bewildered love. This beautiful girl had finally set him free in this outlandish place – so real and self-sustaining – but why? Her integrity had seen beyond his fragile façade and sought out the warrior that lay beneath. Just like Isaac and Jacob and all the guys he had lived with for the last year. True people and true affection – true friends, at last.

Her face was above him and her gentle hands were stroking his convulsing soul. The morning sun cast a glow that surrounded her. Angel. Was she really here with him?

Some of the men had arrived behind her and they were all lit up in the radiance of the sun. Raymond crouched over Isaac's body, unable to comprehend what he saw. They were all panic-stricken but Bird could just see their smiles, emanating tranquillity that pumped life into his decaying heart.

"I could have fallen in love with you," he whispered.

"You still can," she replied with a smile. He moved his hand to hers and their fingers locked together.

All the while, the whispering of a gentle breeze hummed in and out of his ears. In the distance, carried on its flowing soul, the ballad of a harp ebbed and swayed in his distorted mind as Sarah and the men all gathered alongside him. Their faces were calm as she caressed his bloodied brow. The ballad was gradually increasing and becoming clearer, like angels on harps drifting down from heaven above to take the last of this earthly soul. Could it really be angels? He strained himself to listen but the more he tried, the further it went. The effort was too intense, and he was forced to relax and accept the consequences of this melody as it began to stream into his mind more strongly than ever before.

I know this tune.

Its gentle plucking and simple harmony, so distant at first, drew ever nearer on the wind of change. It was clear to him, now – these were not angels with harps at all, these were acoustic guitars strumming out a measure of life that no man could ever ignore. The notes rang out in his mind, flawless and resonant, just the way they'd done when the maestro first played his noble tune. He smiled and gazed at the people around him – the people who loved him with all their hearts. They were stroking his face and nurturing his broken soul as the beautiful ballad immersed the remnants of his mortal being.

The music resounded, sustained and sanctifying – the only language to truly transcend the fountained mosaic of human diversity. The melody strummed as its lyrics came flooding into his heart and the musical beauty of life was all that prevailed.

"Is there really a stairway?"

THE END

GLOSSARY OF AFRICAN WORDS AND PHRASES

Bika pa kyeya	–	*Put on the spotlight*
Bokwe Muchima	–	*Heart of a lion*
Bwana	–	*Boss*
Isamba Noni	–	*Bird talker*
Jamba	–	*Marijuana*
Kachesu	–	*Home-brewed clear alcohol*
Kuwaama	–	*Beautiful*
Muntu	–	*African man*
Muti	–	*African witch doctor charms and medicines*
Muzungu	–	*White man*
Nshima	–	*Maize porridge*
Twasanta mwan-eh	–	*Thank you very much*

South African words

Poes	–	*South African derogatory term*
Skellum	–	*South African slang for undesirable person*

Animals and birds

Lechwe	–	*Medium-sized aquatic antelope*
Mabuki	–	*Greater honeyguide – bird in the woodpecker family, found in sub-Saharan Africa. Known for actively guiding people to bee colonies for the purpose of honey collection.*
Nzovu	–	*Elephant*
Nikuyu	–	*Lanner falcon*
Oribi	–	*Small African antelope*
Puku	–	*Medium-sized semi-aquatic antelope*
Roan	–	*Large horse-like antelope*

ABOUT THE AUTHOR

 Dorian Tilbury is a conservation project manager from Zambia. He has dedicated the last 25 years of his life to understanding, protecting and managing protected areas in Zambia and Malawi to safeguard contiguous links in the regional ecochain. He loves music, birds, Africa and sitting on open grasslands watching lions do nothing other than simply be lions.

CPSIA information can be obtained
at www.ICGtesting.com
Printed in the USA
BVHW030922260919
559481BV00001B/98/P

9 781686 536816